The
Killing
Plains

The Killing Plains

Sherry Rankin

THOMAS & MERCER

Text copyright © 2025 by Sherry Rankin
All rights reserved.

Published by Thomas & Mercer, Seattle

www.apub.com

Amazon, the Amazon logo, and Thomas & Mercer are trademarks of Amazon. com, Inc., or its affiliates.

ISBN-13: 9781662521157
eISBN: 9781662521164

Cover design by Will Speed
Cover image: © Ball SivaPhoto © Papuchalka - kaelaimages / Shutterstock

Printed in the United States of America

For Emily

Prologue

The vultures were waiting that evening—dozens of them riding the thermals high above his head, elegant and still as leaves on water, reflecting a ragged, wheeling crown around the dark form in the pond. Others had settled in the spindly cottonwoods that ringed the shore—so many that the branches sagged under their weight and the ground beneath the trees was painted white with their droppings. They were used to him now. As he emerged through the dry grass with the pack slung over his shoulder, they barely glanced his way but remained focused on their business, hissing and jostling one another for position, close enough that he could see the dust on their wings and the skin of their naked heads, as red and wrinkled as burned flesh.

The birds had been gathering for days. Unable to reach their prize and unwilling to leave it, they eyed him coolly, patiently, during his daily visits. But today was different. They sensed it. As he unzipped his pack and sat to pull on the waders, the vultures ruffled their heavy wings, and when he clambered back to his feet, fumbling to adjust the shoulder straps, a few let out hoarse, expectant croaks.

He picked up the bolt cutters and edged down the bank. In the hoof-pocked mud, dozens of coyote tracks, narrower and more delicate than a dog's, traced a complicated braid along the shoreline. Like the birds, they'd been drawn to the water by the smell of death, which the breeze carried across the sprawling ranchland.

The gorge rose in his throat. Gripping the bolt cutters, he pushed through the reeds into the murky, waist-high water.

The corpse bobbed on its back in the center of the pond, the heavy chain around the torso inadequate to counter the buoyancy of decay. The buttoned shirt strained against the bloat, and the elastic of the socks cut deeply into the swollen, purple flesh. Small fish and turtles had been diligent in their work. He tried not to look at the face.

"It's not Adam anymore," he whispered to himself as he worked the bolt cutters.

Once freed of the chain, the body floated easily across the surface of the pond. The water churned with silt as he struggled up the bank, cursing and grunting, the blackflies rising like smoke from the thick, sucking mud. After falling several times, he managed to tow his burden into the grass.

For a while, he sat, exhausted, not looking at what lay motionless beside him, keeping his eyes fixed on the sun as it sank towards the distant bluffs. He had planned this for days, but now he felt a strange reluctance. It had been peaceful, somehow, the ritual of his daily visits.

Unhooking the waders' straps, he dug into his pocket to find the thing he had brought with him. He unrolled it and laid it carefully on his knee. It had gotten damp in his climb up the bank. He sat for several minutes, smoothing the velvety fur until it was dry.

Finally, from another pocket he produced a length of pale chiffon ribbon, shimmering and pink in the waning light. His hands shook, but he managed to roll up the small, furred object, tie it with the ribbon, and tuck it into the dead boy's hand.

He looked up. The sun had vanished behind the bluffs, and the light was fading fast. With a sigh, he clambered to his feet and walked quickly away through the waving grass. The hiss and squabble of the birds began almost at once behind him, but he kept his eyes fixed on the path ahead. A few minutes later, as he stepped onto the road, he heard a distant coyote begin to wail.

Chapter 1

Pressing his forehead against the cool glass wall, Willis Newland squinted into the gloom of the enclosure. Delilah was playing hide-and-seek again. No matter. He would look till he found her. He needed her comfort tonight. And he could be as patient as she.

Willis wasn't sure how long he'd been standing in front of the herpetarium. Hours, at least. It was after nine o'clock—he knew that without looking. There had been no clocks in his cell, so he'd gotten used to telling time by the feel of the air. Every moment had its own distinct texture, smell, weight. Especially after dark.

"Yo, pervert," Homer used to call from the top bunk. "What time is it?"

And Willis, lying in the gloom on the thin, hard mattress, always knew, which made Homer chuckle. "You the smartest dumbass I ever met."

Homer hadn't slept well on the inside. And Willis hadn't either, for the first year or two, though eventually he got used to the close quarters and clamor and relentless sameness of the days. It was funny, though, how prison followed you home. Lately, he was lucky if he got a couple hours a night. The ranch seemed too quiet for sleeping, now—or if not quiet, the wrong kind of noisy, at least. Coyotes and crickets instead of shouts and clanging metal.

So much had changed. So much *could* change. With no one to tell him what to eat or when to sleep, no one to turn off his lights and lock him inside—the options were endless and disorienting. Like one of those choose-your-own-adventure books Momma had brought him while he was away.

Plus, everything was too big, somehow. The sky seemed vast enough to crush him into the dirt. And he got dizzy thinking of all that land, stretching in every direction outside his door. Nowadays, he stayed in the cabin with the curtains drawn to shut out the thousands of acres of tumbled rock and buffalo grass and mesquite—and most of all, the old stock pond, down at the southern tip of the ranch.

The pond. It was miles away over rough terrain. But Willis could feel it there, like a dark, liquid eye, watching him.

As a kid—back before the trouble—he used to like the pond. He remembered going there with his brothers to catch frogs and grass snakes. And when he got older, he'd go by himself to hide in the tall grass and peer down the hill at the boys from town who came there to swim. He didn't want to hurt them. He just liked to watch their white bodies flashing in the sunlight as they rough-housed and splashed. Then, one time, they saw him.

"Freak! Pervert!" they screamed.

He went home that day with black eyes and two cracked ribs.

"What happened?" Momma asked over and over.

"I fell off the four-wheeler," he said. But he could tell by the creases between her eyebrows that she knew he was lying.

"Willis, you have to be careful. Don't you remember, after last time—that time at church—how people talked?" Momma always referred to it this way. She didn't like to say the Carroway

5

boy's name—didn't like to remind Willis, or herself, of what had happened.

Momma's fears proved justified. News of his encounter with the boys at the pond spread like a grassfire. When his father heard, the beating he gave Willis hurt worse than anything the boys had done.

Willis learned his lesson. For two years, he kept away from the pond, at least in daylight, though sometimes he'd go after dark, when he knew he'd have the place to himself. Until the night they came for Adam's body. Willis heard the sirens over the hill, saw the blue and red lights reflected off the low-scudding clouds.

"Stay in the cabin, Willis," Felix, the ranch foreman, told him. "Don't come out for nothin'."

Willis obeyed, slipping through the door into the dim, humid herpetarium. Delilah seemed to understand his terror. She came to him and slid into his lap, then up his torso, tickling the stubble on his jaw with her flickering tongue. But he couldn't hide forever. The police came the next morning. As they put Willis into the cruiser, his father watched through slitted eyes while Momma stood behind him, her face twisted into a grimace of fear that Willis never forgot, though twenty years had passed since that terrible day.

Willis remembered the time following his arrest as a series of rooms, cramped and windowless, some with tables and chairs, some with beds and medical equipment. All were painted the same cold gray, lit with the same cold light. There'd been a parade of police and lawyers and people in lab coats. He remembered lying still on a hard table while a machine somehow took a picture of his brain. In the cramped gray rooms, they asked him questions he didn't know how to answer. And at the end of that time, in a bigger gray room, a judge stared down at him the way people stared into the big pit of snakes at the Rattlesnake Rodeo.

After the sentencing, his father never visited. But Momma came to see him every week, and his brothers came sometimes, too. Of his three brothers, Willis looked forward to Randy's visits most. Russ and Lowell never had much to say. But Randy would talk to him like he used to, before the trouble. Was Willis getting enough to eat? Was anybody bothering him? Did he need anything? And he told stories about his job at the *Houston Chronicle*, and about his family—his wife, Colly, the detective. And their daughter, Victoria. And later on, little Satchel, Victoria's baby boy, who was born with all the medical problems. Randy even gave him pictures to stick on the walls of his cell. He made Willis feel like he was still part of a family, one that would welcome him back if he ever came home.

But home wasn't like Willis remembered it. His father was dead. Randy was dead. And Victoria, too. Momma was an old lady, now. And Felix, though still ranch foreman, was too arthritic to do much anymore and had handed off most of his duties to his nephew Pete, who avoided Willis and spat in the dirt whenever he saw him.

There were nieces and nephews Willis had never met—never could meet, now, the court order said—though sometimes he caught glimpses of them splashing in the pool or playing on the tennis courts behind the big house. They were all there tonight— his surviving brothers and their families—for Momma's birthday party. Willis could hear the music drifting down the hill.

Tomorrow, when the children were gone, Momma would invite him to the house for leftover birthday cake. She would tell him all about the festivities, if the police hadn't arrested him by then.

On Willis's first day home from prison, Felix had told him to be careful. "Stay near the cabin—and keep away from that damn pond."

A needless warning. Willis's skin crawled at the mere thought of its dark water. For six months, he never went near it. Never went anywhere. And yet history was repeating itself, like a scary movie he'd seen once but was being forced to watch again.

He'd spent the day at the police station, answering the Rangers' questions, though they never seemed to believe him. Just like before, they hooked him to a machine that could tell if he was lying. They asked if he'd killed a boy and left him by the pond—though this time the boy's name was Denny, not Adam.

"No." He made his voice as calm and flat as he could. But the Rangers kept asking, using different words, trying to trick him.

Finally, they brought him home. "We'll be back with the hand-cuffs, soon," they said.

"Don't worry," Felix told him after the Rangers drove away. "That means they don't got nothin'."

But Willis knew it was just a matter of time.

There was only one thing to do, now. Only with Delilah would he find some final moments of peace. The herpetarium was quiet and warm—a few cubic yards of jungle transplanted as if by magic onto the plains of West Texas. A refuge. Inside it, nothing had changed in twenty years, except Delilah herself.

"Where are you?" Willis's breath fogged the glass. She was always hard to spot, perfectly camouflaged in the leaf litter or concealed in the shadowy branches above. She could go days without moving. But Willis always found her in the end.

After prison, it had taken him a while to relearn the trick. On his first day home, he'd rushed to the cabin and gone straight to Delilah's enclosure. But when he put his hand on the glass door, Felix stopped him.

"Best not, till she gets to know you again. I fed her a rabbit, so she shouldn't be riled. But still . . ."

Willis frowned. "I don't see her."

"She's there, in them leaves."

But Willis stared for a long time before spotting her. He'd been looking for something too small. She was no thicker than his forearm when he went away. Now, she weighed more than he did, and he'd mistaken her at first for a fallen tree. She'd become a monster. They both had.

"She'll remember me," Willis said, opening the door.

He was right. She came to him immediately, sliding across the ground to brush against his leg almost like a puppy, tasting him with her tongue. He could see the lump in her belly where the rabbit was. He laid a hand on the cool, dry skin of her back, the muscles constricting beneath his palm with an unhurried power that sent a shiver up his arm.

"I'll be damned." Felix scratched his chin and smiled. "Just you be careful. Don't never go in there when I ain't around for backup."

But Willis trusted her. He always had.

Now, as he wiped the fog off the glass with his sleeve, something caught his attention. In the pool near the back of the enclosure, half-concealed beneath the lily pads, two hooded eyes were watching him. The forked tongue fluttered out, testing the air.

Willis let out a long, slow breath. "Found you," he whispered and opened the door.

Chapter 2

March 4, 2019

Colly Newland stood on the porch of the old farmhouse, cradling a cup of coffee and staring out across the fields. The sun was rising, huge and orange, through a sickle-shaped gap in the distant bluffs, glittering and flashing on the spinning blades of the wind turbines that lined the heights. Mist drifted above the fence line, and a rich, loamy scent of damp earth hung in the air, along with a sharp chemical smell—the ranchers spraying the winter wheat.

Colly shifted uneasily. Beneath the squabbling of crows in the field next to the house, a heavy, aching quiet thrummed in her ears. Accustomed to the hum and rumble of Houston, she found the silence unnerving.

Twenty-five years ago, when Randy first mentioned bringing her home to meet his family, he'd warned her: "West Texas can be a little overwhelming if you're not used to it—all the space and silence. And then there's my family."

"Crazy?" she teased. "I can deal with crazy."

"Complicated. I just want you to know what you're getting into."

"All families are complicated."

"Half of Crescent Bluff works for my father, so being a Newland there—you're under a microscope. Everyone's angling for something. And the family's like a spiderweb you can't escape."

"You escaped. So did Russ."

"Our bodies got out, for now. But up here . . ." Randy tapped his forehead and shrugged. "At least Russ and I tried. Willis and Lowell will be stuck there forever."

Colly hadn't taken his warnings seriously at the time. They were both twenty-one, graduating from college. She was going to be an FBI profiler and Randy a Pulitzer Prize–winning journalist. They'd get married, move out east—to Washington, or New York, maybe. Reinvent themselves. Back then, it seemed inconceivable that anything could stand in their way.

But life hadn't followed the script they'd written for it. Colly remembered with painful clarity precisely when their dreams slipped through their fingers, though neither of them recognized the moment's full significance at the time. She'd been twenty-six, standing in her patrol uniform in the kitchen of their first little apartment, stirring a pot of spaghetti sauce and holding two-year-old Victoria on one hip. They'd just given their landlord thirty days' notice and were packing to move to D.C.

Randy came into the kitchen and sat down heavily. His face was bleak. He stared at the linoleum. "Colly, I can't go."

"What?"

He swallowed. "Momma's going to need the emotional support. Willis, too. Prison'll be tough on him. I'm sorry."

Colly laid down the spoon and brushed her thick, dark hair away from her face, working to keep her voice calm. "Does it have to be you?"

"Dad's no help. Russ is in South Korea, and Lowell's a self-absorbed prick."

"Are you saying you want to move home?"

Victoria began to fuss. Colly was gripping her too tightly. She set her down, and the child immediately began to toddle to her father.

"God, no. But I'd like to be close enough to get home on the weekends when they need me—just till everything's more settled." He stooped to pick up Victoria. "We both have good jobs. It won't kill us to stay in Houston a little longer."

He'd been wrong, though. *A little longer* became two decades, and staying in Houston *had* killed them—had killed Randy and Victoria, at least. And now here was Colly, on her own at forty-six and just as entangled in the Newland web as ever.

Behind her, the screen door slapped open, as loud as a gunshot. Colly jumped, sluicing coffee over her hand. A young boy in black pants and a rumpled t-shirt was watching her from the doorway with solemn blue eyes.

"Ow! Satchel, why?" Colly shook her burned fingers to cool them.

"Sorry." The boy anxiously chewed his lip, a habit that had left one side of his mouth perpetually chapped. He was seven years old but small for his age, with white-blond hair and skin so pale it seemed translucent. A timid boy—so much like Victoria in appearance but so unlike her in temperament. Victoria had been fearless. "I'm ready to go, Grandma." He squinted into the sunrise.

"Get out of the light," Colly snapped. "What on earth are you wearing?"

He stepped back into the shadows. "My trilobite shirt."

"You slept in that. Go get a fresh one from your suitcase."

He shook his head. "It's my lucky shirt."

"Then you shouldn't have slept in it." They stared at each other. After a moment, Colly checked her watch and sighed. "Fine. Take it off. I'll look for an iron."

The darkened foyer of the house was cluttered with dim shapes that slowly coalesced into a jumble of half-unpacked luggage as Colly's eyes adjusted. The boy was bouncing on his toes beside a large suitcase, his now-naked torso glowing in the dim light.

"Maybe the iron's in here?"

Colly shook her head. "I didn't bring one—Uncle Russ said this house was fully furnished. Go brush your teeth and get your sun-sleeves and hat. I'll look around."

The boy tossed Colly his shirt and raced for the stairs.

Colly rummaged through closets, then headed for the kitchen. It was an old-fashioned, cheerful space, with World War Two–era enameled countertops and white curtains festooned with cross-stitched cherries.

Colly checked the pantry and cupboards. "Wonderful. Guess I'm improvising."

She set a heavy stock pot on the stove to heat, then layered several dish towels on the countertop.

A few moments later, Satchel entered the kitchen, still shirt-less but with his backpack slung over a skinny shoulder. He wore a floppy bucket hat and in one hand clutched two dark strips of nylon that looked like a pair of women's stockings.

"What're you doing, Grandma?"

"Ironing."

"With a pot?"

"It's hot metal. What's the difference?" She finished pressing the shirt and inspected it. "Good enough. Take off the hat, buddy."

She popped the t-shirt over his head, then helped him slide the nylon sleeves onto his arms.

"I look dumb. Everyone'll laugh."

"You wear them in Houston."

"People know me there."

"They'll get to know you here, too."

In his pack, she found the tube of prescription sunblock, which she massaged briskly into his face, neck, and the backs of his hands as he grimaced and squirmed.

"Be still for the teacher when she does this today. She's got a lot of kids to deal with."

"It's all gross and greasy. She'll hate me."

"Aunt Brenda explained things to her." Colly dropped the tube into the pack. "Put on your jacket—we're running late."

"What about breakfast?"

"You can eat a granola bar in the car."

"Why do I even have to go to school here?"

"It's just for a couple weeks." Colly rummaged in her purse for keys. "I don't want you to get behind. Besides, you can't stay here alone. I'll be working."

Satchel kicked the doorframe. "You said you retired. You promised."

Colly sighed. "Uncle Russ needs my help. Nothing bad will happen. Let's go, Mr. Worry-Wart."

The town of Crescent Bluff lay only five miles to the west, but it took Colly twenty minutes to reach it over the rutted dirt roads that wound through a patchwork of wheat fields and undeveloped scrubland. Other than the addition of a twelve-pump gas station and adjoining Starbucks out by Highway 208, the place had changed very little since the first time Randy brought her home. As she drove down Market Street, with its antiquated Western-style storefronts, each landmark reminded her sharply of him. She felt her jaw tightening, and she forced herself to relax.

Ten minutes later, Colly parked in the elementary school lot and glanced in the rearview mirror.

Beneath the brim of his hat, Satchel's face was white. "What if the other kids ask why I live with my grandma?"

"Satchel, I'm just forty-six. They'll probably think I'm your mom."

His eyes widened. "With white hair and wrinkles?"

Colly frowned and rotated the mirror until her own gray eyes stared back at her, wary and defiant beneath straight, heavy brows. The outline of her head was blurred by a nimbus of unruly hair—dark brown but threaded with a few undeniable strands of white. Her face looked leaner, tougher than the last time she'd been in Crescent Bluff, the fair skin more deeply furrowed, the once-generous mouth now pressed into a tight, cautious line. It was a guarded face, stripped for action—one that took in everything and revealed nothing.

Colly looked away. "You don't have to tell anybody anything you don't want to, Satch. Come on, let's find Aunt Brenda."

Inside the school's main hallway, Satchel clung to Colly's hand as they threaded through a crowd of raucous children. It was a relief to enter the comparative quiet of the central office suite.

"I'm looking for Brenda Newland," Colly told the middle-aged woman behind the main desk.

The woman smiled pleasantly and regarded them over her half-moon glasses. "She's expecting you?"

"Yes. I'm her sister-in-law."

"Oh." The woman's expression soured. "Mrs. Newland stepped out for a minute. You can wait in her office." She nodded curtly towards a door labelled "School Counselor."

The office was small and meticulously neat. Colly and Satchel sat on a bench in front of the desk. On the opposite wall hung a framed poster of Texas wildflowers, and in its glass, Colly caught another disconcerting reflection of herself. She pulled out her hairband to smooth and retie the thick ponytail.

"How come the lady at the desk was mad at us?" Satchel asked.

"She's mad at me, buddy. Not you."

"Why?"

"Some people here think I did a bad thing."

"Did you?"

"Not now, Satchel. Take off your gear and put it in your pack."

Satchel removed his hat and stripped off the protective sleeves. "Did Grandpa Randy really go to this school when he was little?"

"Yes. Uncle Russ and Uncle Lowell, too."

"Not Uncle Willis?"

"He went to a special school."

"Why?"

"His brain didn't work right. He needed extra help."

Satchel looked at her. "How did Uncle Willis die? You said you'd tell me."

"We'll talk about it later."

"You always say that, but we never do." Satchel scowled and swung his feet.

After a few minutes, the door opened and a slender woman entered carrying a stack of folders. She was in her late thirties with short chestnut hair and the compact, muscular limbs of a runner. Her eyes, dark and intense, were set in a narrow face.

"There you are. I'm so glad." Brenda Newland laid the folders on the desk and hugged Colly and Satchel. "How long has it been?"

"A couple years. Not since the funeral."

Brenda winced. "Sorry to bring that up."

"I love the haircut. You look great, Bren," Colly said, though secretly she thought her sister-in-law seemed tired, her face more deeply lined than Colly remembered.

"You're sweet, but I own a mirror." Brenda ran her fingers absently around the margins of her lips, where the skin had begun to pucker slightly. "Shocking how much divorce ages a person."

16

"How's that going?"

"Nothing's easy. You know Lowell. But we're trying to be civil for the kids' sake." She glanced at Satchel, then mouthed to Colly, "*Later.*" Aloud, she added, "You got in last night? How's the farmhouse? It's been empty for ages. You could've stayed with me."

"I like the quiet. Helps me work." In truth, Colly wanted a refuge from the pressure of other people's unspoken accusations. She needed a safe zone.

"I hope Russ remembered to check the mouse traps and turn on the electricity."

"There wasn't an iron," Satchel said abruptly. "Grandma used a soup pot." He plucked at his shirt.

"You look very nice." Brenda laughed. "Logan and Minnie are so excited you're here, Satchel. They can't wait to see you."

Satchel fidgeted with his backpack. "Okay."

"He's a little nervous." Colly glanced at her watch.

"When are you meeting Russ?"

"I said I'd be at the station by nine."

Brenda nodded. "Satchel, let's find your classroom." She turned to Colly. "Then we'll do the paperwork."

By the time they emerged from the school offices, the central hallway had largely cleared, though a few teachers were still shooing stragglers into classrooms. Colly took Satchel's hand, and they followed Brenda down the hall.

"Here's Mrs. Boyles, one of our second-grade teachers." Brenda waved at a petite, energetic-looking African American woman in flats and a knee-length skirt who was moving briskly towards a classroom.

"Wanice, this is Colly Newland and her grandson, Satchel, the boy I was telling you about."

Wanice Boyles welcomed them warmly. "Why don't you go inside, Satchel. My aide will show you your cubby and desk."

Satchel looked up at Colly and chewed his lip.

She ruffled his hair. "It's okay, buddy."

"Don't forget to pick me up."

"When the bell rings, I'll be waiting. Promise."

"Such a serious little guy," Wanice said after Satchel vanished inside. "Brenda says he's got health issues?"

Colly nodded. "It's a genetic thing—solar urticaria. Direct sunlight triggers a severe histamine reaction. His throat can close up, and he can have seizures. Here's his EpiPen, for emergencies." She rummaged in her purse.

"What about recess?"

"He'll be fine in the shade with his hat and sun-sleeves."

Wanice glanced at Brenda, and then back at Colly. "Is there anything I should watch for? After what y'all have gone through, I'm sure there's been emotional strain."

Though the question was not unexpected, Colly felt her chest tighten. *Strain?* she thought. *Do you want to hear about the night terrors? Bed-wetting? Self-inflicted burns?*

She looked at Brenda, who said, "Satchel's had some struggles, but he's never lashed out at other kids. And he's been better, recently. Right, Colly?"

"Therapy's helped," Colly managed.

The teacher's brow furrowed, but she smiled. "I'm sure he'll do great." She hesitated. "I was so sorry to hear what happened. I knew Randy in high school."

There was no flicker of accusation behind the woman's eyes. Even so, Colly felt her face stiffening into the familiar mask. "Thanks."

◆ ◆ ◆

"I'm so damn tired of people telling me how sorry they are," Colly said when they were back in Brenda's office. "They get this look—it's awful."

"I know. It was the same after Lowell moved out." Brenda rifled through a stack of paperwork. "People mean well. But for them, it's a one-time conversation. For you, it's a constant pity-barrage." She handed Colly a form. "Sign this. I'll be your emergency contact, if you want."

"Pity's the worst." Colly bent over the desk. "I'd rather have them hate me."

"You've come to the right place, then." Brenda smiled wryly. "Most people aren't as nice as Wanice. They hate me, too, if it's any comfort."

Colly handed back the paper. "I doubt that. You didn't get anybody killed. Besides, everyone knows Lowell's an ass."

"But half the town works for him." Brenda gave her another form. "Plus, Iris has been gossiping. I deserve it, I suppose. If I could do things over . . ." An indefinable look crossed Brenda's face, a complicated mixture of wistfulness, regret, and anger. "You'd think a psychology degree would've stopped me making the most humiliating mistakes."

"We all make mistakes, Bren. Even Iris knows that." Colly signed the paper. "Here you go. Oh, by the way, Satchel doesn't want other kids knowing he lives with his decrepit granny. So keep that quiet, if you can."

Brenda laughed as she tucked the form into a thin folder. "There are grannies, and there are *grannies*."

"Which kind am I?"

"You're the badass rock-climbing kind. Come on, I'll walk you to your car."

Out in the parking lot, Colly asked, "How's joint custody going?"

"Tough at first, but getting better. I got a smaller place, and Lowell moved back to the ranch. We're still doing holidays and get-togethers at Mollison like one big, happy family, for the kids' sake. They love spending half their time on the ranch, with all that space to run around, and Iris spoiling them rotten. I don't worry so much about them being there, now that—" Brenda stopped herself.

"Now that Willis is dead?"

"What was the governor thinking, commuting his sentence?"

"Iris is well-connected. Money talks."

"With Willis, another disaster was inevitable. Honestly, that snake of his did us all a favor. Lowell thinks he would've gotten the death penalty this time. I'm not sure Iris would've survived that. As it is, she can believe whatever she wants."

Iris can forgive Willis, but not me, Colly thought. "No mother wants to think badly of her child."

"But she shouldn't be blind to reality. You know Iris was behind this whole re-investigation, don't you? Since Willis died, she's been obsessed with clearing his name. She badgered Russ into dragging you out here. He can't say no to her."

"You think Willis was guilty?"

"Of *course* he was. Denny Knox was found at the pond, just like the Parker boy."

At the car, Colly turned and regarded her sister-in-law thoughtfully. "That's not proof."

Brenda's eyebrows rose. "You don't think it was Willis?"

"I don't think anything, yet. What's the mood in town?"

"Jumpy. People are still keeping a close eye on their kids, worried the investigation might've got it wrong. But the Rangers seemed satisfied. Truth is, Willis was a psychopath. If Iris hadn't pulled strings to get him out of prison, Denny would still be alive."

"You're the psychologist." Colly found her keys and unlocked the car.

Brenda apparently felt she'd said too much. "Sorry, I'm rambling—you know me."

"The distraction's nice. I dread seeing Russ."

"He doesn't blame you for what happened."

"I blame myself. Besides, looking at him is like looking at a ghost."

"Colly, it's just Russ—you've known him half your life." Brenda hugged her. "Don't worry about Satchel. I'm here till noon every day. I'll keep an eye out."

Chapter 3

Driving through town, Colly tried to shake off the heaviness she felt. The visit with Brenda had left her depleted and a little depressed. Her sister-in-law frequently had that effect on her, though Colly wasn't sure why. Their encounters were always friendly but exhausting, as if they were both trying too hard. Acting parts in a play. And Colly hadn't slept well the night before. Satchel, refusing to stay in a separate bed in the unfamiliar house, had kept her awake with his thrashing and muttering. She'd dozed for a few minutes now and then, each time waking to find his hot, sweating little body pressed against her as if he were trying to burrow away from something horrible.

The night terrors had been better since he'd started counseling. Had bringing him to Crescent Bluff been a mistake? He'd looked so small and vulnerable walking through Mrs. Boyles' classroom door, white-faced and clutching the straps of his backpack like a parachute. At least Brenda would be close by in case of trouble. She might be draining to talk to, but she was family.

Colly yawned and glanced at the dashboard clock. No time to hit up the Starbucks on the eastern outskirts of town. She'd have to make do with stationhouse swill.

The police station occupied the oldest building in Crescent Bluff, a nineteenth-century structure that locals still called the

Old Courthouse, though it hadn't served in that capacity since the 1950s. Built of rough-hewn limestone, it sat in a grove of mature live oaks at the west end of Market Street, a little apart from the shops.

Colly parked in the lot next to the station. As she got out of the car, a side door in the Courthouse opened, and a man in a policeman's uniform and western boots trotted towards her, waving. Colly felt something twist painfully in her stomach.

Russ Newland was in his mid-forties, broad-shouldered and powerfully built, with coarse, sandy hair and a weathered face. Colly had first met him six months into her relationship with Randy, when he came to Houston to visit his twin after finishing his first tour of duty in the Marines. She went with Randy to pick up his brother at the airport, and the three of them spent the evening drinking and dancing—not the club dancing she'd grown up with in New Jersey, but Texas "boot-scooting"—at a place called the Silver Spurs Dancehall and Saloon. Colly hadn't known what she was doing and made an absolute fool of herself, but it was fun watching the two men kicking and twirling in their western boots and broad-brimmed Stetsons.

Physically, the brothers had been nearly indistinguishable, Russ being the slightly stockier and more heavily muscled of the two. But their personalities were quite different. While Randy was outgoing and affable, Russ was more reserved. Colly had liked him immediately.

His deep-set eyes were the same piercing blue that Randy's had been. Now, as he approached, Colly found it painful to look at them.

"Saw you from the window," he said. "Glad you made it."

After a quick, awkward hug, they turned towards the station.

"Appreciate you coming out at such short notice, Col. Hope the farmhouse is okay."

"It's perfect, thanks."

"Been empty since Wanda's folks died. I sent Alice to clean it up, but you know teenagers."

Wanda, Russ's wife, had died of breast cancer a decade earlier, leaving him to raise their daughter alone. Colly found it odd that he'd never remarried.

"How old is Alice now? Sixteen?"

"Seventeen. Spitting image of her mother. Hard to look at her, sometimes."

I know the feeling, Colly thought.

She followed him through the station's side door, which opened into a small workroom. On a table beside the copier sat a box of sweaty-looking pastries and a dilapidated coffee maker.

"Want some?" Russ asked. "Costco's finest, but it's caffeinated."

He poured her a cup and then led the way into an open office area, where an elderly receptionist and three uniformed officers sat at their desks—two men and a woman.

The woman caught Colly's eye immediately. She was young—in her late twenties, Colly judged, though she looked younger. Thin and pale, with dark, heavy eyeliner and a purple streak dyed into her straight black hair, she seemed more like a rebellious teenager than a cop. A white birthmark ran down the right side of her face and neck, disappearing beneath the collar of her shirt. She stared at Colly with sullen intensity.

Russ cleared his throat. "Listen up—most of y'all have met my sister-in-law before. You know she was a detective in Houston for years. She's here at my request to review the Denny Knox case. I want you to give her every consideration."

Silence hung in the room. The receptionist and the male officers nodded grudgingly. The pale young policewoman continued to glower.

"Let's get to it," Russ said. "C'mon, Parker, you're with us."

24

The young policewoman stood.

Russ led them down a hallway and through a door marked "Chief of Police." His office was large, and cluttered with papers and files, the only personal touches a spindly cactus on the window-sill and a sun-faded photograph of Wanda pushing a four-year-old Alice on a swing.

Russ shut the door and sat at his desk, waving Colly to a nearby chair. The young patrolwoman planted herself on a stool in the corner.

"Hope you don't mind Avery sitting in. I've asked her to assist with the review. I should stay out of it as much as I can, so it'll be good for you to have someone who—"

"People don't hate?"

Russ's mouth twitched. "I was going to say 'who knows the town.' Avery grew up here, and she's got a special interest in this one. Plus, she's new and could use the experience." He hesitated. "Having a cop along will help. I'm not sure about the legalities, you being retired and all."

Colly glanced at the young woman. She looked anything but helpful, but it would be nice to have an insider's perspective. Maybe she wasn't as ill-humored as she appeared.

Colly turned back to Russ. "I'll trust your judgment."

He nodded. "I didn't tell you much over the phone. I reckon you've got questions."

"Tons." Colly crossed her legs. "Mainly: *why am I here?* The Rangers closed the case. More to the point, you and I are both in the suspect's family. Nothing we conclude will be admissible."

"That's definitely true in my case—but the Rangers respect you. A couple said they'd worked with you before. If you find some-thing they missed, maybe they'll reopen the case. They were so sure Willis was guilty that they wrapped things up and left town right after he died."

"You don't agree?"

Russ shrugged. "The Rangers know what they're doing. But some folks thought the case deserved a second opinion."

"Meaning Iris."

"Been talking to Brenda, huh?" Russ grinned. "Momma encouraged me to call you, I'll admit. But I told her no, at first."

"Why?"

"Lot of reasons. I knew how much you wanted out of police work, after what happened in Houston." His hand momentarily tightened on the arm of his chair. "And, to be honest, I thought the Rangers might be right about Willis."

"What changed your mind?"

"Several things." Russ picked up a file box from the floor beside him and set it on the desk. "How much do you remember about the Adam Parker case in '98?"

"The one Willis went down for? Not a lot, except what was in the news. Victoria was a toddler, so I stayed with her in Houston during the court stuff, and Randy never liked talking about it. I remember Willis admitted killing that boy and later recanted."

"That's the gist, but there's more to it."

"How's this relevant to the current case?"

"I'll get to that." Russ picked up a pencil and turned it in his fingers. "Adam was a troubled kid. Truancy, shoplifting. Nothing too serious, but you could tell there were problems at home. One night, he disappeared—and his house burned down the same night. His mother died in the fire, and his dad and little sister were badly injured."

"Arson?"

"Definitely. Given his history, police figured he torched his own house and ran off—till a month later, when his body turned up at the stock pond." Russ dropped the pencil and opened the file box. He pulled out an 8x10 photo, which he slid across the desk.

"He'd been submerged for weeks. Scavengers had gotten to him, but ID wasn't hard to confirm."

Colly studied the photo—a twelve-year-old boy in rotting, mud-caked clothes lying on the grass, hands folded over a bloated sternum, empty eye sockets staring skyward.

From across the room, the young policewoman inhaled sharply. Her face was flushed, and the birthmark on her cheek and neck stood out in livid contrast.

"Want to see?" Colly gestured to an empty chair beside her.

Avery Parker shook her head and looked away.

"She's seen it," Russ said. "I briefed her on the case."

If she's this squeamish, she's in the wrong line of work, Colly thought.

She turned back to the picture. "They ruled out accidental drowning?"

"He was strangled, weighed down with chains."

"Found in the water?"

"No, that's the thing." Russ pointed to the photo.

Colly's eyebrows rose. "They found him like this? He's been posed."

Russ nodded. "Cops thought the killer did it."

"Why bother weighing down a body, then fishing it out again?"

"Remorse, maybe? It's even possible someone else found him and pulled him out. That's what Avery thinks." He glanced at the young woman, who nodded.

"Then why not call the police? Why leave him for the scavengers?" Colly asked.

"Good question."

Avery stirred. "People do things for lots of reasons. You never know."

Colly laid down the photo. "Was Willis the first suspect?"

"First and only," Russ said. "He was always hanging around that pond. A few months earlier, he got into trouble for spying on some kids swimming there. Plus, he had a history going back to his early teens."

"Molesting that little boy? Randy told me."

"The Carroway kid. Not a kid anymore. Runs his family's farm now. Willis denied it, and Dad paid off the Carroways so they didn't press charges. But everybody knew." Russ grimaced. "Here's what cinched it, though."

He produced a package of blue nitrile gloves from a desk drawer, took two for himself, and tossed the package to Colly.

"What are these for?"

"Just put them on."

He withdrew an evidence bag from the file box and slit the red sealing tape with a knife. When he tilted the bag, a strand of pale pink ribbon slid onto the desk, along with a curled scrap of gray-brown fur.

"What's that, a dead gerbil?"

Russ smoothed the thing flat and pushed it towards her. "This was on Adam's body."

Colly gazed down at the furred object. "What the hell?" She picked it up and spread it on her palm, examining the long, tapered ears and delicate whiskers. Through the dime-sized holes where the eyes should have been, she could see her nitrile-covered hand. The thing seemed to be watching her with staring, bright blue eyes.

"Looks like someone just ripped the face off a rabbit."

Russ met her eyes. "Yeah."

"A hunter, maybe?"

He shook his head. "Turn it over."

"It's been tanned."

"A hunter wouldn't skin the head. Let alone tan it."

"It's like a miniature Halloween mask, only real." Colly shuddered. "Where was it, exactly?"

"Tucked into Adam's hand. Rolled and tied with that ribbon, like a little scroll. State Crime Lab said it hadn't been submerged. It was put there later."

Colly laid down the rabbit mask and picked up the pink ribbon, running it through her fingers. "Chiffon. Maybe off a little girl's dress."

"Or a doll's," Avery said. "I had one with ribbons like that."

Colly regarded her thoughtfully, then turned back to Russ. "Why'd they think this pointed to Willis?"

A muscle twitched in Russ's jaw. "He kept rabbits to feed that damn snake of his. Not even the same kind. Willis's were domesticated. But that's a wild rabbit—some kind of hare, they said. Investigators thought it pointed to a fetish—a *Silence of the Lambs*, serial-killer type deal. Willis was a sex offender with mental problems. He liked to hang around the pond, and he kept rabbits. They figured where there's smoke, there's fire, I reckon." Russ rested his elbows on the desk. "Willis denied everything at first, but he failed a polygraph, so they kept after him. There wasn't any hard evidence. But once he confessed . . ."

"That was enough?"

"Basically. Later, he pled innocent, said he'd been bullied into confessing. But no one believed that, except Momma. She got him an expensive attorney who had doctors do a brain scan. They said Willis had an abnormality that could prevent him from controlling impulsive, violent behavior. The lawyer argued for sending him to a state hospital, but you know juries." Russ picked up the rabbit's mask and stared at it moodily. "They spared him the death penalty, at least."

Colly leaned back in her chair, frowning. "But what's this got to do with Denny Knox?"

"The cases are linked, and there's too much that doesn't add up. Avery convinced me."

"Really?" Colly looked again at the young policewoman. Why on earth would Russ trust the judgment of a kid like that? She was probably fresh out of the academy.

Colly forced a smile. "Russ mentioned you have a special interest in this case?"

"Adam Parker was my brother," Avery said almost fiercely. "I know in my gut Willis didn't kill him. It's why I'm a cop."

Colly stared, her face growing hot. She'd seen it before—victims' family members pushing for further investigation, refusing to accept police findings. To admit a case was over meant recognizing the finality of loss. The hollow inadequacy of justice. It meant letting go. Colly understood the impulse, having experienced it herself. But the notion that her life had been disrupted—her guilt over Victoria's and Randy's deaths leveraged—on false pretenses was infuriating.

Oh God, Russ isn't sleeping with her, is he? She's not much older than Alice, Colly thought. *If he dragged me out here just to please his booty call, I'll kill him.*

Russ seemed to read her thoughts. "I wouldn't have called you if I didn't think Avery's onto something." He leaned forward. "If Willis didn't kill Adam, he didn't kill Denny Knox, either. The same person murdered both boys, and whoever did it is still out there."

The room was silent. Colly swallowed the last mouthful of coffee and set down the cup. "I hate to be the wet blanket, Russ, but that's two gigantic logical leaps. Other than Avery's gut, where's your evidence Willis didn't kill Adam? And how do you know the same person committed both murders? You're not going on the fact that both bodies were dumped at the pond, are you? Everyone in West Texas knew the details of Adam's case—it was all over the news."

Russ peeled off his gloves. "I'd agree, if it weren't for this."

From his desk, he pulled a thick file folder labeled "Dennis Knox." Rifling through its contents, he handed Colly a photo.

It was a close-up of the rabbit mask on a translucent plastic sheet, staring up at her with dead white eyes.

Colly looked up. "So?"

"It's not the same one. That was on Denny, not Adam. Avery took that picture last September, the day we found the body."

He handed Colly a second photograph, this time of a ginger-haired boy, naked, curled tightly on his side, his eyes closed. His pale skin glowed against the hoof-pocked mud on which he lay. He looked asleep.

Russ pointed to one of the boy's cupped hands. "It's there, rolled and tied. Just like Adam's. See the pink ribbon sticking out?"

Colly whistled. Laying the two photos side by side, she inspected them. "Creepy, but it doesn't rule out a copycat."

"Yeah, it does. Back in '98, the cops never released this detail." He tapped on the first photo with his forefinger.

"You mean—?"

"Only the person who planted it on Adam would've known about the rabbit mask. Get it?" Avery said irritably.

Colly suppressed her annoyance at the girl's tone. "That's why the Rangers closed Denny's case after Willis's death?"

"Partly. But it gets worse." Russ ran a hand roughly over his face. "We found a stash of rabbit masks in Willis's cabin the night he died."

"Seriously?"

"Yep. The thing is, Momma alibis him, says Willis was with her the whole day Denny was killed."

"You believe her?"

"Momma's not much of a liar. If anything, she's too honest. And the housekeeper backs her story. Rangers didn't buy it, of

31

course. Thought she was protecting her son. But if she's telling the truth, then those masks were planted to frame him. The killer must've figured if Willis took the fall once, it'd work a second time."

"You think this hypothetical killer murdered Willis, too?"

Russ sighed. "Willis's death was ruled accidental. Rangers thought it was suicide, though, and I agree. Willis knew better than to hand-feed that snake from inside the cage. The Rangers figured he did it out of guilt. But I think he was just scared of being wrongfully convicted again."

"Russ, you can't exonerate someone on a rookie's hunch and the word of the suspect's mother."

"That's why I need the case review. Something's not right, Col. Willis wasn't smart enough to make those masks. And he wasn't dumb enough to leave them in his nightstand. I don't think he killed anyone. But someone went to a lot of trouble to make it look like he did." Pushing aside the papers on his desk, Russ leaned in and lowered his voice. "Momma wants to clear Willis's name. But honestly, that's the least of my worries. I think we've got a serial killer on our hands. This has all the hallmarks—similar victim profile, same method of killing, tokens left to taunt the cops."

"Serial killers escalate till they're caught. They don't go dormant for twenty years."

"Some do," Avery said quickly, dragging her stool towards the desk. "This is just like that BTK guy up in Kansas."

Russ nodded, his eyes on Colly. "The town's on edge. Folks are scared for their kids. To keep the rabbit masks a secret, the Rangers couldn't explain why they closed the case after Willis died. Most people reckon they got it right. But a lot don't. I've heard talk about forming a citizen posse, which would be a nightmare. There's way more guns than people here. And if this killer strikes again . . ." He sat back heavily. "We've got to catch this guy."

Colly nodded, and her gaze wandered to the window. On the station lawn, two gray squirrels, lean from winter and excited by the warm weather, were chasing each other around a tree trunk. They paused, tails flicking in alarm, then shot up into the live oak's dark canopy as a UPS truck rumbled by.

Colly sighed and looked back at Russ. "Okay. Tell me about Denny Knox."

Russ pulled a sheaf of papers from the folder in front of him, but before he could speak, they were interrupted by a knock. The door opened, and the elderly receptionist appeared. "Sorry to bother you, Chief. The team at the pond says they've found something."

Russ's look of irritation vanished. "Tell them we're on our way."

Chapter 4

By the time they emerged from the station, the morning haze had burned off. The sky was now a clear, brassy blue that promised unseasonable heat.

"What team was she talking about?" Colly asked.

Russ settled his Stetson on his head. "The Rangers wanted to dredge the stock pond. But the judge is a golfing buddy of Lowell's and wouldn't give them a warrant, and Momma flat refused. I think she was scared they'd find something incriminating to Willis. I told her she'd have to agree to total cooperation if she wanted your help, though. I sent a couple guys out there this morning." He handed Colly the Denny Knox file he was carrying. "You can skim this as we drive."

He led the way to a dusty black SUV and opened the front passenger door for Colly. Avery, carrying an expensive-looking camera, climbed into the back seat.

As they headed north, Colly dug in her bag for her reading glasses and opened the file. The first document was a typed case summary. She picked it up.

"The Rangers wrote this?"

"Avery did. She's been great on this case." Russ winked into the rearview mirror.

Pretending not to see, Colly put on her glasses and read quickly.

The summary was succinct and well-written: thirteen-year-old Denny Knox had disappeared on a sunny Friday afternoon in early September. He had ridden his bicycle from his home to the Compass Counseling Center for his court-mandated therapy, arriving at noon. His therapist, Brenda Newland, reported that their session was uneventful and that Knox was in a good mood throughout. Both Newland and the office coordinator, Pearl Granley, saw the boy exit through the center's front entrance shortly after one p.m., a fact confirmed by CCTV footage from a daycare across the street. Security cameras from several homes and businesses recorded Knox pedaling rapidly northwards through town. He was wearing jeans, a yellow t-shirt, and a red ballcap, and carrying an army-green canvas backpack. Tom Gunnell, a mechanic at Digby's Automotive on the Old Ranch Way, reported seeing Knox ride past the shop around 1:20 p.m., going north towards Newland Ranch, though Digby's had no cameras, and police could not independently confirm the account. Gunnell's was the last known sighting of Knox, whose nude body was discovered beside the Newland Ranch stock pond at 6:30 the next morning. He appeared to have been strangled with some sort of ligature not found at the scene; his bicycle and clothing (minus ballcap and backpack) were located nearby. Ranch foreman Felix Arredondo discovered the corpse while checking on the cattle and called Chief of Police Ruston Newland to report the news.

Colly stopped reading and looked up. Like most West Texas towns, Crescent Bluff had no suburban perimeter. Its tight cluster of homes and shops thinned to a spotty fringe of junkyards, garages, and trailer parks, and then, abruptly, to rural landscape. They were already past the outskirts and speeding along a straight two-lane highway into open country.

"I didn't know Brenda was Denny's therapist."

Russ nodded. "She works afternoons at the counseling center."

Strange she didn't mention it this morning, Colly thought. "Why was his therapy court-mandated?"

"He started a fire in a school bathroom last spring. District pressed charges. Denny was in trouble a lot. We arrested him for vandalism and petty theft several times."

Colly tapped her pencil thoughtfully against the folder. "His folks didn't report him missing the night before?"

"Avery, what did Jolene say about that?" Russ braked as they approached a dark, feathered lump in the road. An enormous turkey vulture looked up, then hoisted itself in the air to reveal the carcass of a white-tailed deer.

"Interview transcript's in the folder."

"Give me the gist," Colly said.

Avery looked annoyed. "His mom said Denny ran off sometimes, after fights with his stepdad. He'd cool down at his Little League coach's house and come back in a day or two. So she didn't worry."

Russ glanced at Colly. "Sounds neglectful, but Jolene's had her hands full with him. Plus, her husband's been out of work for months, and their relationship's stormy. We've been called out on several domestics, but she won't press charges."

"Who's the coach?"

"Tom Gunnell—mechanic at Digby's Automotive."

Colly rifled through the papers in her lap. "The last person to see Denny alive?"

"Yeah, I don't trust coincidences, either, but this one seems legit. Rangers looked at him hard, but the receptionist at Digby's backed up his story, and he passed a polygraph."

"Maybe so. But he's definitely someone I want to talk to."

A few minutes later, Russ turned onto a gravel road. After crossing a cattle guard and passing beneath a wrought-iron arch that read "Newland Ranch," the road curved north, but Russ followed a rough dirt track that snaked away south. They bumped and lurched through the scrubland, gravel pinging against the metal floorboards, until finally rounding the shoulder of a hill into an open space, where a squad car was parked beside a weathered fencepost hung with a "No Trespassing" sign.

Russ turned off the ignition. "Let's go."

Colly and Avery followed him single-file past the sign and along a narrow cow path. The day was growing warm. Startled grasshoppers leaped around them as they pushed through the sagebrush and stunted cedar. Colly was glad she'd worn jeans and hiking boots.

They emerged from the scrub near a stock pond ringed with cottonwoods. Two officers, sweaty and red-faced, were resting a few yards from the waterside. They had spread out a plastic tarp, on which a metal supply kit sat beside a wet, greenish lump.

The officers clambered to their feet. The taller—a lanky, acne-scarred youth—waved enthusiastically.

"Hey, Chief, look what we got."

The other officer, older and more dignified, mopped his face with a red bandana. "We ain't opened it yet. Figured you'd wanna do that. Jimmy found it," he added generously.

"Good work." Russ leaned over the object for a closer look. Colly joined him.

"It's a backpack," Jimmy, the younger officer, said.

The older one swatted irritably at a pair of blackflies. "They got eyes, Meggs."

"Get some shots of this, Avery," Russ said.

Avery circled the tarp, taking pictures from every angle. "Army-green canvas. Could be Denny's. It wasn't with the other stuff."

Colly looked up. "Other stuff?"

"Denny's clothes were under that tree, perfectly folded. Except for the red baseball cap. We never found that. His bike was over there." Russ pointed.

"The clothes were folded? Interesting."

"Think there'll be DNA?" Jimmy asked.

Colly frowned. "Doubtful. Looks like it's been submerged a while."

Russ bent closer and sniffed. "Smells like it, too." He picked up a stick and poked gently at the backpack. "Something's inside. Gibbins, hand us some gloves and evidence bags."

"A forensics lab should open it," Colly said.

Russ shook his head. "That'll mean calling the Rangers back in. They'll cut us out of the loop. I want to see what's in here." He pulled on a pair of nitrile gloves. Handing some to Colly, he squatted on the tarp.

"Why drag me here from Houston if you won't listen?" Colly muttered, kneeling beside him.

Russ didn't hear, or pretended not to. "Avery, keep shooting," he said, and he began to unzip the pack.

The zipper was badly corroded. After several minutes of coaxing and cursing, he dropped the bag and sat back on his heels. "That's only a couple inches, but it won't go any further without some WD-40."

"You could cut it," Jimmy said eagerly. "I got a Bowie knife."

Gibbins, the older cop, glared at him. "He ain't doin' that, you dimwit."

Russ ignored them both. "You've got smaller hands, Col. Try reaching in."

Colly hesitated. "Are there—?"

"Cottonmouths are the only dangerous water snakes around here, and they stay on the surface."

"Okay. But I won't force anything."

With the sound of Avery's camera shutter in her ears, Colly wriggled one hand through the opening and cautiously groped around. "There's a couple hardcover books. Pages are mush, but the covers feel intact." She explored further. "I've got something stiff and leathery. Baseball glove, maybe."

"Denny played Little League," Jimmy said. "My cousin Tom's his coach."

"Anything you can pull out?" Russ asked.

Avery looked up from her camera. "Little stuff'll be at the bottom."

Colly reached deeper and her fingers closed on something hard. She pulled it through the opening. A Swiss Army knife.

Russ handed her a bag. "We'll find out if it's Denny's."

Another search produced a camo-colored wallet and a fob with what looked like the key to a bike lock.

Colly gave the wallet to Russ, who opened the Velcro flap. "Bingo. School ID for 'Dennis G. Knox.' Plus, six bucks, cash. Robbery wasn't the motive, then. Anything else?"

"I don't think so." Colly did a final check. "Hold on."

She pulled out a small, rubbery object. It was horseshoe-shaped and made of blue silicone.

"What the hell's that?" Russ demanded.

Colly turned it in her fingers. "No clue."

"Parker?"

Avery hunched her shoulders. "Looks medical. Some kind of mouth guard?"

"Gibbins, Meggs, take a look." Russ waved the officers closer.

"That's a shoe insert," Gibbins said immediately. "Got some like 'em for my plantar fasciitis. That one's smaller than mine."

Russ pushed up the brim of his Stetson. "Weird thing for a kid to carry."

Colly dropped the object into an evidence bag. "Did Denny have foot problems?"

"We can ask Jolene," Avery said.

The sun was now high, the mud around the shoreline beginning to crack in the unseasonable heat. Two piebald longhorns had come to the far side of the pond to drink. As Colly stood, they raised their heads to watch her, water dripping from their muzzles.

Colly peeled off her gloves. "Okay, Russ, walk me through the scene."

After sending Meggs and Gibbins back to town with the evidence, Russ led Colly to a spot near the edge of the water.

"Denny's body was here. Felix found it just after dawn. Said he didn't go near it."

"Think that's true?"

Russ nodded. "You could tell by his footprints."

There had been a clear set of prints around the body, though—presumably the killer's—made by a pair of men's rubber boots or waders, size ten.

"What size was Willis?"

"Ten." Russ rubbed the bridge of his nose. "So are Lowell and me, for what it's worth. It's a common size."

"Any barefoot?"

"Nope. Bottoms of Denny's feet were clean, too. There was a set of tracks, like a hand truck's, from the cow path down to the waterside. Rangers figured Willis killed him elsewhere and wheeled him here, but they couldn't find any hand trucks on the ranch that matched."

"Smooth tracks, or treaded?"

"Smooth, I think."

"Any pictures?"

"Avery'll know."

They looked around. The young woman had moved away and was sitting on a grassy rise beneath a cottonwood, hugging her knees and staring across the water.

Colly lowered her voice. "What's her deal?"

40

"She's okay. Let's leave her be."

Colly started to respond, then changed her mind. "Any idea when the body was dumped?"

"Some kids were out here smoking pot till midnight. It wasn't here then."

"So between midnight and six-thirty Saturday morning, when Felix found it?"

"Weird thing is, the ME said Denny died around the time he left Brenda's—an hour after, tops."

"Where was the body all that time?"

"If the Digby's mechanic killed him, he could've stashed him at the garage. But Denny was drugged with Xanax, and we never found evidence that Tom Gunnell had access." Russ met Colly's eyes. "Willis did, though. Momma takes it."

"Half of America takes it." Colly sighed. "You said Iris alibis Willis for the time of death. What about when the body was dumped?"

"He was in his cabin, sleeping. But if he didn't kill Denny, he didn't dump him."

Colly looked around. The two longhorns had finished drinking and were ambling away from the water, grazing on tufts of buffalo grass.

Russ removed his Stetson and fanned himself with the brim. "What are you thinking?"

"Whoever did this is organized, meticulous. Denny's clothes were folded, you said. And it took time and skill to make those rabbit masks. They mean something." She looked up. "You've checked into them as a lead, I guess?"

"The Rangers sent Denny's to the crime lab but didn't find much. Said it looked professionally tanned, for whatever that's worth. We talked to every taxidermist between Midland and Dallas, but they all checked out." He shrugged. "Avery researched 'rabbit heads' online—found a few weird foreign recipes. Plus, some high-end pet food suppliers that sell them as dog treats, believe it or not. City folks pay ten bucks a pop for them—fresh or dehydrated, skin on or off."

"Why city folks?"

"Well, no one in West Texas would buy them, that's for sure. Scrubland's crawling with jackrabbits—you can get as many as you want for free. And our killer's definitely a local. We're on private property in the middle of nowhere." He waved his arm. "This guy knows the area. Anyhow, our masks don't come from any pet food place. They all use domesticated rabbits—we checked."

Colly nodded, staring across the water. Then she asked, "Why did Felix call you directly when he found the body, Russ? The report said he called you, not 911."

Russ stopped fanning. "His English isn't great. I reckon he felt more comfortable with me."

He's not telling me everything, Colly thought. "I'd like to speak to him."

Russ snapped his fingers. "That reminds me, I'm supposed to tell you—Momma wants to have everyone at Mollison for dinner tonight, sort of an unofficial welcome party for you and Satchel. We can hunt up Felix then. He's usually around Willis's cabin that time of day."

Colly, who had been looking forward to a quiet evening at the farmhouse to unpack, inwardly groaned. But a dinner invitation from Iris Newland was more a summons than a request.

"Sounds good."

Russ glanced at his watch. "I've got a meeting in an hour. Anything else you want to see?" He made a sweeping gesture with his hat.

"Not now. Maybe after I've read the whole file." Colly paused. "Where exactly was Adam's body found in '98?"

Russ lowered his voice. "Where Avery's sitting—under that tree."

Colly watched her for a moment. "I don't know about having her help me with the review, Russ. She's got a huge chip on her shoulder."

"You would, too, if you'd had her luck."

"Mine hasn't been exactly stellar."

"I'm just saying there's reasons she's rough around the edges. Apart from losing her mom and brother, her dad was mean as they come."

"She's got some problem with me, and I just met her."

"Misguided loyalty, I expect."

"She blames me for getting your brother killed?"

"If it turns into a problem, I'll talk to her. She wants to be a big-city detective someday, but she needs experience."

"I'm not here to be someone's life coach."

"But you're going to need help. Avery's smart, and she's getting pretty good as a crime scene photographer." He laid a hand on Colly's shoulder. "Give her a chance, maybe reach out a little bit."

Colly squinted up at him. "Russ, if there's something going on between you and her, I need to know."

Russ's eyes widened, and he laughed. "She's half my age, Col. I'm trying to help her make something of herself, that's all." He put on his hat. "I'm starved. Want to grab some gorditas on the way back? There's a great food truck."

His words sounded forced, Colly thought. But it was hard to say whether he was lying or simply embarrassed by her question.

She decided to let it go, for now. "Gorditas sound great. Then, I'd like to see that counseling center."

"Sure thing. Avery'll take you."

As the three of them made the hot trek back up the cow path to the SUV, Colly, walking behind Avery, studied her closely. She seemed more subdued now, her thin shoulders slumped, staring at the ground as she walked. But the hand that gripped the camera's strap was clenched, and her jaw was set in a hard, bitter line. As she climbed into the car, her uniform collar gaped, and in the full sunlight, Colly saw that the pale blotch on her face and neck was not a birthmark but the welted scar of a deep, long-healed burn.

Chapter 5

Outside the Courthouse, Colly followed Avery to one of the cruisers and waited nervously while she unlocked it. Colly had offered to take her own car to the counseling center, but Russ had waved her off.

"People will cooperate better if you turn up in a squad car."

During her career, Colly had developed a cynical view of young drivers, and Avery's purple-streaked hair and aura of barely suppressed rage did nothing to improve her expectations. Sliding into the passenger's seat, she was startled and mildly amused, therefore, to see the girl adjust the mirrors and test the tension of her shoulder harness with care before pulling gingerly out of the lot.

"You said you don't think Willis killed your brother," Colly said as they headed east on Market Street. "Can I ask why?"

Avery's sullen expression vanished. "Because it doesn't make sense."

She's been waiting for that question, Colly thought. "How so?"

"Willis couldn't drive. How would he get Adam to the stock pond? Plus, the chains and gas can used in the crime came from our toolshed." Avery tugged absently at her collar, pulling it higher on her neck.

"You think the perpetrator knew your family's property?"

"Must have. There was no forced entry to the house, either. Investigators thought Adam probably knew the killer."

They stopped at a traffic light. Outside, a woman in a dingy apron emerged from the Blue Moon Saloon to sweep the sidewalk. Colly nodded, and the woman stopped sweeping to stare.

"Maybe your brother was friendly with Willis from church or somewhere."

"Every kid in town knew to stay away from Willis Newland. He was our boogeyman." The light changed, and Avery turned left. "I read Adam's case file and watched the tapes of Willis's interrogation. They didn't threaten him, but they promised he could go home as soon as he confessed. I don't think he understood what was going on."

Colly leaned against the headrest. "Usually, a victim's family is thrilled when someone's held accountable."

"Nobody should be wrongfully convicted, even a pedophile. Prison must've been hell for someone like Willis."

Avery seemed sincere. But Colly couldn't escape the feeling that she was withholding something. "How old were you when Adam died?"

"Eight."

"You didn't hear or see anything that night?"

Avery seemed unsettled by the question. She hesitated. "I was in bed asleep. I only remember my dad carrying me out of the burning house. I was cold, so I got clothes off the clothesline."

Colly said nothing. Instinct and training told her that Avery was lying. It was something about the angle of her shoulders, the overly even timbre of her voice. But why?

Two blocks north of Market Street, they parked in front of a red-brick building ringed with trimmed boxwoods. The sign said, "Compass Counseling Center, Dr. Niall Shaw."

Avery reached for the camera, but Colly shook her head. "We're just here for a friendly chat."

Inside, a grandmotherly woman smiled at them from the reception desk. "Can I help you?" She had just taken a bite of the sandwich she was holding, and she covered her mouth as she spoke.

Colly introduced herself and started to explain the reason for her visit, but the woman cut her off.

"Oh, yes, Detective, Brenda mentioned you might stop by. I'll tell her you're here." She reached for the phone.

A minute later, a door down the hall swung open, and Brenda emerged.

They chatted briefly before Colly said, "I didn't know you counseled here. Russ told me."

"Didn't I mention it? My time's split between this and the school. I'll finish clinical supervision hours this summer."

"And then I'll have to find another way to keep her around," said a deep, male voice.

Colly looked up. A tall, slender man in gray slacks and a crisp Oxford was strolling down the hall towards them. He was African American—in his late thirties, Colly judged—with a handsome, perceptive face and an air of casual confidence. Brenda introduced him as her supervisor and boss, Dr. Niall Shaw.

"More of a colleague." He laughed. "Pearl's the real boss around here." He patted the receptionist affectionately on the shoulder, then extended his hand to Colly. "Brenda explained why you're in town. Happy to help." He gave Avery a friendly nod, clearly recognizing her. She returned it coldly.

What's the story there? Colly wondered. "We're reviewing Denny Knox's movements the day he died. Is this a bad time?"

Shaw glanced at his watch. "Perfect. We never schedule noon clients. Not that I'll be very helpful—I was out of town that whole week. But I'm glad you're here. These last six months have been

46

rough. Parents are scared stiff there might be a killer out there. Here at the clinic, we're seeing more kids for depression and anxiety. I'm treating a kindergartener with an ulcer, believe it or not. Something's got to give." He waved them around the reception desk. "Let's chat in my office. You too, Pearl. Lock the front door."

In contrast with the lobby, Shaw's office felt cluttered and masculine, furnished with deep leather armchairs and walnut paneling lined with bookshelves. An enormous stuffed trout hung on the wall behind the desk.

Shaw noticed Colly staring. "That's Oscar. Beauty, isn't he?"

"You didn't catch him around here, did you?"

"Hardly." Shaw chuckled as he offered them seats. "I'm originally from Montana. I get back there to fly-fish when I can."

Brenda grinned at Pearl. "That's a new record."

"Record for what?" Colly asked.

"They like to see how long it takes me to mention fishing," Shaw said good-naturedly.

Colly found herself warming to his relaxed friendliness. He was an easy person to like—a handy quality in a therapist, she imagined. "I have copies of everyone's statements to the Rangers, but I wanted to go through things in person. You say you were out of town, Dr. Shaw?"

"Please, it's Niall. I was in Phoenix at an APA conference. Brenda called me the morning Denny was found. I caught the next flight home."

"You knew Denny?"

"A little. The woman who cleans our office is his aunt. When Denny got into trouble last year, Carmen asked for my advice. I offered our services to handle his therapy. But I had a sense he'd open up better to a woman, so Brenda took the case."

Colly turned to her sister-in-law. "Did he?"

Brenda glanced uneasily at Niall, who nodded. "I think therapist-client privilege has to be relaxed somewhat in this situation," he said.

Brenda turned back to Colly. "Denny divulged some, but he was guarded." She sighed. "He had the deck stacked against him—learning disabilities, a tough home life. Maybe if he'd gotten help earlier, or if I'd been more experienced . . ."

"You did your best with a difficult case," Niall said gently.

"Walk us through the last time you saw him," Colly said.

Brenda nodded. "It was a Friday noon appointment."

"I thought you didn't schedule noon clients."

"He usually came Thursday afternoons, but his mother said he had a conflict. The dentist or something. So I worked him in. He rode his bike here, and—"

"Wasn't he in school?"

Brenda shook her head. "Expelled last spring. He was attending an alternative program for kids who can't be mainstreamed, but it doesn't meet on Fridays."

"Did he usually ride his bike?" Avery cut in abruptly.

"His mother works nights, so normally she drove him. But that Friday, she was covering a coworker's day shift or something."

"What about the stepdad?" Colly asked.

"Their relationship wasn't good. Denny fended for himself a lot."

"If he wasn't coming from school, why'd he have a backpack? Did that seem odd?"

"I don't remember thinking about it."

"Do you know what he was carrying?"

"The Rangers asked that, too. Denny mentioned something about returning library books, so he must've had those. Not sure what else."

Beside her, Colly felt Avery stir. "Random question—do you know if Denny had foot problems?"

Brenda's eyebrows rose. "No, why?"

"What about his folks?"

"Not that I know of."

Colly and Avery exchanged a look.

Brenda was curious. "What's this about?"

Nosiness—an occupational hazard of therapists, Colly thought. *And cops, too, I suppose.* She ignored the question. "Was Denny here on time?"

Brenda looked mildly disappointed, but she nodded. "He was sweaty from riding. I got him a coke from the fridge and gave him a protein bar because he hadn't eaten lunch. Then we talked."

"Wait, walk me through the scene." Colly stood.

Brenda hesitated, but Niall pushed out of his armchair. "Come on, everyone. You heard the detective."

"Show us where you talked," Colly said.

Brenda led them to her office, a meticulously neat room with a sitting area at one end and a desk and bookshelves at the other. There were few decorations other than a vase of silk flowers on the desk and a brightly colored abstract painting over the sofa.

"I was here." Brenda laid a hand on an armchair. "Denny sat on the couch."

"Nothing unusual happened?"

Brenda frowned. "Not that I remember. We didn't discuss anything heavy that day—sometimes it's good just to chat. Builds trust. When he left, he seemed happy."

"Did he say where he was going?"

"Other than the library, no."

Colly turned to the receptionist, who was standing in the doorway. "You were in the building, too?"

The woman looked slightly indignant. "Certainly." She added that she usually met her daughter for a noon lunch on Fridays, but with Dr. Shaw out of town, she'd remained at work.

"It's our policy," Niall said. "When a therapist's with a client, at least one other person should be in the building."

Colly nodded and turned back to the receptionist. "Did Denny speak to you when he left?"

"No, but that wasn't unusual. He was a rude boy." She compressed her lips. "He gave me a little wave over his shoulder as he went out." She waggled her fingers to illustrate. "He seemed in a hurry. I watched him unlock his bicycle from the telephone pole outside."

"You didn't see him ride away?"

"No, I was gathering my things to go to lunch."

"You said you missed lunch," Avery said sharply.

"I said I didn't go at noon. I went an hour late."

"I didn't have a one o'clock that day," Brenda said.

"You went to lunch, too?" Colly asked.

"No. I stayed to do some paperwork before my two o'clock."

Colly asked if she knew why Denny had been in a hurry, but Brenda had no idea. "He kept glancing at the clock towards the end of our session. But he didn't seem upset. I thought he was excited about the weekend." She smiled sadly.

"Where'd you do the paperwork—your desk?" Avery asked.

Brenda nodded.

"Go ahead, if you don't mind," Colly said.

Brenda went to the desk and sat down.

Colly squinted around the room. "You were completely alone in the building between one and two?"

"Yes." Brenda's face clouded. She reached to straighten the stapler. "Though actually—"

"What?" Colly asked, interested.

"It's nothing, don't get excited. Sitting here, I've remembered—someone else did come in briefly."

Niall's eyebrows lifted. "Really?"

Brenda nodded, more certain. "I heard a noise, which startled me since the front door was locked. I—"

"What time was that?" Avery interrupted.

"Just before two. I remember thinking Pearl must be back from lunch a bit early. I looked out, and there was a little old lady wandering the hall. She must've come in through the alley. She was looking for a bathroom."

"Recognize her?" Colly asked.

"Never seen her before. She seemed lucid and healthy, so I didn't question her. She used the bathroom and left."

"You didn't mention this to the Rangers?"

"I'd forgotten all about it."

Nothing else unusual had happened, Brenda said. Lowell picked the kids up from school. It was his weekend to have them at the ranch. So Brenda had worked later than usual, seeing patients till six. Then she'd sent Pearl home, done another hour of paperwork, and left the center shortly after seven.

"You never saw Denny again?"

Brenda shook her head. At that moment, her phone chirped. She picked it up. "I have a client coming in five minutes. But we can talk more, later."

Pearl returned to her desk while Niall and Brenda accompanied Colly and Avery outside. They strolled towards the curb, chatting.

Halfway down the sidewalk, Avery stopped. "I want to check something." She ducked back into the counseling center.

Niall watched her go. "Can't believe Adam Parker's kid sister is a cop. Seems like yesterday she was playing hopscotch in the street."

"You've known the Parkers a while, then?"

"I lived near them in high school. Budd Parker was a terror, but the mom and kids were sweet. Adam was a few years younger than me and liked to tag along wherever I went. Drove me crazy." Niall smiled wistfully.

"I thought you grew up in Montana."

"We moved here when I was fourteen, after my dad died. Mom wanted to live someplace warm. She had a great-aunt near here."

What was that like? Colly wondered. *Not easy to be a Black person in either location.* "Must've been a culture shock."

Niall hunched his shoulders. "Cowboys are pretty much the same everywhere—and we were already used to living in a bastion of whiteness." He grinned, and Brenda laid a hand on his arm.

"Niall's way too cultured for West Texas. We'll have to get him to cook for us while you're here. He's an amazing chef, and he loves any excuse to show off."

Colly watched her sister-in-law curiously. Was Brenda flirting with her boss? There was certainly a playful familiarity that seemed to go beyond a colleague relationship. But maybe they were just good friends. *Wonder if it's raised any eyebrows?* she thought.

"I'd love to," Niall was saying with apparently genuine enthusiasm. "Maybe later this week."

Before Colly could reply, Avery emerged from the counseling center. She walked quickly to the squad car and got inside without a word to anyone. Niall, apparently taking that as his cue, said goodbye and went back inside, but Brenda followed Colly to the curb.

"Did Russ tell you about dinner at the ranch tonight?"

"You're going, too?"

"One big happy family, like I said." Brenda grimaced. "Why don't you and Satchel come by the house around five-thirty? We can drive out together. Safety in numbers, and all that."

"Great idea." Behind them, the cruiser's engine revved loudly, and Colly rolled her eyes. "That's my ride. See you tonight."

Inside the car, she turned to Avery. "Where'd you run off to?"

"I'll show you." Avery drove to the end of the block and turned, then turned again down an alleyway. She stopped behind the counseling center.

Several cars were parked there. Colly recognized Brenda's green minivan with its Texas Tech sticker in the back window. It stood beside a metal door that led inside.

"I guess that's how the old lady got in," Colly said.

"I don't think so. Look at this." Avery shifted the cruiser into park and jumped out.

Colly followed. "What is it?"

Avery went to the door and pointed to a small red sign: "Fire door: Alarm will sound if door is opened. Do not block."

"Maybe the alarm's disengaged," Colly said.

Avery reached for the doorknob, but Colly grabbed her arm. "*Bad* idea. We can ask about it later." She paused. "Get a picture, though."

Flushed and angry, Avery stamped back to the car. Colly looked around. A CCTV camera hung from the eaves.

She pointed to it when Avery returned. "Did the Rangers download that footage?"

"Why would they? Denny left through the front."

Avery took pictures of the door, and they got back in the car.

"What now?" The girl's voice was sulky.

Pout all you want, kid—it's not my job to coddle you when you do something stupid, Colly thought, glancing at the dashboard clock. She wanted to talk to Denny's folks, but that promised to be a lengthy interview, and Satchel's school let out in an hour and a half.

Satchel. Hours had passed since she'd dropped him off, pale and terrified, at the classroom. She'd been so engrossed in the case that she hadn't stopped to wonder how he was doing. She felt a pang of guilt at the thought.

"Is there time to talk to that mechanic who saw Denny riding towards the ranch?" she asked.

Avery shifted the car into gear and peeled angrily down the alley, kicking up a spray of gravel behind them.

So much for careful driving, Colly thought grimly as they sped through town, heading north.

Chapter 6

In the chaotic aftermath of the Civil War, the town of Crescent Bluff had begun as a minor trading post on a western tributary of the Chisholm Trail, a place for cowboys, driving their vast herds northwards through Texas and the Indian Territories, to stop for supplies and refreshment. A century and a half later, the great cattle drives were gone, and the Chisholm Trail had long ago faded into the grass. But Crescent Bluff remained, and so did the feeder route, though it had dwindled to little more than a farm-to-market road that locals called the Old Ranch Way.

Driving north along it for the second time that day, Colly gazed absently out at the blur of dollar stores, gas stations, and grubby strip malls, and wondered what it would have been like to witness the jostling sea of hide and horn, dust billowing in its wake, as cowhands, heels down in their stirrups, whooped and whistled along the margins of the herd. A romantic image, she mused, but a waste of time to ponder. Life had surely been as brutal and ugly then as now.

She turned away from the window. "Well? Are you going to tell me, or make me guess?"

Startled, Avery jerked the wheel, nearly sideswiping a mailbox. "Tell you what?"

"Your problem with Niall Shaw."

"What makes you think I have a problem?"

"The look you gave him would've curdled milk. Is it about your brother? He mentioned they were friends."

"Shaw doesn't have friends. Just admirers."

Colly waited for more, but Avery was clearly through with the conversation. *If you think this passive-aggressive adolescent crap will fly in a big-city department, you're in for a rude surprise,* Colly thought. But she decided not to press the issue, for now.

On the north edge of town, where seedy businesses thinned into open country, they passed a cluttered salvage yard and pulled into a parking lot beneath a sign for "Digby's Automotive." The shop was the last building for miles, a squat structure with faded blue awnings and two open repair bays. A volley of ferocious barking broke out at the salvage yard next door as Colly and Avery climbed out of the car. They pushed through the door into a disorderly front office, where a young woman was painting her nails and watching a home-remodeling show on a television mounted to the wall.

"We're looking for Tom Gunnell," Colly said.

The woman stared at them without curiosity for a moment, then indicated a side door. "Bay two."

The garage smelled of motor oil and exhaust—vaguely nostalgic to Colly, who had fond childhood memories of playing with cousins in her uncle's repair shop.

"Anybody here?" she called.

An oil-streaked face appeared in the pit beneath a pickup truck.

"Hey, Tom," Avery said.

The man's eyes narrowed. He climbed out of the pit. "Hey, Avery. What's this about?"

Colly sized him up. He was twenty-something, stringy and hollow-chested, with a mop of unkempt ginger hair and a long, hooked nose.

Colly nodded to Avery, who introduced her and explained the reason for their visit.

Gunnell pulled a grimy rag from the pocket of his coveralls and began to wipe his fingers one by one. "I don't know nothin' more than what I told the Rangers."

"Let's hear it again," Colly said. "You saw Denny ride by that day on his bike?"

The man hesitated, then shrugged. "He passed here just after lunch. About one-fifteen, one-twenty."

"Show us."

Gunnell stuffed the rag back into his pocket. "Show you what?"

"Humor me." Colly turned and walked through the open bay door towards the road. The others followed. "You were standing where?"

Gunnell glanced around, then down at his feet. "Around here, I guess. I was fixin' to pull this little Honda into the garage when I saw Denny comin' up the Ranch Way. He was still a good ways off."

"Then how'd you know it was him?" Avery asked.

"Recognized the bike." Gunnell pulled a tin of chewing tobacco from his hip pocket. "He used to ride it to Little League practice."

"Notice anything unusual?"

The mechanic tucked a wad of tobacco under his lip. "He was ridin' fast. But I didn't think nothin' of it."

"He didn't wave or stop to say hello?" Colly asked.

"I hollered, but he kept his head down and sped by."

"That didn't seem strange? You were friends, right? His mom says he'd stay with you when things got bad at home."

"Denny could be moody, especially after him and Jace got into it."

"Jace Hoyer's Denny's stepfather," Avery explained.

Gunnell spat a stream of brown juice onto the dirt. "Some father figure."

56

"You had the impression Denny was upset?" Colly asked.

"Not so much at the time. But after I heard what happened, I did wonder."

Colly gazed up the road. It stretched out, long and straight, to the horizon, distorted and undulating in the heat waves rising off the blacktop. Anything on it would be visible for quite a distance on a clear day. "How long did you stand here watching him?"

"I didn't. Why would I? After he passed, I pulled the Honda inside—owner'd hit a deer, banged up the radiator pretty good." Gunnell paused, and his expression changed. "Come to think of it, I did look for him again."

"When?"

"After I got the car in, I noticed I dropped my rag, so I stepped out to get it. I glanced up the road, but Denny was already out of sight."

Colly frowned. Other than a few scraggly mesquite trees and a fireworks stand a quarter-mile off, there was nothing to block the view. "Did it seem like he'd had enough time to ride that far?"

Gunnell scratched his jaw. "I did wonder if a car picked him up, or if he turned down the dirt road."

"What road?"

"Just a couple ruts in the grass, really. Out past that fireworks stand. Farmers use it to cut across the fields to Salton Road, yonder." He pointed east.

"Why'd you think a car might've picked him up? Did one go by?" Avery demanded.

Gunnell shrugged. "Coulda. Lotta folks use this road. You get so you don't notice."

Colly and Avery exchanged glances. Colly said, "You never mentioned this to the Rangers."

"Reckon it slipped my mind. I got a lot goin' on—gettin' married next month."

Back in the squad car, Avery exhaled sharply. "Damn."

"How well do you know him?"

"I've seen him around with Jimmy Meggs—the skinny cop at the stock pond. They're cousins."

"What's his rep?"

"Tom? Not too bright. Likes to hunt. Never been in any trouble that I know of." She paused. "What are you thinking?"

That, without cameras to back up Gunnell's account, there's no solid evidence Denny made it past this point alive. "His memory's suspiciously selective."

"What now?"

"I want to check out that dirt road he mentioned."

A few yards north of the fireworks stand, Avery braked beside a shimmering expanse of winter wheat bisected by two parallel tracks running perpendicular to the road.

"It really is just ruts in a field," Colly said. "Let's see where it goes."

"Nothing over there but a few family farms. I'm not sure the shocks can handle it."

"Let's find out. If it damages the car, I'll tell Russ you tried to stop me."

Avery nodded and eased the car off the blacktop.

They lurched slowly along the pitted track, the grass between the ruts hissing beneath the car's chassis. Colly's teeth chattered with the vibrations, and she braced herself against the dashboard. Eventually, they emerged onto a strip of cracked gray asphalt.

"Salton Road," Avery said.

"Where does it go?"

"Dead-ends into another field that way." Avery pointed north. "South, it loops past some farms and eventually back to town."

"After what Tom said, we'll need to canvass the farmers."

"The Rangers did. Nobody saw anything."

"We'll do it again." Colly glanced at the dashboard clock. "Later, though. Let's check the fireworks stand."

The stand was little more than a plywood shack, its once-bright yellow paint faded and peeling, the words "Freddy's Fireworks" barely visible on its sides. Back on the Old Ranch Way, they climbed out of the car and Colly shaded her eyes to examine the structure.

"Doesn't look like much. No security cameras." She turned to Avery. "Who's Freddy?"

"There's not one. The Sandleford brothers run it—Sam and Alan. They must've thought the name sounded good."

"Were they interviewed? Maybe whoever was working that day saw something."

Avery shook her head. "It's closed except around Fourth of July."

Colly tested the hatch. Locked. "Do they keep inventory in here year-round?"

"I doubt it. Why?"

"Denny had a record for theft. He might've left the road to try and break in." Colly walked along the front of the stand, examining it. "A little termite damage. No pry marks."

"Maybe we should do a walk-around." Avery picked up a long stick from the grass. "I'll go first. Rattlers get active this time of year."

A cold weight settled in Colly's stomach. *Snakes. Hell.*

Pushing through shoulder-high curtains of dry Johnson grass, the women made their way around the stand. Disturbed from beneath the eaves, a few early wasps hummed around their heads, more curious than angry.

On the shack's rear wall, Colly spotted a faint black streak. "What's this?"

Avery, several feet ahead, turned and came back. "Scuff mark."

"From something rubber?" Colly ran her thumb over the streak. "Yeah, maybe."

Colly stooped to look more closely. "What kind of bike was Denny's?"

"Old, beat-up BMX. Why?"

"Is it at the station?"

"Rangers still have it. But I took pictures." Avery regarded her curiously. "What are you thinking?"

"A BMX doesn't have a kickstand, right?"

Avery shook her head. "You thinking the handlebar grips?"

"If someone leaned a bike here, and it slid down the wall . . ." Colly mimed the action with her hands.

"I can check the photos for damage to the grips."

"Good, good," Colly murmured absently, staring at the ground.

"See something?"

"If Denny parked here, there might be other evidence." Colly knelt and combed through the dense grass, thoughts of snakes forgotten. Avery dropped down beside her, and they searched for several minutes.

Colly sat back on her heels. "It was a long shot." She checked her watch. Already on the verge of being late. She couldn't leave Satchel standing at the curb, waiting and worrying, on his first day. "I need to head back."

They made their way along the rear of the stand, Avery in the lead. After a few steps, she stopped so suddenly that Colly nearly ran into her. Avery pointed to something dull and red in the grass.

"Don't touch. Let me look." Colly stooped and parted the vegetation carefully. A bit of scarlet cloth, sun-faded and rotting, lay half-buried in the dirt.

"Get the camera," she said. "And call Russ. We'll need an evidence team."

"What is it?"

"A baseball cap."

As Avery rushed back to the cruiser, Colly stood and checked her watch again, then pulled out her phone.

"Pick up, pick up, pick up," she whispered as it rang. Finally, to her relief, a familiar voice said, "Colly? Everything okay?"

"Hi, Brenda, I'm running late. When you pick up Logan and Minnie, can you get Satchel, too?"

"I got hung up, myself. A neighbor's picking up my kids. She'd be happy to give Satchel a ride, if she's got room. Want me to ask?"

Colly hesitated. Satchel was such a nervous child. Having a stranger pick him up on his first day would scare him. Besides, she'd promised to be there.

She sighed. "No, I'll figure out something."

By the time the call ended, Avery had returned and was circling the baseball cap, snapping pictures. "Russ says to wait. He'll be here in thirty."

Colly ran her fingers through her hair and tried to think. The panicky feeling was familiar. The men on the force had criticized her, calling her unreliable when Victoria was little and there'd been child-care emergencies—*Mrs. Newland, your daughter's running a fever. You need to come get her.* Always something with kids. It was easier for men. She'd overhear them on the phone with their wives—*Sorry, honey, I can't help. I'm on a case.* Randy had been a good father and reasonably evolved regarding gender roles, by Texas standards. But even he had viewed their daughter's care as primarily Colly's responsibility. Like her male colleagues, he'd "help out" when he could. But if he couldn't, it had been up to Colly to find a way.

She checked her watch again and turned to Avery. "Look, I've got to pick up my grandson. Let me borrow the car. You wait for Russ."

"That's against regulations."

"Fine, you'll have to drive me. We'll be back by the time Russ gets here, if we hurry."

"He said—"

"That hat looks like it's been here for months—it'll be okay for half an hour more."

Chapter 7

When they arrived, the school's visitors' lot had emptied, though a handful of children still loitered on the sidewalk waiting for tardy parents under the watchful eyes of a pair of teacher's aides. Telling Avery to stay in the car, Colly hurried inside. At Satchel's classroom door, she stopped short. The room was empty. As she stood wondering what to do, a noise behind her made her jump. The woman who'd directed her to Brenda's office that morning was staring disapprovingly over her half-moon glasses.

"Mrs. Newland, Mrs. Boyles sent me to look for you. She's with your grandson at the nurse's station."

"Why? What happened?"

The woman shrugged. "Follow me."

The nurse's station was near the main office. Colly crossed the empty waiting area and found Satchel in an exam room, sitting on the edge of a padded table and wheezing raggedly into a paper bag held to his face by Wanice Boyles.

"There you are." Wanice smiled. "See, Satchel, I told you she'd come soon."

Colly looked at her questioningly.

"Everything's fine. We got a little scared, that's all." Wanice patted Satchel's back.

His face was white and tear-streaked. Colly could hear his teeth chattering. He jumped off the table and grabbed onto her, burying his face in her shirt.

"I'm sorry, buddy. I got here as soon as I could." She ruffled his hair.

Satchel hiccupped but said nothing.

A bony woman in a nurse's smock entered the room carrying a file folder. When she saw Colly, she stopped and gave her a look that Colly knew well.

"You're Mrs. Newland? You didn't mention on the health forms that your grandson has asthma."

Colly felt her jaw tighten. "He hasn't had a flare-up in ages," she said with clumsy defiance, thinking, *Having half your family slaughtered by a madman can be distracting, lady. I'm doing my best.*

"Please bring his inhaler tomorrow. Breathing into a lunch bag isn't exactly the standard of care. And since he has anxiety issues, it would help if you'd pick him up on time."

Colly met her eyes coldly. "Thanks." Hoisting Satchel onto her hip, she grabbed his backpack and left the infirmary.

I'm already so sick of this damn town, she thought as she helped Satchel put on his sun-sleeves and hat in the foyer. Did these people really suppose their stares and slights could mean anything compared with the hell of her own conscience?

Colly exhaled slowly. The sooner she finished this case, the sooner she could leave Crescent Bluff and the Newland tribe behind her.

"Grandma, you promised you'd be on time. You *promised*." Satchel was crying again, though he'd stopped in the nurse's station.

"I know, bud. It won't happen again." She stood and zipped his pack.

"Yes, it will."

Colly didn't respond. He was right. It was impossible to shield family from the effects of police work. She hadn't even been able to keep hers alive.

"How was school today?"

Satchel sniffled. "The other kids stared at me."

"Because you're new."

"Because I'm weird."

Colly laid a hand on his shoulder. "C'mon, buddy. Let's go."

When they reached the cruiser, Satchel's eyes widened. "Where's our car?"

"We have to run an errand—then we'll get our car and go home."

Still sniffling, Satchel climbed uncertainly into the back seat but froze when he saw the young patrolwoman behind the wheel. Avery had been smoking, and though she'd rolled down the window, the car reeked of cigarettes. Colly was annoyed.

"Satchel, this is Avery. She's helping with my investigation."

Avery gave Satchel a curt nod through the partition. "Hey, dude."

Satchel stared. "Your hair's purple."

"Yeah, well, your hat's weird. I guess we're even."

Colly chewed angrily on her lip as she helped Satchel buckle his seatbelt. She hadn't expected Avery to be good with children, but was it too much to ask for her not to make him cry again when he was just calming down?

To Colly's surprise, however, Satchel wiped his nose on his sleeve and regarded Avery with interest. "I have to wear it for my solar urticaria." He enunciated carefully, proud of the term.

"Cool." Avery started the car.

Satchel looked pleased but was fighting not to show it. *I'll be damned*, Colly thought, closing the rear door.

As they drove through town, her phone rang. "Hey, Russ, you at the site? I had to get Satchel, but we're heading back."

"Yeah, I'm here. Where's this baseball cap you were talking about?"

"Behind the fireworks stand. It's half-buried, but we trampled the grass pretty well. Shouldn't be hard to find."

"There's trampled grass, all right. But that's all. You'd better get here fast." He hung up.

Why can't men see what's right in front of their noses? Colly wondered irritably. Randy had been maddening about it, always staring into the fridge, bellowing "There's no mustard!" in a vaguely aggrieved and accusatory tone.

Colly glanced at Avery. "Let's go. Hit it."

Avery flicked a switch, and the siren wailed. From the back seat, Colly heard Satchel gasp with delight.

A short while later, they sped past the salvage yard and Digby's Automotive, pulling to a stop behind Russ's SUV, which was parked on the edge of the road near the fireworks stand.

"Wait in the car, Satchel."

"It'll be hot."

"We can't have you traipsing through the evidence. It's just for a few minutes—we'll leave the windows down. You can do your homework."

Grumbling, Satchel stripped off his hat and sun-sleeves.

As Colly and Avery climbed out of the car, Russ emerged from behind the plywood stand, fanning himself with his Stetson.

"We've got a problem," he said without prelude. "Walk that way." He sketched a wide arc with his hat. "Don't disturb the scene."

Perplexed and trying not to think about rattlesnakes, Colly followed Avery through the tall grass. The ground behind the stand was more trampled than they'd left it. A small patch of freshly disturbed earth marked the spot where the cap had been.

"What the hell?" Avery blurted.

Colly's mind was racing. "What time did you get here, Russ?"

"Ten to three."

"Did you notice footprints?"

"Sure, but I assumed they were yours." His voice was grim.

Colly squinted at the ground. "I'm not great at tracking."

"Evidence team's on the way." Russ turned to Avery. "Get the camera—I want to see the pictures." When she was out of earshot, he stepped closer to Colly. "Why the hell did you leave this unattended? I expected expertise from you, not amateur hour."

The patch of skin between his eyebrows had flushed bright red, just as Randy's used to when he was angry. But Colly was not feeling nostalgic. "Was I supposed to ditch Satchel at school?"

"You could've left Avery here."

"Gee, Russ, if only I had your big man-brain, I might've thought of that. Your purple-headed gal pal wouldn't let me take the damn car."

Russ sighed and pinched the bridge of his nose with his thumb and forefinger. "Yeah, okay. I'm just frustrated."

"Whereas I'm having the time of my life." Colly heard the car door slam, and she lowered her voice. "I'm here as a favor to the family, but Satchel comes first. He deserves that much. If you're not happy with my work, I'll gladly go home."

"Okay, okay. I said I'm sorry." Russ put on the Stetson.

"You said you're frustrated. It's not the same."

Avery ran up, oblivious to the tension in the air, and handed Russ the camera.

"Does it look like Denny's cap?" Colly hoped she sounded calm and professional.

Russ shaded the viewfinder with his hand as he scrolled through the photos. "Hard to tell. All the security footage from that day is black and white, but Brenda and the clinic receptionist both said the cap was red. I don't see any logo on this one. That's consistent."

"Maybe his mother'll know if it's his," Avery said.

"Worth checking." Russ handed her the camera and wiped his forehead. "It's too hot for March." He sighed and looked around. "Who could've taken the damn thing?"

Just then, they were interrupted by a shrill scream. "Grandma!"

With a quick stab of anxiety, Colly ran to the cruiser. Satchel lay on his back on the car's rear seat, an open textbook on his stomach.

"What's wrong?" Colly demanded.

He sat up. "I'm *bored*, Grandma."

Colly swallowed her irritation. "Did you finish your homework?"

"The math's different here. I don't know how to do it."

"Do what you can. I'll help later."

She kissed him quickly and returned to Russ and Avery. "Sorry about that. You were saying?"

"Wondering who took the cap." Russ looked annoyed.

Colly frowned. "It was too rotted for someone to find it and think, *Sweet, a new hat.* Had to be an attempt to tamper with evidence."

"Nobody knew about it but us," Avery said.

"Unless someone saw you snooping around." Russ shaded his eyes, looking up and down the road.

Colly sighed. "Let's walk through it. We found the cap around two-fifteen, then I told Avery to get the camera and call you, Russ." She turned to the younger woman. "Did you tell anyone else? I'm not accusing, just covering the bases."

Avery bristled. "Only the chief."

"I didn't speak to a soul," Colly said.

"You called someone about picking up your grandson."

67

"Brenda? I didn't mention the ballcap, or even where we were. You heard me."

"I think we can clear Brenda." Russ smiled. "I notified the evidence team, but that's it."

"You trust them?"

"Absolutely."

"What about Tom Gunnell? He knew we were here. He can see this place from his shop."

All three turned to stare down the road at Digby's. "There's a girl working the desk—she'd know if he left," Avery said.

Colly nodded. "Let's ask. Even if he didn't take the cap, he might've seen someone."

"I'll do it," Russ said. "It'll make more of an impression coming from the police chief."

He's afraid I'll screw it up, Colly thought. She didn't blame him. His anger over the ballcap stung because she knew he was right. This was the Houston debacle all over again in miniature, though she didn't know what else she could've done, in either case. Retiring had been the right call.

A piercing cry penetrated her gloomy reflections. "Grandma!"

"Oh, for God's sake." Colly turned. Satchel had put on his hat and sun-sleeves and was standing on the car's seat, his upper body out the window.

She walked to the car. "What's the matter now?"

"I have to pee."

Colly sighed. "Fine, c'mon." She led him to the opposite side of the road. "Hurry, there's no shade."

Satchel chewed his lip. "I don't want anyone to see."

"They won't. I'll stand guard."

When he had finished, Colly steered him back to the car.

"Grandma, I'm starving. When are we gonna go?"

"In a few minutes."

"But I'm *starving.*"

Colly squeezed hand sanitizer onto his palms and was rummaging in her purse for some food when she heard the drone of an engine. A motorcycle was approaching, ridden by a stocky man in a fringed leather vest. Attached to the bike was an old-fashioned sidecar, in which sat an enormous, fawn-colored pit bull, its jowls flapping as it grinned into the wind.

Colly located a battered package of pretzels. "Here you go, bud. Be back soon," she said, and hurried to rejoin the others.

The motorcycle stopped beside Russ's SUV.

"About time." Russ sounded relieved.

"Who's this?" Colly asked.

Russ didn't answer. He was striding towards the newcomer, waving. Colly followed. By the time they reached the bike, the rider had removed his helmet, and Colly was startled to see that he was, in fact, not a man but a burly middle-aged white woman with silvery braids and a sunburned face.

"Sorry it took me a while," she said in a gravelly smoker's voice. "Had to get Momma out of the tub and wait for the home-health gal to show up."

"Glad you made it."

Russ introduced her as Earla Cobb, forensics specialist for the county. Earla shook Colly's hand enthusiastically, then whistled. "C'mon, fat boy."

The pit bull leapt out of the sidecar and made a beeline for Colly, tail wagging. Like his owner, he was barrel-shaped and slightly bow-legged. Colly, who'd had many unpleasant run-ins with pit bulls in her career, watched him warily, but he seemed friendly.

She scratched the dog's ears. "What's his name?"

"I just said—Fat Boy." Earla pulled an evidence kit from the rear of the sidecar. "We over there?"

She nodded towards the fireworks stand, then, before anyone answered, plunged through the grass towards Avery, who was still glowering at the ground where the cap had been.

Russ and Colly followed. "She's your evidence team?" Colly whispered.

"Earla knows what she's doing."

When they reached the stand, Earla was already surveying the area, while several yards away, Fat Boy paced and whined.

Russ explained the situation. "We need to know who took that cap, Earla."

She grunted, staring intently at the ground. "Lemme see y'all's feet."

She examined and measured their footwear, then donned a pair of nitrile gloves and began to crawl across the dirt. After ten minutes, she stood and removed the gloves with a snap.

"Ground's a mess—this damn Johnson grass mucking things up, and footprints crisscrossing everywhere. But I'm confident there's a fourth set that ain't any of y'all's. Gonna take a while to make sense of it, though. Get along, little dogies—Momma needs some alone time. Gotta think. And smoke."

Russ hesitated, then shrugged. "I'll send someone to cut back the vegetation. Give me a holler when you're done."

"Yes, indeedy."

Back at the vehicles, Avery got into the squad car and slammed the driver's door.

"What's her problem?" Colly asked.

"Probably pissed about missing out on the action." Russ's eyes drifted to the stand, where Earla was unpacking her kit.

"Should we be leaving her here alone?" Colly said quietly. "What if whoever took the cap's still around? Might be dangerous."

70

"If they try to mess with Earla, God help 'em." Russ chuckled. "She's a black belt in karate. Besides, Fat Boy's a sweetheart, but if anyone attacked her, he'd rip their throat out."

"Unless they had a gun."

"I'm going to run across to Digby's and chat with Tom Gunnell. I can keep an eye on things from there." He paused, scratching his jaw. "Want to come?"

Colly declined. She needed to get Satchel home.

Russ nodded and turned to go, but stopped. "Sorry about what I said earlier, Col. I appreciate your help—must've been tough as hell, coming here."

He looked as pained as if he were trying to loosen a rusted fitting with a pipe wrench. Why did men find it so difficult to apologize? She had missed Randy terribly since his death but had not been sorry to leave behind some aspects of married life, and negotiating her way around the male ego was definitely one of them. Russ was sincere, though. That counted for a lot.

"Thanks, Russ. See you tonight."

Chapter 8

Shortly after five p.m., Colly stood in bra and panties at the foot of the bed, staring at the clothes piled beside her suitcase. Why hadn't she brought anything nice? She'd packed anticipating long hours pounding the pavement or traipsing through dusty pastures, not dinner parties with her mother-in-law. No one was more adept at making her feel her penniless roots than Iris Newland.

"C'mon, Grandma, we'll be late," Satchel whined from the doorway.

Colly felt a rush of misplaced anger. "Is five minutes of privacy too much to ask? Go read a book, please—I'll be down soon."

As she closed the door behind him, her phone rang. "Hey, Bren, I'm running late. Wardrobe issues."

Brenda laughed. "Oh, lord, there's nothing more confidence-shattering than facing Iris in the wrong outfit."

Colly sighed. Such a relief to talk to someone who understood. *Wear whatever. No one will care*, Randy would have said with maddening reasonableness. She suddenly liked her sister-in-law immensely.

"I didn't bring any dresses, or even a pair of nice slacks."

"We're about the same size—you can wear something of mine. Come on over."

"Bren, you're an angel."

Throwing on jeans and a t-shirt, Colly grabbed her purse and bundled Satchel into the car. Following Brenda's directions, she pulled up a few minutes later in front of a modest frame house in a leafy neighborhood. Brenda's minivan was parked beneath the carport. A yellow hatchback sat in the driveway behind it.

Satchel ran ahead to ring the bell. A stocky ten-year-old opened the door. "Mom, they're here!" the boy bellowed, then grabbed Satchel's wrist. "Come check out my room."

Brenda emerged from somewhere. "Forgive Logan's manners. He's been so excited to see Satchel."

"I like the new place."

"Thanks. Lowell hates that I moved the kids to the 'wetback end of town,' as he calls it. Such a racist. He thought it was a power play to guilt more money out of him. He can't imagine I'd actually *want* to live here. The neighbors are wonderful."

Brenda led Colly into a small, tidy living room, where a teenage girl sat on the sofa, lazily thumbing through a magazine and watching a curly headed six-year-old girl color a picture.

"Hey, Aunt Colly." The teenager unwound her long limbs and rose. "It's awesome you're helping Dad with the case."

"Alice, my goodness, you're so tall." Russ had been right—with the same striking combination of ash-blond hair and russet skin, Alice Newland had developed into the image of her mother since Colly had seen her last. But she refrained from saying so. She knew how painful it was to be reminded of the dead.

"Minnie, say hello," Brenda urged as the little girl leapt up and buried her face in her mother's dress. "Sorry, we're shy today." Brenda petted the girl's hair. "Alice has offered to take the kids to the ranch early—they want to ride horses before dark. Is that okay with you?"

"Well—"

"Don't worry about Satchel," Alice said. "We'll stick to the trails in the shinnery. It's shady there."

"All right, but keep an eye out. He needs the hat and sun-sleeves, even in the shade. When he's excited, he sometimes forgets."

After Alice and the younger children had driven away in the yellow hatchback, Brenda shut the door and leaned against it. "Finally, some peace. I love my kids, but parenting's just so daily."

Colly laughed. "I'm constantly exhausted. Satchel's higher-maintenance than Victoria ever was."

"He's lucky to have you. C'mon, let's find you an outfit."

A half-hour later, Colly stood in front of Brenda's bedroom mirror, gazing at a reflection of herself in a pale blue scoop-neck dress.

"Perfect," Brenda said. "Luckily, it goes all right with your flats. My feet are bigger than yours."

"This still has the tags on it. Are you sure?"

Brenda grinned. "Absolutely. Iris hasn't seen it, so she won't say anything catty about you borrowing."

Colly squinted critically at herself. Her face and forearms were ruddy from the afternoon spent outdoors, and the spray of freckles across her nose had darkened noticeably.

"I always feel like such a peasant around Iris. I've got a farmer's tan, for God's sake. And look at this." She pulled a bit of dried grass from her unruly mane before retying it in a loose ponytail.

"You look fantastic." Brenda began to readjust the closet hangers, carefully turning them to face the same direction. She saw Colly watching and blushed. "I'm a little bit of a neat freak. It used to drive Lowell crazy."

"Goodness, how many running shoes do you have?" Colly nodded at the long, orderly racks of footwear on the closet floor.

"It's hard getting rid of the old ones. After so many miles together, they're like friends." Brenda sighed. "They should really go in the donation box. If you need anything for Satchel, the thrift shop on South Fourth and Chestnut's great. I'm one of their sponsors. Half the kids' play clothes come from there, these days."

"Was Lowell that stingy with the settlement?"

"I put it in a trust for the kids. I wanted to make it on my own. Things are tight, but supporting myself is unbelievably satisfying. I'll make more money once I finish my supervision hours." Brenda shut the closet door. "We should get going. Let's take my van—it's already covered in ranch dirt. Ready to face the music?"

"Ready as I'll ever be."

The sun was lowering over the scrublands by the time Brenda turned north on the Old Ranch Way.

"I like it out here," she said. "I run this way a lot."

"This is my fourth time on this road today." Colly settled back in her seat. "It was great to see your clinic. Niall seems nice."

"Niall's fantastic, plus crazy handsome. You can see why I was tempted."

Colly looked quickly at her sister-in-law. "Oh, he's the one—?"

Brenda reddened. "I thought you knew. It only lasted a few months. We're just colleagues, now. And friends."

"I didn't mean to pry."

"You didn't. Feels weird to talk about it, though. You have to be so careful in this town." She fell silent, but as Colly searched for a new topic, Brenda surprised her by saying suddenly, "I made a mess of things, Col. All the people I hurt—I never meant to. One night, as we were getting ready for bed, Lowell was griping about something or other. And the thought hit me: *This is as good as life with him is ever going to get.*" She glanced at Colly. "You've probably never felt that way. You and Randy always seemed so happy."

"We were, for the most part. But there were baddish moments."

"A career must've helped. At least you had something of your own—I used to envy that."

"You always said you loved being a stay-at-home mom."

"I love being a mom. The stay-at-home part was an excuse, I think."

"For what?"

"Playing it safe. It took me a while to realize how small my life had gotten. I thought going back to school would help, but then Lowell started drinking more, and gambling. He got controlling about money, and he didn't like that I suddenly had ideas of my own and dinner wasn't always on the table at six o'clock." She passed a hay truck, and a flurry of straw bits swirled against the windshield. "Lowell's meant for the 1950s."

"Lowell's a jerk. No offense."

"Here's the question that haunts me—did he become a jerk over time, or was he always one, and I just didn't see it?" Brenda held up her hand. "Don't answer that. Either way's depressing."

Colly laughed. "I only meant I can understand why you'd be drawn to someone else after a while."

Brenda's knuckles whitened on the steering wheel. "I knew who Niall was in high school, but I didn't really *know* him then. I was fresh out of grad school when I started working for him. He was everything Lowell wasn't, and everything I wanted to be—educated and well-travelled and interesting. You know he was a Rhodes Scholar? Did his postgrad work at Oxford. He writes books on adolescent brain structure. Being around him was like looking through a window into this amazing world, and I wanted it so badly." She smiled wistfully. "I was head over heels, for a while. I loved everything about him—even the little quirks, like talking in his sleep and messing up every dish in the kitchen when he cooks."

Listening, Colly wondered what had triggered this sudden vulnerability. She had learned more about Brenda's thoughts and feelings in the last five minutes than she'd known in twenty years.

Outside, Digby's Automotive flashed by and, seconds later, the fireworks stand. Earla Cobb was gone, but the grass around the stand had been cut short, and a half-dozen marker flags now dotted the scene.

Colly stirred uneasily. "Must be awkward, working with Niall now."

"We've adjusted. Lowell's the one who couldn't cope. You'd think after all *his* indiscretions . . ." Brenda shook her head. "When it came out, I broke things off with Niall and tried to work on my marriage for the kids' sake." She shrugged. "Lowell's so prejudiced—if I'd cheated with a white guy, he might've gotten past it. I don't know."

"I'm sorry, Bren."

"It's okay, now. But it was hell, at first. Logan was angry and acting out. And there was town gossip, and all the legal stuff—not to mention Iris. I started having panic attacks, but anxiety meds helped. Things are better."

"Did you and Niall ever talk about getting back together?"

Brenda's cheeks colored. "It's too complicated. We hang out sometimes. He loves to cook for me. But it's strictly platonic." She flashed Colly a sudden smile. "Life's good. The kids are doing great, and honestly, having a crisis of my own made me a more compassionate therapist. I hate that it's hurt the counseling center, though."

"What do you mean?"

"You know how people are. They figure if I couldn't save my own marriage, how can I help them? Plus, the ones who work for Lowell don't want him thinking they're disloyal."

"You're kidding."

"Denny's stepfather used to be a foreman at the turbine plant. Lowell fired him last year, and a rumor started that it was because Denny was a client of mine."

"Think that's true?"

"I didn't start seeing Denny till after Jace Hoyer was fired. But truth never stopped a good piece of gossip. I don't know why he was let go, but it wasn't because of me."

Colly made a mental note to visit the turbine plant soon.

They were passing a pair of quarter horses grazing in a field, their flanks twitching and tails swishing, when Brenda asked, "Will you speak with Denny's folks?"

"Probably."

"Watch out for Jace. He's got a bad reputation and a big chip on his shoulder. He hates Lowell, and since you're a Newland . . ."

"Guilt by association?"

"He might see it that way. Be careful." Brenda squinted out the side window. "What was up with the question this afternoon about Denny's feet?"

Colly, staring at a distant line of purple mesas and thinking about how much she was dreading dinner, became suddenly alert. Brenda's voice was too casual. She was fishing. If she'd somehow found out about the shoe insert in Denny's pack, who'd told her?

Colly needed time to think. "What do you mean?"

"Avery Parker asked if Denny had foot problems."

"We wondered if he was capable of riding his bike to the stock pond. It's over twenty miles."

"But she asked the same question about his folks."

Colly cursed silently. "I don't know what she was thinking on that one. She's kind of a loose cannon." *And thank God she's not here now.* "Why do you ask? Have you remembered something?"

"I'm a therapist. I'm nosy." Brenda smiled. "About the question, though—if Denny had foot problems, they didn't stop him riding his bike to the stock pond. I know he did it several times."

"Any idea why?" Colly asked.

"That's no mystery. Supposedly, the pond's haunted by Adam Parker's ghost. Teenagers go for thrills, no matter how many 'No Trespassing' signs Felix puts up."

"Hmm." Colly hesitated. "That reminds me—Avery and I went down the alley behind the clinic today and noticed the back entrance is a fire door."

Brenda laughed. "No, it's not. Niall put up that sign to keep clients from bypassing the lobby."

"Wonder why it didn't stop the old lady you told us about? You said she came in the back way."

"I didn't actually see which door she used. I just assumed, since she came down the hall from that direction. She was wearing thick glasses. Maybe she missed the sign."

That's one mystery solved, Colly thought with a sigh, leaning back in her seat.

The light was deepening to a golden haze as they rumbled over the cattle guard beneath the Newland Ranch archway. Passing the track that led to the stock pond, they continued northeast on a paved lane that rambled through the scrubland for several miles.

Images from her last visit churned through Colly's mind—of standing in the grass beside two red mounds of earth, hunched against the winter wind and trying to ignore the sidelong glances and rigid backs, the murmuring voices that hushed when she looked their way. She felt her palms begin to sweat and her mouth go dry.

"How do you deal with this all the time, Brenda?"

"With what?"

"The family, the judgment, the guilt. What the hell am I doing here? I feel sick."

"I tell myself it's for the kids. And if I don't say anything regrettable while I'm here, I reward myself with a very large martini when I get home." Brenda paused, apparently waiting for a laugh. Getting no reaction, she laid a hand on Colly's arm. "Iris may blame you for what happened to Randy and Victoria. But remember—you're here because she needs your help. Iris is very transactional. She may slip in a barb here and there, but for the most part she'll behave till the case review's finished."

"And then?"

"Then all bets are off. It'll depend on what you conclude about Willis."

Chapter 9

The big house on the Newland Ranch, a two-story structure with a long plank porch and a half-dozen gabled dormers, was known in town as "the Mollison Place," and by the family simply as "Mollison." The name derived from Iris Newland's grandfather, Henry Mollison, who had built it in 1927. The precocious son of a Crescent Bluff barber, Henry fought bravely in World War I but was discharged with a Purple Heart after losing an arm in the Battle of Belleau Wood. Upon recovering, he told his father that, since he couldn't earn a living with his hands, he'd have to live by his wits. At twenty-five, Henry boarded a train for New York to try his luck on Wall Street. He returned three years later with a Yankee wife, a baby, and enough money to buy an 8,000-acre ranch and 500 head of cattle.

Henry's run of good luck was short-lived, however. Two years after moving his young family onto the new homestead, he lost his investments in the Crash and was forced to sell the ranch, at a greatly reduced price, to Claud Newland, a prosperous grocer from Amarillo who wanted to get into the cattle business. With few options, Henry took work doing odd jobs in his father's shop. He consoled himself with bathtub gin and gambling, and, in 1938, having betted away the proceeds from the ranch, he put a shotgun in his mouth, leaving his wife and young son destitute.

This ancestral humiliation soaked deep into the psyche of Henry's granddaughter. Iris Mollison grew up poor with a fierce determination to reclaim her birthright, and it was no secret in town that when, in 1970, she married Bryant Newland, grandson of Claud and heir to the ranch, it was for that purpose.

Iris never regretted the decision. Bryant, though a cruel and abusive husband and father, was a shrewd businessman. He foresaw the potential for wind power in West Texas and built a turbine manufacturing company that transformed him from moderately successful rancher to biggest employer in the region.

"Your mom's such a strong woman. Why does she put up with your dad's crap when she could walk away?" Colly had asked Randy early in their relationship.

"Momma's married more to the ranch than to Dad. She'll never leave it," was Randy's blunt reply.

"She'd have plenty of money in a divorce."

"It's not about that. It's about winning back what the universe took. In Texas, what matters is land."

Randy had been right. For forty years, Iris had waited quietly in the shadows, controlling what she could and enduring what she couldn't. And, in the end, her patience was rewarded. With Bryant's death a decade earlier, the universe had folded its cards and walked away from the table, leaving Iris to her patrimony.

Although her son Lowell, who had worked under Bryant for years, continued to oversee the turbine plant's day-to-day operations, Iris was the undisputed head of the Newland family and the legal owner of both ranch and business. She'd paid close attention from the sidelines to her husband's professional dealings, and now, to everyone's surprise, she insisted on the final say in all major decisions. Under her direction, Newland Wind Industries invested in major upgrades and was on track to expand its business greatly. Recently, the deaths of Randy and Victoria had caused Iris to withdraw a bit, and in her grief, her attention to the business had wavered. But according to Russ, his mother was beginning to show an interest once again.

Bryant had been a tightfisted man. During his lifetime, Mollison had fallen somewhat into disrepair. But after his death, Iris poured resources into the place, adding a pool, tennis courts, and guest annex, and remodeling the original structure into a showpiece that had been featured in style and architecture magazines.

Now, riding in Brenda's van up the juniper-shaded avenue that climbed the hill to the house, Colly felt the familiar mixture of intimidation and dull resentment tightening her throat. Even before Randy's death, she'd experienced the burden of Iris's judgment.

"Why does your mom dislike me?" she'd asked as they lay in bed one night after a holiday visit to the ranch.

"It's nothing personal. I'm the only one of her boys she hasn't wrangled back to Crescent Bluff." Randy caressed Colly's shoulder, letting his fingers drift down her arm. "If I hadn't met you, she thinks she could've lured me home."

You're home now, my love, Colly thought as Mollison's gabled roofline appeared above the junipers. *But not the way your mother wanted. Not the way any of us wanted.* She closed her eyes and exhaled slowly.

Brenda glanced over. "You okay?"

"So-so."

"At least it's a school night. We'll have an excuse to leave early. Just stay off politics or we'll never get away. Lowell's drinking is worse, and he's turned completely rabid on immigration—though half the ranch hands are undocumented. Wonderful people, and so hardworking. But self-awareness isn't Lowell's strong suit."

The sun was slipping behind the distant mesas as they pulled onto the gravel drive in front of the house. Alice's hatchback was there, as well as Russ's SUV and Lowell's truck with the company logo on the door. Off to the side stood a black Cadillac that Colly didn't recognize.

"Oh Lord, she invited the judge." Brenda parked a little away from the others and killed the engine.

"Who's that?"

"Iris's arm candy."

"Her *what*?"

"Russ didn't tell you? Iris has been seeing someone, though she swears they're just friends. He was a judge in Odessa, but he retired out here."

"Heavens. How'd they meet? Please don't say eHarmony."

Brenda laughed. "Ballroom dancing society—a hundred-percent geriatric. They get together in the fellowship hall of some church in Big Spring twice a month."

"What's he like?"

"Nice enough." Brenda checked her makeup in the visor's mirror, dabbing at her lip with her little finger. "Mild-mannered, a tad smarmy. Your basic lapdog."

"Doesn't seem like Iris's type."

"I don't know. Bryant was an alpha male, and he treated her like dirt. Makes sense she'd want someone she can control this time around."

Colly unbuckled her seatbelt as she absorbed this information. She'd always seen Iris as something of an archetype—the cool, judgmental mother-in-law, the cunning spider in the center of the family web—not a fully rounded human being. Not someone who might be lonely. Colly felt a twinge of shame but reflexively pushed it away. She needed to stay focused.

"Oh, there's Russ," Brenda said.

Colly looked around. Her brother-in-law had emerged from the breezeway between the house and garage and was striding towards them, a half-dozen ranch dogs at his heels. He had changed out of his uniform into Wranglers and a pastel-yellow Oxford. His sleeves were rolled up, and she glimpsed the tattoo on his inner right forearm—Randy's name in a simple, flowing script.

Colly took a deep breath and opened the door.

"Hey," Russ said. "Saw y'all through the—wow." His eyebrows shot up as Colly climbed out of the van. "You look great." He winced. "Sorry, didn't mean to sound so surprised."

Colly laughed, stooping to pet a half-grown border collie. "Thanks, Russ. I knew what you meant. You look nice, too."

He checked his watch. "The kids aren't back from riding yet. Come around and say hi. Then we can run down to Willis's cabin before supper."

He led them through the breezeway to a stone patio encircling a pool landscaped to look like a tropical lagoon, with areca palms clustered around the edges and a waterfall burbling into the deep end. Nearby, Iris, Lowell, and a plump elderly man with a white goatee sat on lounge chairs in the fading light, sipping cocktails. Iris and the goateed man stood when they saw the new arrivals, but Lowell remained seated, glowering sullenly into his glass.

He's in a fine mood, Colly thought. *Going to be a long evening.*

Iris, tall and elegant as ever, approached with open arms. "Ah, Columba, welcome." She was dressed in linen slacks and a gold lamé blouse. Colly was startled to see how much she had aged in two years. Her cheekbones, always prominent, now stood out like sharp ridges, and her eyes seemed more sunken than before, an impression accentuated by her dark mascara. Only her hair was unchanged—silver-gray and cut in a fashionable shag.

They hugged, and Colly could feel the bones in her mother-in-law's shoulders and spine. "Hello, Iris. You look beautiful as always."

Iris's eyes narrowed, as if she were trying to determine whether the comment had been meant sarcastically. "You, as well. Retirement agrees with you." She held Colly at arm's length. "What a lovely dress. You've expanded your repertoire."

Over Iris's shoulder, Colly saw Brenda roll her eyes.

"I appreciate your coming out here, dear," Iris was saying.

"Happy to help."

As Iris turned to greet Brenda, Colly noticed Russ gesticulating angrily for his brother to get up and join them. When Lowell ignored him, Russ strode across the patio, and the two men whispered furiously together. There had always been antagonism between Russ and Lowell, but this seemed to be about more than the usual sibling friction.

Finally, Lowell swallowed the rest of his drink and pulled himself to his feet. He was a few years younger than Russ, stocky and bull-necked, with a blunt, slightly crooked nose and thinning hair, for which he compensated with a full, dark beard. He'd made no effort to dress for dinner and wore ratty jeans and a work shirt with "Newland Wind Industries" stitched on the pocket.

Lowell gave Colly a perfunctory hug, and nodded, stone-faced, to Brenda before dropping back into his chair with a grunt.

Oblivious to the familial drama, Iris took Colly's arm and introduced the goateed man as Judge Talford Maybrey.

Pink-faced and slightly pear-shaped, Maybrey reminded Colly of Colonel Sanders, minus the white linen suit. Blinking through horn-rimmed glasses, he murmured a polite greeting and surprised Colly by raising her hand to his lips for a moist kiss. She had to resist the urge to wipe her knuckles on her dress.

"Sit down, you three," Iris said. "Care for a drink? My housekeeper makes a marvelous old-fashioned."

"Iced tea for me." Brenda settled herself into a chair at some distance from Lowell.

Russ rubbed the back of his neck. "Momma, we thought we'd run down to the cabin before dark. Colly wants to look at the scene."

A flicker of pain showed in Iris's face, but her voice remained placid. "Of course, dear. We'll eat at seven."

"Not so terrible, eh?" Russ grinned as they followed a flagstone path through a thicket of still-bare crape myrtles on the other side of the pool.

Not if you enjoy catty microaggressions, Colly thought. "What do you mean?"

Beyond the thicket, the path skirted the tennis courts and wound down a grassy slope.

"C'mon, admit you were dreading this." Russ prodded her good-naturedly with his elbow as they started down the hill.

Having lowered her emotional defenses on the drive from town, however, Colly intended to keep them fully raised while here. "Remind your mother that I'm not retired. I'm taking a break, figuring out what I want to do next."

Russ chuckled. "Fine, change the subject."

Colly ignored him. "What was that about with Lowell?"

"His usual jackassedness. He's got the emotional maturity of a toddler who missed naptime."

"Seemed like more than that."

"Forget it." Russ waved dismissively. "What's your impression of the judge?"

"Now who's changing the subject?" Colly muttered. Whatever was going on between the brothers, Russ definitely didn't want to talk about it. "The judge seems okay."

Russ smiled. "He is, as long as you don't get him going about his stamp collection. Lowell can't stand him, thinks he's a gold-digger."

"You don't?"

"I ran a credit and background check. Talford's legit. Momma needed someone. Been a hellish couple of years—losing Randy and Victoria, and now Willis, too."

Colly said nothing. She tried to keep her eyes on the path but felt them inexorably drawn to a distant spot on the hillside, where, beneath a spreading oak, a cluster of white stones glimmered in the twilight. *Such a tranquil scene*, she thought numbly. In a few weeks, it would be covered with bluebonnets waving cheerfully in the breeze—as if nothing but joy could be associated with that place.

Russ followed her gaze, then dropped his arm across her shoulders and drew her against his side. "Sorry, wasn't thinking when I came this way." He hesitated. "Long as we're here, want to go visit them?"

For a moment, Colly almost turned to bury her face in his shoulder. But she couldn't afford to feel anything right now. A breeze ruffled her hair. She inhaled sharply, catching the fresh, chalky scent of the scrublands all around.

"Maybe later," she said and pulled away.

Chapter 10

Willis's cabin, as the Newlands called it, sat at the base of the slope, where the tended lawn gave way to a wild tangle of juniper and mesquite. It had been built in the 1980s as a place for Bryant's mother to live out her retirement. After her death, it sat unused until a teenaged Willis began begging for a pet snake. When Bryant, in a rare moment of parental indulgence, returned from a business trip and popped the Cadillac's trunk, beckoning Willis to look inside a mysterious container, the boy stared, a lopsided grin on his face. Iris refused to allow the young Burmese python in the house, so it was relegated to the cabin, where Willis kept it in a fish-tank terrarium, feeding it mice that he raised in cages stacked nearly to the ceiling.

The snake was the circumference of a broom handle and the length of a child's arm when Bryant brought it home. He had no idea that pythons could live a quarter-century, or that a mature specimen could be twenty feet long and weigh over two hundred pounds.

After Delilah, as Willis called it, outgrew a succession of tanks and graduated from a diet of mice to rats to live rabbits, Iris eventually persuaded Bryant to have the cabin's bedroom turned into a full-blown habitat. Willis was in his mid-twenties then, having graduated from high school only by dint of the fact that he was a Newland. The family had come to terms with the reality that he would never hold down a job or live on his own. Nevertheless, he'd developed an almost savant-like expertise in herpetology. He spent much of his time in the cabin with Delilah, often sleeping there on a cot and sometimes staying for days.

In 1999, when Willis went to prison, Bryant ordered Felix, the ranch foreman, to get rid of the snake. "Chop its head off and feed it to the dogs. I'm tearing this damn place down."

Somehow, Iris managed to change his mind. Keeping Delilah was a way of clinging to hope that her son would someday be released. Occasionally, after Felix fed the thing and Iris knew it would be sluggish, she'd don khakis and boots and head down the hill to sit in the musty room in front of the herpetarium, thinking things she never spoke aloud. And so the cabin remained, as did the rabbits in the hutch behind it. When Willis was finally released, a condition was set that he must stay a hundred yards from the big house whenever children were present. So the cabin became his full-time home.

Dusk was deepening towards darkness as Colly and Russ mounted the cabin's steps.

"Kitchen light's on," Russ said. "Felix must be around somewhere."

Colly followed him inside and wrinkled her nose. The place had the stuffy odor of a house seldom entered, mixed with another smell, acrid and reminiscent of a pet store.

The cabin was furnished as if from a rummage sale, with a threadbare sofa and a wagon-wheel coffee table near the door. A twin bed and nightstand stood against the back wall, half-inside the tiny kitchenette.

"I've never been in here," Colly said.

"Not much to see—in this room, anyway. C'mon."

She followed Russ through a side door, then stopped, astonished.

A few feet inside, running floor to ceiling and stretching the width of the room, stood a thick glass partition, the front wall of an enormous tank, containing what appeared to be a lush tropical jungle. Dense climbing vines hung from the branches of an artificial tree in the center of the enclosure. On the ground below, ferns, sentry palms, and giant philodendrons nodded, their waxy leaves dripping with moisture in the dim light. A pair of fallen logs rested on the leaf-littered floor near the front wall, and Colly glimpsed a recessed pool towards the back.

"Damn, Dr. Livingstone," she murmured.

"It's something, huh? The foundation had to be specially shored up just to support it. Designed by one of the architects who renovated the San Antonio Zoo. He owed Dad a favor, I guess."

Colly laid her palm against the glass. It was cool and dry to the touch, though the other side was beaded with condensation. Leading into the enclosure was a transparent door secured with a heavy padlock. Beside the door was a small, hinged hatch.

"Willis died here?"

Russ nodded.

"Can we go in?"

"If you're okay with snakes. I know they used to bother you." He nodded towards what Colly thought was a fallen log, and she realized with a shock that she was staring down at a head like a shovel blade and a pair of bright, black eyes.

"Jesus God!" She stumbled backwards.

Russ steadied her with his arm. "Woah, there."

"You didn't euthanize that thing? It killed a man." Colly pulled away, trying to regain composure as the blood roared in her ears.

"Momma wouldn't hear of it. Delilah's her last connection to Willis."

Colly brushed the hair off her forehead, and her hand came back wet with sweat. She stared at the giant snake. It lay perfectly still, camouflaged by the patterns on its skin—dark amoeba-shaped blotches against a background of renaissance gold. After a moment, its tongue flicked out and tasted the air. She could see a perfect, convex miniature of herself reflected in its eyes.

What must Willis's last moments have been like? How would it feel to have this Jurassic monster slowly tightening around your throat, the massive weight of its coils compressing your ribcage? To feel the pressure and the blood filling your ears, your eyes, your brain as you clawed at its scaly hide, fighting to breathe or scream, your vision slowly narrowing to black . . .

Colly shuddered. "Just talk me through what happened."

Russ glanced at his watch. "It's a long story."

"Give me the basics."

Russ nodded but said nothing for a minute. When he spoke, his voice was flat and detached, but he never took his eyes off the snake.

Willis had died a few weeks after Denny Knox's murder the previous September. On the night of Iris's seventieth birthday party, in fact. Because of the location of Denny's body and the rabbit-fur mask in his hand, the Rangers quickly homed in on Willis as their prime suspect. They wanted him to come to the station to give a formal statement and take a polygraph, something Iris and the family lawyer refused to allow. Willis couldn't have killed Denny, because he'd been with her the entire day of the murder, Iris insisted. She wasn't going to let the Rangers railroad her boy again.

Lowell was the one who finally persuaded her to relent. Public sentiment against the family was growing and had started to hurt the business. "You can't stonewall forever," he said. "The sooner Willis proves his innocence, the better."

Accompanied by his attorney, Willis had spent that Saturday at the station. He passed the polygraph, and his account of his movements on the day in question matched his mother's.

"I think the Rangers figured if they leaned on him hard enough, he'd confess, like he did in the Parker murder," Russ said. "I watched the tapes. Willis was petrified—kept repeating his story and begging them not to send him back to prison. The DA wouldn't press charges based on the rabbit mask alone, so in the end, they had to let him go." Russ rested his forehead against the glass wall. "Momma was so happy, said it was the best birthday gift she could've gotten."

Colly stared thoughtfully at Delilah. "Who was at the party that night?"

"Everybody—except Willis. He couldn't, because of the kids. But the rest of us were. And Talford."

"Willis stayed here alone?"

"I felt bad about that. He'd had a rough day. I came down before dinner to check on him."

Willis had been afraid, asking if the Rangers would arrest him. Russ had tried unsuccessfully to calm his brother. "He was frantic. I hated to leave him. I tried calling Felix, but he was off somewhere, not answering his phone. So I called Momma, and she sent the housekeeper down with a Xanax pill. I gave him half."

The medicine had helped. By seven o'clock, Willis was calm. "He wanted to spend some time with Delilah and then go to sleep." Russ shook his head, mystified. "I swear, everything seemed fine. I called Felix again and left a message to check on Willis when he got home. Then I left. Wish to God I hadn't."

He stared bleakly into the tank. Colly was searching for something comforting to say when, from the adjacent room, they heard the front door swing open and the hollow tread of boots on the cabin floor.

Russ looked up. "Felix, is that you?"

A moment later, a man wearing faded jeans and a blue denim work shirt appeared in the doorway. He was in his mid-seventies, short and bandy-legged, with leathery skin and salt-and-pepper hair. Under one arm, he carried an enormous gray rabbit, which was working its nose furiously.

The man appeared slightly confused to find anyone in the cabin. "I was gonna feed her. I'll come back later," he said in a heavy Mexican accent.

"No, stay, Felix. It's good you're here. You remember Colly, Randy's wife? She's looking into the Denny Knox case for us. I was just walking her through the night Willis died. She'd love to hear your perspective." Russ turned to Colly. "Felix was the one who found him."

The man nodded, staring inscrutably at Colly. His gaze was unsettling, somehow.

"How did it happen?" she asked.

Beneath Felix's arm, the rabbit began to struggle, unhappy at being confined. Felix opened the hatch in the glass wall and, to Colly's horror, dropped the animal inside.

He closed the hatch and wiped his hands on his shirt. "I was at the movies with my nephew, Pete. When we come out, I seen a message on my phone from Mr. Russ saying Mr. Willis is upset. So when I get back to the ranch, I come here to check on him."

Colly tried to listen, but her focus was riveted on the gray rabbit. It was sitting on its haunches in the herpetarium, its nose and ears twitching as it assessed its surroundings. Ten feet away, Delilah watched, motionless. After a moment, she flicked out her tongue.

"And you—you saw him where, exactly?" Colly stammered. "He was in there?"

"*Si*." Felix pointed to a spot just inside. "Slumped on the ground, half-sitting. His head hanging down." He demonstrated, letting his own fall limply to one side, like a ragdoll's.

In the cage, the rabbit took a slow hop forward, sniffing the leaf litter. The python remained still.

Colly wrenched her eyes away. "Did you go in and check for a pulse?"

Felix shook his head. "No need." He glanced at Russ, who nodded.

"Tell her. It's okay."

"He was purple, swollen," the older man said slowly. "His eyes bulged out. There were tooth marks . . ." He gestured to his neck and head.

Colly's lips felt numb and her palms were clammy. She turned to Russ. "It tried to eat him?"

"Snakes are primitive. When prey's nearby, they get aggressive by instinct, like a shark in a feeding frenzy. That's what the hatch is for." She heard him swallow. "You should never feed one by hand. They're nothing but muscle—even a small constrictor can kill a person. There've been several cases. Google it sometime, just not late at night." He stared into the snake pen.

Growing more comfortable in its new surroundings, the rabbit had begun to explore. It took several tentative hops in the direction of the python, which still did not move a muscle other than its tongue and eyes.

Colly's mouth felt dry. She looked at Russ. "You said the Rangers think it was suicide."

"I do, too. Willis walked in there holding a live rabbit. We found it hiding under a bush in the back, terrified out of its wits." He tapped his finger on the glass. "Willis knew better."

"Could he have gotten confused? Maybe the Xanax—?"

"I didn't give him much. He wasn't loopy when I left, just calmer."

Colly turned to the ranch foreman. "You knew Willis as well as anyone. Could it have been an accident? A mistake?"

Felix's eyes were on the rabbit as it inched closer to the python. He shook his head. "Delilah only eats twice a month. Mr. Willis knew it wasn't time."

"Willis loved this snake more than anything, besides Momma," Russ added. "He took care of it like a baby."

He nodded towards the enclosure. Colly followed his gaze. As they talked, the rabbit had continued to explore. Unaware of its peril, it had hopped closer and closer to the snake and now sat barely a foot from its side, nibbling experimentally at some wood bark. Delilah moved for the first time, shifting her heavy head a few inches towards her prey.

Colly felt a sudden desire to bang on the glass. "Why doesn't she just eat the damn thing, already?"

"Pythons are cold-blooded. They have to conserve energy. They don't move till they're sure of hitting the mark."

The rabbit took another hop towards Delilah's tail, and the snake seemed to contract, the muscles tightening along its burnished flank. It turned, lifted its head a few inches off the ground.

"Here we go." Russ sounded tense, but excited. "If you don't want to see this, look away now."

Colly most definitely did not want to see it, but she was transfixed. It was happening so slowly—like watching the masked killer move up behind some clueless blond girl in a horror film. The blood was pounding in her temples, and she couldn't breathe. She clenched her fists.

When the python struck, it did so with such speed and force that, although Colly was staring right at it, she saw nothing but a golden blur. By the time her eyes refocused, the snake had twisted itself into a surprisingly small, tight knot, from which nothing of the rabbit protruded but its hind feet and tail. The feet twitched, once, twice, then went still as the coils of the snake constricted further. As Colly watched, the pads on the bottoms of the rabbit's feet morphed from bubblegum pink, to dark rose, to deep purple-blue.

Colly, who'd examined brutal crime scenes unfazed, now felt her stomach churn. "Let me out." She stumbled against Russ, willing herself not to vomit on the borrowed dress.

Russ steered her into the adjoining room. "You okay?"

Colly blinked in the brighter light. Her pulse was slowing, but a sharp pain had begun to shoot along the nerve behind her right eye.

"I'm fine. Bit of a headache." She stood up straight. "That's one hell of a way to commit suicide, if it's what happened."

Russ nodded grimly. "Momma believes it was an accident. But once we found those rabbit masks in here, the Rangers considered the case closed."

"Where were they hidden?"

"That's just it—they weren't, really." Russ led her to the twin bed and opened the nightstand's drawer. "They were here, under some magazines. Like we were meant to find them. The Rangers figured—"

"Let's talk about it later."

Russ seemed confused, but nodded. "I reckon we should head back. Felix, you staying?"

The old man was watching them, his wizened face impassive. "Pete's coming to help me clean the pen."

"Lock up when you leave. There's kids at the house tonight."

Felix nodded gravely. "Don't worry, Mr. Russ. I will."

97

Chapter 11

Darkness had fully fallen by the time Colly and Russ exited the cabin. Descending the steps, Colly looked up and was astonished, as she always was when visiting the ranch, by the stars. In Houston, only the brightest were visible, but here they were so thick that they seemed almost oppressive.

"Sorry to cut you off," she said. "Best not to discuss the case around anyone. Even Felix."

"You're right. He's such a fixture here that I didn't think." Russ offered his arm. "The grass is damp. I should've brought a flashlight."

Still fighting a headache, Colly allowed him to lead her across the lawn. "So you think someone besides Willis planted those masks."

Russ sighed. "The Rangers figured he just wasn't smart enough to hide things well, but Willis could be secretive when he wanted to. Dad once found a dirty magazine hidden inside his closet wall when we were kids. He'd made himself a hidey-hole with tools from Felix's shop."

"Where'd he get the magazine?" Colly asked, momentarily diverted.

"Said he found it by the highway. But that raises a good point—where would Willis get those masks? He didn't drive, he didn't have friends. And he damn sure wouldn't know how to tan a rabbit hide."

"He could've googled it."

"He didn't have computer or internet access—that was one condition of his release."

At the flagstone path, Colly released Russ's arm. "If someone planted those masks, you realize what that means?"

"They had access to the ranch."

"Who besides the family has access?"

As they started up the hill, Colly heard Russ snort in the darkness. "Half the town."

"Be serious."

"Okay, I'm exaggerating, but not much. Felix, and his nephew Pete, and Nadine the housekeeper, and a half-dozen ranch hands live on the property year-round. They've all got friends who visit now and then. Not to mention the tradesmen and delivery people in and out all day. Plus Talford, and Momma's bridge-club ladies. And now that Lowell's living in the guesthouse, there's his poker buddies, and sometimes employees from the turbine plant. We had the company picnic here last summer. If it's not literally half the town, it's a fair percentage."

"Great." Colly massaged her temple, where the earlier sharp pain had resolved into a dull throb. "Those masks couldn't have been in the nightstand long, or Willis would've found them himself." She thought for a moment. "Did anything unusual happen at Iris's party?"

She sensed Russ looking at her. "Lowell had one beer too many and got mouthy about politics, like always. But basically, it was a pleasant evening. Dinner, presents, cake. Alice headed out early for a babysitting gig. Brenda took Logan and Minnie home around nine-thirty, as I recall. Talford left around ten. Momma went to bed a little after that, and Lowell and me sat by the pool a few more minutes, finishing our beers. That's when Felix came running up, saying Willis was hurt."

"Hurt? He said that?"

Russ paused. "I think so."

"Tonight, he said he knew right away that Willis was dead."

"Maybe I'm misremembering."

"He's found more than his share of dead bodies recently—first Denny, then Willis." Colly thought of the gray rabbit, of Felix dropping it through the herpetarium hatch as casually as if he were posting a letter. He would certainly know how to catch and skin a wild hare.

They had crested the hill and were passing the tennis courts. The murmur of voices came drifting on the night air from the patio behind the house, along with the shrill laughter of children splashing in the pool.

Russ turned towards Colly, the frown lines on his face accentuated in the dim glow of the distant house lights. "Felix didn't kill Willis—he was his protector. He loved Willis."

"People kill loved ones all the time, Russ."

"Not Felix. Trust me."

And that's the problem with investigating friends and family, Colly thought. *Neither of us should be on this case, but I'm more objective than Russ.* She wondered what he would do if she started poking around in directions he didn't like. It was a subject that needed to be addressed, but not tonight.

From the direction of the house came an especially loud shriek and splash, followed by Iris's sharp voice, carried on the still night air. "That's enough, kids. Come dry off." Then, more querulously: "What's keeping them, Lowell? Run down to the cabin and tell Russ dinner's ready. If Nadine's roast beef dries out, she'll pout for a week."

"That's our cue." Russ offered Colly his arm. "Ready for battle stations?"

Colly sighed and looked up. The Big Dipper hung high above them to the north, tipped as if about to spill the contents of its vast cup onto the roof of the house—*a cup of spiced and foaming wine, full of wrath.* The poetic phrase came, unbidden, to her mind. Was it from the Bible? She hadn't been to church since burying her husband and daughter, yet the verse sounded right. *The grapes of wrath.*

Battle stations, indeed.

She shook off the thought and tucked an escaping strand of hair firmly behind her ear. "Ready."

Ignoring Russ's arm, she walked quickly towards the house.

Entering the gloom of the crape myrtle thicket, Colly was startled to encounter a shadowy figure coming from the direction of the house. To avoid a collision on the narrow path, she stopped abruptly, and Russ crashed into her from behind, knocking her sideways.

In the darkness, the shape in front of her expelled an annoyed grunt, and Colly caught a whiff of alcohol. The figure turned without apology and retreated the way it had come.

"Here they are, Momma—praise the Lord and hallelujah, the roast beef's saved."

"Dammit, Lowell," Colly heard Russ mutter. "You okay, Col?"

"I'm fine." Colly smoothed her dress. "What's Lowell's problem? He's worse than usual."

"I told you, it's nothing. Ignore him." Russ started to move away, but Colly grabbed his sleeve.

"I need full transparency, or I'm going back to Houston. I mean it."

He sighed. "Lowell didn't want me bringing you in on this Denny Knox thing. We had a little dustup over it last week."

"Dustup?"

"He took a swing at me, clocked me pretty good on the jaw. Still a little sore."

"You're kidding."

"It was late, and he'd had a few, of course."

"Why doesn't he want me investigating?"

"Afraid it'll be bad for business. The company's gone through a rough patch recently."

"Why?"

She heard him swallow. "Long story. Let's talk later."

Colly hesitated. The topic had apparently struck a nerve, which surprised her. Russ, like Randy, had always left business worries to Lowell. But now his anxiety was almost palpable.

"Russ, what's going on?"

"Not now, Col. Seriously. Let's go, before Momma sends another search party." He started towards the house, and after a moment, Colly followed.

They emerged from the thicket onto the well-lit patio in time to see Lowell push past his mother and Talford and disappear into the house.

Iris seemed unfazed by her youngest son's rudeness. "There you are." She smiled benignly at Russ and Colly. "Hope you're hungry. The children have worked up quite an appetite."

"A little early in the year for swimming, isn't it?" Colly glanced at the water toys scattered on the flagstones.

"It's a heated pool. The kids stank of horse, so we let them take a dip. Brenda didn't think you'd mind. It's nice for Satchel to have his cousins to play with. I worry about how isolated he is in Houston."

"He has friends," Colly said defensively.

Before Iris could respond, Russ edged between them. "Did I hear something about roast beef? I'm starved."

Arm in arm, Iris and Talford led the way through the French doors into the house. As they entered the living room, Colly was struck by a sense of simultaneous familiarity and strangeness. When Randy had first brought her to meet his family, Colly's impression of Mollison was one of unpretentious, slightly shabby comfort. Then, it was a working ranch house, with piles of boots by the door and the faint odors of diesel, woodsmoke, and sweat permeating the air. A house that had seen four boys grow to adulthood.

Now, she felt as if she'd entered a movie set—some designer's idea of what a ranch house should look like. Brass-studded furniture of walnut and dark leather encircled a cowhide rug, and a row of Navajo saddle blankets hung on the wall, their vivid geometric patterns glowing against the honey-oak paneling.

As Colly scrutinized the room, Iris released Talford's arm and moved closer. "I've redone things since you were here last—ditched those antler chandeliers Bryant loved, and that smelly old rug of his grandmother's. What do you think?"

"Designed it herself," Talford put in. "A woman of hidden talents." He winked at Iris.

Colly hesitated. "It looks very . . ."

"Chic?" Iris prompted.

Proprietary was the word that had come to mind. *This place is yours now, and you're marking your territory.*

Though, after all, Colly thought, *why not?* Bryant Newland had been a domestic tyrant. Iris had a right to a fresh start, and she'd needed a distraction in the wake of so much tragedy. As coping mechanisms went, redecorating the house was harmless.

Colly smiled. "It's lovely." Her gaze was drawn to the fieldstone fireplace. "Oh, wow."

In place of Bryant's prized trophy—a buffalo-head mount that had brooded above the mantel for decades—an enormous oil painting now hung. It was a portrait of Iris done in a bold, Fauvist style and depicting her standing regally beneath a windswept sky, the dormered silhouette of the Mollison roofline behind her.

Iris followed Colly's gaze. "Ah, you've spotted my treasure. A gift from Talford, for my seventieth."

Talford beamed. "Commissioned it from a fellow in Santa Fe. Spot-on likeness, isn't it?"

Colly squinted up at the portrait. Even to her untrained eye, the quality of the work was unmistakable. It vibrated with energy. The artist had seen past the surface of Iris's placid charm and with a few, swift strokes of the palette knife had captured the fierce hunger behind the eyes, the imperious pride in the cambered smile. It was not a warm portrayal, nor a comforting one. The woman on the canvas was intimidating. Frightening, even. Colly could see why Iris loved it.

"It's remarkable," she murmured, taking an unconscious step back.

"I'm so pleased you like it." Iris seemed about to say more but was interrupted by a commotion in the hallway. A second later, the children burst into the room, with Alice and Brenda following.

"Grandma!" Satchel's normally pallid face glowed rosy pink. He ran to Colly and began hopping excitedly, reaching up to pat her cheeks with his fingertips, a habit he'd developed as a toddler when he wanted her attention. "We rode horses—mine was a black-and-white one named Maisie. Alice showed me how to hold the reins. She says I'm a really good rider. Then Grandma Iris let us go swimming."

"I see that." Colly smiled. "Your shirt's inside out. And goodness, your hair." It was still damp and sticking out in all directions. She smoothed it with her fingers.

"Sorry, Aunt Colly," Alice said. "We tried to comb it, but he was too wiggly."

"Come on, buddy." Colly took Satchel's hand. "Let's sort you out before dinner."

Colly led him to the bathroom as he continued to chatter happily. "This is the best place in the whole world. I wish we could stay forever."

"This morning you couldn't wait to get back to Houston. Arms up." Colly pulled off his shirt.

"It's *fun* here. Grandma Iris says I can stay the whole summer with her, sometime."

"She did, huh?" Flushing with annoyance, Colly turned the shirt right side out and popped it back over Satchel's head, then searched through drawers for a comb.

"Why're you mad?" he asked.

"I'm not."

"You're doing that thing with your teeth."

"I'm concentrating." Colly worked to relax her jaw. "Now, will you *please* hold still for two seconds and let me fix your hair."

Chapter 12

Dinner at the ranch was a strange mixture of informality and refinement. Once Alice and the younger children were settled in the den with plates of food and a Disney film, Iris led the adults to the dining room, where a rustic trestle table was covered, somewhat incongruously, with a fine Belgian lace cloth and Iris's best bone china. Wrought-iron candelabras on either end of the table cast long shadows on the walls and lent an ominously gothic feel to the evening.

Colly, who had hoped for a casual cookout on the patio, took her seat with trepidation. Since Randy and Victoria's deaths, she'd grown increasingly lax regarding household routine and was now largely accustomed to takeout dinners in front of the television. Here, she felt strangely awkward with a linen napkin on her knee and an array of forks and spoons to manage. But the roast beef, grilled vegetables, and warm yeast rolls proved homely and comforting; the wine was good; and the conversation remained surprisingly pleasant.

Before they'd sat down, Iris had announced firmly, "I don't want to hear one word about politics or family drama during dinner— there are far too many sharp implements on this table."

This had produced a laugh and set the tone for the meal. Everyone kept to pleasant small talk except for Lowell. He sat, interacting with no one, chewing sullenly with his napkin tucked into his collar and his sunburned forearms on the table. Colly noticed that Russ was watching him closely, frowning as his brother polished off a bottle of Shiraz by himself. The excessive drinking was worrisome, but at least it was keeping Lowell occupied, and Colly hoped Russ wouldn't interfere.

Dessert and coffee were served on the patio. "I love it out here this time of year," Iris said as Nadine, the dour-looking housekeeper, passed around cups of French roast and bowls of warm bread pudding topped with vanilla ice cream. "No mosquitos yet and not too muggy. Which reminds me, Brenda dear—Nadine and I have been spring cleaning. We've got some more things for the thrift shop, if you wouldn't mind taking them."

"Weather's nice *now*," Russ snorted, "but it was hotter than Hades tromping around outside today."

"Rattler weather," Lowell muttered, slurring the words. "They're coming out to bask. Already had a dog bit." He shook his head when Nadine tried to hand him a cup of coffee and held up a tumbler of bourbon he had carried from the house.

Nadine offered the cup instead to Colly. Perhaps it was her imagination, but Colly thought that the housekeeper was staring at her with an odd mixture of apprehension and resentment.

"Time for the Rodeo. Looking forward to some good old-fashioned fried rattler, myself." Talford patted his belly with both hands.

Colly dropped her spoon. "You eat those things?"

Russ chuckled. "We're heathens in West Texas. Can't believe you've avoided the Rattlesnake Rodeo all these years."

"Randy always pestered me to go, but I draw the line at pits of deadly vipers."

"Rattlers aren't bad, if you handle them properly," Brenda said. "We had a blast on the snake hunt last weekend. It was the kids' first time."

"Oh my God."

Brenda laughed. "You'd love the Rodeo, Col—it's like a carnival crossed with a county fair."

Talford nodded. "Less commercialized than that monstrosity in Sweetwater. Ours still has a small-town atmosphere."

"Except when those PETA morons show up," Lowell grumbled.

Iris stirred her coffee placidly. "We should all face our fears, Columba. You're just in time—the Rodeo opens Friday. They've started setting up the pavilions in the north pasture."

How easy it was to be glib about other people's phobias, Colly thought, fighting to suppress a vivid flashback of the rabbit's footpads slowly purpling in the python's coils.

Her mouth felt dry. She gulped coffee too quickly, scalding her throat. "I'll think about it."

She looked appealingly at Russ, who said, "Let's discuss it later, Momma."

Iris didn't seem to hear him. "I've wondered whether it's right to host the Rodeo this year, given all the recent tragedy." She looked up. The housekeeper had finished handing out refreshments and was hovering near her elbow. "We're fine, Nadine. Go put your feet up. That bursitis must be killing you."

"We should definitely have the Rodeo," Talford said as Nadine hobbled back to the house. "Traditions are healing for a community."

"Yes, but should we have it *here*, after two deaths on the property?"

"Gotta clear the snakes one way or another," Lowell mumbled around a mouthful of bread pudding. "Might as well have fun doing it."

"Plus, it raises a lot for charity," Brenda added, unexpectedly supporting her ex-husband.

A spirited debate ensued, the thread of which Colly soon lost in focusing on the interplay of personalities and the shifting eddies of tension and alliance that coursed through the conversation. *Who are these people?* she wondered. They had formed an integral part of her personal universe for over two decades, but any bond she felt was largely illusory, the product of custom rather than true emotional connection. She'd seen almost nothing of them in recent years. From an investigative standpoint, they were practically strangers.

The sound of raised voices pulled Colly abruptly back into the conversation, the subject of which, she realized, had shifted.

"Bullshit, Momma," Lowell was saying, red-faced. "I told you before—that was a freak accident." He gulped a long drink of bourbon.

"How about some coffee, buddy?" Russ stared hard at his brother, who took another pointed swallow from his tumbler.

Iris set down her cup and folded her hands neatly in her lap. "I didn't mean to upset you, dear. But freak accident or no, I think we need an internal audit of our policies and procedures—after the Rodeo, I mean. Better for us to catch any problems than for the Public Utility Commission to find them."

"The PUC's already cleared us. They're not gonna reopen anything unless we do something to provoke 'em, for fuck's sake—"

"*Lowell.*" Russ leaned forward, gripping his coffee cup.

"Every industry has its accidents," Talford said mildly. "At least with wind turbines, they're usually small-scale, not like oil spills or nuclear whatnots."

Iris smiled at him. "True, thank God. Though that's little comfort to the woman's family, I'm sure."

"I think I missed something," Colly said. "What accident?"

An awkward silence followed. Finally, Brenda said, "There was a bird strike on one of the turbines a year and a half ago. A woman was killed. I'm surprised you didn't hear—it was in the papers."

"Not the Houston papers. How on earth does someone get killed by a bird strike on a wind turbine?"

"It was one of those crazy, wrong-place, wrong-time—"

"Not a great dessert subject," Russ cut in.

Brenda waved off the objection. "Colly's used to gory stuff." She followed this with a brief explanation of the incident. A turkey vulture had flown into a blade on a windy day, causing a large piece of it to break off and sail onto a road, where a driver had swerved to miss it and crashed over an embankment.

"I didn't know those turbines were so fragile," Colly said.

"They usually aren't."

"Poor lady."

"She was a single mother, too," Iris added. "Passing through from Oklahoma. A real tragedy."

"Legal nightmare," Lowell grunted. "And cost us a fortune in upgrades."

"How do you upgrade for something like that?" Colly asked.

Lowell glowered into his bourbon and said nothing.

"We had the blades painted black," Iris said. "Supposedly, that helps birds see them. And every turbine had to be gone over inch by inch. The Commission thought all the ice storms that year might have weakened the materials. The woman's family sued, of course, but we managed to settle."

"It's been tough, but we're out of the woods now," Russ said with finality.

Lowell was not ready to drop the subject. "Nearly killed our bottom line—not to mention our reputation. And now, just as we're getting back on our feet—"

"It did *not* kill our reputation," Iris said. "I won't hear that sort of talk. Our good name saved us. But it won't be enough if there's a next time—which is why we need the audit."

"Christ, Momma, we were lucky the Commission didn't shut us down. And now you want to stir the whole mess up again? You have no clue how bad this fucking thing hurt us." Lowell drained his glass.

"Mind your language—the children might hear you," Iris said briskly. "Believe me, Lowell, I'm keenly aware of the damage this has done. In fact, I feel responsible for it."

"We agree on something, then," Lowell mumbled.

Russ turned to his mother. "How's it your fault? Lowell's the plant manager."

"Yes, dear, but I'm the CEO. Since Randy and Victoria died, I haven't been monitoring things like I should. Lowell's tried his best, I'm sure. But—"

"Are you joking?" Lowell pulled himself unsteadily to his feet. "We'd be sunk if it weren't for me. You put me in charge, but you won't stop meddling. You've been driving this company into the ground since Dad died."

"For God's sake, Lowell, that's not true, and you know it," Russ said. "You're making an ass of yourself."

"Right, I'm the ass, while you suck up to Momma and get all the *attaboys*. Let me tell you, Russ—I'm the reason you keep getting those nice, fat checks, so you can afford to run around playing cops and robbers." Lowell was growing increasingly agitated and had begun to pace unevenly on the flagstones.

He's going to fall in the pool, Colly thought. *Which might not be a bad thing.*

In the chair beside her, Brenda was showing signs of growing irritation. "Russ is right, Lowell. You're drunk, and you've been spoiling for a fight all evening. Why don't you sit down and try taking a few deep breaths?"

Lowell wheeled on her. "Why don't you try minding your own goddamn business?"

Brenda stood, her arms stiff at her sides. "It is my business when you're screaming and cursing like a lunatic thirty feet from our children. Will you *please* keep your voice down?"

Lowell laughed. "You didn't seem too worried about the kids when you were running all over town spreading your legs for your boss."

"Who can blame me, considering what was waiting at home?" Brenda's voice shook with fury. "I don't belong to you—I never did."

"You little whore." Lowell's face and neck were dark red and wet with sweat. He took two stumbling steps towards his ex-wife, but Russ leapt from his chair and intercepted him, spinning him deftly around.

"All right, buddy, that's enough. Let's take a walk."

For a second, Lowell resisted. But Russ held firm and finally managed to half-coax, half-frogmarch him down the path towards the tennis courts.

On the patio, no one moved or spoke. Colly's chest ached, and she realized she'd been holding her breath. She exhaled slowly.

Finally, Iris stirred. "And here I was, congratulating myself on how smoothly dinner went." She managed a wan smile at no one in particular. "You'll have to excuse Lowell. He's been under enormous pressure these past few months."

Brenda stared. "You're joking."

Fearing a new outburst, Colly said quickly, "It's getting late. We should get the kids home."

Brenda turned. "I need a minute to clear my head." Sniffling, she walked away into the darkness.

Across the patio, Iris brushed a bit of invisible dirt off her linen slacks. "Well," was all she said.

"And then there were three." Talford seemed cheerfully unfazed. He reached out to pat the back of Iris's hand. "Are you all right, my dear?"

"Certainly. Lowell's hot-tempered, but he always comes around." Iris spoke brightly. *Too brightly*, Colly thought. She felt a sudden twinge of pity for her mother-in-law.

Talford produced a pocket watch and flipped it open. "Colly's right, it's late. I should push off." He stood, buttoning his sport coat. "Unless you need me to stay."

"I'm perfectly fine. I apologize for the scene. We were doing so well, until the end."

"These things happen. Families are like powder kegs—the slightest spark and everything goes *kaboom*." Talford sketched an explosion in the air, then bent to kiss Iris's cheek. "See you Wednesday, for dancing?"

Iris reached up and held his face briefly in her hands. "I wouldn't miss it," she whispered fiercely.

Looking on, Colly thought it was the most authentically human gesture she'd ever seen her mother-in-law make.

Chapter 13

An uncomfortable silence descended over the patio. Somewhere in the crape myrtles, an early cricket chirped fitfully.

And then there were two, Colly thought. All evening, she'd been hoping for a chance to question Iris about the case, but now didn't seem like the right time.

She stood. "I think I'll check on the kids."

Iris, who had been staring absently at the flagstones, looked up and seemed surprised to find anyone there. "All right, dear. I'll come with you."

In the den, they discovered Alice curled on the sofa watching a nature documentary as the three younger children slept on floor-pillows.

"They conked out right after dinner." Alice grinned. "Between the riding and the swimming, they were beat."

"You were sweet to entertain them." Colly glanced around. "I'd like to pay you for your time. Let me grab my purse—it's in the car."

"No way, Aunt Colly. I had a blast." Alice consulted the mantel clock. "I better run, though—I have a little more homework."

When Alice had gone, Colly turned to Iris. "I'll get the kids ready. Wonder where their shoes are?"

Iris laid a hand on her arm. "One minute, dear, I'd like a word."

She led Colly into the dining room. The faint odor of yeast rolls still hung in the air, but the table had been cleared and a Delftware vase of crimson tulips placed in its center.

"It's more private here," Iris said.

"What's up?" Colly asked uneasily.

"I'm concerned about Satchel. When I helped him put on his bathing suit tonight, I noticed quite a few small scars on his thighs and shoulders."

Colly straightened. "Yes, I know. Those are burns. They're self-inflicted."

Iris covered her mouth with one hand. "Why would he—? How was he permitted?"

"He wasn't *permitted*, Iris, but he's clever," Colly snapped. "Ever tried completely eliminating heat sources from your home? You get rid of matches and lighters, but there's still the stove, the iron, the barbecue. His therapist says self-harming's not uncommon in traumatized kids."

"But surely more can be done? Medication—a new environment, perhaps? He was saying just tonight how much he loves the ranch. I know it's been overwhelming for you these past couple of years, looking after Satchel when you're coping with your own trauma."

Colly went rigid. "I'm fine. And while we're on the subject—in the future, please don't tell Satchel he can spend the summer here without checking—" She heard a noise.

Russ was watching them from the archway. "Everything all right?"

Iris smiled and adjusted a tulip in the vase. "Yes, dear. Did you get Lowell sorted?"

Russ looked skeptical, but he nodded. "I left him in the guest-house. He's weepy now, sends his apologies. Brenda's getting the kids ready to go. You're riding back with her, Col?"

Colly nodded. "My car's at her house." She pushed past him without another word to Iris and was halfway down the hall before Russ caught up.

"Sounded intense back there," he said. "You okay?"

"Your mother wants Satchel."

"Nah, she just cares about him."

Like Hitler cared about Poland, Colly thought as they entered the den.

Brenda was there, putting shoes on a groggy Logan. Her brief walk had apparently calmed her. "I couldn't wake the other two. They're out for the night, I'm afraid."

"We got 'em." Russ lifted Minnie in his arms.

Colly picked up Satchel and followed the others out to the gravel drive.

Brenda opened the minivan doors. "Great, my dome light's on the fritz again."

Groping blindly in the dark, they fastened the children into the back seat. Brenda slid behind the wheel and started the engine.

Outside the van, Colly turned to Russ. "What a day."

His smile appeared tired in the muted light from the porch. "Didn't chase you off?"

"Of course not. See you tomorrow."

Russ leaned in and kissed her impulsively on the cheek. His scent and the roughness of his jaw against her skin reminded Colly so potently of Randy that she almost flinched.

She turned quickly and climbed into the van. Russ closed her door. As she pulled the seatbelt, several things happened. A shadow flashed in front of her, and a gust of air hit her face as something large and dark dropped from the ceiling. It brushed against her arm as it fell, landing heavily in her lap.

She shrieked, more startled than afraid.

116

Russ jerked the door open. "What is it?" he demanded as Brenda gasped, "What's *that*?"

"I don't know. Something—"

In the darkness, Colly groped at the thing lying across her knees. It felt rubbery and cool, covered in a wet stickiness. Suddenly she screamed, loudly this time, and thrust the thing onto the floor before scrambling out of the van in a blind panic. Russ's arms closed around her and pulled her away from the vehicle.

"I got you," he was saying. "What's wrong?"

Colly was dimly aware of her own ragged gasps as she wrestled away from him and ran towards the house. Stumbling up the porch steps, she collided with a rocking chair and fell, sprawling on the planking with the chair across her back.

Rushing up the steps behind her, Russ threw aside the chair and pulled her to her feet. "Colly, you okay?" He turned her to face him, and his eyes widened. "Oh, God."

Colly looked down. The front of the blue dress was scarlet. Her extremities felt suddenly cold. "The kids—Russ, get the kids out of there."

"Brenda'll get them. Just stand still." Breathing hard, Russ ran his hands over her shoulders and arms. "Where's it coming from?" He was trying to stay calm, but his voice cracked.

Behind her, Colly heard the screen door fly open. "What's going on?"

"Momma, bring me the first-aid kit," Russ shouted. "And turn on the floodlights."

The screen door banged shut. A second later, halogen lamps affixed to the eaves blazed on. In the harsh glare, Colly saw that the three children had woken up and were piling out of the van, while, behind its wheel, Brenda was struggling to disentangle herself from her seatbelt.

As her initial panic response subsided, Colly's investigative instincts took over. "Kids, stay back," she shouted as the children rushed towards the porch. Satchel's face was white, his eyes fixed on her blood-soaked dress. He stopped and doubled over, vomiting on the ground.

"Satchel, it's okay—just stand still." Colly worked to sound calm. "Russ, I'm not hurt. Something fell on me—it's in the car."

Russ tilted her face into the light and pulled up her eyelids with his thumb to check her pupils. Apparently satisfied, he nodded. "Wait here."

He picked up a lap blanket from one of the rocking chairs and threw it around her shoulders, then turned and descended the porch steps.

Brenda was now out of the van and running towards the house.

Colly waved her off. "Keep the kids back."

Brenda nodded. Satchel was standing a little apart from his cousins, his teeth chattering. Colly gave what she hoped was a reassuring smile. "I'll be right there, buddy. Wait with Aunt Brenda."

Russ had ducked into the van's front passenger seat and was groping blindly on the floorboards. "What the—? Brenda, got a flashlight?"

"In the glovebox."

For what seemed like an eternity, Colly watched from the porch as Russ shone a white beam of light around the van's interior. Finally, he backed out of the door, something long and thin dangling from his fist. He carried it to the base of the porch and threw it on the ground.

"Don't worry, it's dead."

Colly swallowed with effort. At Russ's feet lay a six-foot rattlesnake, its black eyes dull and staring. The diamond patterns on its back were nearly obscured by congealed blood, though Colly saw no visible wounds.

"How'd you kill it?"

"It was dead already. Tucked up inside a cloth pouch the same color as the van ceiling, and rigged to fall when you put on the seatbelt. Fuse for the dome light's been pulled, too. That's why no one saw it." Russ rubbed his forehead, leaving a red smear above his eyebrow.

Colly felt light-headed. She steadied herself against the porch rail. "But—where's the blood coming from?"

"Belly's slit open. See?" Russ rolled the snake with his boot. "There's gore all over the van—spilled out when it fell. The thing's been dead a few hours, at least."

"Who would do that?" Brenda edged closer. She had one arm protectively around Satchel's shoulders, and Minnie was clinging to her skirt.

"That's *cool*." Logan started towards the porch, but his mother grabbed his t-shirt and jerked him back like a puppy on a leash.

"It is not cool—don't say that."

Russ looked at Brenda. "Were the doors locked?"

"No. Why would they be?"

Just then, Iris emerged from the house carrying a metal box with a red cross on the lid. "I couldn't find it at first," she said, then spotted the snake. "Was someone bitten? Are the children all right?"

Russ held up his hand. "No one's hurt, Momma. Stay there."

Heedless, Iris descended the steps. "Was that in the yard? Did you kill it, Russ?" She stooped to peer more closely. "Is that a *cigarette* in its mouth?"

Russ stared blankly at his mother, then pointed the flashlight at the snake's head. Even from her vantage point several feet away, Colly could see the tip of a small, white object protruding from between the jaws. Russ knelt and reached for the snake, but Colly stopped him.

"Got any gloves?"

119

"There are some in here." Iris handed Russ the first-aid kit.

Once gloved, he levered open the snake's mouth and pulled out the white object.

It was a rolled scrap of paper.

With a glance at Colly, he dropped the snake and unrolled the paper on his knee. He stared in disgust.

"What is it?" Colly, Brenda, and Iris asked simultaneously.

Russ stood. His mother reached for the paper, but he held it away.

"Evidence, Momma." He went to Colly and turned the paper so she could see.

Scrawled across it in crude block letters were the words: *1ST WARNING U MURDERING BITCH—GO HOME.*

Chapter 14

Entering the garage, she smells it first—a sharp, raw tang, metallic and sickly sweet—even before she spots the trail of rusty droplets on the floor. The odor, both familiar and shocking, sets the blood roaring in her ears. She lowers the grocery bags to the ground and reaches for her gun.

Where is Satchel? He ran inside ahead of her, but as she enters the house, she hears nothing but the muffled strains of "Frosty the Snowman." The kitchen is oddly dim, filled with a mist that grows thicker as she presses forward, until she finds that she is swimming through cold, turbid water. Ghostly shapes emerge like shipwrecks out of the gloom. Refrigerator. Stove. Table. As she drifts past, they melt back into darkness.

Nothing has any substance except the gun, which feels heavy and solid in her hand. She thinks it is moving of its own accord, pulling her deeper into the house. At the living room door, it stops. The metallic smell is stronger here. She tastes it in the back of her throat. A thing, unseen and horrible, waits in the water—a thing she doesn't want to find but must search for, nevertheless. In the darkness, something slimy brushes her calf. Two shadowy forms rise slowly from the deep, wreathed in a haze of red. As she stares, they tilt up their faces, bloated and fish-belly white, and fix their hollow eyes on hers. Their mouths move soundlessly as they ascend . . .

"Oh God, oh God." Colly lurched upright in bed, breathing hard. A faint gray light glimmered through the curtains. Something touched her shoulder. Satchel sat beside her, blinking sleepily. A smudge of dried blood had crusted on his lower lip where he'd chewed it during the night.

"You were screaming, Grandma."

"Sorry. Bad dream."

Colly pulled him onto her lap. The seat of his pajamas was damp.

"I had an accident." He pressed his face into her chest.

"It's okay, baby." Colly closed her eyes and rubbed his back as she tried to shake off the lingering terror of the nightmare. It was months since she'd had the dream, which never varied and which had haunted her with a sickening persistence for over a year after Randy and Victoria's deaths. In Houston, she'd burn off the emotional aftermath on her stationary bike—but that wasn't an option here. *Finish this case, and you can go home*, she told herself. Perhaps solving it would banish the nightmares for good.

Opening her eyes, Colly glanced at the clock and groaned. She'd slept through her alarm—unsurprising, since it had been three a.m. when they'd finally climbed into bed. The discovery of the dead snake the night before had created a lengthy delay, necessitating a call to Earla Cobb. Arriving at midnight, frowsy-headed and wearing what appeared to be a pair of men's pajamas beneath her coveralls, she crawled through Brenda's van, examining it as best she could in the dark and bagging what bits of evidence she could find, but she held out little hope of fingerprints or DNA.

"Our perp's a careful bastard." She wiped her forehead with her sleeve. "I don't like this, Russ. Stinks of crazy."

"How so?"

"What's the best way to kill a rattler?"

"Chop its head off."

"Exactly. Everyone in West Texas knows that. But this one's spine's been snapped like a pretzel stick." She mimed the action with her hands. "Ain't practical—or safe."

"Think we're looking for someone who's not from around here?"

Earla scratched her ear. "Only a local could find this place. Anyhow, ain't just the snake. There's somethin' about the whole scene. I think the SOB fantasized about this, down to the smallest detail. I'm gettin' a real serial-killer vibe."

Colly felt the gooseflesh rise on her arms as a quick, clear image flashed into her mind—the rabbit mask staring up at her with its demented, hollow eyes.

Russ turned to her. "What d'you think?"

"It does seem pointlessly elaborate. Almost stage-managed."

Earla nodded. "This fella's a couple sandwiches shy of a picnic, if you ask me." She tapped her temple.

"Or wants us to think so," Colly said.

Earla grunted absently. "I wanna reexamine everything in daylight. Got anyone who can keep the scene secure till morning?"

Colly looked at Russ. "What about Avery?"

He shook his head. "She's too involved in the case."

In the end, he called Jimmy Meggs, and it was almost two o'clock when the young officer arrived, bright-eyed but in dire need of a shave. Russ gave him detailed instructions and then drove Colly, Brenda, and the children back to Brenda's house, where Colly's car was parked.

"I'm following you to the farmhouse," he said. "I want to check things out. If this perp knew where you'd be eating dinner tonight, he must know where you're staying."

Even after they cleared the place and Colly shooed Russ away, insisting that she didn't need him to spend the night on the sofa, sleep did not come easily. For once she'd been glad to have Satchel's

123

warm little body beside her as she dozed fitfully through what remained of the night.

Now, leaning against the headboard with Satchel in her arms, Colly felt herself drifting off again. She jerked awake with effort.

"Come on, Satch, let's get you cleaned up." She ruffled his hair. "We're late."

◆ ◆ ◆

Forty minutes later, Colly pushed through the police station door, a Starbucks coffee in each hand. In no mood for small talk, she hurried past the elderly office manager and down the hall to Russ's office, pausing for a moment in the open doorway. Her brother-in-law sat hunched over his laptop, staring intently at the screen. He looked tired, she thought, his face slack and wan, with dark rings under his eyes and a day's worth of stubble on his chin.

He was so absorbed in what he was doing that he jumped when she sat down in the chair facing him.

"I didn't figure you'd be in till later." He pushed the laptop aside.

"Had to take Satchel to school. Might as well get to work." Colly slid one of the paper cups across the desk. "Black with two sugars, right?"

Russ smiled wearily and scratched his stubbled jaw. "Thanks. Get any sleep?"

"More than you, by the looks of it."

"How's Satchel?"

"Not great. He didn't need to see me covered in blood." She shook her head. "I hope bringing him here wasn't a mistake. The therapist thought he'd have separation anxiety if I didn't."

"Kids are resilient." Russ pried the plastic lid from his coffee cup and blew on the steaming liquid. "Alice adapted better than me after Wanda died."

"I just hope his flashbacks don't start again." Colly looked around. "Where's Avery?"

"She texted she'd be late—said she's running down a lead."

"What lead?"

"Beats me. I figured it was something you told her to do."

"Damn kid," Colly muttered. "Any news from Earla?"

"Nothing yet." Russ sipped his coffee. "She's at the ranch now, going back over things. Thought I'd head up in a while, see how it's going. I told Felix to give her access to the security footage. Wish I'd thought of it earlier."

"Since when does the ranch have cameras?"

"I talked Momma into it after what happened to Denny. System's only been up a few weeks, so it slipped my mind last night." He began to turn the coffee cup slowly in his fingers. "You, uh—you okay?"

"I've been called a murdering bitch before—though never so creatively, I'll admit."

"Don't make fun, Col. This wasn't some idiot tossing a brick through a window. If there's a homicidal maniac—"

"Let's not get ahead of ourselves. We don't know that Denny's killer did this."

Russ stared. "Who else could it have been?"

"Think about it. The Rangers closed Denny's case. Most people believe Willis killed him—and Willis is dead. If the real murderer's out there, he'd want to lay low and hope our review flatlines, not build some elaborate booby trap to stir up suspicion."

"Unless he's panicking because you're here. Or he's just crazy."

Colly hesitated. "Various people might have reasons for wanting to scare me off."

Russ frowned. "Got someone in mind?"

"You said yourself Lowell's upset I'm investigating."

"Lowell?" Russ looked shocked.

"He knew where I was last night, and he had plenty of opportunity."

"Are you saying you think Lowell murdered Denny Knox?"

"I'm saying he has motive to plant that snake—I don't know why. Until you give me an explanation, I'm bound to think the worst."

"Lowell would never scare his own kids like that. He knew they'd be in the car."

Colly studied his face. Once again, he'd dodged the subject of his fight with Lowell. But she could tell by the set of his jawline that it was useless to press the issue now.

"He said Iris is driving the company into the ground. What did he mean?"

"Nothing. He was drunk."

"Seemed like more than that."

Russ smiled tiredly. "He and Momma disagree on how to run things. Lowell's like Dad, wants to cut costs to maximize profits. Momma likes to put money back into the business. They've been butting heads about it since Dad died."

"Then why—"

"C'mon, Col, I'm too exhausted for family crap. New subject. *Please.*" Russ drained his cup and set it down with finality.

Colly laughed. "Sometimes you're so much like Randy that it's scary." She settled back in her chair. "Tell me about the fireworks stand, then. Did Earla find anything yesterday? I didn't get a chance to ask you last night."

Russ brightened immediately. He told her that Earla had bagged a few cigarette butts in her search of the area. They were probably unconnected to the case, but they'd been sent for testing. The more exciting news pertained to the mysterious set of footprints identified at the scene. Earla thought they'd been left by a pair of rubber boots or possibly waders—men's size ten.

Colly exhaled sharply. "The same as the ones around Denny's body?"

"Maybe. We're not sure."

"Still, it's interesting." Colly brushed back an unruly strand of hair. "What about Tom Gunnell? Get anything from him?"

"Not much." The mechanic had told Russ that, following Colly and Avery's visit, he'd been under a truck in the repair bay all afternoon. He'd had no idea anything was going on at the fireworks stand till he heard Earla's motorcycle arrive. He'd come out to look because, as he put it, the engine sounded interesting, and he'd been startled to see all the activity up the road.

"He seemed on the up and up," Russ said. "No motive to lie."

"Unless he took the baseball cap himself."

Russ shrugged. "The girl at the desk backed his story." There were no security cameras at Digby's, so their statements couldn't be verified. But both said they'd be willing to take polygraphs. "Besides," Russ added, "Tom's got huge feet—size thirteen, at least."

Colly sighed. "They didn't notice anyone loitering in the area? A customer, maybe?"

Russ shook his head. It had been a slow afternoon at the shop. Both Gunnell and the desk clerk had heard vehicles passing on the road, but since that was normal, they hadn't paid much attention.

"Somebody had to see us find that cap, Russ. How else could it vanish?" Colly considered. "What about the salvage yard next door? Maybe someone was watching from there."

"It was closed yesterday. A couple pit bulls guard it, according to Tom. Both him and the office girl swear they would've heard them bark if there were trespassers. And before you ask—no, it doesn't have a surveillance system, either."

"Jeez. This is modern times."

"Not in West Texas." Russ grinned. "But we're not all stuck in the Dark Ages. Check this out. I was looking at it when you came in." He swiveled the laptop towards Colly. She put on her reading glasses. On the screen was a grainy black-and-white image of an empty road in front of a squat brick building that Colly recognized as the Compass Counseling Center.

She looked up. "What's this?"

"Composite security footage the Rangers put together—all the sightings of Denny Knox on the day he disappeared. I was reading Avery's report on your interviews yesterday, and I got to thinking—"

"She sent you a report?"

"Check your email—she copied you in. Anyway, watch."

Russ started the video. The counseling center door swung open and a slender boy emerged, a ballcap on his head and a bulky pack slung over his shoulder. The image wasn't the clearest, but it plainly showed the boy walking swiftly to a BMX-style bicycle chained to a telephone pole at the curb. He bent over the bike, presumably unlocking it, then jumped on and pedaled rapidly away.

Russ paused the video. "Denny's session with Brenda ended at one p.m. This footage came from a camera on the daycare center across the street. Time-stamped 1:03."

He clicked "Play," and together they watched a series of spliced clips tracking Denny's progress through Crescent Bluff on the day of his death. Some bits of footage came from retail establishments, others from home security systems. Most was of poor quality and taken from a distance. But in every shot, he seemed in a rush, standing on the pedals and pumping hard.

The final seconds of the montage showed Denny zipping through an intersection in front of a convenience store.

"That's on the Old Ranch Way," Colly said.

Russ nodded. "He's heading north. And look at the time stamp—1:12."

"So?"

"Avery's report says Denny told Brenda he was going to the library after therapy to return some books for his mom. But he didn't. Timeline doesn't work. And we found library books in that backpack yesterday." Russ jabbed his finger at the screen. "Something changed his mind."

"Brenda said he was acting antsy. He could've been excited about the weekend and blown off the library."

"Who'd want to lug a bunch of books to the stock pond? That's a long ride on a hot day."

Colly removed her glasses and chewed absently on one of the temple tips. "Too bad he's wearing the hat. If we could see his face, his expression might show—" A noise in the hallway interrupted her thought. Avery was standing at the door, a manila folder under her arm. Her eyes were bright and her face was flushed.

"Sorry I'm late." She grabbed a chair against the wall and pulled it close to the desk. "I've got news."

Russ closed the laptop. "What's up?"

"Last night, I went through the case photos." Avery pulled a color print from the folder and laid it on the desk.

Colly examined it closely—a mid-distance shot of a BMX bicycle lying on its side in tall grass. It was in poor condition, the paint scratched and the saddle wrapped in silver duct tape.

"It's Denny's. I took this at the stock pond the day his body was found. Here's a closer shot." Avery laid a second photo over the first and tapped it with her finger. "See?"

Colly and Russ both leaned in until their heads were nearly touching. A fresh-looking scrape was clearly visible on the tip of the right handlebar.

"Doesn't prove that's from the fireworks stand, I know," Avery said.

"Supports the theory, though." Russ grinned. "Nice work."

Avery waved her hand impatiently. "That's not the big news. Like I said, I found this photo last night. So this morning, I stopped by the feed-and-seed out on Winters Road."

"Ned Sandleford's place?" Russ asked.

Avery nodded. "Sam and Alan Sandleford both work there." She turned to Colly. "They're the ones—"

"—who own the fireworks stand. I remember."

"Well, guess what? Denny used to work for them."

Russ cocked an eyebrow. "When?"

"Last summer. They hired him to staff the stand a couple afternoons a week in the lead-up to the Fourth of July. But get this." Avery paused for effect. "They fired him. Said he was unreliable."

"How'd Denny take it?" Colly asked.

"Not great. Told them they'd be sorry. Then in August, someone broke into the stand and smashed up the place. The Sandlefords thought it was Denny."

Russ crossed his arms. "Why didn't they file a report?"

"They had no proof, and there wasn't enough damage for an insurance claim."

"Did they retaliate?"

"I asked, but they got evasive. There's definitely more to the story than they let on." Avery paused. "Well? This is huge, right? If Denny trashed their place, they've got motive."

"Did you record this interview?" Colly demanded.

"I didn't think of it till after."

Colly glanced at Russ, who cleared his throat. "Did you ask Sam and Alan why they didn't see fit to tell the Rangers all of this in September?"

"I tried. But like I said, they clammed up. I figure we can ask later." Avery hesitated, perplexed. "You'll want to follow up with them, right?"

Colly threw up her hands. "You should've checked with me before doing this, dammit."

Avery turned indignantly to Russ. "What's her problem?"

Russ sighed heavily. "It was a good idea, Parker. But you've got to clear things with Colly first. She's the lead on this case."

"Are you kidding? I bring you a potential breakthrough, and you're lecturing me on how 'there's no *I* in *team*'?"

"Procedure's important. Protocol lapses can ruin a case."

"I moved the case forward—that's what matters. *Jesus.*"

Russ started to reply, but Colly cut him off. "No. What matters is building a case that'll stick. You can't prove the Sandlefords said any of this. If they did kill Denny, you've just put them on notice to—"

"What's done is done." Russ held up his hand. "Won't happen again. Right, Parker?" He turned to Avery.

She stood up. "At least I was out doing something, while you're in here enjoying your frappuccinos." She stalked to the doorway. "FYI, Sam Sandleford wears size-ten shoes. Alan wears nines—I checked." She slammed the door behind her.

Colly and Russ sat in silence as Avery's footsteps faded down the hall. Finally, Colly stirred. "This isn't working out, Russ."

"She's immature, and she screwed up." Russ hunched his shoulders. "But don't you think you're being a little hard on her? She did bring back some important intel."

"Which we can't verify. Now, if the Sandlefords lawyer up—"

"You're retired, Col. You need an active-duty officer with you. Avery's the pick of the litter, believe me."

"Bottom line, I can't trust her." Colly pushed her hair out of her eyes. "She lied to me yesterday, you know. Said she doesn't remember anything from the night her brother disappeared except her dad carrying her out of the burning house."

"Maybe that's true."

"I know when I'm being lied to. She's hiding something."

"She was eight. What could she possibly be hiding?"

"I don't get it, Russ. We might have a serial killer here. Do you *want* the case to fail?"

"I just think you're overreacting a little." Russ rested his elbows on the desk. "Why are you letting Avery get under your skin? This isn't like you. Even good cops make mistakes—you know that."

Colly winced and looked away. "Yeah. And I know how severe the consequences can be."

"Avery needs to learn a little discipline, that's all. I'll talk to her. She'll come around."

Chapter 15

Outside, the air had grown muggy and still. The flags drooped on the pole in front of the station. A flat gray haze hung low overhead, hinting of rain later on. Colly, fidgety with anger, paced the parking lot. When her clothes began to cling to her skin, she leaned against the police cruiser and looked around. Nothing moved on Market Street except for a mail truck trundling down the block. The only living thing in sight was a female grackle busily plucking insects from the grille of an SUV a few yards away. As Colly watched, a male bird landed on the gravel beneath and began to strut, puffing his iridescent blue-black feathers and fluttering his wings in a courtship dance until the annoyed female retreated to the branches of a nearby oak.

Colly's mind drifted back to her conversation with Russ. *Why are you letting Avery get under your skin? This isn't like you.* His words had stung, and that was irritating. He had no right to criticize. He didn't know her—not really. In the past, their relationship had been fairly superficial, always mediated through Randy. Yet Russ's opinion mattered more to Colly than she cared to admit.

Was she being unreasonable? Colly pushed the question reflexively away. She couldn't afford the luxury of a psychological spelunking expedition. Russ was the unreasonable one, leveraging her guilt to bring her here, then saddling her with a sullen and headstrong assistant. Was he subconsciously punishing her for his brother's death? Colly took a deep breath and exhaled slowly. *Trust your training—the rest is noise*, she told herself. Getting to the truth was all that mattered. If Avery jeopardized that process, she would have to go, whether Russ liked it or not. It was as simple as that. Too much was at stake.

Colly's head had begun to throb. She dug in her purse for her sunglasses but looked up when she heard footsteps on gravel. Avery approached, her eyes downcast and her face hot with embarrassment.

"Sorry I acted without your permission."

Colly found her sunglasses and put them on. "From now on, you don't do a thing unless I give the go-ahead."

Avery glared at the ground. "Got it."

"Good, let's go. I want to talk to Denny's folks."

After a silent ten-minute drive, they pulled into Lonestar Estates, a seedy, sprawling mobile-home park on the east edge of town. Avery appeared to be familiar with the area, steering deftly through the labyrinth of narrow lanes without the aid of GPS or map.

"You've been here before?" Colly asked, but Avery said nothing. Colly tried again. "If Denny's parents are friends of yours or something, tell me now."

Avery shook her head. "We've been called out on a couple domestics at their place." She hesitated. "And I used to live here."

"In this park? When?"

"As a kid—with my dad." Her hands tightened on the wheel. "After the fire."

Avery parked the car in a patch of pea gravel beside a double-wide trailer. A row of dead chrysanthemums drooped in plastic pots on the stoop, and the windows were covered with a thick layer of grime. When Colly got out of the car, a scruffy-looking cat that had been lying on the front steps vanished through a hole in the trailer's metal skirting.

"No vehicles," Avery said. "Maybe they're not home."

Colly knocked on the door without response. She turned to Avery. "You said Denny's mom works nights and his stepdad's unemployed?"

"Last I knew."

They were descending the porch steps when a dented hatchback turned into the yard. The driver, a thin-faced woman, eyed them uncertainly. Finally, she killed the engine and climbed out, a bag of groceries in her arms. She appeared to be in her mid-fifties. Her face was lined and her hair streaked with gray. But as she drew closer, Colly realized that she was at least a decade younger than that, though the years had not been kind.

"Denny's mom?" Colly whispered.

Avery shook her head. "I don't know her, but I've seen her around."

"Then you lead."

The woman stopped at the bottom of the stairs. "Can I help you?"

Avery presented her badge and explained their purpose. "We need to talk to Jolene and Jace."

The woman identified herself as Carmen Ortiz, Jolene Hoyer's sister. "Jo's probably still in bed. Give me a couple minutes—I'll get her up." She mounted the steps and dug a key from her pocket. "Jace is probably tinkering out back. You can check, if you want."

Colly and Avery followed a pair of tire tracks around the trailer and through a weedy lot towards a prefab metal garage.

"Anything I need to know before we talk to this guy?" Colly asked.

"The Rangers looked into him. He had no alibi for the afternoon Denny died. But in the end, they ruled him out in favor of Willis."

Two massive pit bulls slept in the dirt beneath a pecan tree next to the garage. They lifted their immense heads, then stood and walked to the end of their chains, growling. The garage door was open, and a cherry-red pickup fitted with all-terrain tires was backed partway inside, blocking most of the entrance. Colly noted mechanically that the truck, though filthy and mud-splattered, was an expensive one and fairly new. It seemed out of place amid the general air of seedy destitution that characterized the property.

"Hello," Colly called.

When no one answered, she sidled through the gap between the truck and the doorframe. Avery followed. The interior of the garage was cool and comparatively dim, smelling of motor oil, sawdust, and something else—a familiar odor, earthy and sharp, that put Colly instantly on high alert. As her eyes adjusted, she became suddenly aware of a massive shape looming over her. She gasped and jumped back, reaching reflexively for her sidearm before she realized what she was seeing.

Avery rushed up, pistol in hand.

"It's okay," Colly said. "Look."

Above them, dangling by its hocks from a homemade hoist welded to the bed of the truck, hung the half-skinned carcass of an enormous wild hog. Its belly had been slit open, and beneath it sat a plastic tub filled with blood, offal, and strips of hairy hide.

Colly glanced around the garage. A row of four chest freezers hummed against the left wall. Against the right stood a workbench topped with a butcher block. On a pegboard behind it hung an array of meat hooks, cleavers, and knives. A stainless-steel band saw sat in the center of the space, a halo of blood spatter ringing the sawdust floor beneath it.

"Damn," Colly whispered. "Freddy Krueger's playhouse." She cleared her throat. "Anybody here?"

After a few seconds, they heard a toilet flush, and a man emerged from a door in the rear of the garage, zipping the fly of his coveralls. After the stories she'd heard about Jace Hoyer, Colly expected a hulking giant, but this was a short, wiry white man with coarse, mud-colored hair and a nose that looked as if it had been broken several times.

Seeing Avery, he stopped, and his eyes narrowed. "What do *you* want?"

Avery introduced Colly, then said, "What's going on here, Jace?"

"What's it look like?" Jace Hoyer began washing his hands at a utility sink by the workbench.

"I didn't know it was hunting season," Colly said.

Hoyer cast her a scornful look and turned off the water with his elbow. "Not from around here, are ya? Ain't no rules with hogs. Hell, you can shoot 'em from a chopper, if you want." He pointed at the half-skinned animal. "I cornered that one with my dogs this morning, then stuck it through the eye with a knife."

As Colly pondered a reply, Avery waved towards the line of freezers. "You're not selling meat out of your garage, I hope?"

"Who's gonna hire me in this town anymore?" Hoyer grabbed a leather apron from a hook and threw it over his head, tying it behind his back. "Jolene ain't worked in weeks—just lays around popping her damn pills. Gotta keep the lights on, somehow."

"You know you need a license," Avery said. "Has the DSHS inspected this?"

Hoyer's eyes flashed. "Go to hell, why don't ya, and leave us alone. Ain't we been through enough?"

Colly stepped forward. "This won't take long. We're trying to wrap up a few loose ends regarding your stepson's death."

"That case is closed. I got nothing to gain by talking to y'all."

"You've got plenty to lose if you don't." Avery jerked her chin towards the freezers. "If I were you—"

Colly cut her off. "We're not trying to jam you up, I promise."

"As long as I cooperate?" Hoyer spat in the sawdust. "I ain't falling for that good-cop, bad-cop shit from someone who got her whole family killed. How're you still a detective?"

Colly met his eyes. "It's just a few questions, Mr. Hoyer."

Jace Hoyer stared back at her for a moment, then shook his head and grabbed a long knife from the workbench. Colly's gun-hand flinched, but Hoyer picked up a whetstone and began running it along the blade. "Fuckin' Newlands, you're all alike. What do you wanna know?"

"I understand you worked at the turbine plant."

"Till your goddamn brother-in-law fired me."

"Why?"

"He wanted a cat to kick, and I was handy."

"Meaning—?" Avery prompted.

Hoyer shrugged. "Screwups ain't ever Lowell Newland's fault, that's all."

"You're talking about the accident on the highway a couple years ago?" Colly asked.

Hoyer stopped sharpening the knife. "Wasn't my fault that lady got killed. Lowell called the shots—I just followed orders."

"I thought it was a freak accident."

He cast her a sly look and wiped a trickle of sweat from his temple with the heel of his hand. "Sure, freak accident. But the company was taking flak, anyhow. Lowell needed a scapegoat, so he drummed up a bullshit excuse. Fired me on a technicality. Then went around giving folks the impression that the real reason he let me go was that I caused the accident." The insinuations had been subtle, Hoyer said—nothing overt enough to allow for a defamation lawsuit. But a few winks and nods from Lowell to the right people had been enough to render Hoyer unemployable.

He tossed the whetstone onto the workbench. "I can't even defend myself, 'cause he made me sign a goddamn NDA."

"How come?" Avery asked.

Hoyer laughed harshly. "Lowell ain't the business genius folks think he is, and he ain't no choirboy, neither."

Colly took a step closer. "If Lowell did something illegal, the NDA's not binding. You'd be covered by whistleblower statutes."

"Think I'm stupid? Who'm I gonna make a report to, Russ Newland and his Ranger buddies? *You?* I already lost my house, and I reckon they'll repo my truck any day now. When a grand jury subpoenas me, I'll tell 'em all about it. Till then, I got nothin' more to say on the subject." Hoyer tested the knife blade with his thumb, then strode over to the hog and began to score long, thin strips in its hide.

Colly followed him and leaned against the truck. "Okay, new subject, then. Talk to me about Denny. I heard the two of you didn't get along."

"Denny didn't get along with nobody. Kid needed a lot more ass-whuppin' than he got."

"And that's where you came in?"

"Done my best, but Denny'd go crying to Jolene, and she'd get pissed at me. She wanted us to bond. I tried it her way—used to let him tag along to the factory, sometimes. But how can you bond with a kid who gets his kicks setting fires and blowing up frogs? Something wasn't right upstairs." Hoyer tapped the knife against his temple. "Ain't just my opinion. The shrinks at that clinic done some kind of brain scan on him. Kid was a psycho."

"That's pretty harsh. Where were you on the afternoon he disappeared?"

"Right here, working on my truck from lunch till after dark. Then I came in and drank myself silly."

"The Rangers never verified that," Avery said.

"How could they? I was alone, for Chrissakes. Jolene was working a double. Denny was a little shit, but I didn't kill him. If I did, I woulda made damn sure to have a better alibi than the one I got."

Colly thought for a moment. "What about last night?"

"What about it?"

"Where were you between six and ten?"

Hoyer hesitated. He hunched his shoulders. "Home. Jolene and me watched the Mavs game then went to bed."

"She'll vouch that you never left the house?"

"She better—it's the truth." He dropped the knife into his apron pocket and seized a strip of hog skin, pulling it down in one long, smooth motion to reveal a layer of glistening white. "Best way to flay a hog's to peel it like a banana. This way, you don't rip off the fat. It's how the old-timers do it. Those YouTube morons with their tutorials don't know shit."

"Ever do anything with the skin?" Avery asked abruptly.

Hoyer shrugged. "Hog's hide ain't much use for tanning. Too greasy. Sometimes I sell the bristles on eBay. Folks use 'em for fishing flies and whatnot."

Avery started to ask another question, but Hoyer waved them away. "That's enough, now. Leave me alone and lemme work, before this hog rots on the gambrel."

The women walked back towards the trailer in silence. They stopped beside a rusty clothesline, where a lone floral sheet hung limply in the still air.

"What do you think?" Colly asked. "He's got a motive. Sounds like he couldn't stand the kid."

Avery shrugged. "Small feet, though—definitely not size ten."

140

"True, but he'd know how to make those rabbit masks." Colly ran a hand through her hair. "Let's talk to the wife, see if their stories match up." She paused. "Good work getting Hoyer to talk, by the way."

Without waiting for a reply, Colly turned and led the way up the path towards the trailer's front door.

Chapter 16

When Colly knocked on the door of the trailer, Carmen Ortiz, the woman they'd met earlier, opened it almost immediately. She wore a pair of rubber gloves slick with suds, which she wiped nervously on her apron.

"This ain't a good time, actually. Jolene don't feel much like company."

"I understand. But it's important," Colly said.

Carmen glanced over her shoulder, then shook her head. "Some other day."

She started to close the door, but Avery pushed forward. "You do the housekeeping for the counseling center, right? I'd think twice about blowing off Brenda Newland's sister-in-law."

Colly laid a hand on Avery's shoulder, pulling her back. "We know your family's been through a lot, Ms. Ortiz. This won't take long."

Carmen hesitated, chewing her lip. Finally, she stepped aside.

The place was poorly lit and reeked of cat litter and stale cigarette smoke. Carmen waved them towards a shabby sofa, where two cats were curled on a blanket. Avery shoved them to one side and flopped down on the center cushion. Colly, who was allergic to cats, joined her more tentatively, her eyes itching. She looked around.

A frail-looking woman sat in a recliner on the other side of the room. She was staring down at her folded hands and seemed oblivious to the visitors. Like her sister, Jolene Hoyer appeared prematurely aged. She couldn't be past forty, Colly thought, but her hair was dull and the skin of her neck was already beginning to slacken. She was dressed in a housecoat of the sort worn by elderly women, and an old-fashioned knitted throw covered her legs. On a nearby table sat a box of tissues next to a framed school photograph of a stocky, ginger-haired boy.

Carmen lowered herself into a rocking chair beside her sister. "Sorry, Jo. They said it couldn't wait." She removed the rubber gloves and laid them across her knees.

Colly leaned forward. "Mrs. Hoyer—"

"Useless bitch! You freakin' psycho!" a voice shrieked.

Colly jumped, her pulse racing. In a corner of the room, a large gray parrot was watching them from a stand that Colly had taken for a floor lamp.

The woman in the recliner looked up. She wore bright pink lipstick; the effect in the haggard face was garish and macabre. "Don't mind Fred," she mumbled.

"Some mouth he's got," Avery said.

"He picks things up from TV."

"From Jace, more like—"

Colly cut Avery off. "Mrs. Hoyer, I'm very sorry for your loss. Did Carmen explain why we're here?"

The woman stared with unfocused eyes. "I already told the Rangers everything I know."

"We're reviewing their findings."

"Shut your hole, freakin' psycho!" Fred screamed.

The bird's voice was piercing and toneless, like something mechanically generated. Forcing herself to ignore it, Colly sized up Jolene Hoyer. She was clearly distraught and possibly under the

143

influence of some drug; a hard-hitting interview would probably backfire, though a soft touch might work—as long as Avery didn't blow the whole thing up. *We should've worked out a game plan beforehand*, Colly thought, rubbing her watery eyes.

"What can you tell me about Denny, Mrs. Hoyer?" she asked. "The police file doesn't give me a very rounded picture."

A ghost of a smile flitted across Jolene's face. Her eyes drifted to the photograph on the table. "Handsome, wasn't he? All them freckles. Denny looked like a boiled shrimp after ten minutes out-side, but he was so stubborn about sunblock."

"My grandson's the same way." Colly thought she saw a brief, responsive flicker in the other woman's eyes. She pressed on. "I know you saw a side of Denny nobody else did."

"He was a handful." Jolene touched the frame with her fingertips.

"The more you can tell me, the better."

The room grew silent except for the muttering and clucking of the parrot, who was now preening itself on its perch. Avery shifted impatiently. Finally, Jolene cleared her throat. When she spoke, her voice was flat and dull.

Denny had worried her from the start, she said. Even as an infant, he would fly into rages, screaming until he made himself sick. Later on, he struggled in school. He had trouble reading, and being big for his age, he took out his frustrations on the smaller kids. When she married, Jolene hoped that having a man in the house would help, but Jace and Denny never got along. In the last couple of years, he'd fallen in with a bad crowd—older boys who spent their days smoking pot and getting into trouble. She'd pushed him to sign up for baseball, thinking that a hobby might help.

"He liked it okay, but he felt out of place. Most of them kids been playing since the peewee leagues. Denny just wanted to belong somewhere. No one ever gave him a chance."

"The Sandleford brothers did," Avery said suddenly. "They hired him at the fireworks stand, but he trashed the place."

The lines around Jolene's eyes deepened. "Them boys thought 'cause their daddy's on the town council they could call Denny 'white trash' to his face. What'd they expect?" She sighed. "The only place he fit in was the turbine plant."

Colly sat back in surprise. "Really?"

"Jace was the foreman there, till a year ago," Jolene said. She'd goaded him into taking Denny along a few times during school vacations, hoping it might improve their relationship. The workers were sweet to Denny, letting him do odd jobs and calling him "Little Man," even taking him on a few installation runs.

"It was the first time he found something he was good at. He'd come home grinning, wanting to tell me all about it. He was crushed when Jace was let go."

Jolene had been crushed as well, she admitted. She'd hoped her son might have a future with the company.

"Jace says he was fired for a technicality," Colly said. "What was it?"

Jolene picked with her fingers at the blanket on her lap. "Lowell said he breached protocols bringing Denny to the factory. No warning, no two weeks' notice. Denny'd been going up there for months and Lowell never said nothin' before. I know he's a relative of yours, but Lowell Newland's a bastard, and that's the truth."

"Bastard!" Fred shrieked. "Tan your hide, you little bastard!"

Avery stirred. "When exactly did that happen?"

"Last March, just before the Rattlesnake Rodeo."

"Denny torched the school bathroom the next week, right?"

"He was upset." She looked at Colly. "You know what kids are like."

Jolene had begged the authorities for lenience. As the school counselor, Brenda had also argued on Denny's behalf, since no one was hurt and only minor damage was done to the school. Nevertheless, the district had pressed charges, and Denny was convicted of arson. Rather than sending him to a juvenile detention center, the judge paroled him on the condition that he receive therapy. But with Jace unemployed, the Hoyers couldn't afford it. Brenda must have spoken to Dr. Shaw about the situation, because a few days later he called Jolene and offered the clinic's services to Denny, pro bono—if she'd allow him to conduct certain tests and use the data in his research.

"He's writing a book about troubled kids," Jolene explained. "He said Denny fit the profile." She pressed her lips together. Her eyelids drooped. Carmen stood and seemed prepared to end the interview.

"That's helpful, thanks," Colly said. "Can we see Denny's room before we go?"

Carmen frowned. Jolene opened her eyes. "Okay, but it's nearly packed up."

Clutching her sister's arm for support, she led the way down the hall to a cramped bedroom cluttered with items of clothing, books, and toys, some packed into boxes and plastic bags, others sorted into piles on the floor. Blobs of blue sticky-tack pocked the walls where posters had once been.

Jolene hung back in the doorway. "Folks said it'd be comforting to keep his room like he left it. But I hate that idea. Makes it seem like he's coming back. I thought if it was something different—a sewing room, maybe." Her face was bleak.

Colly moved gingerly through the room, looking but touching little. Detective or not, it felt disrespectful to root through a dead child's belongings while his mother and aunt looked on. Avery, who appeared to have no such qualms, began opening boxes and bags without waiting for permission. Jolene watched, chewing her cuticles.

On a bookcase next to an empty fish tank sat a colorful heap of plastic cigarette lighters. Jolene saw Colly looking at them, and reddened. "I found those under his bed. Denny'd steal mine. Don't know why."

"He liked playing with fire?"

"Since he was little. Nearly burned the house down a couple times—not on purpose, just messing around. Had burn scars all over his fingers." Jolene hesitated. "It worried Brenda."

Colly's chest felt tight. "How so?"

"She didn't say. But when I told her about the lighters, she asked if he ever wet the bed. Seemed like a funny question."

"They're both symptoms of juvenile psychopathy," Avery said bluntly. She was digging through a cardboard box on the dresser. "So's cruelty to animals. Jace said Denny liked to blow up frogs—maybe Brenda was concerned."

Jolene looked horrified. She covered her mouth.

"Do you have a psychology degree I don't know about?" Colly snapped. "And go easy with those things. We're guests here."

Flushing, Avery pulled a framed 8x10 photograph from the box and studied it before handing it to Colly.

It was a team photo—rows of boys in front of a dugout. All were dressed in blue caps and jerseys embossed with a cartoonish demon brandishing a baseball bat. Denny stood squinting into the sun beside Tom Gunnell, whose arm was draped over the boy's shoulders.

"The Blue Devils." Colly turned to Jolene. "Did he ever play on a team with a red uniform?"

"No. Why?"

"He was last seen in a red ballcap."

"Denny didn't have no red caps."

"It's all on video," Avery said, moving towards the closet. "Maybe you didn't know him as well as you thought."

Jolene scowled. "What are you playin' at? My boy's the victim."

"No one's implying otherwise, Mrs. Hoyer." Colly tapped the picture. "What did you think of his coach?"

Jolene shrugged. "Tom never screamed at the boys, like some of them coaches do. Used to take them for ice cream after the games."

"Did you ever worry—"

"He ain't no pervert, if that's what you mean." Jolene pulled the photograph from Colly's hands, then stopped, distracted. "What are you doing?"

Avery had opened the closet door and was on her knees, rummaging through a pile of shoes. "Did Denny have foot problems, wear corrective inserts in his shoes, anything like that?"

"'Course not."

Avery picked up a grubby sneaker and peered inside. "What about you and Jace?"

Jolene was growing agitated. "N-no. Now, put that down—I didn't let you back here so you could go making insinuations and pawing through Denny's things."

"Avery, that's enough," Colly said.

To her relief, Avery rose without protest, dusting off her hands. "Mind if I wash?" she asked, and left the room before anyone answered.

"Sorry about that," Colly said.

Jolene was still frowning, but the energy of her outburst had left her. She stared bleakly at the pile of shoes. "The Rangers were the same—tearing up the place, showing no respect."

"We didn't mean to offend."

"Denny was a good boy." Jolene sat down on the edge of the bed, still clutching the photograph.

Carmen turned to Colly. "My sister's tired."

"We won't keep you much longer." Colly's phone chimed with a text. She switched it off without reading the message. "While

I'm waiting for my partner, let me ask—did you notice anything unusual the day Denny disappeared? Sometimes people don't mention critical details because they think they're irrelevant."

"I've thought about it a million times," Jolene murmured. "It was a normal Friday."

"Brenda told me Denny's regular appointment was on Thursdays." Colly shut the closet door. "Why'd you change it?"

Jolene looked up. "I didn't. The clinic called, asked if we'd mind switching the schedule that week 'cause Brenda had a conflict."

"Did that happen often?"

"A few times. I didn't think nothin' of it."

She'd been picking up extra shifts on Friday afternoons that month, Jolene explained, working days as well as nights to cover for a fellow aide on maternity leave. That morning, she told Denny he'd have to ride his bike to his counseling appointment at noon and asked if he'd return some library books while he was out.

Jace and Denny had argued all week; so when Jolene got back from work shortly after seven the next morning and learned that Denny hadn't been home, she wasn't overly concerned. "I figured he was coolin' off somewhere, probably at Tom's."

"Tom Gunnell?"

"He used to let Denny crash at his place when things got bad."

Colly approached the bed and knelt so that she was eye-level with the grieving mother. "This is a tough question, but I have to ask: is it possible Jace—"

"No." Jolene leaned in so that Colly smelled her breath, a sour mixture of coffee and toothpaste. "Jace has a temper and drinks too much. But if he hurt Denny, he woulda told me."

"Jace was here when you got home Saturday morning?"

Jolene nodded. "Asleep on the couch. We talked a few minutes, then I made some eggs. We was finishing our coffee when Russ Newland knocked. I couldn't make no sense of what he said, at first. I told him it must be some other boy by the pond." She looked away.

Watching her, Colly had a brief, vivid memory of standing at her own living room door, clutching her handgun and staring without comprehension at the scene in front of her.

She pushed the thought aside and turned to Carmen. "Did you see Denny at the clinic when you cleaned it that day?"

Carmen shook her head. "I didn't get there till after dark. I do it last on Fridays, 'cause the counselors stay late sometimes, finishing their weekly reports. No one was there. I went in the back door—"

Colly looked up. "Was it unlocked?"

"I have a key. I remember thinking it'd be a quick job with Dr. Shaw out of town. His office wouldn't need much. But there was play-therapy toys all over Brenda's office. She keeps them in a suitcase in her office closet, but the closet was locked, so it took me a while to find a box to put them in." Carmen had finished by ten o'clock and, a half-hour later, was home, watching TV in bed, unaware of her nephew's death until the next morning.

Colly heard a sound and looked up. Avery was leaning against the doorjamb, her hands in her pockets. She met Colly's eyes and jerked her chin towards the exit. She seemed excited. Colly stood, her knees cracking.

Back in the living room, they thanked their hosts. As she started to follow Avery out the door, Colly paused. "Mrs. Hoyer, can you tell me where you and Jace were yesterday evening?"

Jolene blinked. "Right here, watchin' the basketball game. Why?"

A sudden, shrill scream and a whir of beating wings cut off Colly's response. She felt a rush of air as the parrot shot past her face and landed on Jolene's shoulder.

"That thing flies?" Colly gasped.

150

"Jace won't trim Fred's wings—says it's cruel."

"But he's fine with stabbing a hog through the eye," Avery murmured in Colly's ear.

The bird cocked its head and glared at them with a yellow-ringed eye. "Tan your hide, bitch! Shut your hole!"

"You're sure Jace was with you the whole evening, Mrs. Hoyer?" Colly asked. "Could you have dozed off?"

"I—I was awake."

The parrot began to bob its head rapidly. "Useless bitch. Better not, better not."

"Good game last night," Avery said. "Fourth quarter was a real nail-biter, huh?"

Jolene nodded distractedly. "If something happened last night, Jace didn't do it. I dunno why folks are so quick to think the worst of him."

"Because it saves time," Avery muttered.

Fred chuckled. "Freakin' psycho."

Colly thanked Jolene and followed Avery outside.

"Like *hell* she was awake," Avery said when they were back in the car. "That game was dull as dirt after halftime. She was probably drugged out of her mind." Avery pulled out her phone and thumbed through her apps. "This was in the bathroom." She showed Colly a photograph of an orange pill bottle.

"You rifled their medicine cabinet?"

"I texted to ask if it was okay, but you didn't answer. It's not like I stole anything."

Colly sighed and took the phone, enlarging the photo with her fingers. "Xanax, huh?"

"Filled a week ago, but there's only a few pills left. Jolene's over-medicating."

"Or someone's stealing."

"Either way, proves Jace had access. He could've drugged Denny."

"Assuming Jolene had the meds in September. But that's easily checked." Avery's phone began to ring in Colly's hand. She glanced at the caller ID as she handed it back. "It's Russ."

Colly was slightly annoyed until she remembered that she had switched off her own phone in the house. Checking it, she saw that Russ had tried to call her first. She also had a missed call from Brenda. Alarmed, she jumped out of the car and hit redial.

"What's wrong?" she demanded when Brenda answered.

"We've had a little incident. Don't worry—" Brenda added quickly, "Satchel's okay. Just a little shaken up. But we need to have a conference before I can let him back in the classroom. Can you come by the school?"

Colly glanced at her watch, then through the windshield at Avery, who was still on the phone, listening intently. She looked excited. When she saw Colly watching, she gestured for her to hurry.

Telling Brenda she'd be there soon, Colly hung up as Avery climbed out of the cruiser, her camera over her shoulder.

"Be right back," she said and raced up the driveway, disappearing behind the trailer.

As Colly was considering whether or not to follow her, Avery returned. "Boss wanted some shots of Hoyer's truck." She buckled her seatbelt. "Hope Jace didn't see me."

"What's up?"

Avery was already backing down the drive. "We're supposed to get to the ranch, ASAP. Earla found something."

"I'll have to catch up later," Colly said. "Run me by the station—I need my car."

Chapter 17

Too impatient to search for a space in the crowded lot, Colly parked on a side street and hurried to the school. Brenda was waiting at the entrance.

"What happened?" Colly demanded.

"We haven't gotten the whole story yet." Brenda led her inside and down the hall. "Satchel brought matches—from the farmhouse, I assume. Or maybe from Iris's. He won't say."

"Oh, God. Is everyone all right?"

"Satchel's got a couple minor burns, but Wanice caught him before anything horrific happened."

"It's been months—I thought we were past all this. Do I need to take him out of school?" Colly wondered how she would manage a murder investigation with a seven-year-old in tow.

Brenda paused at the door to the central office suite. "Hopefully not, but we've got to be sure he won't do it again. We thought if you talked to him—"

"Where is he?"

"Wanice's with him. The other kids are at lunch."

Colly followed Brenda past the front desk and through the door marked "School Counselor." The office appeared empty; it took a second for Colly to spot the top of the teacher's head.

Wanice Boyles was seated on the floor behind the desk. Hearing the door open, she clambered stiffly to her feet and smiled.

"Satchel, look who's here." Wanice met Colly's eyes and pointed downward.

"No hurry," Brenda said. "We'll be in the classroom."

After they'd gone, Colly stepped behind the desk. Satchel was curled in the cramped space beneath it, hugging his knees and sniffling into the crook of his arm. His white-blond hair glowed in the dim light.

Colly sat cross-legged on the floor. "Satchel, what were you thinking?"

The boy shivered.

"You're not in trouble. Tell me what happened. Where'd you find the matches?"

Satchel said nothing.

"I'm not mad."

"Yes, you are," he murmured into his sleeve.

"I'm not, I promise." She reached beneath the desk to rub his back. "Where were they?"

"Your purse."

"My *purse*? You know that's not—" Colly stopped herself. "When?"

"This morning. You were in the bathroom."

"Satchel, why? Look at me." She tried to pull his arm away from his face, but he resisted, hugging his knees more tightly. Colly caught a glimpse of his bandaged fingers.

"A boy called me a bad name," he whispered. "Everyone laughed."

"What bad name?" Colly waited. "Never mind. Remember how to put up your forcefield like Dr. Bracken showed you?"

"That doesn't work."

"Neither does burning yourself."

"It makes me feel better. I don't know why."

Colly's head had begun to ache. She pinched the bridge of her nose. "You can't play with fire, buddy. You just can't."

"Why'd my mom give me such a stupid name?"

"You're named after a great baseball player. And don't change the subject. Promise you won't play with fire."

Satchel looked doubtful. He hunched his shoulders, then nodded.

"Say it."

"I promise."

"Good boy." Colly pulled him onto her lap and kissed his forehead. "Let's go."

They found Brenda and Wanice in the second-grade classroom, talking quietly at the teacher's desk.

"Satchel has something to say." Colly nudged him forward.

He stared at the floor. "Sorry. I won't do it again."

"Thank you, Satchel. That's very brave." Brenda extended her hand. "You're probably starving. I'll walk you to the cafeteria. We can have a chat while we go."

Satchel looked uncertainly at Colly but allowed himself to be led away.

When they were gone, Colly turned to Wanice. "I don't know what got into him."

The teacher smiled sympathetically. "Brenda mentioned there was an incident last night that could've triggered something?"

"He saw some blood. But I never thought—" Colly's head throbbed. She felt her phone vibrate in her pocket with an incoming text, but she ignored it. "I understand if you're not comfortable keeping him in class."

"He's a sweet little boy. I'd love to have him if Brenda okays it. She's the expert."

Brenda returned alone after a few minutes. "I think he'll be all right now. I should've anticipated how traumatic last night might've been."

"You're not the one with matches in your purse," Colly said. "I switched bags before we left Houston. I must not have checked it well."

"That's where he got them?"

"He says so, but it's odd. I'm always so careful." She suddenly remembered that she had left her purse in Brenda's van during dinner the night before. Was it possible that whoever booby-trapped the van had left the matches as well?

"Goodness, there's no telling what's in my old handbags," Wanice was saying.

"Mine either." Brenda laughed. "I'm always running late for something when I switch purses, so I never clean them out properly. Come on, Col, I'll walk you out."

Outside, the air was still muggy, but the sky had lightened to a pale, hazy gray, and the threat of rain seemed to have lifted.

Colly glanced at her watch. "What a day, and it's only eleven-thirty. I'm glad you were here, Bren. From now on, I'll frisk him every morning." Colly chewed her lip. "I heard that fire-starting and bed-wetting are early signs of—of psychopathy. Is that true?"

Brenda shot her a quick look. "Studies do indicate *some* link between those traits and antisocial personality disorder."

Colly's phone buzzed again. She ignored it. "Should I be worried?"

Brenda hesitated. "Kids harm themselves for lots of reasons, Col—I've seen it at the clinic. When they can't find a way to process emotional pain, they try to externalize it."

"I know. But what do I *do*?"

"Sports can be a good outlet."

"Sunlight's a problem, though."

"There are indoor sports. Karate, maybe. Or bowling."

I'm scared he's turning into Ted Bundy, and you want him to roll a ball at some sticks? Colly thought. She remembered the pile of lighters in Denny Knox's bedroom. Was Brenda the reason Jolene had pushed him into baseball?

"I'll look into it."

"I know his Houston therapist says he's doing well, but after what happened last night, it might help to have him talk to someone here. I'd be happy to do a couple sessions with him, if you want."

"I'll think about it."

Colly's phone buzzed again. She pulled it out and saw that Russ was calling. She'd missed several calls from him, as well as a text from an unknown number.

She apologized to Brenda and answered the phone.

"Where've you been?" Russ demanded irritably. "I've been calling for fifteen minutes."

"Emergency at school."

His voice softened immediately. "Is Satchel okay?"

"He's fine. What's up?"

"Jace Hoyer was at the ranch last night—around the time we were at Willis's cabin."

"He's on security footage?"

"Yep. Parked down the hill and walked towards the house. Face isn't real clear, but it's him, all right. Tire tracks match his truck's."

"Does the video show him planting the snake?"

"Brenda was parked in a blind spot. But Jace was heading that way. It's circumstantial, but let's talk to him."

"Tell Avery to meet me at the Hoyers' trailer. We'll bring him in for an interview."

"He'll never agree—"

"Then I'll arrest him for criminal trespass, or for the illegal meat sales."

"I'll get to the station and cue up the video."

Colly hung up. "Gotta run, Bren." Unlocking her car, she glanced down at the anonymous text and froze.

"What's wrong?" Brenda asked.

Colly clutched the phone. "Nothing I have time to worry about now. Thanks for the advice about Satchel—I appreciate it."

She drove a few blocks, then stopped and put on her glasses to reread the text, which had been sent while she was talking to Wanice Boyles: *SECOND WARNING. YOU DON'T WANT TO SEE THE THIRD.*

Driving towards Lonestar Estates, Colly tried to clear her mind and focus on the task ahead. What were the chances that Hoyer would come to the station voluntarily? She hoped she didn't have to arrest him. He had guns on the property. A standoff—or worse, a shoot-out—in a trailer park would be a nightmare. They'd have to keep things low-key, if possible. Friendly and non-threatening.

She pulled over beside the entrance to the park and texted Avery: *Approach w lightbar off.*

Fifteen minutes later, the patrol car pulled up next to her, and Avery rolled down the window. She looked tense but eager. "What's the plan?"

"We've got the advantage of surprise. Let's keep guns holstered but block their drive. Go ahead—I'll follow."

I should've reminded her to take it easy, Colly thought. But trailing the cruiser through the narrow lanes, she was pleased to see that Avery drove slowly, as if on casual patrol. Whatever her failings, Russ was right—the girl had strong instincts.

Carmen's hatchback still sat in the Hoyers' drive. Colly pulled up close behind it, while Avery parked across the track leading to the garage. As they started around the trailer, Colly caught a flash of movement in one of the windows. A pair of eyes peered through a gap in the blinds. So much for the advantage of surprise.

Entering the back lot, they saw that they were too late. Jace Hoyer's red truck had vanished, along with the two pit bulls. Inside the garage, a large, stippled lump lay on the ground—the hog carcass, growing slimy in the heat and crawling with blowflies.

"He left it to rot? Gonna be some stink by tomorrow." Avery exhaled sharply.

"Guess we spooked him."

"Should we search the place? It's open."

"Let's wait for a warrant. Play it safe. I'll—"

Colly was interrupted by the thud of running footsteps and a sudden, piercing scream. She turned. A figure rushed towards her brandishing a long, dark object. Colly raised her arm to fend off the blow, but before it struck, something ploughed into her ribcage, knocking her aside. The ground rushed up, and her skull smacked into the hard-packed earth with a sickening crunch and a burst of white light.

Stunned, Colly rolled onto her back. At first, she could make little sense of what she saw—a blur of color and frenzied motion that slowly resolved into the image of two forms battling above her. Avery was trying to wrestle a baseball bat away from the attacker, who, Colly realized with a shock, was Jolene Hoyer. Still in her housecoat and slippers, Jolene shrieked and gibbered as she clung to the bat.

Fighting nausea, Colly sat up, but before she could climb to her feet, someone else raced past her and seized Jolene from behind, pinning her arms.

"*Stop* it, Jo." Carmen was trying to haul her sister backwards.

With Jolene partially immobilized, Avery yanked the bat away and tossed it angrily into the weeds.

"What the *fuck*, Jolene? You don't have enough problems without adding 'assaulting a police officer' to the list? You're lucky I didn't shoot you." She handcuffed the struggling woman and turned to help Colly to her feet. "Sorry I knocked you over. You all right?"

"Little dizzy." Colly dabbed cautiously at her forehead.

"I shoulda killed you," Jolene sobbed, still in her sister's arms. "You wrecked your own family, now you're wrecking mine? Why don't you ask Lowell Newland who killed my Denny?"

"What's that supposed to mean?"

Jolene continued to cry but said nothing.

Colly brushed the dirt from her jeans. "Avery, take her to the car."

"With pleasure." Avery seized Jolene by one arm and hauled her off.

Carmen moved to follow, but Colly stopped her. "What's going on?"

Carmen chewed her lip. "Jace left."

"What—when?"

"After he saw y'all taking pictures of his truck, he loaded it up and took off—told Jolene he was sick of her and this town and everyone in it."

"Know where he went? Any relatives or friends he'd run to?"

Carmen shook her head.

"Did he take any weapons?"

"Jace don't go nowhere without his guns."

Colly sighed. "What did Jolene mean when she said to ask Lowell who killed Denny?"

Carmen shrugged, looking genuinely mystified.

Colly's head was pounding. She swayed, suddenly dizzy, and Carmen steadied her. "Should you go to the ER?"

"I want to talk to your sister."

In the driveway, they found Avery leaning against the cruiser.

Colly glanced through the rear window. The energy of Jolene's rage had left her. She lay slumped on her side, her stringy hair obscuring her face.

"Get anything?" Colly asked.

Avery shook her head. "She wants a lawyer."

"You arrested her?" Carmen's voice held an edge of panic.

"Damn straight. She attacked police with a freakin' baseball bat."

"Please—she's not herself." Carmen appealed to Colly. "*You* know what it's like, losing a kid."

Colly looked again at Jolene. She appeared unconscious, or asleep. "Let her go."

Avery's jaw dropped. "What?"

"Do it."

Grumbling, Avery jerked the door open and removed the handcuffs.

Carmen rushed forward. She pulled Jolene from the car and half-dragged, half-carried her towards the porch steps.

"What the hell?" Avery hissed once the sisters had gone inside. "She nearly brained you."

"She won't be any more trouble. I don't want to waste time getting her to the station and booking her." Colly pulled out her phone and dialed.

Russ answered quickly. "Got Jace?"

"Put out a BOLO. He's in the wind, and he's armed." Colly briefly narrated the events of the last half-hour. "Any idea why Jolene thinks Lowell knows something about Denny?" The line was silent. "Russ, you still there?"

Russ cleared his throat. "Avery said Jolene's taking drugs."

"I think there's more to it than that." Colly glanced at her watch. "I'm heading to the turbine plant."

"Right now?"

"I want to talk to Lowell."

"He's not at the plant—he's supervising an installation."

"Where?"

There was another silence. "You should get checked for a concussion first."

"Where's the goddamn installation, Russ?"

She heard him sigh. "You've had a head injury. I'll take you."

"What happened to you staying out of things?"

"I said I'd try. Don't bring Avery. Lowell will be more candid if it's just you and me."

"I'll be at the station in ten." Colly hung up.

"No way," Avery spluttered after hearing the plan. "I'm coming, too."

Colly shook her head. "I want you at the turbine plant. Find Jimmy Meggs, take him along for backup. With Lowell gone, it's the perfect time to interview the workers."

Avery's eyes widened. "What do I ask?"

"Get them talking, see what turns up. Jace didn't tell us the whole truth about why he got fired. I want the real scoop."

Chapter 18

The electronic sign at the Ranchland Community Bank across the street read "12:04 p.m., 84°" *when Colly pulled into the police station parking lot.*

She found Russ staring out of his office window and speaking quietly into his phone. When she cleared her throat, he shoved the phone abruptly into his pocket and said with brisk cheerfulness, "Hungry? I thought we could—" His eyes widened. "*Damn.*"

"What is it?"

He nodded towards a small mirror behind the door. Colly glanced at her reflection. Since she'd checked it at the trailer park, the swelling on her forehead had doubled in size and turned a mottled purple-blue.

She touched it gingerly. It felt puffy and loose, like an under-filled water balloon. She pressed harder, and a bolt of pain blazed along her brow ridge. "Ow!"

"You need a doctor."

"I'm fine. I took ibuprofen."

"Randy always said you were the stubbornest woman on earth, besides Momma." Russ grabbed his hat. "Let's get some ice on it, at least."

On the way out, they cut through the breakroom, where Russ rummaged in the freezer for a cold pack.

"Whew, it's as hot as yesterday—and even more humid," he said as they climbed into the SUV.

Colly fastened her seatbelt. "Where are we going?"

"The bluffs. They're installing turbines east of the ravine."

"Good spot. Wind's always howling up there."

Russ pulled out onto Market Street. "That's where Randy proposed, isn't it?"

Ignoring the question, Colly rummaged for her sunglasses. "You're hiding something. Is it about Lowell?"

In her peripheral vision, she saw Russ look hastily her way. "Nah. I was going to tell you—Sam and Alan Sandleford lawyered up. Station got a hand-delivered letter from their attorney an hour ago."

Colly leaned against the window, pressing the cold pack to her head. "Didn't waste time, did they?"

"Go ahead, say it."

"I told you so."

"Those boys didn't murder Denny."

"Then why'd they lawyer up?"

"Probably their old man's idea. Sam and Alan were in diapers when Adam Parker was killed."

Despite her sunglasses, the hazy glare was making Colly's head ache. The air felt sticky and warm. She rolled down her window. "They still could've killed Denny."

"But Adam's killer's the only one who knew about the rabbit mask."

"Some killers brag. Whoever murdered Adam might've told the Sandlefords. I don't see how we can rule out a copycat situation."

Russ turned south onto Whiskey Creek Road. "We went over this yesterday. Do you know how hard it is to keep a secret around here? If you tell anyone other than your priest or your lawyer, you might as well post it online. And the Sandlefords aren't famous for discretion. There's only one way to keep something this big under wraps for twenty years."

"Shoot, shovel, and shut up?"

"Exactly. This killer's stone-cold. Sam and Alan have gone too far with a prank, now and then, but nothing worse." Russ braked at a red light behind a roughly idling pickup.

"Would they consider anonymous texts a prank?" Colly pulled out her phone and handed it to Russ.

He cast a cursory glance at the screen, and his face darkened with disgust.

"It came while I was talking to Satchel's teacher."

"Hell." Russ handed the phone back. "I doubt it's the Sandlefords—more likely Jace Hoyer. We'll try tracing it."

"Probably a burner."

"We'll find out where it was bought, at least. I'll get Edna started on the paperwork."

Russ called the station and rattled off instructions. When the light turned, he hung up, dropping his phone into the cup holder as the truck in front of them roared away in a cloud of diesel exhaust.

Colly coughed and rolled up the window. "Linking Jace to the phone might support harassment, but not murder."

"It'd be a hell of a red flag, though. Jace wants you out of here—why else would he plant that snake?"

"Maybe he didn't. The video's circumstantial, at best."

"It looks bad. He'd know how to make those masks. Plus, he's got a motive for killing Denny, and no alibi. Now he's skipped town. Men have gone to prison on a lot less."

"It's not proof. You think Jace murdered Adam, too? How old would he have been in '98—fifteen? Sixteen?"

"Old enough to kill."

"If the two of them ever met. Avery didn't mention it."

"She was a kid. She might not have known." Russ glanced at Colly. "The pieces fit, don't they? Why are you pushing back so hard?"

Because I know what can happen when detectives cut corners, Colly thought bitterly. *You're tossing a stone in the water with no idea where the ripples might go.*

"Think about the crime scenes, Russ. They're staged, almost playful. Those masks were meant to taunt us, like a twisted little 'catch me if you can' game. I think we're looking for someone emotionally controlled, maybe well-educated. Does that sound like Hoyer? If he murdered—" Colly stopped. Her head was pounding, and the smell of diesel exhaust was making her sick. She took a breath, exhaling slowly.

"You're pale. Have you eaten?" Russ asked. "We can grab a couple burgers at the Dairy Queen."

Colly's stomach roiled. "Please shut up." She pressed the heels of her hands against her temples. "Stop the truck."

Russ pulled over. Colly threw the door open, but Russ grabbed her arm. "Put your head down, Col."

Too nauseated to object, Colly complied, resting her head against her knees.

"Breathe through it," Russ said. "Nice and steady."

For a few seconds, Colly had the odd impression that it was Randy seated next to her, speaking soothingly and rubbing her back. When the queasiness passed, she sat up.

"Have some water." Russ produced a bottle from the center console.

Colly took a drink. "Thanks."

"Better?"

"I'm fine. Let's go."

Russ frowned. "If you're still dizzy when we get back, I'm taking you to a doctor, whether you like it or not."

◆ ◆ ◆

The Crescent Bluffs, a long, low ridgeline some twenty miles southeast of the eponymous town, were named for the narrow ravine that sliced through them—which, from a distance, appeared as a scimitar-shaped gash of blue sky in the red rock surrounding it. Through that ravine ran Whiskey Creek. At most times a dry wash, the creek transformed into a boiling, rust-colored torrent after heavy rains.

As the SUV crept up the switchback road that mounted the bluff-face east of the ravine, Colly, still fighting a headache and nausea, stared out of the window, hardly aware of the sweeping vista beneath. She was preoccupied instead with holding at bay the painful memories—of a bright autumn afternoon nearly a quarter-century ago.

She'd been queasy that day, too, already three weeks pregnant with Victoria, though she hadn't known it yet. Thanksgiving 1996—a year into her relationship with Randy. She'd been to the ranch twice before, but this was her first major holiday visit. After an enormous midday meal and an afternoon nap, she and Randy had gone for a hike up the bluffs to watch the sunset.

"You won't regret it," he'd insisted. "The view's spectacular."

There was no road then—only a steep footpath up the talus slope. The climb was slow going. Juniper bushes, stunted and warped by the wind, clung to the escarpment, their roots burrowing into cracks and dislodging stones that tumbled onto the path below.

After an hour's sweaty scramble, they'd crested the ridge. And there, in a broad, empty tableland of sage and switchgrass, beneath a sky of pale autumnal blue, Randy pulled a jeweler's box from his pocket and dropped to one knee, while the wind whipped around them and the whole world seemed spread at their feet . . .

"I hate these hairpin turns," Russ said, wrenching Colly abruptly back to the present.

She looked around. "How do they bring up the installation equipment? No tractor-trailer's coming this way."

"There's an industrial-haul access ramp out towards the gravel quarry, but this is quicker for us." Russ downshifted up the last, steep slope and braked at the top.

Colly leaned forward, squinting into the hazy glare. Once an undeveloped expanse of grassy scrub populated only by jackrabbits, lizards, and red-tailed hawk, the blufftop had been transformed into something like the surface of Mars. The ground was rutted by heavy equipment, the plant life trampled into the red clay. A line of gleaming turbines now marched down the center of the ridge, their tapered blades spinning slowly in the wind.

The closest was still under construction. Though several hundred yards away, it seemed impossibly tall, its headless mast towering into the sky alongside a gigantic crane. Smaller cranes, bulldozers, and portable toilets ringed the area. A dozen men in hardhats crawled over a flatbed trailer, though Colly couldn't tell what they were doing.

"Is this the last installation?"

"On this side. They'll start west of the ravine after this. That's on a separate ranch, but both owners agreed to lease us the land. We nearly lost the westside contract after the bird-strike accident. Lucky for us, Talford knows the owner and pulled some strings."

Russ let out the clutch, and they lurched slowly along a pitted track towards the construction site. He parked a football field's distance from the work zone, and Colly now saw that the flatbed trailer held a single turbine blade, which the workmen were apparently preparing to unload.

"That thing's huge," she said as they climbed out of the SUV.

"Everyone says that when they first see one up close."

"No, really. Randy took me to the factory once, but I don't remember the blades being like *that*."

"We were probably still making 126-footers then. Other manufacturers have lengthened their blades to boost power output, but Dad was too cheap. After he died, Momma decided we should upgrade. We're a lot more competitive now."

"The retooling must've cost a fortune."

"That's why Dad dragged his feet. Lowell's just like him. He fought Momma like blazes about it, but she insisted."

"What did you think?"

"I stay neutral. There's enough cooks in that kitchen."

Some things never change, Colly thought as they walked towards the worksite. It hadn't been easy for the brothers, growing up in the shadow of a man like Bryant Newland. Each had coped in his own fashion. Russ was the peacemaker.

They stopped a few dozen yards from the flatbed. Lowell was pacing beside it, shouting orders as a half-dozen men attached harnesses to the cradles holding each end of the blade, while others maneuvered two cranes into position nearby. When he saw Colly and Russ, Lowell nodded at them but kept working.

Colly started forward, but Russ stopped her. "Once the blade's down, he'll be less distracted."

Lowell didn't seem particularly surprised to see them there, Colly thought. "You didn't give him a heads-up, did you?" she asked.

"Don't be silly."

For twenty minutes, they watched as the cranes slowly lifted the turbine blade from the truck and lowered it onto the packed earth. Lowell walked its length, running his hand over it and occasionally stopping to peer closely at something. Apparently satisfied, he nodded to the workmen, who began unhooking the cradle straps.

Lowell strode towards Colly and Russ. He was sweating and exuded a faint odor of Scotch.

"Glad that's over. Easy to ding the fiberglass getting it off the truck." He took off his hard hat to mop the back of his neck with a red bandana, and for the first time appeared to notice Colly's bruised face. "What the hell happened to you?"

"Bumped my head. No biggie," she said. "The blades are fiberglass? I thought they were metal."

Lowell stared suspiciously at her eye. "Fiberglass is stronger, more flexible. No welds or rivets to worry about."

"If they're so strong, why'd a bird strike break one apart?"

Lowell muttered something inaudible and spat in the dirt.

"Don't be an ass, Lowell." Russ turned to Colly. "We had an especially harsh winter that year—the PUC thought the heavy ice buildup weakened the epoxy, somehow. We considered suing the supplier, but that would've kept the story in the news. We needed it to die."

"Epoxy? The blades are glued together?"

"If you want a turbine-construction tutorial, go watch a damn YouTube video," Lowell snapped. "Y'all got any important business?"

Colly's head was throbbing like an engine. "We do, as a matter of fact. Where were you the afternoon Denny was killed?"

Lowell flushed a deep, mottled red. He turned to Russ. "What the hell?"

"It's routine, Lowell. She's questioning everyone."

"Probably why someone popped her in the eye. You let her interrupt an installation to hear the same shit I told the Rangers six months ago? She can read, can't she?"

"You sure you gave the Rangers everything?" Colly asked. "I hear you know more about Denny's murder than you reported."

"Hear *where?*" Lowell demanded, still addressing his brother. "Who the hell's saying that?"

Colly moved closer and caught a whiff of sour sweat. "Just answer the question."

"You can't listen to Jace Hoyer, if that's who it was—he's pissed because I fired him."

"It wasn't Jace."

"Who, then? His pill-popping wife?"

"Where were you?"

Lowell threw up his hands. "It was my weekend for the kids. I picked them up from school and took them to the movies in Big Spring. We had pizza after that, and then we went back to the ranch—like I told the Rangers."

"What about earlier, before you picked up the kids?"

Lowell looked at Russ, who cleared his throat. "He was with me. Dove season just opened. We took the day off, went hunting out at Paint Rock. Left before dawn and got back just as school let out."

"Why Paint Rock?"

"Felt like getting away."

Colly's phone began to vibrate. She reached into her pocket and switched it off. "What about that evening?"

Lowell shrugged. "I put the kids to bed, then fell asleep watching Netflix."

"You didn't go out at any point during the night?"

"Why the hell would I?"

"Can anyone verify that?"

"I was sleeping alone, if that's what you're asking." Lowell wiped his face with the bandana and stuffed it in his pocket. "I didn't see Denny that day. Jace neither. Hadn't seen either of them in weeks."

"Jace said you fired him because of Denny."

Lowell swallowed. "This again? I explained everything to the Rangers. I got a business to run." He put on his hard hat and turned to go.

Colly was losing patience. "It'll waste more time if I have to drag you to the station to finish this."

Lowell turned back, furious, but Russ cut in. "We're almost done, Lowell. Cooperate, so we can wrap this up."

Lowell glared at them. He pulled a pack of cigarettes and a lighter from his pocket.

Colly took that as a go-ahead. "How long was Jace your plant foreman?"

"Twelve years."

"Was he any good?"

Lowell shook a cigarette from the box and lit it. "He was an ungrateful sonofabitch, but he had his strengths."

"Such as?"

"Whenever Momma'd come up with some bonehead idea that shot our overhead through the roof, Jace had a knack for finding ways to offset the costs. The foreman I got now ain't half as good." Lowell took a long drag and exhaled in Colly's direction.

"If Jace was so talented, why'd you fire him?"

"He started taking liberties—thought the safety regs didn't apply to him. Kept bringing that kid to the plant, even after I said not to. Distracted the workers."

"Seems pretty minor, all things considered."

"If a man breaks small rules, he'll break big ones, too."

"Like what?"

"I meant hypothetically."

"He says you spread a rumor that he caused the turbine accident."

"Bullshit. He's lying." Lowell spat a bit of loose tobacco off his tongue and glanced at the worksite. The men had finished removing the harnesses from the turbine blade and were milling around, chatting and smoking.

Lowell flicked his cigarette away. "That's all I know. We finished yet? I'm paying those bozos by the hour."

Colly scrutinized his face. In some ways, the interview had raised more questions than it answered. Lowell was concealing something, she was sure. He fidgeted, avoiding eye contact one moment and meeting her gaze belligerently the next. But she sensed she'd get nothing more from him now.

"Go ahead. We'll talk again later."

Lowell grunted and walked away, yelling, "Y'all quit screwing around and prep the damn rotor hub."

"Hang on, I need to ask you about the Rodeo setup," Russ called after him. "Be right back," he said to Colly before hurrying to catch his brother.

Damn, this headache, Colly thought as she climbed into the SUV. She checked the visor mirror. The bruise on her forehead had darkened and spread around the orbit of her eye, but the swelling had subsided a bit and the queasiness was gone.

Colly pushed up the visor. Outside, Russ and Lowell had stopped walking. Russ had his hand on Lowell's shoulder and was speaking earnestly in his ear. Whatever they were discussing, she thought it wasn't the Rattlesnake Rodeo.

As she watched them, Colly heard an electronic chirp. It wasn't her phone—she'd turned the sound off. Looking around, she spotted Russ's, still in the cup holder where he'd dropped it earlier.

Colly picked it up, and the passcode screen appeared. Going through someone's phone without their permission was risky. But she needed to be sure about Russ. Pushing guilt aside, she typed in Russ and Randy's birthday; then Alice's; then, after a few moments' struggle to recall it, Russ and Wanda's anniversary.

"Damn it," Colly muttered, rubbing her eyes.

She looked out of the window. Russ and Lowell appeared to be wrapping things up. They'd moved a little apart and were chatting more casually, though Russ's hand still rested on his brother's shoulder. Even from that distance, Colly could see the faint dark smudge of Randy's name tattooed on his outstretched arm—Russ's tribute to his lost twin.

Colly's heart raced. Her own phone buzzed, but, ignoring it, she typed "010317" into Russ's keypad. Instantly, the passcode screen vanished and the home screen appeared. She tapped the messages app. At 11:54 a.m.—immediately after she'd called him from the Hoyers' driveway—Russ had texted Lowell: *GOTTA TALK NOW.* She checked the phone log. Lowell had called his brother at 12:01 p.m.—three minutes before Colly arrived at the station. Russ had been on the phone when she'd entered his office. She remembered the look on his face, how quickly he'd hung up when she walked through the door.

Colly looked up. The brothers had concluded their talk and parted ways. Russ, his hands in his pockets, strode slowly towards the SUV.

Colly's phone began to vibrate again.

"Finally," Avery said when Colly answered. "I've been calling forever."

"We're leaving the bluffs now."

"Going to the station? I got some intel at the factory you and the chief need to hear."

Russ had reached the SUV and was rounding the front bumper. When he saw Colly watching him, he smiled.

"Don't go to the station, and don't talk to anyone." Colly checked the time. "I've got to pick up Satchel. Can you meet me at the farmhouse at four?"

There was a heavy silence. "Russ's in-laws' old place?"

"I'm staying there."

"What about Russ? Shouldn't—"

Colly cut her off. No time to debate the issue. Russ was outside, fumbling for his keys.

"Don't tell him anything, yet—I want the first briefing. I'll explain why later." She hung up and reminded herself to smile as Russ opened the driver's-side door.

Chapter 19

Arriving at the school shortly after the dismissal bell rang, Colly found Satchel, in his sun-sleeves and hat, waiting with his cousins beneath the covered walkway. They laughed and shouted as they bounced a small rubber ball back and forth in an improvised game.

Colly paused in the crowd of jostling children to watch. Satchel's cheeks were rosy with exertion as he ran after the ball, catching it with the heels of his hands to safeguard his bandaged fingers.

After a few moments, Colly felt a nudge.

"Kids are amazingly resilient, huh?"

Colly turned. Brenda stood at her elbow.

"Oh God, your eye—what happened?"

"It's nothing. Looks worse than it feels." Colly was getting tired of the question. "Satchel did okay this afternoon?"

"He must have. I've been at the clinic, but Wanice would've called if anything happened." Brenda hesitated. "I hope you don't mind—I told Niall about the matches incident. Childhood compulsive disorders are his specialty."

"Did he have any advice?"

"He's giving it some thought. Which reminds me, he wants to cook for us Friday night."

"I don't know, Bren. I shouldn't socialize with someone I've interviewed in a current case."

"It's impossible to keep clear boundaries in Crescent Bluff." Brenda laughed. "You don't suspect Niall, do you? He wasn't even in Texas when Denny died."

Colly shrugged noncommittally and glanced at her watch. Avery would arrive at the farmhouse in just over an hour. Colly longed for a nap, or at least a shower, before then. "I should get Satchel home."

"What do I tell Niall about Friday?"

"I'll let you know tomorrow."

Though he'd seemed happy enough while playing ball, Satchel was subdued on the ride home, answering Colly's questions about his day with hunched shoulders and a mumbled "I dunno."

Newland males have been stonewalling me this whole damn day, Colly thought irritably as she turned up the long drive. *Is it genetic, or what?*

The sight of a navy-blue Jeep in front of the farmhouse inter-rupted her musings. Through the tinted windows, she could see the outline of a man's head.

Colly hit the brakes. "Stay here, Satch."

Climbing out of the car, she approached the unfamiliar vehicle with a hand on her pistol. When she was fifteen feet from the Jeep, its driver's-side door opened and a tall, slender figure emerged, looking out of place in a well-tailored suit and black wingtips.

Colly was both relieved and annoyed. *Can't I get five minutes to myself?* She released the gun and said with more irritability than politeness, "What are you doing here, Dr. Shaw?"

Shaw appeared unperturbed. "Please, it's Niall. I—wow, are you okay?" He gestured towards her forehead.

"Yeah, but I need to get a t-shirt that says, 'You should see the other guy.'"

"One of those days?"

"You have no idea."

"I won't keep you long. Brenda told me what happened this morning with your grandson." He reached into the Jeep and produced an orange gift bag.

Colly heard a noise and turned. Satchel was standing beside the car, staring curiously at the stranger.

He pointed to the gift bag. "What's that?"

"Get out of the light, Satchel." Colly hurried towards him.

"But it's cloudy," he whined as she pushed him into the car.

"That doesn't matter."

Colly drove the car beneath the red oak near the house and hustled Satchel onto the porch, motioning for Niall to join them. She introduced him as "a friend of Aunt Brenda's."

Niall smiled and shook Satchel's hand. He held out the gift bag. "This is for you."

Satchel's eyes narrowed. "Today's not my birthday."

"I thought you might not have many toys here."

Satchel looked at Colly. When she nodded, he reached for the bag, extracting a rectangular object made of clear plexiglass set in a blue stand. He turned the thing in his hands. "What is it?"

"An ant farm. You can watch them build their tunnels and nests. The queen's there, in the corner, see?" Niall pointed. "She controls the worker ants, and those white things are her eggs. Careful, don't shake it."

Satchel held the plexiglass frame near his face, then looked up at Colly. "Can I take it inside?"

"Sure." Colly unlocked the door. "Aren't you forgetting something?"

"Thank you," Satchel murmured over his shoulder as he went into the house, holding the ant farm like an overfilled cup he was afraid might spill.

Colly closed the door behind him. "He loves it."

Niall stood and dusted his knees. "It's been in my office for years. The kids I treat for anxiety find it soothing."

"Why?"

"I don't know. Maybe because it's a hermetically sealed little world where all the rules work."

"I'll be sure to return it before we go back to Houston."

"It's a gift. I'll get another one." Niall hesitated, smiling. "At the risk of sounding forward, it's hard to believe you're a grandmother."

Colly frowned. The remark was more personal than she liked, but it seemed well-intentioned. "My daughter was fifteen when Satchel was born." She changed the subject. "Brenda says you specialize in compulsive disorders?"

"That's my therapeutic focus. I research the links between brain structure and impulse control in kids with antisocial tendencies."

"Psychopaths?"

"That's not a clinical term, but essentially, yes—kids with potential in that direction, anyway."

Remembering her earlier conversation with Brenda, Colly felt the familiar pang of worry. She wanted to ask more questions, but Avery, who disliked Shaw intensely, was due at the farmhouse soon. Colly didn't want to risk a tense encounter while Satchel was within earshot.

"Well, thanks for the ant farm," she said a little abruptly. "It was kind of you to think of Satchel."

Niall took the hint without offense. "Not at all." He trotted down the steps, then paused. "Did Brenda mention dinner Friday? I hope you're free."

"She did. But I don't know."

"It'll be a nice break. Great food, pleasant company, Walmart's finest Pinot." He grinned.

Colly murmured something noncommittal.

"No pressure. Things are complicated, I realize." Pulling a pen and business card from his pocket, he jotted something down and handed the card to Colly. "My personal number. If Satchel's struggling, call any time."

◆　◆　◆

Inside, Colly found Satchel in the living room, sitting on the floor with his chin on the edge of the coffee table. He'd set the ant farm in front of him and was staring intently at it.

"Pretty cool, huh?" Colly ruffled his hair.

He looked up. "We didn't ask what to feed them."

"We'll google it."

"What if Google's wrong?"

"I'll ask Dr. Shaw, then." Her head throbbing, Colly checked the time—fifteen minutes until Avery would arrive. No time for a nap, but with luck she could grab a shower.

She went to the kitchen, returning with apple slices and cheese crackers on a plate. She set them on the coffee table. "There you go, buddy. I'm going upstairs to clean up."

Satchel rubbed his bandaged fingers against the edge of the coffee table. "Can you change my bandages first? They're itchy."

Colly sighed. "Okay, but hurry."

In the second-floor bathroom, she carefully unwrapped the gauze from his fingers and was relieved to see that the burns were minor, the skin red and in a few places blistered but otherwise intact. She held his hands under cold water and scrubbed them vigorously with antibacterial soap.

"Ow!"

"Sorry, bud. We have to keep these clean."

After patting his fingers dry, she retaped the wounds with fresh gauze from a first-aid kit she found in the cupboard. As she

180

was putting it away, she heard a sharp knock on the front door downstairs.

Satchel stiffened. "Take out your gun, Grandma."

Colly glanced out of the bathroom window. A squad car sat by the carport.

So much for a shower, she thought. "It's just Avery, Satch."

"The girl with purple hair?" He sounded hopeful.

Colly nodded. "Go show her your ant farm. I'll be down in a sec."

Satchel raced for the stairs. When he'd gone, Colly checked herself in the bathroom mirror. The entire orbit of her eye had turned dark indigo-purple. She looked, Colly thought, like the bad guy in a Bugs Bunny cartoon. She took two more ibuprofen, then washed her face and changed her dirt-stained top. As she started down the stairs, she heard voices and paused on the landing to listen.

"You did it on purpose? That's dumb," Avery was saying.

"It helps."

"Bullshit."

"Grandma thinks I'm crazy, too. I can tell."

"I didn't say crazy, I said dumb—it tells everyone you're weak and scared. They'll pick on you worse."

A long pause. "You don't know."

Torn between curiosity and the urge to intervene, Colly crept low enough on the stairs to peer through the archway. Avery was on the sofa. Satchel sat on the floor with his back to her, staring at the ant farm on the coffee table. His cheeks were bright pink, and he seemed to be fighting tears.

"Think I never got teased?" Avery leaned forward suddenly, tapping Satchel on the shoulder so that he turned to look. "They used to call me 'Two-Face.'" She pointed to the white scar on her cheek.

"What *is* that?"

"A burn. Happened when I was about your age."

Satchel's eyes widened. "Can I touch it?"

"Don't be a jerk."

"What did you do when they teased you?"

Avery shrugged. "Beat 'em up. Tried to, anyway."

"I'm a lot smaller than the boy who called me names."

"Who was it?"

"His name's Clay."

"Clay McReedy?" Avery snorted. "He's a little shit—all the McReedys are. What did he call you?"

Satchel gnawed his lip. "*Sasquatch*. He said that's what my name sounds like. Hey, stop that."

Avery had fallen back against the cushions, laughing. "Sorry, dude." She wiped her eyes. "Don't be such a baby. You gotta stand up for yourself."

Satchel turned back to the ant farm. "I don't know how."

"If you can't use your fists, be a smart-ass. Tell Clay, 'I'd rather be a Sasquatch than a pile of wet dirt.' That's what *his* name means."

Satchel smiled, but he shook his head. "He'd hurt me."

"You're gonna get hurt no matter what. But you can take the fun out of it for him."

Okay, that's enough, Colly thought, continuing noisily down the steps.

When she entered the living room, Satchel jumped up. "Did you hear what we were talking about?"

"Do I look like an eavesdropper? Listen, Satch, Avery and I need to discuss something. We're going to walk around the yard. You can play with your ant farm, or watch TV." Colly handed him her phone. "If you need me, call Avery's number—I've pulled it up."

In the kitchen, she pulled two longnecks from the fridge. "Russ stocked the place with some basics. I think we both could use a beer." Colly rummaged in a drawer for a bottle opener.

"You shouldn't drink with a possible concussion."

"I'll risk it."

Carrying their beers, they went out through the carport and around to the backyard. Colly was surprised to see patches of blue sky through breaks in the clouds.

"Let's get farther away. I don't want Satchel hearing this."

Behind the house, the weed-choked remnants of a footpath led through a pasture to a timber-pole barn. Its wooden siding was ragged with dry rot, the tin roof dimpled by countless hail storms.

"Think it's safe to go out there?" Colly asked.

"There's probably rats."

"I don't care about rats. It's snakes I can't handle."

"Where there's one, there's usually the other. But this time of day we should be fine. Just watch your step."

The air was surprisingly cool inside the barn. The ground, a pulpy humus of decayed dung and straw, sank beneath their feet, giving off a sweet, musky odor. Colly looked around. Piles of corroded machine parts and rotted tractor tires lined the walls. Doves cooed in the hazy dimness of the rafters.

An overturned metal water trough sat beside a support pole near the door. Colly brushed away the cobwebs and sat down.

"Thanks for meeting me here. From now on, I think it's wise to keep things between the two of us as much as possible."

Avery crossed her arms. "Why are we cutting Russ out of the loop? He's my boss."

"Russ has a conflict of interest."

"No more than he did yesterday."

"Yesterday I didn't know he's Lowell's alibi for the afternoon Denny was killed."

"Haven't you read the file?"

"Not thoroughly. I haven't had time." Colly paused. It was difficult to know how much to say. But she needed Avery to understand the necessity of discretion. "I know we haven't gotten off to the best start. But you need to trust me."

"You think Russ is part of some cover-up?"

"We should err on the side of caution."

"You're talking in riddles. Did something happen?"

Colly sighed. "Yes, but it may have an innocent explanation, so I'd rather keep it to myself, for now."

"I don't like it."

"We won't cut him out entirely. As a practical matter, we can't. But he's under pressure from a lot of directions. Let's do what we can to minimize it—for his sake, and for the investigation's."

Avery scowled at her boots. "I'll play it your way, for now."

"Thank you." Colly exhaled. "Okay, tell me what you found out at the turbine plant. We'll compare notes."

Avery brushed back a strand of purple hair and sat down on the trough. "No one would talk to me at the plant. But after I left, one of the fiberglass packers called me. Lori Lambreth. I went to high school with her. She said Lowell's been erratic the last year or so, losing his shit for no reason, coming to work drunk. And get this—last March, he got into a shouting match with Jace Hoyer. They were in Lowell's office. All the line workers heard them. Then Lowell came out and announced Jace was fired."

"We already knew that."

"Yeah, but a few minutes later, Lori walked by Jace's workstation when he was packing up. She saw him log into his computer and print some papers, and she asked what he was doing. He said he'd be damned if he'd let Lowell throw him under the bus—he was taking some insurance with him."

"She doesn't know what the papers were?"

"Spreadsheets of some kind."

"Did Lowell give an explanation for firing Hoyer?"

"He sent around an internal memo saying Jace broke safety regulations bringing Denny to the plant."

"Lowell confirmed that today at the bluffs."

"Lori says that was a load of crap, though. Jolene was right. Denny'd been coming around for months. Everyone liked him, even Lowell. He was the plant's unofficial gofer."

"Does Lori know why Lowell lied?"

"If she does, she didn't tell me. There was another big blow-up a few weeks later. Lori wasn't there, but she heard about it. Jace showed up at a job site, screaming and carrying on. Punched Lowell in the face. The workmen had to pull them apart."

"What was that about?"

"No idea." Avery tipped up her longneck and swallowed. "What do you think?"

"It's odd neither Lowell or Jace mentioned any of this." Colly narrated a quick rundown of her interview with Lowell. "We need to talk to both of them again—Jace first, if we can find him."

She checked her watch. Satchel was alone in the house and she needed to get back. She stood too quickly, and her vision darkened. The floor pitched like a wave. Colly stumbled, and Avery grabbed her arm.

"You okay?"

"Just a headrush."

Avery started to answer, but then her phone rang. She pulled it out, and her face reddened. "For you."

Colly took the phone and glanced at the caller ID. "'Queen Bitch'? Seriously?" She raised it to her ear. "What is it, Satch?"

"Uncle Russ is here." His voice dropped to a whisper. "I think something bad happened. He looks upset."

Chapter 20

Returning to the house, Colly and Avery found Russ pacing the entryway, his Stetson in one hand and his phone in the other. Sounds of a children's cartoon emanated from the living room.

"What the hell?" Russ demanded when they entered. "I hear you sent Avery to interrogate the workers at the turbine plant without checking with me first?"

"Why would I need to check with you? That wasn't part of the deal."

"The last thing we need—"

"Satchel can hear you," Colly hissed. "Go outside—I'll be right there."

Russ glared at her, then banged out of the door.

Avery started to follow but instead said, "Can I use your bathroom?" and trotted up the stairs without waiting for an answer.

Colly went into the living room. Satchel was on the sofa, balancing his ant farm on his knees and watching TV.

He looked up. "Is Uncle Russ mad at you?"

"Everything's fine. We're going to talk outside. Stay here, okay?"

"It's scary by myself."

"I'll be on the porch. Tonight, we'll have pizza and a movie, just me and you."

"No, we won't. Something'll happen."

Colly ruffled his hair. "Not this time, buddy. I promise."

When Avery came downstairs, the women went outside. Russ was sitting in a wicker armchair, balancing his hat on his knee and drumming his fingers impatiently on the crown.

He jumped up when he saw them. "Y'all want to tell me what the hell's going on?"

"You said to run the investigation as I see fit," Colly said.

"Yeah, but I thought you'd have some common sense about it. The turbine plant—"

"You never said the plant was off-limits. Denny hung out there. It had to be checked. I thought I'd streamline things and send Avery while you and I went out to the bluffs."

Russ turned to Avery. "Get anything useful?"

She shrugged uneasily. "No one would talk to me out there."

"Well, okay. But it would've been nice if y'all had asked me first, that's all." Russ's shoulders had relaxed, but his voice was still peevish. "The company's had enough bad press lately. If word got out—"

Colly lost patience. "Oh, for God's sake, Russ, let me do my job, or send me home. I don't have time for PR bullshit. You drove all the way out here to gripe about *this*?"

Russ sighed and scratched his jaw. "No. Brenda phoned a few minutes ago. Carmen Ortiz called her, hysterical. She ran some errands, and when she got back to the Hoyers' trailer, Jolene was unconscious. Looks like she took a bunch of pills and washed them down with a bottle of vodka. Carmen was scared to call 911, afraid we might change our minds and arrest Jolene for assaulting you. Brenda talked her into it, but Jolene's in rough shape."

"Will she make it?"

"Don't know. She's being medevacked to Abilene."

"I'll get the car—we can be there in an hour and a half." Avery started down the porch steps.

Colly checked her watch. "I can't, I promised Satchel."

"What if she dies? You said yourself she was hiding something."

"Jolene's unconscious," Russ said. "No point going tonight."

"We could talk to Carmen." Avery looked at Colly. "Can't you get a sitter?"

"Carmen won't be in a fit state. Hopefully, Jolene will be awake tomorrow." Colly turned to Russ. "Any word on Jace?"

"Nothing yet. I alerted the Abilene police, in case he shows up at the hospital."

"He might go home. Let's set a guard on the Hoyers' place," Colly said. "And see about getting a search warrant. Maybe there's something on the property that'll tell us where he went."

Colly awoke the next morning to a dull headache. A strange, ruddy light filtered through the bedroom curtains. She stumbled, bleary-eyed, to the window. Over the farmhouse scudded dark, ragged clouds, stained blood-red with the coming sunrise.

"Red sky in the morning, sailors take warning," she murmured. It was part of a rhyme her grandfather, a marine in World War II, had taught her as a child. The hairs rose on the back of her neck. The sky had looked like that on the day Randy and Victoria died.

"It's just atmospheric particles and light waves," she told herself, turning away from the window.

After dropping Satchel at school, Colly permitted herself the minor indulgence of a detour to Starbucks for a flat white before heading to the police station. Raindrops began to pock the dust on her windshield as she pulled into the parking lot, where Avery and Russ were waiting.

Russ looked annoyed. "You're late."

"Too bad I'm doing this pro bono, or you could dock my pay." Colly swallowed a mouthful of coffee. "Good morning to you, too, by the way."

"Sorry." Russ scratched his cheek. "Your eye's looking better. Feel okay?"

"Bit of a headache."

Avery, who had begun to fidget, now threw up her hands. "Can we get to work?"

"What's our status?" Colly asked.

"Jolene's awake—for now, at least," Avery said.

"And we're cleared to search the Hoyers' place," Russ added.

"The warrant came through?"

"Don't need one. I called Carmen. Turns out the trailer's half hers. She gave consent. She's pissed as hell at Jace and wants us to find him."

"Still nothing on his whereabouts?"

Russ shook his head. "How should we do this?"

Colly thought quickly. Despite her growing doubts about Russ, she couldn't afford to alienate him until she knew more.

"Jolene used my skull for batting practice yesterday—I doubt she'll talk to me. You go to Abilene. Avery and I'll take the property search."

Russ frowned. "If you figure out where Jace is, don't confront him on your own."

A thin drizzle was falling as Colly and Avery turned into the Lonestar Estates. They found a squad car in the Hoyers' drive. Inside it, Jimmy Meggs was asleep with his forehead on the steering wheel and a rope of drool dangling from his lower lip.

Avery rapped on the window, and Meggs jumped. "You scared the shit out of me," he gasped, wiping his mouth on his sleeve as he opened the door. "Are you my relief? I been on watch all night." He clambered stiffly out of the cruiser and stretched.

"On watch?" Avery said. "Hoyer could've come and gone ten times, for all you'd—"

"We're here to search the place," Colly interrupted.

Meggs brightened. "I can go home?"

"Sorry, we need the backup. Hoyer's armed. Can't run the risk he'll surprise us."

"Can I take a leak?"

"When we're finished."

"And stay awake, numbnuts," Avery added.

Grumbling, Meggs climbed back into his car. Colly handed Avery a pair of nitrile gloves.

"I've never done this before," Avery said.

"We don't have the time or personnel to do it right. We're just doing a quick scan for clues to where Jace might've gone. Grab some evidence bags from the car. I'll start with the house. You take the garage."

"Great—you get the air conditioning, I get the rotting hog?"

Colly laughed. "Fine, we'll stick together. Garage first."

Rounding the corner of the trailer, they were struck by an odor so foul that it seemed to have physical mass. As a homicide detective, Colly had gotten used to the smell of death, but as they neared the humming, fly-shrouded mound in the garage, Avery went pale and covered her nose and mouth.

"Breathe normally," Colly said. "After a while, you won't smell it."

Their eyes watering, they edged past the carcass. Inside, Avery found the wall switch, and two banks of fluorescent bulbs winked on.

"You start at the back. We'll meet in the middle," Colly said.

With the furious drone of the blowflies buzzing in her ears, Colly moved slowly along the wall, surveying the shelves of tools and other equipment. Jace Hoyer seemed to have left in a hurry.

The butcher table was littered with knives and cleavers, shreds of desiccated meat still clinging to their blades. Hoyer's leather apron lay in a heap on the floor.

"Empty gun safe," Avery called from the rear of the garage. "Big enough for six long guns. Not much else of interest. I'll check the bathroom."

Colly grunted and glanced into the utility sink. A stiffened shop rag and grimy bar of Lava soap suggested a hasty cleanup.

Suddenly, she heard a gagging noise. Avery emerged quickly from a door in the rear wall. "Hoyer's not coming back—didn't even bother to flush."

"Thoughtful of him to leave the mess for Jolene." Colly was examining a set of utility shelves, bare except for some bits of trash and a few dead insects. "Something big was here." She swiped a gloved finger across the surface. "Till recently, too."

Avery stopped rooting through a barrel of garden tools and joined her. "Truck box or storage bin, maybe?"

Colly looked up. "What do people keep in storage bins in the garage?"

"Stuff they don't use much. Christmas decorations, things like that."

"I can't picture Jace getting sentimental over a box of ornaments."

Avery reached for something on the shelf that Colly had taken for a scrap of paper. "What's this?" She flattened the object on her palm.

It looked like a miniature sack the size of a wine cork, open at one end and made of fine, white mesh.

"Bag it up," Colly said. "Maybe Meggs will know."

Avery complied. "There's nothing here. Let's try the house."

"Hang on." Colly moved towards the chest freezers on the opposite wall.

"Seriously?"

"I found thirty grand and a dead chihuahua in one of these, once. Owner was a bank robber."

"That doesn't explain the dog."

"It was his mother's. The guy said he got sick of the barking."

Three of the freezers contained nothing but packages of meat, neatly wrapped in white butcher paper and organized by date and type of cut. The packages in the fourth, however, looked as if someone had hurriedly rummaged through them. Wedged between two bundles labeled "tenderloin" was a torn manila envelope.

Colly picked it up gingerly. Empty.

"I bet that was the 'insurance policy' Lori Lambreth mentioned—the one Jace printed at the plant," Avery said.

"Maybe." Colly tucked the envelope into an evidence bag.

Back at the trailer, they found Jimmy Meggs' squad car abandoned, its doors unlocked. "I bet that moron's off taking a piss," Avery muttered, locking the car. "At least he didn't leave his gun laying on the seat."

Colly sighed and turned towards the trailer. "How do we get in?"

"Carmen said there's a key on a nail under the top step."

The trailer, like the garage, showed signs of a hasty departure. Groceries were scattered on the floor just inside. A vomit-stained pillow and a knitted throw lay beside the couch; several prescription bottles and a nearly empty fifth of cheap vodka littered the coffee table nearby.

"Damn," Colly murmured.

"Got a grape?" a tinny voice shrieked. From his perch in the corner, Fred the parrot cocked his head and bobbed excitedly.

"Poor guy's alone," Avery said.

"We'll call Animal Control. Search here. I'll check the bedrooms."

"Get lost, dumb bitch!" Fred chortled as Colly started down the hall.

In the master bedroom, both the floor and the unmade bed were strewn with men's clothes, footgear, and wire hangers. Colly picked up a boot and examined it, then opened the closet. Not much was inside. On a high shelf sat an empty handgun case.

When she returned to the living room, she found Avery inspecting a side-table drawer. On her shoulder, Fred was preening a strand of purple hair and mumbling, "Pretty feathers, pretty feathers."

"New BFF?" Colly asked.

Avery looked up. "I gave him a saltine from the kitchen, and now he won't leave. Anything in the bedroom?"

"Looks like Jace packed some clothes and a Glock 19. He wears a size-eight shoe."

"I found this." Avery handed her a slip of paper. "Receipt for a burner phone—purchased last April."

Colly examined it. "Did Jace disclose this to the Rangers?"

"Nope." Avery closed the drawer and stood. "No sign of the phone itself."

"He must have it with him, wherever he is." Colly moved towards the door.

Avery reached for the bird on her shoulder, but Fred squawked and lunged for her fingers.

Colly laughed. "He wants more quality time with your hair."

In the end, they used a broom to force the parrot back onto his perch.

"Poor guy's lonely," Avery said.

When they emerged from the trailer, the drizzle had stopped, though a faint rumble in the distance indicated more rain on the way. Jimmy Meggs was leaning against his squad car, smoking a cigarette.

"You were supposed to watch our backs," Avery snapped.

Meggs reddened. "Sorry, I was about to bust."

"Never mind." Colly handed him the evidence bag containing the white mesh object from the garage. "Any idea what this is?"

Meggs flicked the butt of his cigarette into the gravel and held the bag up to the light. "Mantle for a propane lantern."

Colly and Avery exchanged looks. Colly reached for her phone.

"You at the hospital yet?" she asked when Russ answered.

"Almost."

"Looks like Hoyer's taken his camping gear—he may be roughing it. Ask Jolene and Carmen where he'd most likely go." She hung up before Russ could reply.

"Have you checked the lease?" Jimmy asked. "Jace and some other guys from the plant went in on a hunting lease over in Coke County, on Whitebone Creek. I went out there with Toby Peterson once—bagged a ten-point buck."

Avery threw up her hands. "Dammit, Jimmy—Jace has been missing since yesterday and you're just now telling us this?"

"How was I s'pposed to know he took his camping gear?"

"Forget it," Colly said. "Draw us a map. Then get Animal Control and Solid Waste Management over here—there's a parrot and a dead hog to deal with."

Chapter 21

Although heavy on facts about the Revolutionary War, Thomas Edison, and the wreck of the *Hindenburg*, the textbooks employed in the New Jersey school system of Colly's childhood had painted the history of Texas with a very broad brush. What knowledge she'd acquired on the subject had come through a middle-school history project she'd once helped Victoria complete. West Texas had always seemed to Colly like a dreary, arid wasteland—but it had seen its share of action and atrocity.

At the outbreak of the Civil War, federal soldiers had abandoned the forts guarding the old Butterfield Overland stagecoach route and hurried east to fight, leaving the Texas frontier largely unprotected. The Comanche, displaced by the government decades earlier, seized the opportunity to push southward from the Indian Territories and reclaim vast swathes of the stony scrubland that comprised their ancestral Comancheria.

After the war, General Philip H. Sheridan was charged with expelling the tribe once again from West Texas. Lacking the troops to accomplish the task militarily, he decided to starve the Comanche into submission. Federally authorized and munitioned hide hunters slaughtered the great herds of buffalo by the millions, skinning the humps and leaving the carcasses to rot in the sun.

The tactic was brutal but effective. The Comanche who survived the ensuing famine were driven off. And in the years that followed, white settlers lured to the area by the promise of cheap land were astonished to find it strewn so thickly with bleached buffalo skeletons that the ground seemed covered with snow. Homesteaders gathered up and sold the bones by the ton to fertilizer companies, who ground them into meal so that gardeners in the more "civilized" parts of the country could compost their vegetables with the evidence of a federally sanctioned genocide.

Every inch of this desert is soaked in blood, Colly thought, gazing absently out of the window as Avery navigated the squad car along the backroads of Coke County. *And for what? Who'd want to live here, let alone kill for the privilege?*

"Think we've gone too far?" Avery asked.

Startled out of her musings, Colly squinted at Jimmy Meggs' crudely drawn map. "We're supposed to 'turn at the buffalo skull'— Meggs said we can't miss it."

"Jimmy couldn't find his own ass with both hands and a flashlight." Avery nodded towards the ominous blue-black cloudbank flickering like a paper lantern in the distance. "Hope *that* holds off till we're back on asphalt."

After a few more miles, they came to a dirt track that branched away from the road on their right, ducking beneath a rustic archway of cedar logs. A gigantic horned skull loomed over the passage, its blank round eye sockets gazing down at them from the arch's crossbeam. Staring at it, Colly felt gooseflesh rise on her arms.

They followed the track down a slope and back up to the top of a shallow ridgeline, where it plunged into a forest of dark juniper dotted with stands of still-leafless mesquite.

"We should have an SUV for this," Avery muttered as they lurched over deep, dried ruts. She glanced at Colly. "What's the plan—just drive up to Hoyer's camp and hope he doesn't open fire?"

Colly was well-trained in urban tactics but had little wilderness experience. "I'm not sure. Any suggestions?"

"Visibility's shit in here. I could approach in the car while you cover me on foot. With any luck, Jace wouldn't see you."

"Good idea—but I'll take the car."

"You'll be more exposed."

"I've been shot at before, but I don't know the first thing about sneaking up on someone in the woods."

Avery shrugged and stopped the car. "Give me the map." She studied it carefully. "Jimmy says Jace likes to set up here." She tapped on a large *X* in the upper corner. "Stupid of him, but good for us. That close to the creek, he won't hear us coming."

Tossing the map back to Colly, Avery eased the cruiser forward.

A few minutes later, she stopped again as they approached a blind curve. "Hoyer's camp should be just ahead."

They climbed out of the car, and Colly walked around to the driver's side. Avery had drawn her service pistol and was checking the magazine.

"Handguns are no match for what Hoyer's probably got, but they're better than nothing." She looked up. "I'll follow on the left. Go slow or you'll lose me." Avery turned and stepped quietly into the forest.

Colly climbed behind the steering wheel. Unholstering her own gun, she laid it beside her, then shifted the car into gear. Around the bend, the track ran beside a narrow, swift-flowing stream that chuckled over moss-covered stones and fallen logs. The ground was damp here, and Colly spotted recent tire tracks. In her excitement, she accelerated for a few seconds before remembering herself. She stopped and waited for a minute, then continued at a crawl that she hoped would match the pace of someone on foot in the dense vegetation.

A hundred yards further on, the road curved again, following a bend in the streambed. Rounding the curve, Colly's pulse quickened. In a grassy clearing ahead, Jace Hoyer's pickup sat beside a lime-green pop-up tent. Hoyer was nowhere in sight. The door and windows of the tent were zipped closed, and the firepit beside it had not been recently used.

Colly shifted into park and quietly opened the car door. Outside, she understood Avery's earlier comment about Jace's choice of campsite. Whitebone Creek was surprisingly noisy for its size. It would easily obscure the sound of an engine or the crack of a twig.

Colly peered through the trees to her left. No sign of Avery. *We should've arranged a signal*, she thought.

Though in Houston she'd followed armed men down dark alleyways and into crack houses without hesitation, here Colly moved forward nervously, clutching her sidearm. She hadn't gone three steps when a horrible baying erupted. Two enormous pit bulls scrambled from beneath Hoyer's pickup and raced towards her. Colly stepped backwards, raising her gun. Her heel caught on an exposed tree root. She fell, landing hard on her back. The impact knocked the gun out of her hand. It flew beneath the squad car.

The dogs were almost on her. Colly instinctively flipped onto her belly to protect her throat and vital organs. As she scrambled for the pistol, a pair of massive jaws closed on her ankle. Even through her boot, the crushing pressure sent a shock of pain up her calf. The second dog went for the back of her neck but was hindered by her thick ponytail. It clamped down on a mouthful of hair, nearly ripping it from her scalp.

As Colly struggled to pull away, a voice shouted, "Tank, Trigger—*heel*."

Immediately, the dogs released her. Colly rolled onto her back. Jace Hoyer stood blinking in front of the now-open tent flap, a double-barreled shotgun in his hands. His mud-colored hair was disheveled, and he wore nothing but faded cutoffs and a pair of unlaced boots.

The dogs had run to stand beside him, but they stared at her, whining eagerly and ready to lunge on command.

Hoyer stepped forward. "How'd you find me? Jolene don't even know about this place."

Colly raised herself cautiously on her elbows. "Why'd you run off, Jace? It looks bad."

He pointed the shotgun at her chest. "*I'm* doing the asking. Don't reckon you came out here alone. Where's your sidekick?"

Great question, Colly thought, fighting the urge to glance towards the woods. There was no way to reach her pistol; even if she could, she'd never be able to get Hoyer and both dogs before they got her first. She could only stall for time and hope Avery turned up.

"Don't do anything stupid, Jace. It's not worth it."

"I got nothin' to lose—I'd rather get sent up for killing a cop than a kid." Hoyer racked the shotgun.

Colly felt a bead of sweat roll between her shoulder blades. "So it's true you killed Denny?"

"Truth's got nothin' to do with it. I'm being set up. There's no fighting the Newlands—y'all get what you want."

"No one's setting you up, Jace."

"Then why'd that purple-haired bitch take pictures of my truck yesterday?"

"Maybe the bitch wants to find out why you're lying to us," shouted a disembodied voice.

Hoyer wheeled around as the pit bulls lunged, snarling, towards the thicket across the road. Seizing the unexpected opportunity, Colly groped beneath the squad car for her pistol. As her hand closed on it, she heard two sharp gunshots and a chorus of terrified yelps.

She scrambled to her feet. The dogs were racing back towards their owner with their tails tucked. Two puffs of dust rose from the center of the dirt track, where the bullets had struck.

"Next shots won't miss," said the voice from the trees.

"Kill my dogs and I'll gut you," Hoyer screamed, waving his shotgun wildly at the dense wall of juniper.

Colly aimed at his back. "Drop it or I'll shoot, Jace."

Hoyer froze. The muscles in his arms and shoulders tensed.

Colly's hands were sweaty on the gun grip. "Don't do it, don't do it," she murmured. To her relief, after several seconds, Hoyer put down the shotgun.

Avery stepped out of the thicket. Her uniform was filthy, her hair mussed. A deep, bleeding scratch cut across the white scar on her cheek.

She trained her pistol on Hoyer. "Kick the gun away."

He obeyed, and Avery moved closer. "Now, put those dogs inside your truck—slow, or I shoot them."

Glowering, Hoyer seized the pit bulls by their collars and towed them towards the door of the pickup.

"Sorry I'm late to the party," Avery said a few moments later as she snapped the handcuffs on Hoyer. "Terrain's rougher than I thought."

"Worked out okay." Colly holstered her gun. "Sit him down."

Avery jerked Hoyer to his feet and pushed him onto the tailgate of his pickup. Above their heads, they heard the low rumble of approaching thunder.

"What do you want from me? I ain't done nothin'," Hoyer grumbled.

"We want to know why you lied," Avery snapped. "You weren't watching basketball Monday night. We've got you on security footage creeping around the ranch."

Hoyer swallowed, his prominent Adam's apple rising and falling beneath the leathery skin. "Ain't no cameras out there."

"They were installed a few weeks ago, jackass."

Hoyer stiffened defiantly. "Gimme a lawyer."

"Have it your way."

Colly sighed and nodded to Avery, who shrugged and said, "Jace Hoyer, I'm arresting you on the charge of criminal mischief, and on—"

"Criminal mischief? What the—"

"You did a lot of damage inside Brenda Newland's minivan," Colly said.

"The hell I did. I wasn't even—"

"Save it for the judge. We can't take your statement once you've lawyered up. You're also being arrested for aggravated assault, threatening police with a deadly weapon." Colly nodded to Avery. "Read him his rights and put him in the car."

"What about my dogs, goddammit?" Hoyer's voice held a sudden edge of panic.

Colly shook her head. "They attacked me. We'll send Animal Control to pick them up. They'll be euthanized."

"You ain't hurt. Lemme call Jolene to come get 'em."

"Jolene's in the hospital in Abilene." Avery tugged Hoyer towards the squad car as the thunder rumbled again, louder this time. "You have the right to remain—"

"The hospital? What the hell happened?"

"She tried to off herself," Avery said coldly.

The color drained from Hoyer's face, and his knees buckled. Colly jumped forward and grabbed his other arm.

He jerked away. "You done this, snooping around, stirring things up. Jolene ain't—"

"She did it because you left her. According to Carmen, anyway," Colly said.

She opened the car's rear door, and Hoyer sank onto the seat, his face gray. "I gotta get to Abilene. I gotta get to Abilene."

"Put your feet inside, before I slam the door on them."

"Please, I'll tell you whatever."

"Are you saying you withdraw your request for an attorney?" Colly asked.

Hoyer looked up. "Yeah, sure. I'll tell you everything. Just let me go."

Colly glanced at Avery, who was shaking her head furiously. "No way."

Colly shut Hoyer inside the car. "Let's clear the tent."

They found three more long guns, a pistol, and a cache of ammunition. As they were putting them in the cruiser's trunk, Colly whispered, "He knows something, and right now, he's motivated. We won't get another chance."

"He'll just make up a bunch of crap," Avery hissed. "Cut him loose, and we'll never see him again."

As she spoke, another crack of thunder, much louder this time, sounded directly overhead. A sudden gust of cold wind blew through the juniper, sending dirt and dried leaves skittering. A few fat raindrops struck the hood of the cruiser, and the women dove inside the car as the sprinkling became a driving downpour.

In the front passenger seat, Colly swept the damp hair out of her eyes. "You're under arrest, Hoyer. We can't let you go. But give us your statement on the way back—the truth, this time—and we can discuss getting you to Abilene."

"What about my dogs?"

"They'll be fine where they are for a couple hours. We'll have your truck towed back to town."

"They're gonna go nuts. They're scared of thunder."

Avery laughed and started the car.

Colly turned to look at the sullen prisoner. "Poor babies, that's a shame. Now fasten your seatbelt, and start talking."

Chapter 22

The dirt track was slick with mud by the time they emerged from the tree line. The cruiser's tires spun and fishtailed as Avery coaxed the car up the slope to the buffalo-skull archway.

Once on the road, Colly turned in her seat. "Well?"

Hoyer stared out of the window. "It's a long story."

"Start with Monday night. Why'd you lie about where you were?"

"You woulda slapped me in cuffs if I didn't."

Behind the wheel, Avery snorted. "You're in cuffs now, genius."

Hoyer said nothing for a minute. "I drove to the ranch Monday night, but I didn't do nothin'."

"What was your plan? To talk to Lowell, try to get your job back?" Colly asked. "Or did you think you'd have better luck with Iris?"

"That old hag? Not likely."

"Then why were you there?"

Hoyer's shoulders hunched. "Jolene and me was watching San Antonio wipe the floor with the Mavs, which was pissing me off. And—" He swallowed. "And Carmen come by earlier, saying she heard y'all was up at the clinic that afternoon, asking questions. Like I said, I figured I was being set up. More I thought about it, the madder I got."

Avery glowered at him in the rearview mirror. "So you figured, 'What the hell, I'll put a dead snake in Brenda Newland's car'?"

"I told you, I never done that. I didn't have no plan, really. Jolene fell asleep, so I just thought I'd drive up to the ranch, maybe piss in the pool."

"We're supposed to believe that?" Colly asked.

"Believe what you want. I'd had a few beers by then."

Colly considered. "When you got to the ranch, where'd you park?"

"Bottom of the hill, below the Mollison place. I walked up the drive and seen somebody standing by a van messing with something in the front passenger seat."

"Know who it was?"

Hoyer shook his head. "Too dark. I saw the beam of a flashlight moving around. I must've stepped on a stick, because all of a sudden, the guy swung the light my way—"

"The guy? It was a man?"

"Just saw the silhouette. Thought it was Lowell, at first. Dude was kinda short, wearing a Stetson and one of them square-looking field jackets. Lowell's got a coat like that. Didn't act like Lowell, though."

"What do you mean?"

"Lowell'd never abide strangers wandering up to his mama's place in the dark. He would've come after me. Shouted, at least."

Unless he had reason to keep things quiet, Colly thought. "What did he do?"

"Never made a peep. Just swept the flashlight back and forth in my direction, slow and methodical, like he was hunting for me. Gimme the willies."

"Did he see you?"

"Dunno. I dove behind one of them big junipers by the drive and hightailed it back to my truck."

"And then—?"

"Then nothin'. I went home. Jolene was still asleep. Never knew I left."

"That's the whole story?"

"Yup."

Colly studied his face. He seemed to be telling the truth. As she contemplated her next question, she felt a vibration in her pocket and heard a faint mechanical chirp.

"Must be back in range," Avery said.

Colly pulled out her phone. There was a text from Russ: *At hospital. Will call soon.*

She had also missed a call from Brenda. School had been out for nearly thirty minutes. In the excitement of the past two hours, she'd lost track of time. Cursing softly, she hit redial.

When Brenda answered, Colly apologized and explained. Could Brenda possibly watch Satchel till Colly got back to town? Brenda hesitated. She had to get her own kids to baseball and ballet, but she'd take Satchel with her. He could hang out at the clinic while she did paperwork, and Colly could pick him up there.

"Is he upset?" Colly asked.

Another hesitation. In the background, Colly could hear children's voices.

"A little. Let's talk later."

Colly thanked her and hung up. "*Shit.*"

Avery looked at her questioningly, but Colly shook her head.

"Any news on Jolene?" Jace was leaning forward, his face lined with worry.

"Not yet. When our interview's finished, I'll call the hospital."

"I told you everything."

"I want to hear the real reason you were fired."

Jace sat back and crossed his arms. His earlier mood of eager capitulation had vanished. "I bet you do."

Colly sighed. "I know you think I'm part of some plot to frame you. But honestly, I don't give a crap about clearing Willis's name. He may be family, but he was a pedophile."

"Then why're you here?"

Colly stiffened defensively but forced herself to relax. Vulnerability with a suspect was sometimes more effective than confrontation. But it was much more difficult.

"Because of guilt, if I'm honest," she said after a moment.

"That business in Houston?"

Colly nodded. "I cut some corners, and Russ lost his brother. When he asked me to review Denny's case, I thought I owed him that much. But I'm not here to play along with any Newland PR campaign."

Jace was watching her through narrowed eyes. "If I incriminate myself, do I get immunity?"

"That's not my call. But I promise things will go better for you if you cooperate."

Jace stared down at his cuffed wrists. "Okay. But you gotta drive me to Abilene—not *maybe*, not *we'll see about it*. Drive me there now."

"I've got to get back to Crescent Bluff. Tell us your story, and I'll have an officer drive you to see Jolene as soon as we've booked you at the station. That's the best you're going to get, Jace. Take it or leave it."

He shifted in his seat and finally shrugged. "You talked about cutting corners. I reckon I did, too. But it ain't my fault. Like I said, Lowell's good at making a mess for other folks to clean up."

"What kind of mess?"

"Embezzlement."

Colly and Avery looked at each other. "From his own company?" Colly asked.

"His old man was grooming him to take over. After Bryant's first stroke, Lowell was running the show pretty much unsupervised. That's when it started."

"He's been embezzling for fifteen years?"

Jace hunched his shoulders. "Lowell gambles, but he ain't no good at it. He got himself in a hole, so he raided the piggy bank."

"He never got caught?"

"Who's gonna catch him? Bryant was half-gaga by then, and Lowell was in charge of the business accounts. Newland Wind Industries is a decent-sized company, but the old man was a control freak—never took the thing public 'cause he didn't want no shareholders breathing down his neck." Jace smiled grimly. "Came back to bite him in the end. As long as Lowell made payroll and kept the place humming, he had nothing to worry about."

"Sweet deal," Avery muttered.

"It took a toll. Not at first, 'cause Lowell convinced himself he was just borrowing. Whenever he'd have a winning streak, he'd put the money back. But you know how that goes. The wins got fewer, and his drinking started getting out of hand."

"If no one knew about it, how'd you find out?" Colly asked.

"Got to be too much for him. Ain't easy, juggling two sets of books. He needed help. Lowell had the final say on everything, but by the time his old man croaked, he had me overseeing production, purchasing, the whole shebang. I was in it up to my neck—but he made it worth my while."

Avery was glowering skeptically at Jace in the rearview. Colly leaned back in her seat and gazed thoughtfully out of the window. The storm had moved on. A black wall of flickering cumulus still towered behind them, while in the sky ahead, long streaks of sunlight streamed through the ragged shreds of cloud, turning puddles into patches of dazzling gold.

Colly reached for her sunglasses. "I don't buy it, Jace. If you had so much dirt on Lowell, why would he fire you? He's not that stupid."

Jace snorted. "Wanna bet?"

"Explain."

"I gotta take a leak first."

Avery shook her head. "We'll be at the station in half an hour."

"I ain't pissed since last night. You want a mess back here?"

Avery glanced at Colly, who checked the time. "Make it fast."

Outside, the air was now clear and cool. Red-winged blackbirds squabbled in the reedy ditch along the roadside, and the gravel crunched wetly beneath Colly's shoes as she rounded the front of the cruiser. Avery was opening Jace's door.

He emerged and looked around. "Gimme some privacy, will ya?"

"Don't push your luck." Avery planted a palm between his shoulder blades and propelled him towards the ditch. "And don't ask me to take the cuffs off, either. You can unzip yourself just fine."

When he was finished, Avery spun him around. "Let's go."

At the car door, Jace stopped. "I'd remember better with a smoke."

Avery hesitated, chewing her lip.

She wants one, too, Colly thought. *Maybe it'll keep Jace talking.* She checked her watch again. "Fine, but not in the car."

Avery lit two cigarettes and handed one to Jace.

"Explain why Lowell would fire you if you could send him to prison with one phone call," Colly said.

"I couldn't. He woulda taken me down with him. Not just for embezzlement."

"Meaning?"

Jace leaned against the car door and exhaled white smoke. "Manslaughter, maybe negligent homicide."

Colly and Avery stared.

"You *did* kill Denny," Avery said.

"I ain't talking about Denny."

"Who, then?"

Jace tapped his cigarette to dislodge the ashes. "Gimme another one of them coffin nails."

Colly snatched the pack from Avery and shook out a cigarette. Tucking it behind his ear, Jace stared out across the rain-drenched scrubland. "To understand, you gotta put yourself in Lowell's shoes," he said slowly. Lowell's biggest fear, after his father's first stroke, had been that the old man would get well and discover the embezzlement before Lowell had time to pay back the money. Bryant would've disowned him, maybe even pressed charges. So when Bryant had his second stroke and died, Lowell thought his troubles were over—or at least postponed. Though everything went to Iris, Lowell thought she'd leave him to run the business. But Iris had other plans. A few weeks after the funeral, she called a family meeting. She intended to play a hands-on role in the company moving forward. She asked Lowell for copies of all the business records so she could get up to speed. Lowell panicked. He gave her copies of the dummy books, not the real ones.

Bryant had been a miser. He'd always resisted putting money into development, preferring to keep overhead down and profits high. But Iris turned out to have a shrewd business sense of her own, and she did her homework. Longer blades were the industry standard now, she said. The business couldn't stay profitable unless they kept up with the times. According to the records Lowell gave her, the company appeared to be sitting on a mountain of capital, and Iris decided to invest a large part of it in upgrades.

"We're talking a major retooling, millions of dollars," Jace said. "Problem was, a big chunk of that money wasn't really there. Lowell was fit to be tied."

"What'd he do?" Avery demanded.

Jace squinted up at the sky, where a red-tailed hawk circled lazily. "He was in too deep by then. I was, too. I thought we should come clean and hope Iris's motherly instincts kept her from doing anything too rash. But Lowell wouldn't hear of it. Too much pride, I reckon. So he started scrambling."

Lowell had taken out a second mortgage on his house without telling Brenda; sold his hunting cabin, his boat, his ski lodge in Colorado. He ordered Jace to lay off dozens of workers, paring back to a skeleton crew and slashing benefits to the bone. But it wasn't enough.

"Then one day, Lowell called me into his office," Jace said. "He looked bad—sweating Scotch, white as a ghost. Told me if I didn't find a way to cut the cost of Iris's upgrade by twenty percent, we was both going to prison. I said, 'How the hell am I supposed to do that?' But he didn't want to hear it. Said he didn't know and he didn't *wanna* know—just get it done." Jace spat out a loose bit of tobacco. "So, I did."

Colly pursed her lips. "How?"

"Called in some favors, leaned on suppliers that were hungry for our business. But we was still short by a good bit. Then I had my bright idea." Jace scowled and kicked at the gravel. "When you make turbine blades longer, you gotta use a stronger, more expensive kind of epoxy, see? Which meant we was gonna have to throw out a couple hundred grand worth of the old stuff we had on hand, or sell it at a huge loss—ain't much market for it nowadays. I figured if I mixed the new stuff with our existing stock—not diluting it much, mind you, just a little—I could make it stretch without really weakening the blades."

Avery looked pale. "Christ."

Jace removed the second cigarette from behind his ear and lit it with the butt of the first. "They over-engineer materials for them longer blades to hold up in extreme environments—tundra, open ocean, you name it. I figured West Texas weather ain't near as harsh as them places."

"A woman died, Jace," Colly said.

"Yeah, been eating me up—it gimme a damn ulcer." He jabbed a thumb at his gut. "But how was I supposed to know? I had my guys run months of stress tests on the prototype blades. Everything held up fine. Till we had that crazy winter. Once-in-a-century fluke, they called it. With weather like that, stuff goes haywire."

"Did Lowell sign off on all this?"

Jace glanced sidelong at Colly. "Damn straight. I wasn't gonna be left twisting in the wind if things went sideways. But Lowell didn't really know what he was signing. His marriage was cracking up, and he was drunk most of the time. I'd copy him on everything and try to explain what I was doing, but he'd wave me off."

Then came the turbine accident. Jace was terrified that the PUC would uncover what he'd done; but by some miracle, they missed it. He'd thought he was out of danger until last March. When Lowell started talking about suing materials manufacturers, Jace was forced to come clean.

"I explained everything, showed Lowell his signature on the purchase orders. He hit the roof, said I tricked him. Told me to clear out my locker and get off the property. That was my reward for saving his ass."

Avery flicked her cigarette butt into a puddle. "That explains the first fight. What about the second?"

"Huh?"

"Someone said you and Lowell had another fight later, at a job site."

"Oh, that." Jace looked annoyed. "I went to talk to him when I found out he was bad-mouthing me around town. But he wouldn't listen."

"I heard you sucker-punched him."

211

"He made threats. I got a right to defend my family."

"What kind of threats?" Colly asked.

"I told him I'd go public about the embezzlement unless he stopped spreading lies about me. It was right after Denny got arrested for that school fire. Lowell said he was buddies with the judge, and he'd pull strings to get Denny locked up if I didn't watch out. Denny was a punk, but I'm damned if I'll let someone like Lowell Newland blackmail me."

"Seems like the blackmail worked," Colly said. "You kept quiet, and Denny got probation with mandated therapy."

"I kept quiet for Jolene." Jace laughed suddenly. "And Brenda Newland ended up being Denny's shrink. Lowell must've been shittin' himself."

"Why?"

"Brenda would have him by the short hairs if Denny told her about the embezzlement."

"Denny knew about that?"

Jace shrugged. "I didn't tell him, but he could've overheard me and Jolene arguing about it. She was pretty pissed off."

This angle had not occurred to Colly before. It opened up a new set of possibilities.

Avery's mind was apparently on a similar track. "That's why Jolene thinks Lowell's involved in Denny's murder?"

Jace nodded. "She don't reckon he done it himself, but he coulda paid someone."

"You must've been just as worried as Lowell about Denny blabbing," Colly said. "Maybe you teamed up to kill him. Innocent men don't run—and they don't need burner phones. We found the receipt for one in your house."

She expected an explosive reaction to this, but Jace seemed amused. "Sure, I got a burner—I run an off-license meat store out of my garage, for Chrissakes."

"Where's the phone now?"

"In my truck." Jace jerked his head eastward. "Y'all won't find nothin' more interesting on it than the price of pork tenderloin."

Colly and Avery exchanged looks.

"Suppose Lowell says you embezzled, and he didn't find out till after the fact," Colly said. "Can you prove any of this?"

"Hell, yes. I knew Lowell would scrub the records, so I printed hard copies. They're hidden someplace safe."

"Where?" Avery demanded.

Jace folded his arms. "Someplace safe. Y'all can have 'em after I see Jolene."

Colly opened the car door and rummaged in her purse. She pulled out the plastic evidence bag containing the torn manila envelope. "Hiding stuff in a freezer's the oldest trick in the book, Jace."

"If you found that, you know I'm telling the truth."

"It's empty." Colly shook the bag to illustrate.

Jace's expression of annoyance morphed into one of almost comical astonishment. "What the *fuck*?"

"You didn't take the papers?"

Jace shook his head. He was still staring at the evidence bag. "Thought if I got collared and Russ Newland found them on me, he might burn 'em. Figured they was safer where they was."

"Who else knew this was in the freezer?"

"Just Jolene. I told her where to find it in case I ever got arrested."

A shrill ring interrupted the conversation. Colly pulled out her phone and checked caller ID. "Hey, Russ. Any news?"

From two counties away, she heard him exhale heavily. His voice was flat and weary. "Jolene didn't make it. I'm heading home."

Chapter 23

It was nearly five-thirty when Colly arrived at the Compass Counseling Center to pick up Satchel. She'd been reluctant to leave Avery on her own to manage Jace Hoyer. His reaction to the news of his wife's death had been unsettling. He'd grown very quiet, dropping his head and staring down at his hands for the rest of the drive. By the time they reached the police station, he had sunk into a torpor so profound that they needed the help of two patrolmen to get him out of the squad car. Colly had insisted on calling a doctor. It wasn't until Jace had been evaluated, booked, and given a sedative that she felt comfortable leaving.

She rehearsed an effusive apology as she trotted up the sidewalk and through the empty waiting room, but she had no need to use it. She found Brenda at her office desk working on her laptop, while Satchel played with a pile of toys next to a large dollhouse on the floor. When Colly entered the room, they both looked up. Satchel waved distractedly and resumed playing.

Brenda pushed away from the desk. "There you are." Her voice was cheerful. She showed no sign of annoyance or fatigue.

"What a day." Colly collapsed into an armchair. "I owe you, big-time, Bren."

Brenda smiled sympathetically. "How's Jolene? Carmen said they were taking her to Abilene."

"She died a couple hours ago. Carmen was with her. I just notified Jace."

"Oh, no. He fell to pieces, I imagine."

Colly was startled. "How'd you guess?"

"Sometimes the abusive ones are the most fragile. They bluster, but they don't have much ego-structure of their own."

Colly wondered whether Brenda was thinking of Jace or of Lowell. Did she know about the embezzlement? Had it been the last straw that ended the marriage? Colly needed to find out, but now wasn't the time.

She leaned forward and tousled Satchel's hair. "What are you playing, buddy?"

Satchel hunched his shoulders without looking up. He had arranged two action figures—an Iron Man and a Wonder Woman—on the sofa in the dollhouse living room, and was moving a plastic grizzly bear stealthily through the kitchen towards them, growling menacingly through his teeth.

Colly felt suddenly cold. "Is he okay?" she mouthed to Brenda.

Brenda nodded and stood. "It's almost time to put up the toys, Satchel. You can have five more minutes while I talk to Grandma."

She led Colly across the hall into a breakroom. "Those are therapy toys I use to assess trauma in young kids. I wasn't trying to diagnose him or anything. He was bored, and I thought he'd enjoy playing with them."

"But did you see? I think he's reenacting—"

Brenda held a finger to her lips and pulled the breakroom door nearly closed. "It's okay, it's normal."

"He's using a *bear*."

"They all gravitate to that bear—the ones who've gone through major trauma, I mean. That's why I have it. It's a way for kids to express adult behavior that's too monstrous for them to process."

"I thought he'd worked through all that. He's seemed so much better lately."

"Trauma recovery's never a linear thing." Brenda's brow furrowed. "But I don't mind telling you—I am a little concerned. I think he's struggling more than we realized."

Colly sighed. "Is it because I'm working a case? Or is it more than that?"

"I don't know. Like I said yesterday, I'd be happy to do a couple sessions with him."

Colly chewed her lip. "I'd hate to confuse him, Bren. He's used to the Houston therapist."

"I get it. But if you change your mind, let me know."

They returned to Brenda's office, where she wheeled an enormous suitcase out of the closet and laid it on the floor by the dollhouse.

"Let's put away the toys, Satchel."

Satchel clutched an action figure against his chest. "Iron Man doesn't want to go in the suitcase. He hates the dark."

"Would he rather go home with you for tonight?" Brenda asked.

Satchel nodded.

On the drive home, Colly tried to engage him in conversation, but Satchel was in an odd mood, distracted and remote. Back at the farmhouse, however, he seemed to return to normal. He sat at the kitchen table and chatted about his day as Colly made grilled cheese sandwiches and heated a can of tomato soup.

It wasn't until later, when she had helped him into pajamas and was reading him a bedtime story, that Satchel abruptly asked, "Do you ever dream about bears, Grandma?"

He spoke the words quickly, and his voice sounded strange—simultaneously nonchalant and tentative.

Colly laid down the book. "Not very often. Do you?"

Satchel nodded. He was propped against the pillows, balancing his ant farm on his chest and staring intently at it. The Iron Man toy lay beside him on the comforter.

"Scary bears? Or nice ones?" Colly asked.

"Mostly scary."

"What do the bears do in your dreams?"

Satchel shrugged and appeared suddenly to lose interest in the subject. He set the ant farm on the nightstand and picked up Iron Man.

Colly hesitated. "Satchel, do you remember the day Mommy and Grandpa Randy—the day they got hurt?"

He seemed not to hear her; he was absorbed in making Iron Man combat-crawl over the quilt.

Colly tried again. "Did you like playing with the toys at Aunt Brenda's office?"

"I guess." Satchel made an explosion sound. Iron Man flipped in the air and dove for cover beneath a fold of blanket.

"Would you like to play there again?"

"Okay." Suddenly, Satchel turned and extended the action figure's arm towards Colly, aiming it like a gun. "Pew, pew, pew!"

"Why is Iron Man shooting me?"

Satchel giggled. He shoved the toy closer to Colly's face. "Pew, pew, pew!" There was a manic edge to his voice.

Colly started to move his hand aside, but he shrieked and jerked it away, hurling the toy at her head. It bounced off her cheekbone and onto the floor.

"*Ow*—that was too hard, Satchel." She stooped to pick up the figurine. Satchel lunged for it, but Colly stuffed it in her pocket. "I think you're overtired. Time for lights-out."

Satchel immediately burst into hysterics, sobbing and flailing. Colly tried for a while to calm him, but her efforts only made him more upset, so she turned off the lights and left the room. She paced the hallway, listening to him cry until, after half an hour, he wore himself out and fell asleep, still sniffling and hiccupping fretfully into the pillows.

Exhausted, Colly went downstairs and collapsed on the sofa. She took out her phone and held it uncertainly for a minute. Finally, she dialed. Brenda answered on the first ring, and Colly gave her a summary of the evening.

"I don't know what got into him, Bren. Maybe some therapy sessions aren't a bad idea."

Brenda seemed pleased to help. She had an online conference the next day, she said, so she wouldn't be at school for her usual morning hours; but she thought she'd be done by the time school was out. With Colly's permission, she would pick up Satchel and take him to the clinic. "I cleared my schedule tomorrow because of the conference, so we'll have as much time as we need. I can get a friend to take my kids for a couple hours."

Colly hung up, relieved, and checked her watch. Nine o'clock. She was beyond tired but too keyed up for bed. Maybe she'd take a closer look at the case files. But first, she needed a stiff drink. Was there any liquor in the pantry? She was heading for the kitchen when a loud knock on the front door shattered the quiet.

She grabbed her pistol. "Who's there?" she shouted.

"It's me."

Holstering the gun, she unbolted the door. "Dammit, Russ, don't scare me like that. Text first next time."

Her brother-in-law stood on the porch, a slender brown paper bag in one hand. "Sorry. You busy?"

"I'm tired. Can't it wait?"

"I'm not here on business." Russ wiped his boots on the mat. "I came to apologize for being a jackass yesterday. I shouldn't have accused you of going behind my back." He pulled a bottle of wine out of the bag. "Peace offering? The guy at the Booze Shack said it's pretty good."

Colly hesitated. "Okay, but outside. If Satchel heard us and woke up, that would be the last straw."

By the time she returned with two tumblers, Russ had settled on one end of the porch swing and was opening the bottle with the corkscrew attachment on his pocketknife.

Colly sat beside him. "I couldn't find wine glasses."

"Wanda's folks were teetotalers." Russ poured the drinks and held up his tumbler. "Here's to the end of one hell of a day."

"I'll drink to that."

They sipped for a while in silence. A few early crickets chirruped in the grass and a gentle breeze rattled the dry leaves still clinging to the branches of the oak tree in the yard.

"Did you talk to Jolene before she died?" Colly asked finally.

Russ shook his head. "She was unconscious when I got there. Never woke up again."

"What about Carmen?"

"I tried, but she was in no fit state. Let's give her a day or two."

But the trip to Abilene hadn't been a total waste, Russ said. While he was there, he'd gotten word about the burner phone that had sent Colly the threatening text. It'd been purchased less than a week ago at a convenience store outside Colorado City—not much of a detour for Russ on his way back to Crescent Bluff, so he'd decided to stop by.

"No video footage, unfortunately," he said. "But the kid working the register remembers selling two phones that day."

"Cash transactions?"

"Yep. The kid said one was bought by a woman about his mom's age—in her forties, slender build. Could be either Carmen or Jolene."

"Or Brenda, or me, for that matter. Did he get hair color? Eye color?"

Russ shook his head. "He didn't seem real detail-minded."

"What about the other phone?"

"Bought by a thin Black man who looked like 'a banger,' he said. In his twenties, maybe thirties."

"Damn."

"At least we know that text wasn't sent by Hoyer's phone—not the one you found the receipt for, anyway. He could have another one we don't know about."

"I doubt it. You said the phone was bought a week ago? That's before I got here. Our perp must've known I was coming. Jace didn't." Colly swallowed the last of her wine.

"We don't know that. Gossip spreads fast in a small town." Russ refilled her tumbler. "I'm not thrilled you went looking for him today without telling me, by the way. That was risky."

"I've been a cop longer than you. I know what I'm doing."

"You're not a cop anymore. I feel responsible."

"Jace is in custody, isn't he? You said you'd stay out of things and let me investigate my way."

Russ sighed in the darkness. "It's harder than I thought." He half-turned towards her and laid his arm on the back of the swing. "It's nice having you here, Col. I've missed you these last couple years."

His hand dropped to her shoulder. It was an innocuous gesture, but the casual intimacy of it felt disquieting, somehow, at the end of an exhausting day.

Colly stood up, setting her glass on the porch rail. "Let's walk around a little. I'm getting sleepy."

She led the way down the steps into the damp grass. The storm that afternoon had cleared the air, and the night was cool and fine. The waxing moon hung over the black line of the eastern bluffs, bright enough to obscure the stars around it and bathe the land in a cold, pale light. Away from the house, the breeze was stronger. Colly shivered as she ambled in the direction of the big oak.

Russ strolled beside her, carrying his drink. "You and Avery get anything out of Jace today?"

Colly hesitated. Should she ask if Russ knew about the embezzlement? No. Not yet. She'd talk to Lowell first. "I got an earful about Newlands in general and Lowell more specifically. Hoyer's not a fan."

Russ laughed. "I reckon not."

"He did say Lowell's drinking is out of control. I've noticed it, myself."

"I know." Russ sighed. "He fell apart after the divorce. He blames Brenda, but she wouldn't have had the affair if he wasn't such a mess. I've tried to get him to join AA."

They reached the oak, and Colly leaned against it. The bark was rough and solid through her shirt. "Is he fit to manage the company?"

Russ's face was hidden in darkness, but his feet shuffled restlessly. "Did Jace say he wasn't?"

"I just wondered. I have a vested interest, too, you know."

"Momma keeps an eye on things. The company'll be all right."

"I asked you this yesterday, Russ, but I'll ask again—could Lowell have killed Denny Knox?"

"Is that what Jace says?"

"He has his suspicions."

"You can't trust his word—he hates Lowell."

"That's why I'm asking you."

"I told you, Lowell's alibied for that day. He was with me in Paint Rock till just before school let out, and with his kids after that."

"Hypothetically, then. Is he capable?"

Russ swallowed the last of his wine in a noisy gulp. "Anyone's capable of anything, under the right circumstances. Put me in a room with that nutcase who killed Randy and Victoria, and I'd have blown his head off without thinking twice—if he hadn't beaten me to it."

"That's different. Denny was a child."

"Lowell can't be in two places at once."

"There's such a thing as a contract kill."

Russ ran his free hand roughly up and down the back of his head. "Oh, come on, this is Crescent Bluff. Besides, he's got no motive."

"Sure he does. Lowell fired Jace, and then Brenda started counseling Denny—all while she and Lowell were in a nasty custody dispute. You don't think Lowell might've been scared that Denny could tell her something damaging, something he overheard from Jace?"

"Like what?"

"Maybe that Lowell drinks on the job," Colly said. "Jace was my prime suspect. But I don't think he did it. I have to question who else had cause. I need to rule Lowell out so I can move on."

"Yeah, okay. I just didn't expect—I mean, I brought you in to clear Willis, not—"

"You brought me in to find the truth. That's what you said, anyway."

Russ emitted an exasperated sigh. "Dammit, Colly, Lowell's not the killer."

"How do you know?"

"Lowell couldn't have killed Adam Parker in '98—he was away at college when it happened. And nobody but the police and the killer knew about the rabbit mask."

Unless you told him, Colly thought. Would Russ do that? *Anyone's capable of anything, under the right circumstances*—he'd said so himself. Assumptions based on trust could be fatal to an investigation. Russ was not Randy, though the fact that they looked alike made it harder to remember.

Somewhere in the darkness, an owl hooted mournfully. Colly pulled out her phone and checked the time. "It's ten o'clock. I looked over the case files last night, but I want to spend more time with them before bed."

They moved towards the house. "What's the plan for tomorrow?" Russ asked.

"I've got to figure out who's stalking me. We've come up empty on the snake in the van and the anonymous text. That just leaves the red ballcap. If Tom Gunnell didn't see who took it, maybe the farmers on Salton Road did. I thought Avery and I might knock on a few doors. Maybe we'll get lucky."

"Watch out. Dave Carroway's place is over there."

"Carroway? Isn't that—?"

"Yep. He's the kid Willis molested at church. That was thirty years ago. His folks are gone, and he runs the farm now. He went through a rough patch—bar fights, drugs, a few DUIs. Served a stint for assault. Seems pretty stable these days, but tread lightly. He hates Newlands."

"Good to know."

They mounted the porch steps, and Russ faced her. "I'm glad you're okay, Col. See you tomorrow." He leaned in suddenly and kissed her cheek before turning and striding back to his truck.

Colly watched with her hand on the doorknob until his taillights vanished in the distance.

"Shit," she murmured. Then she opened the door and went inside.

Chapter 24

Thursday dawned chilly and damp. The pale disc of the sun struggled to penetrate the thick fog blanketing the scrubland. As she drove Satchel to school, Colly was relieved that his volatile mood of the previous evening had dissipated, and he was acting like himself.

"Do I have to wear my sun-sleeves? It's not sunny," he whined as he climbed out of the car, the Iron Man toy clutched in his hand.

Colly raised the brim of his bucket hat and kissed him on the brow. "The fog'll burn off by recess." She wiped away the lip-balm smudge she'd left on his skin. "Remember, Aunt Brenda's picking you up after school for another playdate at her office."

Satchel's face lit up, and he trotted into the building without further protest. Back in the car, Colly phoned Avery and explained her plan—Avery was to find Jimmy Meggs or another available officer and interview the farmers on Salton Road. Being a local, she'd have better luck than Colly would.

"Find out if they saw anything suspicious Monday when the ballcap disappeared. And ask about the day Denny was killed. That's a long shot, but it's worth a try."

"Where are you going?" Avery asked.

"Turbine plant. If I can catch Lowell off guard, maybe he'll corroborate some of Jace's story. It's best if I fly solo," she added before Avery could object. "He'll be mad that you interviewed his employees the other day without his say-so."

The Newland Wind Industries manufacturing facility lay west of town on a barren plain between two stony ridges. It was a large complex composed of some dozen windowless metal buildings, each the size of an airplane hangar. Acres of asphalt skirted the facility, dotted with storage sheds, heavy equipment, and neat rows of turbine blades awaiting transport. Colly parked in the visitors' lot near the road. Entering through the glass doors of the closest building, she found herself in a lobby decorated with potted ficus trees and framed posters extolling the virtues of wind energy. Colly introduced herself to the young receptionist and asked her to tell Mr. Newland that she wanted to see him regarding a police investigation. *That'll piss him off*, she thought. An angry Lowell would be less careful of his words.

The girl looked startled and uncertain. She reached for the desk phone, then changed her mind.

"Wait one moment," she said, and vanished through a door behind her desk.

She returned nearly five minutes later accompanied by a plump, olive-skinned young man with round glasses, a powder-blue bowtie, and dark, short-cropped hair. He introduced himself as Manny Pareja, head of community relations. He was delighted to meet his boss's sister-in-law. Unfortunately, Mr. Newland wasn't available. But he, Manny, would be happy to help.

"Great, I've got plenty of time," Colly said. "I'd love a tour of the place while I wait."

Manny blinked rapidly, but his broad smile never wavered. "Certainly."

He ushered her down a nondescript office-lined hallway—the "managerial hub," he called it. "But the real magic happens back here." Colly followed him around a corner and through a pair of heavy doors. Manny stopped and gestured theatrically. "The molding floor."

They were standing in an immense room, longer than a football field, though narrower. Forklifts, golf carts, and strangely shaped vehicles of unknown purpose maneuvered along a series of crowded workstations, the sounds of their motors echoing in the cavernous space. High above, the ceiling bristled with catwalks and steel tracks supporting enormous gantry cranes. Down the center of the space marched a series of gigantic shell-like molds. They were long—fifty yards each, Colly estimated—broad at one end and tapering at the other, as if a turbine blade had been filleted like a trout and laid, open-faced, on a long metal platform. Inside the mold nearest Colly, workers in gray coveralls were arranging long strips of white fabric in an overlapping pattern.

"These are the packers," Manny explained. "They're laying fiberglass sheeting. When it's hardened, it forms the outer blade wall."

"Do you only make blades?"

"Nowadays, yes," Manny said. "I understand we used to manufacture more of our own components. But in a globalized economy, you've got to specialize. We import what we don't make—and of course we sell and install the final product."

He commandeered a passing golf cart and drove Colly slowly down the length of the room, explaining the purpose of each workstation with a flood of jargon that Colly made no attempt to decode. However, as they approached the last two blade molds in the line, she caught a term she recognized.

"Epoxy? This is where they add the glue?"

Manny stopped the golf cart. "Industrial epoxy-resin, yes."

At one end of the blade mold, beside a computerized panel, stood a half-dozen white plastic tanks, each as large as a washing machine. From them, hoses ran to connectors attached to the mold.

"The computer mixes the proper ratio of epoxy and hardener, and vacuum suction pulls the mixture into the blade to saturate the fiberglass," Manny explained. "At the next station, we fasten the two halves of the blade together. Then it goes to another building for grinding and painting."

Colly climbed out of the golf cart to peer more closely at the plastic tanks. "I've heard that these longer blades need a stronger epoxy than the shorter ones."

"Absolutely correct. We had to replace our inventory when we upgraded the blade length." He beamed ingenuously. Whatever Jace and Lowell had done, Manny Pareja clearly knew nothing about it.

"Where's the epoxy stored? In this building?"

"No, there's a warehouse outside. Why?"

"Who has access to the warehouse?"

Manny frowned, and Colly quickly added, "Just curious. I've heard my in-laws talk about the business for ages, but I've never known much about it."

"Sure, I get it." Manny sounded uncertain. "Everything's operated by key card. The plant foreman and the floor manager have access—and Mr. Newland, of course. I'm not sure who else."

Colly was wondering how far she could push this line of questioning when they were interrupted by a loud and furious "Hey!"

She turned. Lowell was barreling down the production line towards them, his face red with fury. As he approached, Colly saw that his eyes were bloodshot. There was a smear of dried oatmeal on the placket of his shirt.

"What the hell's going on, Pareja? She shows up, and you roll out the red carpet without calling me?"

Manny swallowed. His bowtie bobbed up and down. "She's your family. I figured—"

"She's not here for a tour, you moron—she's doing an investigation."

"I came to talk to you, Lowell," Colly said. "It's not this guy's fault you don't stumble in to work till ten o'clock."

Lowell glanced up the assembly line. Most of the workers were watching them with open interest.

"Where's the damn floor manager?" he snapped. "Get them back to work, Pareja."

"Yes, *sir*." Manny spun the golf cart in a tight U-turn and sped away up the line.

When he was gone, Lowell lowered his voice. "You've got some nerve, coming here to embarrass me in front of my employees."

"You don't need my help for that," Colly said. "I tried to be discreet the other day, and you gave me the runaround. If you want to be left alone, talk to me."

Lowell raised his Newland Industries ballcap and ran a hand through his thinning hair. "Fine. But not here."

He grabbed her arm and hurried her through a door marked "Exit" at the end of the room. The morning fog had dissipated. The sun now shone bright in a cloudless sky. Lowell led the way across a wide span of tarmac and into a labyrinth of finished turbine blades that were lined up on metal cradles in long, parallel rows like gigantic knives in a drawer. The blades towered above them on either side, blocking the sunlight, and with no visible point of reference, Colly soon felt lost.

"That's far enough," she said, pulling away from Lowell's grip.

He turned to face her, crossing his arms. "Ask your damn questions."

She squared her shoulders. "I want to know why you planted that dead snake in Brenda's van Monday night. Did you really think that would chase me off?"

Lowell's eyes widened comically. "What the hell?"

228

"I have a witness who saw you do it."

"Then they're either blind, stupid, or lying. Get a lawyer, depose me if you want—I'll swear to it."

Colly studied his face. His outrage seemed genuine. She didn't think he was the shadowy figure Jace had seen by the van that night.

"You don't deny you're upset that I'm investigating?"

"I don't care what you do, as long as you're not a pain in my ass."

"Then why'd you punch Russ for bringing me here?"

Lowell laughed. "If I punched Russ every time I wanted to, he wouldn't have much of a face left."

"That's no answer."

Lowell shrugged. "Been a rough year for the company. I didn't want him stirring things up."

"Were you scared I'd find out you embezzled?"

This time, nothing changed in Lowell's expression, but his face grew rigid. "What?"

"Don't play dumb. Jace Hoyer has the proof. Or didn't you know he kept hard copies of all the documentation? They were in an envelope in his freezer—I found it yesterday when we searched his place."

Bluffing was always risky, but Colly knew immediately that the gamble had paid off. Lowell's eyelids flickered, and he opened and closed his mouth.

"Hoyer's making a big deal about nothing," he said finally. "It was a cash-flow problem, that's all. I borrowed—and I was paying it back."

"Is that how Iris would see it?"

"Gimme a break—she would've loaned me the money if I asked."

"Why didn't you?"

"Didn't need the guilt trip." Lowell took off his cap, waving it for emphasis. "Dad wanted me to run the business, but she waltzes

229

in after he died like it's one of her little home-renovation projects, throwing her weight around with no idea what the hell she's doing."

"Just when you're up to your neck in debt. Bad time for an embezzlement scandal."

"Like I said, I was paying it back. I just needed time."

"If only Iris hadn't screwed everything up, insisting on those upgrades, huh?" Colly stepped closer. "You raised what money you could and ordered Jace to work his magic for the rest?"

"Keeping overhead down was part of his job."

"He was good at it, too, wasn't he? Everything was humming along, till that turbine accident. I bet at first you thought, *This is my golden ticket—I'll sue the epoxy manufacturer for all they're worth.* You were going to let them take the blame for that woman's death and pay you enough in damages to get you out of the hole. Must've been a shock when Jace told you what he'd done, how he mixed the old and new epoxy to save money. How *you* signed off on it because you were too damn drunk to know better. Now Iris is pushing for an internal audit that could bring the PUC breathing down your neck, maybe even land you in prison. Your life's a house of cards, Lowell, and it's coming down."

Lowell's face was white. Beads of sweat stood out on his forehead. "Hoyer tricked me into signing those orders. I was going through a divorce, for Chrissakes. I was still in shock from what happened to Randy and Victoria."

At the mention of her family, Colly felt the blood rush to her face. "Man up, Lowell. Take some responsibility for once in your life."

Lowell's right hand balled into a fist. He took a half-step forward, but when Colly laid a hand on her sidearm, he stopped.

"Say what you want." He pulled a handkerchief from his pocket and wiped the back of his neck. "That woman's blood's on Hoyer's hands, not mine."

"The law would take a different view. So would Brenda."

"Meaning—?"

"I bet it was an ugly surprise when she started counseling Denny Knox. You were scared of what he might tell her, right? Maybe scared enough to kill him?"

"I wasn't even in town that day."

"You might've hired a hitman."

"Are you crazy? Think I wanted the Rangers crawling around, prying into our business? Besides, if I killed Denny, I sure as hell wouldn't dump his body on my own land. How dumb do you think I am?"

Colly shrugged. "Dumb enough to embezzle."

Lowell made a sound of disgust. "I can't change that now." He shoved the handkerchief into his pocket. "You arresting me?"

"I'm not a cop anymore."

Lowell swallowed. "You gonna tell Momma and Brenda?"

It's gone beyond that, Colly thought. *Avery knows, and Jace, and God knows who else. There's no un-ringing this bell.* "You didn't mention Russ," she said aloud. "Is that because he already knows?"

A flicker of some strong emotion—fear, perhaps, or anger—crossed Lowell's face. "Ask him yourself. I'm done talking."

"I think I will. And if I get even a whisper of a hint that you've tipped him off, I'll call the Rangers and report everything."

But Lowell was already moving away. "I got work to do," he said over his shoulder. "Find your own way out."

Back at her car, Colly phoned Russ.

"Hey, what's up?" His voice was cheerful.

"Where are you?"

"Heading to the ranch. Told Momma I'd look in on how the Rattlesnake Rodeo setup's going." He paused. "Everything okay?"

"Not exactly. I'll meet you there."

Chapter 25

Still tense and angry, Colly sped north along the Old Ranch Way. Damn Lowell. He'd cost her three days' work on what increasingly appeared to be nothing more than a complicated red herring. But she had to be sure. Gripping the steering wheel, she worked to slow her breathing and relax her aching jaw muscles. When she arrived at the ranch house, Russ's SUV was parked in front of the garage. The rear hatch stood open, and he was digging through a toolbox in the back.

As Colly climbed out of her car, he looked up, smiling. "Just got here, myself. How fast did you drive?"

"We need to talk."

Russ pulled a pair of leather work gloves from the toolbox and closed the hatch. "What about?"

"I came from the turbine plant." Colly glanced towards the house. Nadine the housekeeper was watching them from the dining room window. "Is there someplace more private?"

Russ stuffed the gloves in his back pocket. "I'm riding up to the north pasture—I want to get there before the setup crew breaks for lunch. Come along. We can talk on the way."

Colly hesitated. "On horseback?"

"You can ride Maisie. She's gentle."

Colly, who'd spent most of her childhood in the urban sprawl of New Jersey, had rarely seen a horse before her first visit to the ranch with Randy. Even if she'd been a confident rider, conducting an interrogation on horseback wasn't ideal. "Can't we take the highway up to the access road?"

"Access road's blocked with equipment. Come on, even Satchel rode Maisie."

Colly sighed. She didn't want to cool her heels at Mollison, making small talk with Iris until Russ returned. Pushing aside her misgivings, she followed him around the garden walk and along a path to the barn. It was a handsome fieldstone structure designed in the traditional western style with a breezeway down the center. One side was unpartitioned and served as a makeshift machine shop for the repairing of ranch equipment, while the other held a dozen stalls and a tack room.

As they entered, two barn cats darted for cover behind a tractor tire. The air smelled of hay and manure. Colly sneezed into the crook of her arm while Russ saddled a fidgety bay gelding and a pinto mare.

He helped her onto the pinto and adjusted the stirrups. "You won't fall off Maisie unless you jump."

"I'm not good with reins."

"Just hang onto the horn. She'll follow me."

"We can't talk if I'm ten feet behind you."

"I know a place we can talk on the way back."

Russ mounted the gelding and led the way out of the barn. To Colly's relief, Maisie followed placidly. At the bottom of the hill, they turned onto a trail heading north. Russ's mount, frustrated at being held back, snorted and tossed his head but eventually settled into a walk.

Russ was a relaxed and confident rider, Colly thought. He moved with the animal as naturally as if he'd sprouted from the saddle, hitching one shoulder slightly higher than the other, just as Randy used to. It was these little similarities that got to her the most, especially when she wasn't prepared for them. Why had Russ lied to her the other day? Did he know about the crimes at the turbine plant? If he was complicit, then what? The thought made her stomach churn. She felt nothing but contempt for Lowell. But it was different with Russ. Though she seldom admitted it even to herself, Colly was lonely. And in the last few days, there'd been moments with him when she'd felt—something. Was it only that he looked like Randy? Was her treacherous subconscious making some pathetic substitution, trying to recover what she'd lost?

She couldn't afford to think about it now. With an effort, she forced herself to focus on the rocking rhythm of the pinto's easy gait.

For half an hour, they rode through the scrubland. The ground began to rise, gently at first and then more steeply. Finally, they crested a ridge, and Colly found that they were on top of a low bluff overlooking a grassy plain. Near the base of the bluff stood an enormous white circus tent surrounded by booths and food trucks. Shading her eyes, Colly saw workmen, ant-like in the distance, stringing lights along walkways and marking off a makeshift parking lot with orange traffic cones. At the booths, vendors busily arranged merchandise. A crew of men in hardhats was assembling a Ferris wheel at the eastern edge of the grounds. From the top of the bluff, the whole scene looked like a child's toy model.

"I pictured something smaller," Colly said.

Russ nodded. "When Dad was a kid, it was one tent and some bleachers by the highway. Now we get hundreds of people."

"Ever have trouble?"

"Not much. A few pickpocketing incidents, maybe a fight or two. I have every cop I can spare running security, plus a few guards from the turbine plant."

"I meant with the snakes."

"Oh." Russ laughed. "A handler got bit on the thumb a while back, but never any civilians. We keep a paramedic and some anti-venom on-site, just in case. Are you coming?"

"Satchel's begging me, but I don't know. When does it start?"

"Tomorrow night. Runs all weekend. Lowell and me will be here most of that time keeping an eye on things."

He goaded the gelding forwards. The bluff, which appeared steep, actually shelved down to the plain in a series of jagged stair-step formations. They descended a switchback trail along these natural steps.

At the main entrance to the big tent, they dismounted. Colly rubbed her backside. "I forgot how sore that makes me."

Russ grinned. "Only cure's practice."

He tied their horses to a signpost, and they went inside. A few workers were moving about, but the preparations seemed fairly complete. Bleachers ran along the two longer sides of the tent, while at either end, booths, tables, and portable kitchens were clustered. In a line down the center of the huge space stood four circular enclosures, like the rings of a circus. The walls of the rings were chest-high and fitted at intervals with plexiglass windows so young children could look inside. From within the ring nearest to them came a muted buzzing noise, like a thousand maracas being shaken in the distance.

Colly moved instinctively backwards. "Is that what I think it is?"

"It's okay. Come on."

Russ took her hand and led her across the grass. As she peered over the wall of the ring, Colly went cold. The floor was covered a foot deep in a dappled tangle of writhing snakes. Some lay motion-less. Others squirmed on their backs, trying to right themselves, their pale bellies making cream-colored streaks in the dark, mottled heap. A few slithered over the top of the living mass like crowd-surfers at a concert. A strong, rancid odor rose from the pen. Colly cupped her hand over her nose and mouth.

"This is the holding pit," Russ said. "Don't worry, they can't climb the walls."

"Are—are these all from the ranch?" Colly stammered.

Russ shook his head. "Only a couple hundred. Most are from off-site. We pay by the head, so the locals bring them to us. Helps with population control in the area."

As he spoke, a young Latino workman wearing a greasy straw Stetson and dusty Wranglers entered from behind a partition marked "Staff Only." He was carrying a broad, flat plywood box.

"Hiya, boss," he said to Russ.

"Hey, Pete. How's the prep going?"

Pete grimaced. "Some of the new crew's the laziest SOBs I ever seen—but I been ridin' herd on 'em. We'll be ready."

Balancing the box on the edge of the snake pit, Pete flipped it over, and a hatch dropped open. A knot of rattlesnakes slid out onto the writhing heap, setting off loud rattles of protest.

"How many this year?" Russ asked.

"Over two thousand. Gonna be a good Rodeo." Pete shook the box to make sure it was empty, glancing curiously at Russ and Colly as he did so. Colly realized that Russ was still clasping her hand. She pulled it away.

"This is my sister-in-law, Colly," Russ said belatedly.

Pete nodded and tipped his hat. "Y'all have a good one." He left the tent with the snake box balanced on his shoulder.

"Pete's Felix's nephew," Russ said. "He's taken over most of the ranch-foreman work since Felix's arthritis got bad."

"You trust him?"

"Pete grew up here. He's one of us."

Whoever murdered Denny is probably one of us, too, Colly thought. "What's in the other rings?"

"The next one's the show pit, where the snake handlers do demonstrations." Russ pointed down the row. "After that's the slaughter pit, and the last one's the skinning pit. The meat gets cooked and served at the food-prep stations, and the skins go to make wallets and belts and things."

Colly's stomach heaved. "This is barbaric."

"You'd feel different if you lived around here. Every year someone reaches into a woodpile or steps in the wrong spot and ends up maimed or dead. This makes a lot of money for charity. Serves a scientific purpose, too. C'mon, I'll show you."

He led Colly across the tent and past the "Staff Only" partition she'd noticed earlier. They went through an opening into a long, narrow side-chamber that, in the tent's circus days, had been used as a staging area and informal greenroom. Five or six people, all in their mid-twenties, sat on upturned five-gallon buckets around a card table at the far end of the room, chatting and eating what looked like carnitas wrapped in soft taco shells. When they saw Russ, they looked up briefly to wave hello.

"More ranch hands?" Colly asked.

"Grad students from A&M. This room's the research station."

Worktables laden with stainless-steel scales and other scientific instruments lined the walls. Not far from where the students were eating stood another round plywood pit, like the ones in the big tent, but smaller, with slightly shorter sides.

"Every rattler's weighed, measured, and sexed before it goes into the holding pit," Russ said. "And they're milked for antivenom. The data's sent to Texas Parks and Wildlife, and the antivenom's shipped to hospitals all around. The Rodeo's a win-win for everyone."

"Except the snakes."

Russ laughed. "Don't talk like that around Lowell. Last year, some animal-rights folks showed up with signs and a bullhorn. I had to stop him running them off with a shotgun."

For an hour, Colly tagged along as Russ made the rounds, inspecting the progress of the setup and chatting with the crew. It was after one o'clock when they mounted their horses for the ride back.

"You said there's someplace we can talk?"

Russ turned in the saddle. "Up ahead."

They reached the foot of the bluff and picked their way slowly up the switchback trail.

Halfway to the top, Russ stopped. "There's a good spot along here, but it's safer on foot."

They dismounted at a wide place in the trail and tethered the horses to a scrubby cedar growing out of the cliff face. Colly followed Russ down a path that ran along one of the natural shelves of rock, hugging the crumbling wall on her left and trying not to think about the dizzying drop on her right. After a while, they rounded the shoulder of a stony outcrop. There, the shelf widened out to a platform a dozen feet wide, north-facing and shaded by the cliff behind it.

"Randy and me used to come here when we were kids. It was our hideout." Russ picked up a chunk of flat sandstone the size of a dinner plate, turned it over, and handed it to Colly. It was covered in faded but still legible characters scratched in a child's hand. The characters were unfamiliar to Colly. She looked questioningly at Russ.

"Our secret outlaw-code. Randy made it up. He was the smart one." Russ sighed. "I don't come here much anymore." Throwing himself on the ground, he leaned against the cliff wall and stretched out his legs. "What'd you want to talk about?"

Holding the stone covered in her husband's childish scrawl, Colly felt suddenly depressed. She sat down facing Russ and gathered her thoughts.

Finally, she laid the stone aside. "I know everything, Russ. I know about the money Lowell took, and about Hoyer cooking the books for him—and why a random bird strike was enough to make that blade come apart and kill that woman."

Russ said nothing. The color drained from his face, but he nodded for her to continue. In a low voice, she recited the details of her conversation with Lowell that morning and with Jace Hoyer the day before. Russ listened quietly, staring off into the hazy distance.

After a few minutes, Colly paused. "None of this is news to you, is it?"

She waited, but Russ didn't answer.

"Well?"

His eyes darted quickly to hers. "What do you want me to say?"

Colly's earlier ambivalence vanished in a flash of anger. "Were you involved in this mess?"

Russ sighed. Taking off his Stetson, he set it on the ground and rubbed his eyes. "Not on purpose."

"What the hell does that mean?"

"I was an accessory after the fact, I guess you'd say." He tilted his head back against the stone wall. "I should've seen it coming. I knew Lowell gambled. Then his drinking got worse, and he was pissed off all the time—but I figured it was the divorce. I should've guessed."

"When did you learn the truth?"

Russ exhaled slowly. It was last April, he said, a month after Jace Hoyer's dismissal. Lowell had called and asked to talk. They met on the porch of Willis's cabin one evening while Willis was up at the house with Iris. Lowell blurted out the whole ugly story. He'd just found out that Denny Knox was seeing Brenda for therapy. What if

Denny knew something? If Brenda found out about the embezzlement, she'd destroy him—he'd lose his kids, maybe go to prison.

"How'd you react?"

"I cussed him out, said something like, 'Do you realize the bind you're putting me in? If I don't arrest you, I'm an accessory. I've got to send you to prison or break the law myself.'"

"And you chose option two."

Russ paused. "A lot was at stake, Col. Momma'd been so depressed since Randy and Victoria died, but she was finally coming out of it—going to dance classes, dating Talford. The scandal would've destroyed her and the company both. I was thinking about the kids, too. All the kids, including Satchel. Their futures would've been gone, just like that." He snapped his fingers. "I did my best. I insisted on a generous settlement for the dead lady's family, more than they asked for. And I told Lowell that if Brenda, or Jace, or anyone else blew the whistle, my hands would be tied—I'd have to turn the matter over to the county sheriff."

"That's awfully noble. How'd Lowell respond?"

"All he cared about was stopping Denny from blabbing anything to Brenda. The judge in Denny's arson case is a friend of the family. Dad helped him out of a financial jam once. Lowell wanted me to trump up some parole violation against Denny, then get the judge to incarcerate him."

"You're joking."

"I said if I found out he so much as nodded hello to Judge Appleton, I'd tell Brenda the whole story myself."

Colly sighed. Her initial anger was draining away, leaving a cold, sick feeling in its place. "Tell me the truth, do you know who killed Denny?"

"No, I don't."

"Could it have been Lowell?"

"I don't see how."

Colly chewed her lip. "Then explain why Felix called you instead of 911 when he found Denny's body. You said it was because his English is bad. But that doesn't pass the smell test, to me."

Russ winced. "You caught me off guard with that question the other day."

"Tell me now."

Russ picked up a pebble and rolled it between his fingers. The situation had turned out to be more complicated than he knew, he said. When he and Lowell met that night on the cabin porch, they'd had no idea that Felix was inside, cleaning Delilah's pen. The windows were open, and he'd overheard them talking. Considering it none of his business, he'd kept the knowledge to himself. But months later, when he found Denny's body by the stock pond and recognized him, Felix immediately understood the implications. A second murder at the ranch would bring a lot of scrutiny, particularly to Willis. But the fact that the victim was Jace Hoyer's stepson would put the company—and Lowell—under the microscope, as well.

"Felix has worked for us since before I was born," Russ said. "He's loyal as hell, especially to Momma. I think he's always been half in love with her. He didn't want her getting hurt."

It had been early morning when Felix called Russ, who raced to the ranch to examine the scene. "At first, I didn't notice the rabbit mask. I was afraid Lowell might've snapped and done it. I called him out to the pond. I wanted to look him in the eye when I asked him."

"And?"

Russ shook his head. "Lowell's got no poker face—that's why he's a rotten gambler. When he saw Denny, he was floored. He thought Willis did it, which made sense to me, too, at the time."

The brothers had debated what to do. Lowell wanted to bury the body on the property and pretend nothing had happened. When the Hoyers reported Denny missing, Russ could go through the motions of a search, conclude the boy ran away, and leave it at that. Delinquents ran off all the time.

But Russ had refused. He'd notified the county sheriff, who'd called in the Rangers.

"It's nice to know you draw the line somewhere."

Russ scowled and tossed the pebble over the cliff. "Keeping mum about Lowell is one thing. But you think I'd let Jolene Hoyer suffer not knowing what happened to her boy? Besides, once I saw the mask, I knew we had a serial killer. Whether it was Willis or somebody else, I couldn't let some maniac go around killing kids."

Colly studied his face. "I want to believe you. But you've lied from the beginning." She gave him a hard look. "Is there anything else I need to know?"

He shook his head. "Nothing. I swear."

"For God's sake, Russ, the case was already closed. Why'd you ask me to investigate if you didn't want this stuff coming out?"

Russ's forehead puckered into a frown. "Momma and Avery convinced me Willis didn't kill Denny. And I knew Lowell couldn't have, because he didn't know about the first rabbit mask, back in '98. A killer's running loose. He might—"

Colly cut him off. "Wait—you said Lowell was with you in Paint Rock the day Denny was killed."

Russ nodded, confused.

"Now you're saying you knew he couldn't be the killer because of the rabbit mask? Why would that matter if he had an airtight alibi?"

Russ stared. "Like you said, he could've hired a hitman—"

Colly scrambled to her feet. "That Paint Rock alibi's bullshit, isn't it?"

He pressed the heels of his hands into his eyes and said nothing.

"Russ—*why*?"

He was silent for so long that she thought he wasn't going to answer. Finally, he sighed. "Lowell claimed he was in bed with a hangover most of that day. If the Rangers uncovered the embezzlement, I was afraid they'd think—" He shrugged lamely. "I didn't see the harm in saying he was with me since I knew he didn't do it."

"I'm not the Rangers, Russ. Why'd you lie to me? You just swore there was nothing else."

"It seemed simpler." He looked up at her bleakly. "I know how that sounds. But if I told you I lied to the Rangers, you'd want to know why. The embezzlement's got nothing to do with Denny's murder. So I thought—"

"You thought you could use me to solve your problems while you made sure the family's dirty laundry stayed in the hamper," Colly snapped. "Is that why you showed up with wine last night? To play on my emotions, find out how much I know?" She felt something on her cheek and dashed the tears away angrily with her fingertips.

"Of course not." Russ climbed to his feet. "I didn't want to put you in the same bind I was in. Ignorance is bliss, and all that. I'm sorry, Col. I thought I was doing the right thing."

"That's your problem, Russ—you're weak. Weak people are dangerous because they can always convince themselves they're doing the right thing."

Russ stared at her miserably, then stooped to pick up his hat. "What are you going to do?"

"I don't know. I need to think. I should demand your resignation. For now, you're going to recuse yourself."

"From this case?"

"From all police work. If you don't want me telling everyone why, you better get the flu or think up some other excuse for taking a few days off."

Russ was staring at the horizon, rotating his Stetson by the brim. "Okay."

"Now get me the hell out of here. I want to go home."

Chapter 26

They rode back to the barn in silence. Leaving Russ to unsaddle the horses, Colly walked quickly towards her car, hoping to get away without being spotted. Nearing the house, she was dismayed to see Iris, in brightly colored garden gloves and a wide-brimmed sunhat, pruning the rose bushes by the porch.

Her mother-in-law greeted her cheerfully. Where was Russ? What did Colly think of the Rodeo grounds? How was the investigation going? When was Satchel coming back to the ranch for another visit? Colly and he must both come soon. What about tomorrow evening? It was Lowell's weekend to have Logan and Minnie. He'd be helping with opening night at the Rattlesnake Rodeo, and Iris had promised to babysit. Alice would be there, as well. They could grill burgers and then all take the children to the Rodeo.

Colly hedged, murmuring something about a possible dinner with Brenda and her friend.

Iris's face lit up. She clapped her gloved hands. "I'll babysit Satchel. No, no, I insist. He can spend the night."

Over Iris's shoulder, Colly spotted Russ walking slowly up the barn path. His shoulders sagged and his eyes were on the ground. Hastily, she thanked her mother-in-law and hurried to her car.

A few minutes later, she was speeding south on the Old Ranch Way when her phone rang. It was Avery. She'd finished canvassing the farmers on Salton Road and had turned up some curious bits of information, but she wasn't sure of their significance. Did Colly want to meet at the police station to debrief?

Colly hesitated. Lunchtime was long past, and she smelled like horse. "How about the farmhouse? Have you eaten? We can have a sandwich while we talk."

"I'll be there in ten," Avery said.

When Colly reached the house, Avery was leaning against the squad car smoking a cigarette. Colly pulled into the carport, and Avery joined her there.

"Get anything good at the turbine plant?" she asked as Colly emerged from the car.

"I wouldn't say *good*. Definitely interesting." Colly rummaged in her purse for the house key as she climbed the short flight of steps to the side door. "Come on in. Let me wash up before—"

Something crunched beneath her boots, and she froze. The door stood slightly ajar. A small windowpane near the doorknob had been broken out, and glass shards littered the steps. Colly turned and laid a finger on her lips. Avery nodded, and they drew their sidearms. Colly handed her the house key and motioned towards the front door. Avery nodded again and slipped noiselessly out of the carport.

Using her elbow, Colly pushed gently on the door. It swung open with a nerve-racking squeak. She stepped carefully over the broken glass into the kitchen. The tumblers used as last night's wine glasses still sat by the sink beside a partial bowl of soggy Cheerios, the remnants of Satchel's breakfast. Other than a couple of faint muddy boot prints on the linoleum, the room appeared undisturbed.

Colly cleared the pantry and checked the dining room. She found Avery in the foyer, gripping her gun. In front of her stood three suitcases, lined up by size like a row of nesting dolls. They were Colly's. When she'd left the house that morning, they'd been lying half-unpacked on the bedroom floor upstairs.

Colly's skin crawled, but there was no time now to wonder or to process. She did a quick sweep of the living room, then led the way up the stairs. The women split up. Colly checked the bathroom and the bedroom designated for Satchel, though he'd never slept in it, while Avery checked the master bedroom.

"All clear," Avery called, her voice unnaturally loud in the stillness. "Come look at this."

Holstering her gun, Colly hurried up the hall and stopped short in the bedroom doorway. She was not a morning person. It was usually all she could do to get herself and Satchel washed, dressed, and out the door. When she'd left the room that morning, there'd been a heap of towels and discarded clothing piled on an armchair by the window. Satchel had wet the bed again during the night, and Colly had stripped the sheets and dumped them in a corner to be dealt with later.

Now, the bed was made, and the clothes on the chair had vanished. The room was immaculate except for a small pile of debris on the bed—some type of granulated material mixed with shards of transparent plastic or glass. A claw hammer sat on the nightstand nearby. The identity of the shattered object didn't register with Colly until she noticed ants crawling on the comforter.

For a long time, she stared numbly at the pathetic little heap of wreckage. Then, her emotions caught up, and she felt herself shaking with rage. For several minutes, she paced the room, venting her indignation in a long stream of profanity.

"What the *hell?*" she realized she was spluttering over and over. She wanted to hit something. Without thinking, she reached for the hammer, but Avery stopped her.

"Better not touch anything. Russ'll want to get Earla out here. Come on, let's go."

Colly clenched her fists and nodded. Following Avery outside, she leaned wearily against the squad car. The initial burst of rage had dissipated, and a deep sense of violation was setting in. There was something appallingly calculated about the scene. The prim neatness of the packed suitcases and tidied bedroom—juxtaposed with the frenzied annihilation of the ant farm—suggested a kind of horrible lunacy. And yet that felt wrong, somehow.

She became aware that Avery was speaking.

"Shouldn't we call Russ?"

Pushing emotion aside, Colly checked the time: three-thirty. She was in no mood to see or speak with Russ right now, but it couldn't be helped. He might be recused from police work, but he couldn't be cut out of the loop on this. He owned the farmhouse.

She dialed, and he picked up immediately.

When she told him what had happened, his voice was grim. "Hang tight, I'll be there soon."

Colly started to dial Brenda next, then remembered she was in the middle of a session with Satchel. Instead, she texted: *Call when you can.*

"Think Denny's killer did this?" Avery asked. Her eyes were bright and her face was flushed with excitement.

How simple life was for the young, Colly thought. She couldn't remember a time when she'd had the luxury of such single-minded eagerness untainted by the angst of responsibility. There was something to be said for the unattached life in police work.

"I think it's the same person who rigged the snake and texted the anonymous threat."

"Gotta be the killer, right?"

Colly's head was throbbing. She rubbed her temples. "Probably."

"Why smash an ant farm, though?"

Because threatening me directly didn't work, Colly thought. *God, I dread telling Satchel.* "Who knows?" she said aloud.

"Bright side—this proves Hoyer's not the guy. He's in jail."

Colly looked at her. "You're right, that's something." She pulled herself together with effort. "Tell me about Salton Road."

Avery eagerly recounted her morning's work. None of the Salton Road farmers remembered seeing anything unusual Monday afternoon, when the baseball cap was taken, other than the police activity around the fireworks stand. There'd been no sightings of suspicious characters or unfamiliar vehicles in the vicinity.

"So that's a wash, unless someone has a sudden brainstorm," Avery said. But when she'd questioned them about the day Denny was killed, the results had been more intriguing. One farmer reported that he and his wife had seen an older woman heading south on Salton Road that afternoon.

Avery paused. "The lady was on foot, dressed up in church clothes and carrying a giant purse over her arm. Road dead-ends north of their house, so either they missed her when she came up from the south, or she cut across the fields from the direction of the fireworks stand. They figured she was a neighbor's relative, since their dogs didn't bark at her."

"There's no mention of this in the case file," Colly said sharply.

"I know. They left for Colorado to visit their daughter a couple days after the murder, so the Rangers must've missed them in the canvass. By the time they came home, the investigation was focused on Willis." Avery chewed her lip. "What do you think?"

"Denny was a big kid. I doubt an old woman could kill him."

"Maybe she's connected to the killer somehow. He might've dropped her there when he put Denny's bike behind the fireworks stand."

"Leaving her toddling through the pastures for anyone to spot?"

"Maybe they argued. Or maybe he didn't want her seeing where he dumped the body."

"Whoever she is, we need to talk to her. Let's track her down if we can," Colly said. "Anything else?"

Avery's face clouded. "Nothing solid. But I got a weird vibe from Dave Carroway. He was evasive, practically slammed the door in my face."

"He was never a suspect?"

Avery shook her head. "The Rangers checked him out because of his history with the Newlands. But his alibi was good."

"Think he's upset we're looking into the case? Willis molested him when he was little—makes sense he wouldn't want Willis's name cleared."

"Maybe." Avery sounded unconvinced.

"We'll let him stew a couple days and try again."

Avery asked about Colly's interview with Lowell at the plant. Colly told her the story and was wondering how much, if anything, to mention about the talk with Russ, when they heard tires on gravel. Russ's SUV was coming up the drive. He parked behind the squad car and jumped out.

"Earla's on her way. Y'all all right?" His question was inclusive, but he was looking at Colly.

"We're fine," she said. "Nothing stolen, as far as I can tell. Only the window and ant farm were damaged. But there's something twisted about it."

She described their search of the house. Russ was still asking questions when Earla arrived on her motorcycle, accompanied by

Fat Boy in the sidecar. Colly and Avery were obliged to go over the story again while Earla unloaded her kit and donned coveralls, gloves, and shoe covers.

"Y'all wait here," she said. "Stay, Fat Boy." When she disappeared into the house carrying her evidence kit and camera, the dog flopped down on the porch with a groan.

The wait was awkward. Colly wanted nothing to do with Russ, but since she wasn't prepared to explain the situation to Avery, she was forced to act like nothing was wrong. Russ tactfully asked no questions about the case, though the break-in at the house made it impossible to avoid the subject entirely.

It was nearly five o'clock when Brenda called. She'd been in session all afternoon and had just seen Colly's text.

Colly was surprised. "You weren't with Satchel that whole time, were you?"

Brenda lowered her voice. "I thought he could use it. He's . . . struggling."

Colly's throat tightened. "Is he okay? He scared me last night, the way he acted."

"Let's talk later. Need me to bring him home?"

"I'm not sure what to do." Quickly, Colly told her about the break-in, though she omitted most of the details.

"Oh God, that's awful."

"Can Satchel stay at your place tonight? I'll bring his things later."

"Absolutely. You'll stay too, I hope?"

"I'm not sure yet. Let me talk to Satch."

After what Brenda had said, Colly expected Satchel to sound upset. But he seemed happy when he took the phone, and he was thrilled at the prospect of spending the night with his cousins.

"Bring my ant farm when you come—I wanna show Logan and Minnie."

Colly replied evasively and hung up, feeling both guilty and reassured.

The sun was sinking towards the horizon when Earla emerged from the house. She looked tired, her silvery braids frazzled.

"Almost done," she said.

Russ stood up. "What did you find?"

"No suspicious fingerprints. But our pal Mr. Size Ten Boot's been here. Break-in's staged, too. Window's smashed from the inside."

"I locked up when I left this morning," Colly said.

"A baby could pick that lock with a teething biscuit. Or maybe the perp had a key. Who's got access?"

Russ scratched his head. "My in-laws lived here sixty years. God knows how many keys they handed out or lost. They kept a spare on a nail in the carport. Probably still there."

"You never changed the locks after they died?"

Russ looked abashed. "I always meant to."

Colly sighed. "This town's a criminal's paradise."

Earla grunted in agreement. "Y'all come in a sec—I need input."

They followed her inside. The three suitcases, still unopened, now lay prone on the foyer floor. Stepping around them, Earla led the way up the stairs into the master bedroom. Colly glanced around. The remnants of the ant farm had been bagged. Blankets, sheets, and mattress pad were peeled back, exposing the bare mattress.

"Are these the same sheets you took off the bed this morning?" Earla asked.

Colly nodded. "They were urine-soaked."

"They're clean, now. Perp must've washed 'em." Earla rubbed her forehead with the back of her gloved hand. "I didn't open the suitcases yet. Wanted you there for that."

251

They followed her downstairs. Earla knelt and unzipped the largest case. The clothes lay in immaculate order—jeans, tops, socks, and panties carefully folded; bras nested in a neat stack.

"This look right?" Earla asked.

Colly flushed angrily. "It's mine, but when I left the house this morning, half this stuff was in the hamper."

"Christ Almighty," Russ muttered.

The middle-sized case contained more of the same—Colly's clothing, washed and meticulously repacked. The smallest was Satchel's, and when Earla unzipped it, everyone froze. A folded sheet of white printer paper lay within, and beside that, on top of a stack of child-sized t-shirts, was a brown-gray swatch of fur the size of a human hand. Through its empty eyeholes, the red fabric of the topmost shirt was visible, giving the thing a glaring, demonic look.

"Oh, *shit*," Avery said.

No one else spoke. Colly was aware of the noise of blood rushing in her ears. Finally, Earla raised her camera and began to take photographs.

"You've got gloves on," Russ said after a few minutes. "See if something's written on that paper."

Without a word, Earla set down her camera and gingerly unfolded the page, laying it on the open suitcase. On it was scrawled in rough block capitals: *FINAL WARNING. IT'S HARD TO GET BLOOD OUT OF THE WASH.*

Russ and Colly exchanged glances, and Avery cursed again. Earla picked up the camera.

An hour later, after documenting the scene, bagging the mask and note, and examining the other contents of the small suitcase, the forensics specialist stood with a groan, her knees cracking.

"I'll be honest, Russ, I'm out of my league here. The DPS crime lab should take over."

"No," Russ said firmly. "The Rangers had their chance." He shot Colly an embarrassed look. "But it's your call."

"I think I agree," she said slowly. "We're not going to solve the case through forensics. This break-in's the act of someone who's either terrified or cocky. He's taking stupider and stupider risks, which is good for us. Bringing in the Rangers might shut him down."

Russ nodded. He turned to Earla. "You're okay with releasing the scene?"

She shrugged and pulled off her gloves. "Nothing more I can do."

The four of them went out onto the porch. The sun had set and the azure sky deepened to a dark periwinkle. A few stars were already shining.

"What are you thinking, Earla?" Russ asked.

"That I could use a smoke." She patted her pockets absently.

Avery produced a pack and took a cigarette for herself, then offered one to Earla.

"I'll take one," Russ said.

Earla's brows rose. "Thought you quit."

"Yeah, well." He lit up and leaned against the porch rail. "Okay, Earla, what do you think?"

Earla dropped heavily onto the porch swing. "It's the same whackadoodle who rigged up that rattler."

"Why?"

"Who breaks into a place in broad daylight and stays long enough to do a couple loads of laundry? Same nutcase who stands in front of a house full of people rigging a booby trap in a minivan. This perp's got cojones."

"Psychotic?"

Earla frowned. "If he was irrational, he woulda got caught already."

"You think a sane person did this?" Avery sounded incredulous.

"I didn't say *sane*. Rational. Could be some upstanding-member-of-the-community type who passes for normal. But whoever it is, they're definitely a half-bubble off plumb. Probably fantasizes about going down in history as the 'Rabbit Face Killer' or some such nonsense." She turned to Colly. "Don't you reckon?"

"I'm not sure. I get the feeling there's some ideology behind this—I just can't figure out what it is."

Colly sighed, staring eastward through curling tendrils of cigarette smoke. Low in the sky, the moon, two days from the full, hung above the bluffs, where a long line of wind turbines turned slowly in the cold gray light.

Chapter 27

It was almost nine o'clock when everyone left the farmhouse. Colly packed pajamas, a toothbrush, and a change of clothes for Satchel and headed for town, her mind in turmoil. She'd always been able to reason her way to decisive action. But since the moment she'd seen the vacant red eyes staring up at her from Satchel's open suitcase, her brains had felt scrambled, and a heavy sense of dread and uncertainty had settled in her gut.

Until now, she hadn't been convinced that the person trying to frighten her off with dead snakes and threatening texts was the killer. But the appearance of this latest rabbit mask seemed to remove all doubt. What was the point of the break-in? Just to threaten her—*back off or I'll go after your grandson*? Or was it an elaborate attempt at misdirection? Either way, she could presumably protect Satchel by sending him back to Houston.

On the other hand, if the killer had decided to target Satchel— not to intimidate Colly, but for his own perverted reasons—there was no guarantee that distance would provide safety. They were dealing with the murderer of two young boys, after all. The thought that Satchel could be followed back to Houston by a psychopath while Colly remained 400 miles away in West Texas, helpless to protect him, was unbearable. Her only options were to keep him with her or abandon the case and take him home—an irresolvable dilemma. She wouldn't be able to live with herself if another child died in Crescent Bluff because she gave up the case. She knew what it felt like—a failure of that magnitude. How could she trust any decision she made? The thoughts churned, bringing little clarity. This place—so desolate and barren, with its rattlesnakes and thorns and haunted past—was getting under her skin in a way she couldn't afford. Her head throbbed. She hunched forward, gripping the steering wheel until her hands ached.

At Brenda's house, Colly knocked softly. Her sister-in-law answered the door in her robe and slippers.

"The kids are asleep. Satchel wanted to wait up for you, but he was exhausted. I put him to bed in some of Logan's old pajamas."

Colly swallowed her disappointment. At least she wouldn't have to explain to him why she hadn't brought the ant farm. She thanked Brenda and handed her the bag of Satchel's things. Brenda looked startled.

"Aren't you staying, too?"

Colly shook her head. "Things are developing fast. Anyone around me is in danger until we catch this nutjob."

"Tell me you're not going back to that creepy old farmhouse."

"I'll be fine." Colly patted her sidearm. "How was therapy today? You sounded concerned on the phone."

Brenda's face clouded. "I want to show you something."

She led Colly into the kitchen. A briefcase lay open on the table, and she rifled through it.

"This is an exercise Niall uses for assessing trauma in kids. I had Satchel draw a picture of what other people see when they look at him, and a picture of what he feels like on the inside."

She laid two crayon drawings side by side. The first was a child's sketch of a smiling boy with rosy cheeks and lemon-yellow hair. He was dressed in a bright orange t-shirt and blue pants and held a purple flower. The second was hard to make out at first. Most of the page was covered with dense black scribbles. In the bottom corner, a tiny gray stick-figure crouched, its arms thrown over its head. The figure had no mouth, and its eyes were huge and terrified. Red-orange flames lapped at its feet and sides.

Colly stared at the drawings. Tears stung her eyes. "I thought he was doing better. His therapist's been so encouraging."

"Most family counselors aren't really qualified to assess this level of trauma. I'm not, either," Brenda added quickly. "But Niall is. His post-doc work's on the link between childhood trauma and psychopathy."

"Satchel's no psychopath," Colly said hotly.

"I just meant he's been through a lot—and there's a specialist here. You're coming to dinner at Niall's tomorrow, right? We can pick his brains then."

Colly stared down at the drawings. "I guess it wouldn't hurt."

Before leaving, she looked in on Satchel, who was asleep on a trundle bed beside Logan's. She brushed back his hair. He looked innocent and vulnerable curled on his side in pajamas two sizes too large. She thought of the cowering, mouthless stick figure in the drawing, then of the rabbit mask with its leering red eyeholes. A wave of nausea seized her. *I can't screw this up. He's got no one else.* She kissed him and tiptoed out.

"I hope he doesn't have an accident," she said to Brenda at the door. "The bed-wetting's gotten worse."

"Doesn't matter at all." Brenda switched on the porchlight. "Are you sure you don't want to stay? I worry about you out there alone."

"Thanks, but I could use the quiet time. I'm missing something about this case—I need to think."

Pulling up the farmhouse drive a half-hour later, Colly was glad she'd left the lights on. Russ had nailed a board over the broken windowpane in the kitchen door before he'd left, but even so, Colly drew her pistol and cleared the house before feeling comfortable enough to relax.

She was exhausted and very hungry, having eaten nothing but a couple spoons of peanut butter since early morning. She took a long shower. Then, donning yoga pants and an old sweatshirt of Randy's, she microwaved a macaroni-and-cheese cup, opened a longneck beer, and curled on the sofa with her laptop. She typed "childhood trauma and psychopathy" into the search bar of her browser, but stopped herself. That was not a topic to research at night if she hoped to get any sleep.

She put down the computer and sat chewing macaroni without tasting it, staring vacantly at the wall and trying to think. She'd run down so many leads and uncovered so many crimes and potential motives in the last twenty-four hours that she thought she must be nearing some kind of breakthrough in the case. In light of all she'd learned, Jace, and Lowell, and even Russ made for credible murder suspects. And yet their stories, though each pathetic and damning in its own way, had struck her as wholly plausible. Even if she was wrong, and one of them had killed Denny Knox, what possible motive could any of them have for killing Adam Parker so long ago?

With a grunt of frustration, she tossed the empty macaroni cup onto the coffee table and picked up her purse. Finding her keys, she went outside and retrieved two file boxes—one labeled "Adam Parker" and the other "Dennis Knox"—from the trunk of her car, where she'd put them for safekeeping when Russ agreed to let her take them to study. She'd read through the files a couple of times, but experience had taught her to go back to the beginning when she hit a wall.

Returning to the living room, she put on her reading glasses and, laying a fat three-ring binder on her knees, she began to read slowly and methodically through the first report.

Adam Parker, aged twelve, a boy with a history of truancy and vandalism, disappeared from his home sometime during the night of July 30, 1998. That same night, the Parkers' house burned to the ground. Connie Parker, aged forty-five, died in the fire. Budd Parker, fifty-two, suffered burns over 70 percent of his body but survived. Avery Parker, eight, received third-degree burns to her face and neck and minor smoke-inhalation damage to her lungs. Blood tests showed that Connie Parker had legally prescribed sedatives in her system, though at double the prescribed dosage, which explained why she did not wake up in time to escape the fire. Budd Parker was heavily intoxicated with alcohol.

The fire was determined to be arson. An accelerant had been used to start it, and the point of origin was the living room carpet. Law enforcement had found an empty gasoline container belonging to the Parkers in the front yard. Investigators thought that Adam had started the fire before running away, so a warrant was issued for his arrest. But nearly a month later, on August 25, Newland Ranch foreman Felix Arredondo noticed an unusual amount of vulture activity around one of the property's stock ponds and, upon investigating, discovered Adam's badly decomposed body lying on the bank.

The medical examiner determined that Adam had died by strangulation, probably on the night of his disappearance. He'd been badly beaten shortly before death and submerged almost immediately thereafter. He was fully dressed in the clothing he'd worn on July 30, though signs indicated that he had been dressed after death by someone else. The body had apparently been weighted down with chains to prevent it from floating. The chains, which were found at the bottom of the pond, had been cut with bolt cutters, then the body removed from the pond and posed on the bank. What appeared to be the hide of a rabbit's face, tanned on one side, had been rolled and tied with pink ribbon and placed in the dead boy's hand. The hide had not been submerged in water and was presumably put there by the same person who'd posed the body. Investigators believed that this was done by the killer for unknown reasons, since an innocent person who discovered a corpse would naturally notify police. The hide was determined to have come from a type of wild hare native to Great Britain.

Colly took off her glasses and chewed thoughtfully on one of the temple tips. *Great Britain?* The mystery of the hares' masks was by far the weirdest aspect of these cases, and their presence on both bodies the most striking similarity—but there were others. Both Adam and Denny had a history of truancy and troubled home lives; both had been strangled; both were found at the stock pond by Felix; neither had foreign DNA on his body.

However, there were important differences, as well. Denny, unlike Adam, disappeared in broad daylight while riding his bike; he was found less than twenty-four hours after his death; he was naked, had sedatives in his bloodstream, and was never submerged in water. There were no injuries to his body other than a ligature mark around the neck.

Colly dug through the box and found a fat envelope of 8x10 color photos. She looked through a large sheaf taken at the stock pond, then through some taken at the hospital the night of the fire. One showed a stringy man lying naked on a gurney. Ropes of skin hung off his charred limbs like tattered clothing. A respirator obscured his blackened face. Another depicted a young girl wrapped in a white sheet and huddled in a wheelchair. Her hair was singed to the scalp, and a raw burn covered her right cheek and throat. She was staring at the camera with huge dark eyes, the expression on her face one of absolute desolation. Colly looked at it for a long time. Avery had been only a year older than Satchel, then. She knew what it felt like to have one's life disintegrate in a single moment. No wonder Satchel was drawn to her.

The next set of photos, taken by fire investigators at the Parker home the following day, showed the still-smoking husk of a small frame house. It sat back from the road in a weedy lot. Shots of the interior revealed that some parts of the house had been completely consumed. The living room was a jumble of black and blistered wood. In the master bedroom, all that remained of the bed on which Connie Parker had died was a set of scorched steel springs. But other areas had fared better. A photograph taken in the room shared by the children showed only moderate damage. In the foreground stood a pink daybed with a little soot-streaked comforter and sheets depicting characters from *The Lion King*. A pillow lay on the floor nearby, covered in flecks of ash.

Colly started to set the photo aside, but then stopped. She grabbed her phone and scrutinized the photo for several seconds with the magnifying app.

"Oh my God." She checked her watch. Eleven-thirty. "Screw it," she muttered, dialing the phone.

It rang five times before she heard Avery's voice, groggy and annoyed. "Yeah?"

"I need you at the farmhouse—*ASAP*."

For a moment, the line was silent. "Did something happen?" The younger woman was alert now. Colly heard the rustle of blankets being thrown back.

"Yes."

"On my way. What—"

But Colly hung up before Avery finished speaking.

Chapter 28

Colly paced the porch for twenty minutes until she spotted head-lights coming up the drive. A dusty Volkswagen pulled into the yard. Avery climbed out in ratty Converse sneakers, jeans, and a rumpled t-shirt with "Whatever" printed on the front. She wore heavy-rimmed glasses, and her purple-streaked hair was tied back with a scrunchie.

She looks like a ninth-grader, Colly thought.

Avery walked towards the house. "What's up?"

Colly was in no mood for pleasantries. "You know what happened to your brother, don't you? You've been lying about it for twenty years."

Avery stopped at the bottom of the porch steps. Her face was ashen. "What—"

"No more bullshit—I'm sick of it." Colly threw open the screen door, and Avery followed her warily into the house. In the living room, she stopped when she saw the crime-scene photos on the coffee table.

"Sit down," Colly said.

Avery lowered herself cautiously onto the sofa. Colly sat beside her and picked up the photo of Avery's childhood bedroom. "You told me you were in bed asleep when that fire broke out—that you only remember your father carrying you out of the house. That's what you told investigators in '98, as well." She thrust the photo under Avery's nose. "I want to know what really happened."

Avery stared down at the image of the blackened walls and ash-covered bed, and her brows knotted.

"You're going to make me drag it out of you?" Colly jabbed with her forefinger at a small pink shape in the photo, clearly visible at one end of the bed. "That's a folded nightgown. I do that, too—put my pajamas under the pillow in the morning. You were in street clothes when the EMTs arrived. The other day, you said you were wearing your nightgown when your father carried you outside, but you changed into clothes you got off the clothesline. That didn't make much sense to me. Then again, people do weird things in a crisis." Colly shrugged. "But in that case, your nightie should be outside the house, not here."

Avery's eyes were large. She said nothing.

"I'm giving you a chance to explain. If you're going to be stubborn, I'll call Russ." Colly dropped the photo and reached for her phone.

"Don't," Avery said quickly. "Please."

Colly crossed her arms. "I want the truth."

Avery nodded, but said nothing for a while. When she spoke, her voice was so quiet that Colly had to lean in to hear. "My old man was a drunk. He never had a job that I remember. My mom had three, but if she spent too much on groceries and not enough on booze, he'd hit her. He hit all of us. I used to wear long sleeves to school to hide the bruises, no matter how hot it was. But Adam got the worst of it. He'd try to protect us."

Avery's scowl softened. Adam had been a good kid, she told Colly. He'd gotten into trouble a lot, of course, not having a decent role model. He was so starved for male attention and approval that he'd latch onto anyone who paid him the slightest notice. He used to follow the high-school boys around like a shadow—a lot of his vandalism and truancy were attempts to impress them. Of all the older boys, he had particularly admired Niall Shaw.

Colly sat back. "Shaw?"

Avery's face darkened. "Adam thought he was the coolest. He was from out of state, so he seemed different—more sophisticated, I guess. Even in high school. He'd talk about Montana. And England, where his dad came from. Adam loved listening to him, and Shaw liked having his own personal fan club. Even at my age, I could see it."

"That's why you don't like him?"

"Shaw's an asshole. He'd let Adam tag along on his fishing trips and be his gofer—but not really his friend. He made that clear. Adam always came home depressed after being with him."

"We're getting off track. What happened the night of the fire?"

Avery looked away. It had been a typical evening, she said. During dinner, her father had lost his temper and started beating her mother over some little something—the tuna casserole was too hot, or not hot enough. Adam was twelve, big for his age. He'd begun to intervene more assertively in recent months.

"Adam actually pulled a knife on my dad that night," Avery said. "And it worked. The old man backed off." Their mother, shaken and in pain from the beating, went straight to bed. "I guess she took sedatives, but I didn't know that, then." Avery sighed. "Dad went out to the Blue Moon after supper, as usual. That was our favorite time of day, Adam and me. He had an old Nintendo Mom found at the thrift store. We played Donkey Kong till pretty late. Finally, Adam said we should go to bed since it was a school night. He got into his pajamas, but I was being a brat, dragging my feet." She swallowed. "That's when the old man came home."

Several hours of heavy drinking at the saloon had not improved Budd Parker's temper. He walked through the door spoiling for a fight, and when he saw dirty dishes and congealed casserole still on the table, he exploded.

"He came into our room screaming and went after me with the belt," Avery said. "Adam jumped in to stop him. Dad was still pissed about what happened at dinner, I guess. He yelled, 'I'll teach you to pull a knife on me, you little bastard.' He dropped the belt and started punching Adam, kicking him, hitting him with anything he could find. Finally, he grabbed the belt, but instead of flogging Adam with it, he started choking him. I was crouched down between my bed and dresser. I saw the whole thing. The old man was holding him up off the ground, and Adam was thrashing, clawing at the belt. I watched his face turn red, then purple. His tongue was sticking out, all fat, like a sausage." Avery hesitated. "Then he stopped thrashing, and his arms dropped. He was looking right at me when he died."

Colly realized she'd been holding her breath. She exhaled sharply. "Your father murdered Adam."

Avery nodded. She was staring at her fingers plaited in her lap. "Mom slept through the whole thing."

A thousand questions flooded Colly's mind, but she set them aside. "Then what?"

"It's a little fuzzy—I must've been in shock. I remember my father dropping Adam in a heap, like a rag doll. He wasn't angry anymore. He just stood there. Then he nudged Adam with his boot and said, 'Enough playacting. Get up,' or something. He was drunk—I guess it took a while to sink in."

When he finally realized what he'd done, Budd Parker shifted into self-preservation mode. "He stripped off Adam's pajamas and put his clothes back on him," Avery said. "It's hard to dress a dead body. He wanted me to help, but I couldn't move. Then, he threw my brother over his shoulder. He grabbed my arm and dragged me along. He carried Adam to the truck, and he told me to get some old chains out of the toolshed. My teeth wouldn't stop chattering. I thought he might kill me, too. He put the chains in the truck, and he made me get in. I don't know why. Maybe he was scared I'd call 911 if he left me at the house. I asked where we were going, but he didn't answer. We drove up the highway, swerving like crazy. I can still see the yellow centerline waving like a ribbon. If a cop had stopped us, maybe . . ." Avery shrugged. "We ended up at the stock pond. The old man wrapped the chains around Adam and waded out to the middle. He pushed my brother under and watched to make sure he stayed down. Then we drove home. On the way, he said if I ever told anyone, he'd kill me and my mother, both. He said when people asked, I should say that Adam was in the house when I went to bed, and when I woke up, he was gone."

Avery stopped and looked up. Her eyes were dry, her expression dazed and vacant. She seemed stupefied with the effort of reliving that night's events.

"I'm sorry," Colly said gently. "Look, I get why you kept quiet as a kid. But Russ said your dad's been dead for years. You *knew* Willis was innocent—of murder, anyway. Why didn't you tell anyone? Your story would've gotten him a new trial, at least."

Avery twisted her fingers miserably in her lap and said nothing.

Colly felt a surge of weary irritation. "This changes everything. I've been investigating under the assumption there's just one killer, and you knew that isn't true."

Avery remained silent. As Colly sat wondering what to do or say next, the crime-scene photos on the coffee table caught her eye. A sudden thought struck her. "How did the fire start?"

Avery stiffened. Her eyes darted to Colly's.

"It was you, wasn't it? You torched the house," Colly said.

She could see the pulse pounding in the younger woman's throat. After a minute, Avery gave a barely discernible nod.

"Tell me."

Avery nodded again but seemed unable to start.

"You got back from the stock pond," Colly prompted. "Then what? Your mother was still asleep?"

"Yeah." Avery cleared her throat. "The old man drank a few stiff ones and was out cold on the couch in fifteen minutes. By then it was three a.m. I went back to my bedroom. It was a wreck, broken stuff everywhere. Adam's pajamas were still on the floor. They were wet. The room stank of urine.

"As I stood there, some switch flipped in my brain. I hated my father—I wanted to hurt him like he hurt Adam. I remembered seeing the gas can in the shed when I got the chains out. I didn't think—I just ran outside and got the can. It was half-full. I poured it all over the living room."

Avery's mouth was dry. She licked her lips. "My father's lighter was on the coffee table. I—I lit it and tossed it on the floor. Then I picked up the empty gas can, and I ran.

"I stood outside, watching the flames through the living room window. I could hear the smoke alarm shrieking. And that's when it dawned on me that my mother was trapped in there, too. I'd been so focused on revenge that I'd blocked everything else. I banged on her bedroom window, but nothing happened. So I ran back inside. I made it partway down the hall, but the smoke was so thick. Fire was everywhere." She touched her scarred cheek. "Everything went black. Next thing I knew, someone was carrying me outside. It was my father. He laid me on the grass and ran back into the house. I guess he tried to get my mother, but the place was an inferno by then. When he came out, he rolled in the dirt, screaming. That's all I remember till sirens woke me up, and we were in the ambulance."

"You never told anyone?"

Avery shook her head slowly.

"Why not?"

"I killed my own mother."

"You were a traumatized kid."

Avery said nothing.

Colly picked up the photo of Budd Parker, burned and blackened, on the hospital gurney. She stared at it thoughtfully. "The Rangers thought Adam's killer got him out of the pond. But that's impossible."

Avery's eyes flickered with a hint of their usual animation. "Exactly—Dad was in the hospital for six months. Someone else found Adam and posed his body with that rabbit mask—then twenty years later, the same psycho killed Denny."

Colly leaned back and sighed. "Maybe the Rangers were right about Willis, after all. I thought there was no way he could've transported Adam to the ranch—but this means he didn't have to. He could've found Adam floating in the pond, already dead. Maybe that somehow got him fixated on the idea of murder."

Avery frowned. "It can't be Willis."

"Why not? The doctors who evaluated him said he had an antisocially disordered brain structure—whatever that means. If he was already predisposed, finding Adam could've triggered him, somehow. Then he had twenty years in prison to fantasize about it. Maybe when he saw Denny hanging out at the stock pond last fall, the temptation was too much."

"But Willis had a solid alibi, and he passed a polygraph," Avery said. "Besides, who else but the killer could've broken into the farmhouse today and left that rabbit mask in Satchel's suitcase?" Avery's eyes, larger and darker than usual through the heavy-rimmed glasses, shone with impatience. "This is why I pushed Russ for the case review. I owed Willis that much, at least. I knew the Rangers had it wrong. I thought if we could prove Willis didn't plant that mask on Denny, everyone would realize he couldn't have planted the one on Adam, either. Don't you see?"

Colly experienced a quick flash of anger. "Sure, I see. You wanted to free your conscience without having to fess up to the whole truth. So I had to waste four days finding it out for myself."

Avery flushed. "Are you going to report me?"

"*Report* you? I should have you arrested. You're guilty of obstruction, at the very least."

Avery was silent. She stared at her feet. After a minute, she cleared her throat. "What happens now?"

"I don't know." Colly leaned back and stared at the ceiling, thinking hard. Avery's story answered some questions. But it raised many others. It had been difficult enough to imagine a single-killer scenario that explained all the evidence. But two killers? The person who'd found Adam's body was strong enough to pull him out of the pond—presumably an adult male or possibly more than one person. He, or they, must have cared about the boy and wanted his body discovered—yet for some reason didn't call the police. That was riddle enough. But what was the hare's mask about? And why would a person like that murder another boy two decades later in a similar way? Willis's sexual deviance and brain abnormalities might explain it; but if Willis was innocent, Colly couldn't imagine a scenario that accounted for all the variables.

A bump, followed by a faint clattering noise, interrupted her train of thought. The women leapt up, and Colly snatched her holstered pistol from the coffee table. "That came from outside."

Avery nodded. "I'm not armed."

"Stay behind me, then."

Colly moved quickly to the foyer and opened the front door. A white envelope fell onto the mat. Ignoring it, Colly stepped outside. In the moonlight, a dark figure was running very fast down the long drive towards the road.

"Stop—police!" Colly started down the steps.

The screen door slammed, and Avery flew past.

So much for staying behind me, Colly thought. *Hell's bells, that kid can move.* She followed as quickly as she could in her sock feet but was only halfway down the drive when Avery tackled the fleeing man. He went down with a loud grunt. By the time Colly reached them, Avery was sitting on the man's back and twisting his arm in a hammerlock.

"I've got you covered," Colly said. "Check him."

Avery rolled the man onto his back and patted him down, then stepped away. "He's all right."

"Get up," Colly ordered.

The man climbed slowly to his feet, cursing softly and rubbing his shoulder.

Avery switched on her phone's flashlight app and turned it on the stranger, who quickly raised his hand to shield his eyes.

"Who are you?" Colly demanded.

The stranger remained silent.

"Lower your hand."

The man obeyed. Avery shone the light full in his face, then let out a long, low whistle of surprise.

Chapter 29

For several seconds, the captive stood blinking in the glare of the flashlight. He was a stranger, Colly saw—a white male in his mid-thirties, broad-shouldered and dark-haired, with the tanned face and pale forehead of a hat-wearing outdoorsman.

"Well, well. Dave Carroway," Avery said finally. "What the hell are you doing here?"

Colly stared. "Dave *Carroway*?"

"Leave me alone—I didn't do nothing."

"How'd you get here? Where's your truck?" Avery demanded.

"Down yonder." Carroway gestured towards the road. "I just come to leave a note. Read that, and lemme go home." He turned, but Avery blocked the way.

"Someone broke into this house today, and now you're snooping around. You've got some explaining to do."

Carroway spat. "Have it your way. I ain't no burglar. Just get that damn light out of my face."

They walked back to the farmhouse in silence. The white envelope still lay on the mat. Colly picked it up. In the living room, she sat on the couch. Avery flopped down beside her and pointed Carroway to an armchair.

Colly studied the newcomer. The indoor lighting revealed a pinched, sharp-featured face and arms pocked with blotchy scars—from long-healed meth sores, most likely. The knees of his jeans were dirty and ripped where he'd landed on the gravel outside. She glimpsed blood through the torn place.

"Why'd you run away?" she asked.

Carroway gestured sullenly towards the envelope in her hand. "Just read that."

Colly tapped it thoughtfully against her palm, then dropped it onto the coffee table. "I'd rather hear it from your own mouth."

"Aw, hell, read it, will ya? You can ask me questions after." Though his tone was hostile, Carroway seemed more anxious than angry. He glanced wildly towards the door and leaned forward, ready to bolt.

Beside her, Colly felt Avery shift, preparing to give chase again.

"Relax, David. Everything's fine," Colly said. "The sooner you tell me what this is about, the quicker you're out of here."

Carroway stared blankly at her for a minute, then ran a hand roughly over his face. "Yeah, okay."

Colly waited, but he seemed unable to begin.

"Need some water?" Avery sprang up without waiting for an answer and headed for the kitchen, returning momentarily with a glass.

Carroway drank half the water in one long swallow. "Thanks." He took a deep breath and looked at Colly. "I reckon you know about me?"

"I know you own a farm on Salton Road, and you've had a few run-ins with police. And I know my brother-in-law Willis molested you when you were a kid."

"No, he didn't."

Colly wasn't sure what she'd expected to hear, but it wasn't this. "Excuse me?"

Carroway reddened. "That's the story, all right. But Willis Newland never touched me. I kept my mouth shut for thirty years.

272

But when she come by the farm asking questions this morning"—
he nodded towards Avery—"it stirred things up."

Colly stared. "You lied?"

"Yes—no. I don't know. Not at first."

Colly held up her hand. "Start from the beginning."

Carroway shifted uneasily. "My family and the Newlands went
to the same church when I was a kid. Willis was seven or eight years
older than me, but he was kinda slow, so mentally we weren't so far
apart. I liked him. We used to play together, sometimes." Carroway
took another quick gulp of water. "One day, when I was six, Willis
was pushing me on the swing set after church. I needed to take a
piss, so he took me inside to find my mom. But we couldn't find
her. I was about to wet my pants, so Willis took me to the bathroom. Nobody else was in there. I had trouble with my zipper, so I
asked him for help. My dad walked in just as Willis was unzipping
my pants.

"I reckon you can imagine what happened next. My old man
didn't ask questions. He just scooped me up and carried me straight
to Willis's folks. He told them what he saw—what he *thought* he
saw. I think he threatened to call the cops. I was scared and confused. I couldn't understand why he was so mad.

"That night, Mr. Newland called my father. He made some
kind of settlement offer if we'd keep things quiet and leave the
courts out of it." Carroway looked up. "I found this out years later."

"Your parents never asked you what happened?"

"Sure they did. But I thought they were mad at me, so I didn't
tell the truth for a while. When I finally did, my old man didn't
believe me, just said, 'I know what I saw.' And he told me to keep
quiet." Carroway sighed and shook his head. "I don't know what
my folks really thought. But after they died, I found out that the
money from the Newlands kept the farm from going bust that
year."

Carroway fell silent, turning the water glass in his hand.

"Why didn't you clear things up when you got older?" Colly asked.

"I wanted to. But I was afraid the Newlands might sue my folks. Then, after Willis killed that kid and went to prison, I told myself my story didn't really matter no more."

He had gotten into drugs to numb the guilt of the lie, he told them, but he was clean now. "I been seeing a shrink in Sweetwater the past couple years. He says I gotta tell the truth to Willis's family if I want to get free of the past. Today when you knocked, I figured it was a sign. Now or never."

Carroway gestured towards the envelope on the coffee table. "I've had that written a long time." He met Colly's eyes. "I heard you were staying out here. Since you ain't a Newland by birth, I thought . . ."

"You thought I'd take it better than the rest of the family."

Carroway blushed. "I figured I could stick that letter in the door and you wouldn't see it till tomorrow."

Colly stared hard at him. "How do I know all this is true? Everyone who could corroborate your story is dead."

Carroway's eyes flashed. "I got nothing to gain by lying. If you don't believe me, ask my shrink."

"I think I will, if you'll authorize it. What's his name and address?"

"You serious?"

For answer, Colly pushed the white envelope across the table, along with a pencil. "Write it down."

Scowling, Carroway consulted the address book on his phone and did as she asked.

When he was done, Colly took back the envelope. "I want you to call him in the morning and give him permission to talk to us.

He'll want you to sign release forms, I'm sure, but hopefully it can be done electronically. Tell him I'd like a face-to-face."

After Carroway left, Colly checked her watch. It was just past one a.m. She turned to Avery. "What do you think?"

Avery studied her uncertainly. "Does this mean you're not reporting me or—or having me arrested? I'm still on the case?"

Excellent question, Colly thought. Avery had lied to her from the beginning, which was reason enough to drop her. But Colly had already sidelined Russ for the same reason. There was no one else she could turn to, and the job was too big for one person. *I suppose it's not fair to report Avery and keep quiet about Russ*, she thought. *Besides, nothing about this is by the book—it's an informal review. I only need to gather enough to convince the Rangers to reopen the case.*

Aloud, she said, "You've told me everything? No more surprises?"

"No more surprises, I swear."

Russ said the same, Colly thought grimly. Hopefully, with Avery, it was true. "I haven't decided what to do," she said finally. "Let's finish the investigation, and we'll see. Consider yourself on probation, for now. One more screwup and you're out."

Avery's shoulders sagged with relief. She nodded. "What next? You gonna tell Russ about Carroway?"

Colly shook her head. "I'm not tossing that grenade into the family till I verify it."

"Does it matter now if Willis groped the kid or not? He didn't kill Adam, and he's got an alibi for Denny. Once we find the real killer, Willis is in the clear."

"As long as people around here think he was a pervert, he'll be suspected, no matter what evidence we bring. Let's do what we can for him—he deserves that much."

◆ ◆ ◆

That night, Colly was reluctant to sleep in her own bedroom after the events of the afternoon. She lay down on the living room sofa, her gun by her side, but couldn't fall asleep. It wasn't the fear of an intruder that kept her awake. Her brain churned with the flood of new information in the case, and she couldn't switch it off.

In a day filled with remarkable revelations, Dave Carroway's had hit her the hardest. For as long as Colly had been part of the Newland family, Willis had been its most shameful secret—a sexually deviant convicted murderer. Colly herself had only seen him a few times, and not at all since his murder conviction two decades earlier. She remembered him as a podgy, rather quiet young man with straight, flaxen hair and large, very pale blue eyes. Only Iris had wholeheartedly believed in his innocence. After his release, he'd been barred by law from meeting his nieces and nephews or joining in family events. Instead, he'd been banished to the cabin, where his only companion, a monstrous snake, repaid his love by killing him. The town, and most of his family, had been relieved at his death. Colly remembered her own callous reaction—Willis was a pedophile, and the world was better off without him.

But if Dave Carroway was telling the truth, Willis was as much an innocent victim as Adam and Denny. His life had been an unmerited hell. There could be no amends for that.

With these gloomy thoughts roiling in her head, Colly eventually dozed off. She woke, groggy but restless, before the alarm sounded. Showering quickly, she drove to Brenda's house in the hope of catching them before they left for school.

Satchel was thrilled to see her and babbled happily as she applied the prescription sunblock to his pale skin. When she told him that he was going to spend that night with his cousins at the ranch because Colly and Aunt Brenda had a dinner engagement, he clapped excitedly.

"Grandma Iris and Alice are going to take you to the Rattlesnake Rodeo after supper," Colly explained as she helped him with his sun-sleeves.

Brenda looked up from packing lunchboxes. "No, that's off. Alice has a date, and Iris doesn't want to wrangle three kids at the Rodeo by herself. They're going to swim and watch movies, instead." Brenda had promised to take Logan and Minnie to the Rodeo the next afternoon. Satchel was welcome to join them—and Colly, too, if she liked.

Colly shuddered and said she'd think about it.

Reassured by Satchel's happy mood, Colly hugged him good-bye and drove to the station, where Avery was waiting for her in the parking lot, a Starbucks cup in each hand.

"Triple-shot latte." Her face bore an abashed, uncertain expression. The coffee was a peace offering after last night's revelations.

Colly forced a smile. "Triple-shot? I hope you brought a defibrillator." They got in the car.

"I talked to Carroway a few minutes ago," Avery said. "His shrink can see us if we're there before noon." She latched her seatbelt. "I don't see why we can't just call the guy, though."

"Shrinks are like cops—they're used to getting information, not giving it. I want to see his face, read between the lines."

They drove in silence along Market Street. Once on the highway, Avery engaged the cruise control and glanced at Colly. "What are you thinking?"

"This case has me stumped." Colly leaned against the headrest. "We've got two dead boys and two rabbit masks—not counting the ones in Willis's cabin and Satchel's suitcase. Before last night, I thought we were probably dealing with a serial killer, and the masks were a signature. But there *is* no serial killer. So what are the masks about? I can't make the puzzle pieces fit."

"Maybe Denny's murderer's not a serial killer, but he's still a psychopath. Last night you said Willis could've been so messed up by finding Adam's body that it triggered some homicidal urge."

Colly sipped her coffee and grimaced. "You nixed that theory."

"I said it couldn't be Willis. But what if someone else found Adam—someone young and impressionable?"

"A budding psychopath with a rabbit fetish?"

"Why not? Whoever posed Adam might've been excited by the uproar it caused and wanted more, but this time, he had to kill to get it." Avery changed lanes and began to edge past a slow-moving cattle truck. "Maybe Earla's right—the murderer leaves the masks because he wants a cool nickname."

Colly reached to close the vent as the stench of cow manure filled the car. "Except police never released that detail to the press."

"Maybe the killer figures it'll come out eventually. Or maybe he just wants to play catch-me-if-you-can with the cops."

"That doesn't feel right. There's something tender about the way Adam was posed. I think whoever did it cared about him. With Denny, it was different."

"Twenty years is a long time." Avery eased back into the right lane. "Maybe the killer changed. Maybe he's conflicted. Psychopathic criminals are emotionally complicated, right?"

Colly set her cup in the cup holder. "They're *not*—that's the thing. There are smart ones and stupid ones. But I've never met one that's deep. The ones I've arrested are like cardboard cutouts of people."

"Dangerous, though."

"To a point. They have no feelings for anyone but themselves, so most of them go through life pissing off the people who know them best. They leave a trail a mile wide, if you know what you're looking for."

"Then why are serial killers so hard to catch?"

"Because they usually choose their targets at random. And some of them like playing games, which stirs up a lot of publicity. That complicates things. But once you do identify a suspect, it's not hard to build your case. They don't talk and act and think like normal people. Interrogate them for five minutes, and you spot it. They're like bad poker players—they can't hide their tells."

"You don't think we're dealing with a psychopath here?"

"If we are, it wouldn't be the worst-case scenario."

"What would be?"

Colly pushed a strand of hair behind her ear. "My opinion? A zealot. Criminal psychopaths trip over their own egos. Zealots don't. And they'll justify anything for their cause—they'll die for it themselves, even. The 9/11 hijackers wiped out more people in one morning than all the serial killers put together, and they felt like heroes doing it."

"There's no radical extremists in Crescent Bluff."

"Don't be so sure. Nowadays, a lot of them are regular people who got sucked down some internet rabbit hole. They're gullible, but they can be dangerous." Colly turned and stared absently out of the window at the green-gray blur of the scrubland rushing by. "They get in their chatrooms and cut themselves off just as much as if they followed Charles Manson into the desert. You hardly notice them till something explodes, and you're left picking up the pieces and trying to figure out what the hell happened."

Chapter 30

The trip to Sweetwater was less productive than Colly had hoped. David Carroway's therapist, an elderly gentleman with a grizzled goatee and an impassive face, believed that his client was being truthful about the incident with Willis, but he volunteered no additional details or insights. Colly asked about the possibility of a false or altered memory. Was there any chance that Willis had, in fact, molested Carroway, who later recast the event in his mind as something innocent? But the therapist didn't think so, giving a long, jargon-laden explanation that Colly didn't bother to untangle.

"Waste of time," Avery grumbled when they were back in the cruiser. "What's the plan?"

Colly rummaged for her sunglasses. "How far is it to Colorado City from here?"

"Probably half an hour."

Colly checked her watch. "No time now."

"For what?"

"The burner phone that sent me that threatening text was bought at a convenience store there last Saturday. The clerk told Russ he sold two phones that day—one to a middle-aged white female and one to a younger Black male. That's all he remembers, and the store has no cameras. But whoever bought the phone could've made more than one stop. If we backtrack along the route from there to Crescent Bluff, maybe we'll find someone who saw something—maybe even get video footage."

"Sounds like the mother of all snipe hunts, to me."

"I know it's a long shot, but we're out of leads. Identifying who bought that phone might be the break we need."

Avery conceded the point with a shrug. "Why can't we do it now?"

"School lets out in a couple hours."

"Tonight, then?"

"I've got a dinner thing with Niall Shaw and Brenda—I'm hoping to pick their brains a little more about Denny. Sometimes when you hit a wall, it's best to go back to victimology." Colly chewed her lip. "Let's do this: drop me in town, and then you drive the route to Colorado City. Stop everywhere. Talk to as many people and gather as much footage as you can. We'll comb through it at the station tomorrow."

Although Brenda had offered to pick up Satchel after school, Colly wanted to do it herself. Brenda's account of the therapy sessions had alarmed her, and she couldn't get Satchel's crayon self-portraits out of her head. Colly had barely seen him in forty-eight hours, and they'd be apart again that night and much of tomorrow. Some quality time together would be good for them both.

"How was school?" she asked when he climbed into the car.

He shrugged noncommittally but brightened when she suggested a trip to Dairy Queen. A few minutes later, they were seated at a picnic table under the ice cream shop's faded awning drinking strawberry milkshakes.

Satchel chattered excitedly about spending the night at the ranch. "Minnie got a new hamster named Toby. He's funny—he rolls around the house in a clear plastic ball. She's gonna take him to show Grandma Iris tonight." He wiped his mouth with the back of his hand. "I wanna take my ant farm to the ranch. Can we go get it?"

Colly sighed. She'd been dreading this conversation. The ant farm had gotten knocked off the nightstand and broken, she told him. But she'd get him a new one. He listened solemnly and asked no questions. When she finished explaining, he began to talk about going to the Rattlesnake Rodeo the next day as if he hadn't heard what she'd said.

She drove Satchel to Brenda's house at four-thirty and kissed him goodbye. "Be good for Grandma Iris. You're going to stay there with Logan and Minnie till Aunt Brenda comes to take you to the Rodeo tomorrow afternoon."

"Aren't you coming to the Rodeo, too?"

"Maybe, buddy—I'll have to see. I've got lots of work to do."

Brenda walked Colly to her car. "Go home and clean up. I'll take the kids to the ranch and pick you up around six. Niall lives kind of far—it's easier if we go together."

When Colly returned to the farmhouse, she was startled to find that she couldn't unlock the door. She double-checked to make sure she had the right key, then tried again. The key went into the lock but wouldn't turn. The memory of yesterday's break-in still fresh, she cursed and drew her pistol. She circled the house, but all the doors and windows were secure. Pulling out her phone to call Russ, she saw a missed text from him. He'd changed the locks that morning. The new key was under the gas can in the carport.

Feeling relieved and a bit foolish, Colly found the key and went inside. After showering, she surveyed her clothing options before pulling on a pair of clean jeans and a simple plum-colored top. She was just tying her thick, unmanageable hair into a loose ponytail when Brenda rang the bell.

"Thank God you're in jeans, too," Colly said as they climbed into the rental sedan Brenda had been driving since the snake incident. "There's no way I was going to ask to borrow something again, after what happened to your blue dress Monday."

Brenda turned the ignition and put the car in reverse. "Casual clothes are mandatory at Niall's. Chances are good he'll drag us outside to admire his fishing hole."

"His what?"

"He calls it that. It's actually a lovely little pond behind his house."

"Should we take a bottle of wine or something?"

"I had one, but I forgot to bring it. Niall won't care. He's very laid-back."

Niall Shaw lived thirty miles northwest of town, in a sparsely populated knot of cedar-clad hills. The sun was setting as Brenda turned off the main road onto a narrow lane. It wound for half a mile through the hills before ending abruptly in a broad patch of pea gravel edged with boulders. Niall's navy-blue Jeep was parked there, but Colly saw no sign of a house.

Brenda parked the car, and they walked to the row of boulders. Colly found herself looking down into a grassy, saucer-shaped hollow. At the bottom was a stand of dark cedars close to a reed-edged pond. She followed Brenda down a graded path that led through the trees to a small, neat house a hundred yards from the pond. It was painted dark gray and built in a retro, mid-century modern style, with floor-to-ceiling windows along the front. Through these, Colly glimpsed the warm glow of walls paneled in honey-colored oak. Despite its modern design, the place seemed like an organic part of its rustic surroundings. Colly had seen nothing like it in West Texas.

"Did we go through some wormhole and come out in California?" she asked as they climbed a short flight of steps to the door.

Brenda laughed. "Niall designed the house. He's one of those annoying people who's talented at almost everything."

"I had no idea psychology paid so well."

"I think he got some kind of inheritance from his folks. His dad made a tidy bundle in the mining industry in Montana."

Brenda rapped on the door and pushed it open without waiting for an answer. "Hey, it's us."

"I'm in the kitchen—come on back," Niall shouted.

Colly stepped inside. They were standing in an open-plan living room, cleanly furnished with a red leather Chesterfield sofa and two Eames lounge chairs. Framed textiles splashed with stylized designs of birds, lizards, and gazelles hung on one wall, while densely packed bookshelves ranged along two others. The window at the far end of the room looked out on a lawn that sloped towards the pond.

She followed Brenda through the living room and around the corner into a white-tiled kitchen with a dining area at one end. Niall, wearing a chef's apron over jeans and a t-shirt, was at the stove, stirring something in an enameled Dutch oven.

"What's that heavenly smell?" Brenda plopped down on one of the barstools lining the counter.

Niall adjusted the flame under the pot and turned to greet them, wiping his hands on his apron. "Coq au vin."

Brenda clapped her hands. "You're spoiling us."

"I always default to French food when I'm hoping to impress a new acquaintance." He smiled at Colly.

"I love your house. Those textile hangings in the living room are amazing."

"They're Korhogo mud cloths from the Ivory Coast. My father was born there. That's how I got interested in French cuisine."

"How'd your family end up in the States?"

Niall opened a cupboard and began taking out plates. "Dad studied hydraulic engineering in England, then moved to Montana to work for a mining company. He met my mom at a ski resort near Red Lodge while she was visiting a friend. And the rest is history, as they say."

"The other day you said you moved here after your dad died?"

Niall nodded. "My mom wanted to be near family. She had an aunt in Falroy, about thirty miles from here. We bought a house in Crescent Bluff because it had a better school system. I hated it. Siblings would've helped. I was the only Black kid in my eighth-grade class. We're thin on the ground in Montana, too," he added with a wry smile. "But at least there you've got the mountains and rivers for compensation. When I moved back here after grad school, I bought this property because it doesn't feel like West Texas, to me. It's green, anyway. And I can escape from people when I want. It's tough being different."

"But everyone knows you. And you provide such a great service to the community," Colly said.

Niall hunched his shoulders. "The South is the South. It's true, most people are very nice, though there's always some low-grade stupid stuff. But even with the best, I sometimes get the feeling they're thinking of me as their *Black* friend." He pushed the plates across the bar to Brenda. "Make yourself useful and lay those out, will you?"

"What should I do with all that?" Brenda gestured towards the glass-topped table, which was strewn with books and papers.

"Oh, I was working earlier. Just pile everything on the bar."

Colly moved to help. Many of the papers she gathered up were printouts of multicolored blobs. She held one up. "More art from the Ivory Coast?"

Uncorking a bottle of wine, Niall looked up and laughed. "No, PET scans. I'm writing a book with a neuroscientist friend of mine at UC Irvine on the correlation between brain architecture and violent crime. A lot's been done on that in recent years, but we're focusing specifically on adolescents. My co-author's a researcher, so he's covering statistical aspects on the neurological side, and I'm handling the clinical work."

Colly looked closely at the PET scan in her hand. Now that she knew what it was, she could clearly discern the distinct folds and valleys of the human brain, lit with gaudy splashes of red, yellow, green—and one very large patch of dark blue.

"What do the colors mean?"

"Warmer ones indicate greater blood flow, which means higher neural activity in that area. See that gigantic blue blob on the right side?" Niall leaned across the bar to point.

"Low blood flow there?"

"Almost none. That region of the frontal lobe's associated with morality, empathy, and self-control."

"A psychopath?"

"Basically, yes, though that's a term cops and reporters use, not scientists." He nodded towards the page in Colly's hand. "That's the brain of a seventeen-year-old who killed his grandparents over a jar of loose change. He's in a state prison, but the majority of our study participants are at the juvenile correctional facility in Brownwood. I go out to meet with them once a month."

"I'm glad that kid was tried as an adult," Brenda said as she wiped down the table with a damp cloth. "I'd hate to think someone like that could be back on the streets soon."

Colly handed the scan to Niall, who took it with a sheepish grin. "Sorry, I've been droning. I get carried away." He laid the paper with the rest and opened a cupboard.

"It's interesting. Jolene Hoyer mentioned you did a brain scan on Denny. Was that for this project?" Colly asked a little nervously.

"Yes and no." Niall handed a stack of placemats and napkins to Brenda and took wine glasses from another cupboard. "Denny was really too young—the study's cutoff is fifteen. But I told the Hoyers that the clinic would handle his therapy pro bono if they'd let me enroll him. I figured it'd hurt their pride less if they thought I was getting something out of the deal. I just wanted to help." He filled the wine glasses and handed one to each of his guests.

"Would it be ethical to show me Denny's PET scan?" Colly asked.

Niall hesitated, then shrugged. "If you think it might help solve his murder." He rifled through the scans, then pushed one across the bar. Colly recognized the signature dark blue blotch in the frontal lobe.

"Denny was a psychopath?"

"He definitely lacked empathy and impulse control. But he was a thirteen-year-old boy. That's kind of their thing. The brain changes so rapidly during puberty that it's impossible to say how typical or atypical he was without scanning a lot more kids his age."

"In Denny's case, there were other worrying signs, though," Brenda said. "Cruelty to animals, bed-wetting, arson—all typical traits of ASPD in kids."

"ASPD?" Colly asked.

"Antisocial personality disorder. In layman's terms, psychopathy. I was definitely concerned."

Colly's mind went to Satchel's recent behavior. She felt suddenly queasy.

"Not everyone with ASPD's a criminal," Niall said, as if reading her thoughts. "Many—probably most—live fully integrated, productive lives. A grad-school buddy of mine scanned himself out of curiosity a few years back and found out he has a so-called psychopathic brain. The *Smithsonian* did an article on it. I still tease him."

"But he's not—?"

Niall looked up from slicing a baguette, and laughed. "He's a little cut-throat on the rugby field, but that's the worst of it."

A kitchen timer rang, indicating that the coq au vin was ready, and the conversation turned to other things.

Colly was surprised at how much she enjoyed the dinner. The food was excellent, and Niall proved to be well-read and widely traveled. He conversed intelligently about a range of issues and showed a lively interest in her, as well, asking many questions about her life and career. The more they talked, the more Colly found herself wondering about him. Why would someone so bright and cosmopolitan bury himself in a dried-up backwater like Crescent Bluff?

After dinner, Niall suggested a stroll down to the pond before dessert. Outside, the air was cool, and the stars hung thick and bright. The moon was rising, and a glowing yellow nimbus hovered on the eastern rim of the hollow. From the direction of the pond came the melancholy *chuck-chuck-chuck* of a leopard frog.

The path to the pond led past a small log cabin a few dozen yards from the house. "My fly-tying shed," Niall explained. "It's a hobby."

Brenda laughed. "It's an *obsession*. You should see it, Col. Feathers and beads and fur and more frou-frou than the dressing room of a Hollywood starlet. Open the door, Niall—give her a peek."

Niall good-naturedly agreed, and they crossed the lawn to the shed. A motion-sensitive light beneath the eaves flickered on. The door was padlocked, and Niall felt along its upper casing for the key.

Inside, he switched on the lights. The interior of the shed was crowded with gear yet seemed neatly organized. Dozens of expensive-looking fly-rod cases lay across the open rafters above. Reels, waders, vests, nets, and baskets hung on one wall.

On another, rows of shelves were stacked with plastic containers, each carefully labelled. In the corner, beside an enormous wheeled plastic case of the sort used to convey sporting equipment, stood a plywood workbench fitted with a vise and magnifying glass, both on hinged arms. A large pegboard on the wall above it held spools of thread and wire, bobbins, pliers, scissors, tweezers, and other tools of obscure purpose. Given the remoteness of the property, Colly had initially been surprised that Niall bothered to lock the shed. Now she understood.

There must be fifty grand worth of stuff in here, she thought.

"What did I tell you?" Brenda said. "And to think Lowell used to gripe about my teeny little scrapbooking closet."

"How long have you been collecting this stuff?" Colly asked.

Niall leaned against the workbench. "I started as a kid. Fly-fishing's huge in Montana. But most Texas rivers are too hot for trout. After my mom and I moved here, I used to get so homesick that I'd cast a line in every piddly little pond within biking range, even though there's nothing in them but bluegill and turtles."

Colly had wandered across the room and was examining a framed photo of an eleven- or twelve-year-old Niall standing knee-deep in water and holding up an enormous fish.

"Sounds like you still miss Montana."

"I go up there to fish a couple times a year."

"Why didn't you open your practice there, if you don't mind my asking?"

Niall was quiet. Colly turned. He was watching her, an odd expression on his face. "My standard answer—there aren't enough mental-health services in this area. I wanted to help. But if I'm being totally honest, I'm partly here to do penance."

Colly waited, thinking of what Avery had said about him the previous night. "Penance for what?" she asked bluntly when he volunteered nothing more.

"It's no deep, dark secret. Just garden-variety regret." He gave her a sad smile and picked up a hook-shaped tool from the workbench, turning it in his fingers. "Did I tell you I knew Adam Parker? He used to follow me around. I wasn't always very nice to him. After he died, I felt bad about that—especially when I got old enough to realize he was just looking for a role model. I can't help thinking that if I'd been a better friend, he might still be alive. His sister thinks so. I've apologized, but she's never forgiven me." Niall tapped the hook thoughtfully against his palm. "Adam's the reason I got interested in psychology. I sat through every minute of Willis Newland's trial, wanting to understand why someone would do what he did. His trial was one of the first in the country to use brain-scan evidence as a defense. They showed his PET scan in court—it looked exactly like the ones in my kitchen. I was fascinated." He tossed the tool on the workbench.

Colly glanced at Brenda, who was regarding Niall intently from her seat on the rolling gear box. "You were here back then, too, weren't you, Bren?" she asked.

Brenda jumped. "I—I was a high-school senior. I didn't know Adam, but his death made a huge impression."

"What do you—?" Colly was interrupted by a vibration in her pocket. She checked her phone. "It's Iris."

Iris did all of the talking. Colly listened, then said, "We're on our way." She hung up with a sigh.

"Are the kids okay?" Brenda demanded.

Colly felt suddenly very tired. She set the phone on the shelf beside her and rubbed her eyes. "They had a fight or something. Iris tried to explain, but there was a lot of yelling and crying in the background. She sounds frazzled."

They returned to the house for their purses, and Niall walked them back up the path to their car.

"Sorry to miss your crème brûlée." Brenda kissed him on the cheek.

"Gives us an excuse to do this again." Niall turned to Colly and extended his hand. "I hope everything's okay with the kids. Let me know if there's anything I can do—anything at all." In the moonlight, Colly had the impression that he was observing her closely. They shook, and he waited politely while she got into the car and put on her seatbelt before he closed her door.

As they drove away, Colly glanced in the side mirror. Niall was standing silhouetted against the stars, watching their taillights recede into the night.

Chapter 31

It was past ten o'clock when Colly and Brenda drove up the juniper-lined drive and parked in front of the ranch house. Lights shone in most of the ground-floor windows, though the upper story was dark. Expecting to walk into chaos, Colly was surprised when Iris answered the door seemingly at ease in a rose-colored dressing gown and slippers.

"The children finally settled down." She led them to the den, where the stoic housekeeper was gathering playthings into a laundry basket. "I tried calling to tell you, but both your phones went to voicemail."

"What happened?" Brenda demanded. "The kids usually get along great."

A shadow crossed Iris's face. She turned to the housekeeper. "Nadine, where did you put it?"

"Garage, ma'am."

"Bring it in, please."

The housekeeper set down the basket and limped from the room, returning with a cardboard shoebox, which she laid on the coffee table.

Without waiting for Iris's explanation, Brenda seized it and opened the lid.

"Oh, no." She sank onto the sofa and held out the box to Colly.

A tan-and-white hamster lay curled on a bed of folded newspaper. Except for a smear of dried blood on its nose, it looked asleep.

Colly sat down beside Brenda. "How did this happen?"

Iris pursed her lips. She hadn't seen it, she said. The children had all told slightly different stories. Minnie's hamster had been rolling around the den in its little plastic ball. While Iris was in the kitchen with Nadine, Satchel and Logan had gotten into a fight, though neither would tell her what it was about.

"I heard shouts, then a crash and a scream. When I got in here, the ball was smashed and the hamster was dead on the floor. Logan said Satchel got mad and kicked the ball against the fireplace. Minnie was wailing, and Satchel was huddled in the corner with his fingers in his ears, banging his head on the wall. That's when I called you." Iris threw up her hands in a gesture of helplessness. "They finally exhausted themselves enough that Nadine and I were able to get them to bed."

Colly stood. "Where's Satchel now?"

"In the olive room. But perhaps you shouldn't—"

Without waiting to hear the rest, Colly headed for the stairs.

The olive room, named for the color of its curtains and bedding, was at the end of the second-floor hall. The door was closed. Colly opened it partway. In the nightlight's glow, she saw the outline of a small figure on the bed. A shock of white-blond hair glowed against the dark pillowcase.

"Satch, are you awake?"

The figure sniffled but said nothing. Colly crossed the room and sat on the edge of the bed. "Hey, bud, heard you had a rough night." She stroked his hair. "Want to tell me about it?"

Satchel whimpered and drew himself into a tight ball, hiding his face in the blankets.

"That's okay. I'll just sit here with you for a while."

Colly rubbed his back, humming softly until his breath became slow and even. Thinking he was asleep, she kissed the top of his head and stood to go.

"Logan says you killed Mommy and Grandpa Randy. Uncle Lowell told him." Satchel's voice was muffled through the bedclothes.

Colly's throat tightened. "Is that why you kicked Minnie's hamster?"

"I didn't mean to. I was trying to kick Logan."

Colly sighed and sat down again. She tried to pull the covers away from his face, but he held onto them fiercely. "You can't kick people, Satch. No matter how mad you are."

He was quiet for a long time. Finally, he whispered something inaudible.

"I can't hear you, bud."

"You didn't kill them, did you?"

Colly hesitated. "No, sweetie. I didn't kill them."

"Then why'd Uncle Lowell say so?"

"Sometimes Uncle Lowell says things without thinking."

There was another long pause. "When can we go home, Grandma?"

"To the farmhouse?"

"No, to Houston."

"I thought you liked it here."

Beneath the blankets, Satchel shook his head. "You're different here. You seem mad all the time. I wanna go home."

"Me too, bud. We will as soon as I finish this case." She rubbed his arm. "Do you still want to stay here tonight? Or would you rather come back to town with me?"

Satchel emerged from the blankets and wiped his eyes with the heels of his hands. "I wanna stay so I can go to the Rodeo tomorrow."

"In the morning, you'll have to apologize to Minnie for hurting her hamster."

He sniffled loudly. "Okay."

Colly sat with him a while longer, singing his favorite songs until he dozed off. Downstairs, she found Brenda and Iris talking quietly. Brenda had checked on Logan and Minnie, who were both asleep.

They said goodbye to Iris and headed back to town. The drive was a quiet one. When they pulled up in front of the farmhouse, Brenda broke the silence.

"You were upstairs with Satchel a long time."

"He was pretty worked up." Colly told her about the conversation. "We'll buy Minnie a new hamster, of course." She paused. "I'm sure there's no point asking Lowell to be more discreet. But you might have a chat with Logan about what really happened in Houston."

"I will."

"I'm worried about Satchel, Bren. Honestly, this case is more than I bargained for. I've got some lunatic stalking me, and Satchel's falling apart. It's not safe for him here, and I don't want to send him back to Houston alone."

"You could go with him."

"You mean quit the case? I can't."

"Why not?"

"I made a commitment."

"You made one to Satchel, too."

"There's a killer on the loose, Bren. He's got to be caught."

"Do *you* have to do it?" Brenda hesitated. "I know there's a lot at stake. But is it possible you're pushing yourself so hard in an attempt to make up for what happened in Houston?"

Colly felt herself flush. "I had my psych eval, thanks. I don't need you to redo it."

"Don't get defensive. I've spent a lot of time with Satchel these last few days—enough to form a pretty solid opinion about his mental state. Colly, he's not okay."

Colly leaned against the headrest, staring vacantly out of the window at the moon shining through the dry, brown leaves of the oak above them. She felt a deep weariness settling over her like a fog. "I can't think about this now, Bren. If you're concerned about Satchel being around your kids, he doesn't have to go with you to the Rattlesnake Rodeo tomorrow."

"Don't be ridiculous." Brenda sounded hurt. "I'm just trying to help."

"I know." Colly exhaled wearily and unfastened her seatbelt. "See you tomorrow."

It was nearly midnight when Colly said goodbye and went inside. Despite the new locks, she checked and cleared the house before she felt relaxed enough to undress. It wasn't until she emptied the pockets of her jeans that she discovered her phone was missing. She picked up her purse and dug through it.

"Are you kidding me?" she muttered.

Closing her eyes, she worked back through the evening. She'd answered Iris's call in Niall's fly-tying shed. Had she used it since then? She checked the tracking app on her laptop, which showed that her phone was thirty miles northwest of town. Niall's place. There was nothing to be done until morning.

The bed was still stripped from the previous day's break-in, and Colly was too tired to make it. She pulled on her pajamas and stretched out once again on the living room sofa. But despite her exhaustion, she lay awake for a long time, staring at the dappled confusion of moon-cast shadows on the ceiling. Maybe Brenda was right. Colly had vowed never again to put her family at risk for the sake of her work. She couldn't afford to let history repeat itself. Satchel deserved better. She would call Russ in the morning and tell him she was quitting the case.

◆ ◆ ◆

Colly woke up to sunlight in the room and lay blinking for a moment, wondering why she was on the sofa and why the preset alarm on her phone had not gone off. She sat up, disoriented, but the sight of the disconnected charger cable on the floor brought back her memory, and she cursed as she kicked off the blankets. Retrieving her phone from Niall's place would kill half the morning. But there was one crumb of comfort, she reflected, climbing the stairs to the bathroom. Without a phone, she'd have to put off the call to Russ. A night's sleep had not altered her determination to quit the investigation, but she dreaded breaking the news to him.

She showered quickly and brushed her hair. In the bathroom mirror, her expression was tired and defiant. She'd come to Crescent Bluff to make amends to the Newlands, but instead she'd uncovered their ugliest secrets. What would Randy have wanted her to do now? Would he expect her to close ranks with his brothers, or expose them?

Wait till tomorrow, came the sudden thought. It was hardly fair to tell Russ she was quitting now, while he was absorbed in overseeing the Rattlesnake Rodeo. She'd give it one more day. Maybe, by then, she'd see some way forward. With a sense of relief, she dressed hurriedly, grabbed her holstered sidearm, and headed for the car.

The dashboard clock read eight a.m. as she pulled out of the carport—too early to show up unannounced on Niall Shaw's doorstep on a Saturday morning. She considered going by Brenda's house and using her phone to call him, but decided against it. Brenda would insist on driving to Niall's with her and would want to continue the previous night's discussion. Colly wasn't in the mood. What was the point of more talk?

Wondering if Avery had tried to contact her, she drove by the police station and saw the girl's shabby Volkswagen in the parking lot. Colly parked near the door and went inside. The place seemed almost deserted. Everyone was out policing the Rattlesnake Rodeo, the office manager said.

Colly found Avery in Russ's office, hunched over a laptop. She looked up, bleary-eyed. "Where've you been? I texted you like five times."

"Misplaced my phone. Anything to report?"

Avery leaned back in the chair and rubbed her eyes. "Not yet. Yesterday, I drove up to Colorado City, like you said. Stopped in every dinky little shop and gas station along the route. But nobody remembered anything. Most places didn't have security footage that far back, but I got what I could." She nodded at the laptop. "Slow going, though. I'm glad you're here to help."

"Sorry, can't stay. I've got to run out to Shaw's." Colly explained the situation.

"Get anything useful from him last night?"

"I found out Denny was a psychopath."

Avery's eyebrows rose. "For real?"

"According to the brain scan. Jace was telling the truth about that."

"Think it's relevant?"

"No idea. It's interesting, though."

"Maybe the killer's a psycho who hunts psychos."

"As good a theory as any, right now." Colly turned towards the door. "Keep checking that footage—I'll help when I get back."

Colly bought a half-dozen donuts on the way out of town and by nine-thirty was driving up the long, narrow road towards Niall Shaw's place. Relieved to see that his Jeep was still parked where it had been the night before, she made her way down the path to his house and knocked on the door. He answered, barefoot and wearing shorts and a white t-shirt.

Colly quickly explained her errand. "I think my phone must be in your shed. Here's a peace offering for crashing your morning." She held out the bag of donuts.

"What a nice surprise." Niall grinned, waving her inside. "I'm on a video call with my co-author, but we're nearly done."

Colly followed him through the living room and into the kitchen. The table was once again strewn with brain scans, papers, and books, as well as an open laptop.

Niall pulled a mug from a cupboard and handed it to her. "Make yourself at home." He sat down at the table and addressed the laptop screen. "Okay, Gary, I'm back."

Colly poured herself some coffee and, not liking to eavesdrop, wandered back into the living room. She was perusing the bookshelves ten minutes later when she became suddenly aware that the drone of voices from the other room had stopped. She turned quickly. Niall was leaning against the doorframe, watching her.

"Sorry to startle you," he said. "Finished my call. Come help me eat those donuts."

But Colly politely declined. She needed to get her phone and head back to town.

"No rest for the weary, eh? Let me grab some shoes. I'll walk you out to the shed."

He disappeared down a hallway and returned a minute later carrying socks and sneakers. He sat on the Chesterfield and began to pull on his socks. "How'd everything go at your mother-in-law's last night?"

Colly briefly recounted the events at the ranch the evening before. "The kids seemed fine by the time we got there, but it rattled Iris. Me too, honestly."

"Sounds like a run-of-the-mill kids' squabble, if you ask me." Niall laid a shoe on his knees and worked to unknot the laces.

Colly eyed him nervously. "Brenda says fire-starting, bed-wetting, and hurting animals are all signs a kid might be a psychopath."

Niall set aside the shoe and waved Colly to a seat. "The hamster was an accident, right?"

"According to Satchel."

"You said you believed him."

"Even if it's true, he still lashed out and tried to kick Logan."

"If every little boy who got into a fight was a psychopath, there'd be more prisons in this country than Starbucks." Niall chuckled.

"Brenda wasn't laughing. She thinks something's seriously wrong with him. I can tell."

Niall studied Colly's face. "Look, Brenda's going to be a great clinician. But she's new at this."

"Meaning?"

"She's got a touch of New Therapist Syndrome—lots of head-knowledge, but not much clinical experience, yet. The real world doesn't always match what it says in the textbooks."

"Satchel has the same symptoms Denny had. You said yourself that Den—"

"Denny tried to burn down a school, and he got his kicks bullying younger kids and torturing small animals. That's very different from a child who inflicts minor burns on himself and accidentally kills his cousin's hamster."

Colly looked doubtful but said nothing.

"Satchel's a sensitive kid who's experienced major trauma. He's got a loving family. He's getting the help he needs. He'll be fine." Niall picked up the sneaker again and bent to put it on. "For the record, I don't think Denny was beyond hope, either. No kid's hereditarily doomed to be a monster, no matter what their PET scan shows. If I thought they were, I wouldn't be in this line of work." He straightened and gave Colly a penetrating look. "Did Satchel say what the fight was about?"

Colly felt suddenly hot. "Logan repeated something he heard—about me."

"About how your husband and daughter died?"

"Of *course* you've heard about it."

"Brenda never said anything, in case you're wondering. But yeah, rumors fly in a small town."

"I didn't hire anyone to kill my husband and daughter for the insurance money, if that's what you heard."

Niall laughed as he tied the second shoe. "I did hear that, as a matter of fact. And I dismissed it out of hand." He sat up and cocked his head, studying her face. "What's the real story? Can I ask?"

"Why not? The truth's not as bad as the rumors." Colly ran her fingers distractedly through her hair. "Abridged version—I made a mistake in an investigation, and my family got killed because of it."

"And the unabridged version?"

Colly sighed. "A few years ago in Houston, we had a series of strangling-murders of young women and girls." She spoke slowly, staring into space. "The victims were mostly prostitutes, drug addicts—people who don't always get reported missing right away, which complicated things. For months, we had nothing. Then finally, we got a lead on a suspect, but the guy was very slick about covering his tracks. He lived with his elderly mother. She had dementia and never went out, but she had a storage unit that the son visited a lot. That seemed strange. I thought if we searched it, we were bound to find something. But no judge would give us a warrant. Called it a fishing expedition."

Colly stopped. Niall was sitting with his legs crossed and one arm along the back of the sofa, his face registering nothing but friendly interest. He nodded encouragingly.

"One day, a sixteen-year-old vanished while walking home from a babysitting gig. Janie Krause was her name. She didn't really fit the victim profile, but the MO was similar. And unlike the rest, she was reported missing the night she disappeared, which gave us an edge. We knew the others had been held somewhere for a few days before they were killed, so I thought there was a chance our suspect might have her tied up in that storage unit. I talked the manager of the place into giving me access. I figured a search was justified as an exigent circumstance. If the girl was in there, she could be dead by the time I got a warrant."

"Did you find her?"

Colly met his eyes. "Not then. Hunters stumbled on her remains three months later. But we found other things—a trove of evidence. Including proof the guy was already stalking another victim."

"You saved a life—maybe a lot of lives. How's that a screwup?"

"Judge didn't see it that way. He was a real hard-liner. When it came to trial, he wouldn't let us use any of the storage-unit evidence, even though other judges had ruled similar searches legal in the past. So the bad guy walked. You should've seen him smirk. All the victims' families were extremely upset, of course. Most blamed the judge. But Janie Krause's dad blamed me—went out of his mind. He wanted me to know . . ." Colly's throat contracted. She looked away.

"He wanted you to know how it felt to lose someone you loved?" Niall asked gently.

Colly nodded. "Victoria and Satchel were living with us then, while she finished community college. She and Randy were at the house alone that afternoon—I'd taken Satchel with me to the store.

When we got home, the door inside the garage was standing open. Before I could stop him, Satchel ran inside. He saw them first."

"That's horrible. Poor kid."

Colly rubbed her palms on her knees. "The cops found Krause dead in his garage an hour later. Shotgun under the chin. He left a letter addressed to me." She winced. "That was two years ago. After that, I resigned from the force. Couldn't do it anymore. Since then, I've just been taking care of Satchel and trying to figure out my next move."

"Crescent Bluff blames you for everything, eh?" Niall said. "What about the Newlands?"

"Russ and Brenda have been kind. Iris and Lowell, so-so. I dread the day Satchel finds out the details."

"Aren't you being a little hard on yourself? You made a judgment call in a high-stakes situation, and it backfired through no fault of your own. Most people—" Niall was interrupted by a ringtone. He pulled out his phone and checked the screen. "I'm so sorry, I've got to take this. I'm on call this weekend."

Colly stood up. "I need to get back to town, anyway. Mind if I go look for the phone myself?"

"Remember where the key is?"

Colly nodded. As Niall answered the call, she walked back to the kitchen and exited through French doors into the bright morning light.

Chapter 32

The grassy lawn behind the house was still slick with dew, and Colly picked her way carefully along the path to the shed. Standing on tiptoes, she groped along the door's upper casing until she found the key.

Inside, the air was chilly. A faint, dusty light filtered through a curtained window high on the north wall. Colly groped for a switch, and a bank of florescent work lamps hummed to life. She glanced around. Nothing in the shed appeared altered since she'd seen it last; but in the densely packed confusion of tackle, fly-rods, tools, and other equipment, she saw no sign of her phone.

Where had she left it? Colly crossed the room to the wall of metal shelves stacked with shoebox-sized plastic bins. She'd been standing here when Iris called. Presumably, the bins contained fly-tying materials, though the descriptions on their labels were cryptic: Foam Bodies, Grizzly Hackle, Eyes, Chenille. Familiar terms, though contextually unenlightening. Others—Dry-Fly Dubbing, Zonker Strips, Tippets—communicated nothing to her mind. She noted them automatically as she ran her hands over the tops of the bins and shifted them to check the gaps in between.

After five minutes of searching, she was getting frustrated when a soft buzzing noise drew her attention to a bin labeled "Goose

Biots." Her phone sat beside it, vibrating insistently. Relieved, she picked it up.

"Finally," Brenda exclaimed when Colly answered. "I've been trying to reach you for ages." There'd been a change of plans, she said. Thunderstorms were now forecast for the early afternoon, so Brenda, Alice, and Iris were going to take the kids to the Rattlesnake Rodeo now.

Colly could hear children chattering excitedly in the background. "Sounds like they're over their fight."

Brenda hesitated. "I think so. Chocolate-chip pancakes this morning helped."

"It's pretty sunny, at the moment."

"Iris has Satchel's EpiPen, and she's buttering him with sunblock as we speak."

Colly checked her watch. "I'll try to meet you out there for lunch, if I can."

"Oh." A brief silence. "Are you sure? I figured you've had enough of snakes this week."

"Satchel really wants me there. Don't tell him, though—I don't want to disappoint him if I can't make it."

They said goodbye, and Colly stuffed the phone in her pocket. As she turned towards the door, she caught sight of the last bin on the bottom shelf. She froze, then knelt for a closer look at the words printed on the label. An adjective and a noun. A thousand bees began to buzz inside her skull. She touched the words to make sure of what she was seeing. "Hares' Masks."

Standing up, she moved quickly to the door and peered cautiously towards the house. Through the windows, she caught sight of Niall pacing the kitchen, still on the phone. Closing the door again, she took out her own phone and snapped a few photos of the bin on its shelf before carrying it to the workbench.

Her heart thudded as she removed the plastic lid. The faces of a half-dozen flayed rabbits stared up at her with empty eyes. Colly reached for the masks, then stopped, struck suddenly by the vulnerability of her position. She took a picture and texted it to Avery—*Need backup, Shaw's place. NOW.*

She loosened her gun in its holster. Had Shaw forgotten that the masks were here? Cocky bastard to label the things. Or was it a calculated move? Did he want her to find them? Was it some sort of confession—part of some sick game? Whatever the case, he might be off the phone any second. If there was more evidence, she needed to find it now.

Colly looked quickly around. From hooks behind the door hung two sets of waders. A pair of rubber boots stood on a mat beneath them. She checked them all. Each had a clearly legible "10" stamped on its instep.

Her phone vibrated. A text from Avery: *ON MY WAY.*

It'll take her a while to get here, Colly thought. *I was stupid to come alone.*

Her eyes fell on the hard-sided equipment case near the workbench. Denny's body had been moved to the stock pond by something with wheels—a dolly, the Rangers thought, though the tracks had been smooth, and most dolly-wheels had treads. Was this case large enough to hold a child? Satchel, yes. But Denny? Colly knelt for a closer look. Smooth casters. And muddy.

She tried the lid. Locked. Why keep it locked inside a padlocked shed? Maybe the key was hidden nearby. Colly felt along the edges of the workbench, then began to rifle through the numerous small containers on its surface. Dumping the contents of a battered metal Folgers can, she sorted quickly through them. No key. But among the empty thread spools, beads, and bits of colored foam, a small strip of iridescent pink ribbon fluttered out. Colly picked it up. Was it the same as those Russ had shown her—the ribbons wrapped around the masks found on Adam and Denny?

She was hunched over the desk, oblivious to all but the scrap of ribbon on her palm, when she heard the shed door open quietly behind her. Colly froze. The door opened wider, and a bright blade of morning light fell across the workbench. On the wall in front of her loomed the silhouette of a man. He held something in his hand.

The shadow moved. "What are you doing?"

Almost without thinking, Colly turned and drew her sidearm in a single, smooth motion.

Niall stood just inside the shed, one hand on the doorknob. In the other, he clutched his phone. Seeing the gun, he took a half-step backwards. "What the hell?"

"Hands up. Turn around."

"Colly, what's going on?"

"Turn around, damn you."

Niall pivoted slowly to face the wall and placed his palms against it.

"If you have a weapon, tell me now," Colly said.

"Phone, keys, wallet. That's it."

"Don't move."

She approached him cautiously. Pressing the gun against his spine, she took his phone and stuffed it in her pocket, then patted him down with her free hand, emptying his pockets and tossing the contents onto the workbench.

"Can I turn around now?" he asked when she stepped away.

"Shut up. Stay where you are."

"Colly—"

"I said shut up." A decrepit rolling office chair stood in front of the workbench. Colly shoved it behind his knees, then stepped back. "Sit down, then turn very slowly. Keep your hands on the armrests."

307

He obeyed, his dark eyes fixed on the gun's muzzle. "Am I under arrest?"

"I'm not a cop anymore. But police are on the way. Meanwhile, it's your choice if you want to talk to me."

Niall didn't seem to hear her. He had torn his gaze from the gun, and his eyes were roving around the shed, scanning the floor, ceiling, shelves, workbench. "At least tell me why—" He spotted the bin labeled "Hares' Masks," and froze. "Oh . . ." His eyes met Colly's, and he moved to stand up.

Colly raised the gun. "Don't."

He checked himself. Suddenly, all the energy seemed to drain from him. He looked sick. "I—I forgot those were here."

"You're a good actor. You really had me going with that sophisticated-psychologist routine." Colly lowered herself onto the edge of the workbench, keeping her gun trained on his chest. "Why'd you do it?"

"I didn't kill Adam."

"No. You just pulled him out of that pond and left him for the scavengers, with one of these creepy things in his hand." She jerked her head towards the bin of masks beside her.

Niall looked up. "It was a mistake, but it doesn't warrant holding me at gunpoint—it was twenty years ago."

Colly ignored this. "Why didn't you call the cops when you found him?"

"You won't understand."

"Try me."

"You're making me nervous. Put the gun away, and I'll talk."

Colly shook her head. Her fingers tightened on the weapon's grip.

Niall shifted impatiently. "Look, you've already searched me. What am I going to do, attack you with a fish hook?"

"I won't shoot unless you do something dumb."

"Speaking as a Black man, that's not reassuring." Niall watched her for a moment. "Colly, it's me. An hour ago, you were telling me your life story. If you jump ahead of your evidence, you'll be making the same mistake you made in Houston."

Colly pursed her lips, hesitating. Finally, she laid the weapon on the bench, pointing the muzzle towards the wall but keeping her hand on it.

Niall's shoulders relaxed. "Thanks."

"Why didn't you report finding Adam's body?"

"I was scared."

"Of—?"

"Of the all-white police force, what do you think? I figured it was safer to keep my mouth shut—at the time."

"Oh, come on."

Niall smiled grimly. "You don't get it. Nobody knew us in Crescent Bluff, and I was a fatherless Black adolescent—the most suspicious demographic in America to the average white cop."

"Avery says everyone admired you."

"In high school, sure. Other kids hung around me because their parents told them not to. I was the bad boy, if you can believe it. *Me*." He laughed sourly.

"You were scared to report finding Adam because you're Black—you're sticking to that?" Colly asked.

"I was also grieving and confused." Niall's eyes flashed with the first sign of anger. "Is it that hard to believe? Jesus, I thought maybe you were different."

"Right, I'm the bad guy. What's your excuse with Denny and Willis? You weren't a teenager when *they* died."

Niall stared at her blankly. "Denny and Willis?"

Colly picked up a hare's mask. "Police never released this detail to the public. You're the only person who knew."

309

Niall frowned. "Are you saying hares' masks were found with Denny and Willis, also?"

"Don't play dumb."

"I had no idea—I promise you." He held up his hands, palms outward.

Colly reached for the gun. "Don't move."

"Sorry—you caught me off guard." Niall returned his hands to the armrests. "Look, I pulled Adam out of the pond and put the mask in his hand—but that's all. I never met Willis, and I was at a conference seven hundred miles from here when Denny died."

He looked so genuinely bewildered that Colly felt a stirring of doubt. "Why would you leave a rabbit face on a little boy's corpse? That's pretty sick."

"They're used to make flies. If you'll let me up, I'll show you." He nodded towards a tackle box by the wall.

"Stay there." Keeping her eyes on him, Colly carried the gun with her as she fetched the box and set it on the workbench. She opened the lid. Inside, in divided compartments, were dozens of tiny barbed tufts of fuzz. She looked inquiringly at Niall.

"See the brown and gray ones on the bottom left?" he said. "They're dry flies made with turkey tail feathers and fur from an English hare. The pink wings come from strands of chenille ribbon. My own invention—the 'AnNiallator.'"

"AnNiallator?"

"Dumb, I know. I was twelve when I named it. I've caught some great trophy trout with those." Even in the stress of the current moment, there was a note of pride in his voice.

"There aren't any English hares in Texas."

Niall blinked in surprise. "I don't kill and skin the things myself. Sporting-goods stores carry hares' masks—at least up north, they do. But I got mine online. They're perfect for dry-fly tying because they have so many types of fur on them—guard hairs, underfur, whiskers, hackles."

Colly squinted at him, deliberating. "Your waders are size ten, just like the footprints by Denny's body."

"I told you, I was in Phoenix. Take the waders, run any tests you want."

"What about this rolling case?" Colly gestured towards the black box by the workbench. "Why is it locked?"

"My custom fly-rods are in there. They're worth more than my Jeep. You've got my keys—see for yourself."

Colly did as he suggested. "Okay, okay." She sat back down. "Let's say I buy your story. I still don't understand why you'd leave one of these masks on Adam's body. Were you trying to mess with the cops?"

"Of course not."

"Then why?"

Niall was quiet for a minute. "I told you last night that Adam was my little shadow."

"You said you felt guilty because you weren't very nice to him."

He nodded. "I was in high school when Adam started tagging along on fishing trips. He wanted to help, though mostly he got underfoot—asking a million questions, scaring off the fish, generally being a pest. Normal kid stuff, but I wasn't very patient. He wanted to learn to tie flies, and he ruined a bunch playing with them, which really annoyed me. Finally, I told him if he touched my gear again without permission, he wouldn't be allowed to help anymore.

"One day, we were at the stock pond. I waded out to unsnag my line, and when I turned around, Adam was playing with a hare's mask from the tackle box. He had his fingers through the eyeholes, pretending it was a puppet. Acting silly."

A shadow crossed Niall's face. "He didn't damage it in any way. But it pissed me off. More than pissed me off. I blew up, told him I was through with him. Sent him home." Niall sighed. "That was the last time I saw him. When he disappeared a few days later, I thought he started that fire and ran away because of me."

"Did you tell anyone?"

Niall shook his head. "Too ashamed." He looked away. "About a month after Adam vanished, I went back to the stock pond—to fish a little, get my mind off things. The vultures were circling, and something was floating in the water. A mannequin, I thought." He swallowed. "I waded out. Adam was face-up, wrapped in a chain. All bloated and purple, like he'd been submerged for weeks. Unrecognizable."

"Then how'd you know who it was?" Colly asked.

"He was the only kid missing. Besides, I recognized his clothes." Niall stared at the floor, reliving the moment. "I don't remember getting back to shore, but I remember puking my guts up in the reeds. I sat on the bank for hours, trying to decide what to do."

Colly didn't have to coax him to tell the rest of the story. Right away, he'd understood that it was murder—that much was obvious. But he'd been terrified to report it. He felt responsible, somehow, and assumed others would think so, too. He returned to the pond day after day, hoping each time that the body had been discovered.

"I was sure someone would see the vultures, but no one did. I was afraid the body would sink again when the bloat subsided. It might never be found." Niall looked up. "So, one day, I took my waders and a bolt cutter out to the pond." He winced. "It's not a pleasant memory."

Colly nodded. "And the hare's mask you left in his hand?"

Niall smiled sadly. "My guilt offering, I guess you'd say. My apology to Adam." He sat up straighter. "You may not believe this, but it never occurred to me to wonder what the cops would think of it. I definitely didn't imagine they'd take it as some perverse psychopathic signature."

Colly studied him, chewing her lip. "Who else knows about this?"

"No one."

"Not even a friend? Therapist? Priest? Your mother? Think carefully."

"No."

"What about Brenda—when you were dating?"

"You're the first to hear about it. I swear. It was just between Adam and me—a private thing." He looked at her. "That sounds crazy, I know."

Not that crazy, Colly thought. Aloud, she said, "Then how do you explain those masks showing up with Denny and Willis?"

"I can't. But anyone could've ordered them—they're on Amazon."

"I don't believe in coincidences. None ever went missing from your shed?"

"Not that I'm aware." Niall paused. "You said the cops didn't officially release the detail of the mask. But maybe one of them let it slip."

"Cops understand how vital it is to keep a secret like that."

"Yeah, but there had to be quite a few in on it. It only takes one careless comment."

Colly's mind strayed uneasily to Russ. He'd lied to give his brother an alibi. Could he have told Lowell about the hares' masks, too? He had vehemently rejected her suggestion that Denny was murdered by a copycat. Was he trying to steer her away from some inconvenient truth?

"I'll look into it." Colly stood and holstered her gun. "I'd like to take these in as evidence, if that's okay." She picked up the bin of hares' masks.

"Does this mean you believe me?" Niall asked, pushing out of the chair.

Colly looked at him. A trace of bitter watchfulness still lingered in his eyes, but his expression was open, ingenuous. If he was a liar, he was an extraordinarily talented one.

"Let's go back to the house." She handed him his phone and other belongings. "Avery'll be here any minute." She started towards the door but stopped at the threshold. "Look, I'm sorry. This investigation's got my nerves on edge. I thought you were the killer."

"I know."

"It's nothing personal."

"Maybe it should be," he said flatly. "I like you, Colly. I like you a lot. But it's demoralizing, always having to revise my expectations downward."

Colly said nothing. As she stepped outside, her eyes were momentarily dazzled by the bright morning sunlight, and she ran into the dark form before she saw it. She reached for her gun, but someone grabbed her hand.

"Relax, it's me."

As Colly's eyes adjusted, she saw that Avery was standing, weapon drawn, beside the doorway.

"I got here a few minutes ago—in time to hear this sonofabitch admit to leaving my brother out for buzzard bait." She stared darkly at Niall, who was emerging from the shed. "You were getting good info, so I didn't interrupt."

"If you heard that, then you heard why I did it," Niall said.

"They ate his eyes out, you asshole."

"I know. I'm sorry."

"You—" Avery started, but Colly laid a hand on her shoulder.

"Now's not the time. Let's stay focused."

They said goodbye to Niall at the house, and as they climbed the path to their cars, Colly summarized the parts of the story that Avery had missed. Her derisive snorts and mutterings showed plainly that she was skeptical of Niall's account, but she didn't argue.

"Any update on that video footage?" Colly asked.

"Nothing useful. I haven't found anyone matching the descriptions the store clerk gave Russ," Avery said. Some of the cameras had captured the road, and four vehicles showed up repeatedly between Crescent Bluff and Colorado City—a dark green or possibly blue minivan; a diesel pickup pulling a cattle trailer; a black SUV; and a very dirty Jeep of indeterminate color—but Avery hadn't seen the drivers or gotten any license plates. All the videos were too fuzzy and distant.

Colly sighed. "It was a long shot, but it had to be checked."

They reached the top of the hill and leaned against the cruiser to catch their breath. The sun was still shining brightly above their heads, but a line of clouds, towering and dark, loomed ominously to the west.

"That's heading this way. Gonna put a damper on the Rodeo," Avery said. "What now?"

Colly checked her watch. "Let's go over Adam's case file one more time. If we can make a list of everybody who knew about that first hare's mask, we can try to track them down, see if anyone'll admit to blabbing."

"That was twenty years ago."

"I know. But we're out of leads." Colly searched her purse for her sunglasses. "Go get yourself some lunch, first. I promised Satchel I'd try to swing by the Rodeo—" Suddenly, she stopped. "Tell me again about those vehicles on the video. Did any have distinguishing features?"

Avery replied. Then, seeing the expression on Colly's face, she said, "What? What is it?"

Colly didn't answer. She yanked her phone from her pocket and pulled up her list of contacts, fumbling and nearly dropping the device more than once. Finally, she found the number she was looking for and placed the call. When it was answered, she blurted without preamble, "You talk in your sleep, don't you?"

She listened tensely to the reply.

"Oh my God." Beneath her feet, the ground seemed to tilt. She dropped the phone.

Alarmed, Avery grabbed her shoulders, steadying her against the cruiser's frame. "What is it?"

But Colly only shook her head.

Avery picked up Colly's phone and held it to her ear. "Who the hell is this?"

She got the answer, but it gave her no insight.

"We have to go, we have to go." Colly wrenched herself out of Avery's grip and scrambled into the patrol car. "I know who killed Denny."

Chapter 33

Colly was aware of very little except the roar of the squad car's engine and the rushing sounds of wind and road as they raced towards the Newland Ranch. She sat in the passenger seat, staring into the distance. Random phrases, seemingly insignificant at the time, churned into her consciousness with a new and terrible relevance.

"Denny looked like a boiled shrimp after ten minutes outside . . ." "They figured she was a neighbor's relative, since their dogs didn't bark . . ." "We've got some more things for the thrift shop . . ."

Colly's shoulders were hunched and aching. She forced herself to relax the muscles, but that didn't stop the barrage of memories. They slipped into place like scraps of a torn photograph magically reassembling itself as she watched.

"Denny didn't have no red caps . . ." "There was play-therapy toys all over . . ." "He was going to the library to return some books for his mom . . . something changed his mind . . ." "No kid's hereditarily doomed to be a monster . . ."

"Shouldn't we call ahead?" Avery asked. "Practically all the local cops are there—they could make an arrest."

Colly looked up. "Too risky. Might scare the killer into doing something rash."

Hours seemed to pass before they spotted the streamer flags announcing the entrance to the Rattlesnake Rodeo. A long line of vehicles idled on the shoulder of the Old Ranch Way, waiting to enter. A police deputy stood at the entrance, directing traffic.

"Nice and easy," Colly said. "Don't want folks thinking there's any emergency."

Avery grunted and stepped on the brake. Skirting the line of cars, they waved to the deputy and turned onto the dusty track that the Newlands opened once a year to serve as the event's access road. After jolting across the ranchland for half a mile, they spotted the white roof of the circus tent with a Lone Star flag flying from its peak. Passing the crowded makeshift parking lot, they stopped at the construction fence that circled the Rodeo grounds.

"What's the plan?" Avery asked.

"I'll start on this end. You go around to the employee entrance. We'll work towards the middle. You know who we're looking for."

Avery chewed her lip. "Yeah, but I don't know how you're so sure. It'd suck to make a mistake—considering who it is."

"It's no mistake. I'll explain later. There's no time now." Colly leapt out, slipping through the main gate as Avery drove off in a cloud of red dust.

Although she'd seen the Rodeo being set up just two days earlier, Colly was unprepared for the size of the crowd or the assault on her senses. Country music blared from speakers fixed to tall posts, competing with shouting children, barking dogs, and a cacophony of tunes emanating from numerous booths and arcades. The odors of hot dogs, cotton candy, and beer hung in the air, mixed with the acrid smells of cooking grease and sun-ripening garbage. Vendors dressed in all sorts of outlandish costumes shouted and waved in an attempt to attract the milling crowds to booths selling everything from t-shirts and ballcaps to rattlesnake-leather wallets, belts, holsters, and Bible covers.

There must be a couple thousand people here, Colly thought, pushing her way through the hot, jostling crush.

It was just past noon. The clouds on the western horizon had darkened to a menacing blue-black. They were closer but hadn't yet obscured the sun, which beat down through the haze like a disk of tarnished silver. The air was muggy and oppressive. After ten minutes and only a hundred yards of progress, Colly was sweating profusely. She stumbled over an obese basset hound and was apologizing absently to its owner when she caught a glimpse of ash-blond hair and long, tanned legs across the way.

"Alice!" she yelled, but her voice was drowned in the surrounding hubbub. Disentangling herself from the dog's leash, Colly fought her way through the crowd to a booth where her niece and several other teens were attempting to toss horseshoes around a row of stakes for a prize.

She laid a hand on Alice's shoulder, and the girl turned. "Aunt Colly—I didn't know you were here."

"Thought I'd come see what the fuss is about." Colly wiped her forehead. "Have you seen your dad?"

"A few minutes ago. He and Uncle Lowell were heading to the big tent."

"What about Grandma and Aunt Brenda?"

Alice shrugged. "Gran's judge turned up while we were buying the kids some balloons, and after that I got separated from everyone, somehow."

"Who has the kids?"

"Logan went to the Ferris wheel with some friends. Satchel and Minnie were with Gran and Aunt Brenda, last I saw."

"If you run across any of them, text me, okay?"

Alice cheerfully agreed, and Colly pushed once more in the direction of the massive tent. A wide area around its entrance had been left free of booths and stands to create a sort of improvised plaza. Here the crowd thinned slightly. Seeing no one she knew, Colly moved towards the tent's entrance. Standing beside it was a uniformed officer—Jimmy Meggs. Looking hot and slightly hungover, he greeted her with an irritable nod. But when she pulled him aside and murmured some instructions in his ear, his eyes widened.

"I think the person I'm looking for is probably inside this tent," Colly said. "Whatever happens, don't let them get away. Tackle and cuff them, if you have to. But keep them here—and contact Avery or me ASAP. Got it?"

"Who approved this?" Meggs croaked. He looked scared.

"I'll take responsibility." Colly nodded towards the entrance. "Is this the only door?"

"There's one on the north side, too."

"Who's on duty there?"

"Some turbine-plant security guard, I think."

Colly frowned. "I'd rather have a cop. Who's on-site? Is there someone trustworthy we can put on that door—someone discreet?"

Meggs fidgeted with the brim of his hat. "Gibbins is around somewhere."

"Radio him to meet you here. You know what to tell him."

Colly turned and slipped through the entryway. Inside, the tent was crowded and stifling. The stench had worsened considerably since Thursday, a fetid brew of snake blood, offal, greasy food, and sweat. Fighting nausea, Colly assessed her surroundings. It was the worst possible venue for a confrontation. The killer could be armed, and a gunfight would be disastrous. Clear sightlines were impossible in a place like this. Hundreds of civilians—of which at least a third were children—were crammed into a comparatively small area with poor entrance and exit routes, not to mention open pens of lethal vipers. The open-carry laws in Texas meant that dozens in the crowd likely had weapons, and with the walls of the place made of canvas, people both inside and outside the tent would be in danger.

Colly cursed softly and began to work her way towards the north end of the big top. A ring of spectators surrounded the holding pit that she'd seen on Thursday with Russ. She elbowed her way to the plywood wall for a better view of the faces gathered there. The pit still held hundreds of snakes, though fewer than Colly remembered. Inside it, a man and a woman, both in Kevlar gloves, tall boots, and camo-colored gaiters, were using long-handled tongs to load the creatures into large plastic bins, which they handed over the wall to workers who carried them away.

Colly saw no one she recognized either there or at the second ring, where a heavily bearded man was demonstrating snake-handling techniques. At the third ring, workers in blood-spattered rubber aprons stood at butcher blocks made of tree stumps, methodically beheading snake after snake with machetes and tossing the fanged heads and still-writhing bodies into separate buckets. Children pressed their sticky faces against the plexiglass windows of the enclosure and shrieked with each decapitating chop. There were more people at this pen than at any other, and Colly spent several minutes circling it hopefully before giving up and moving on.

At the last ring, workers were skinning and gutting the headless snakes before passing them on to the fry cooks in the food court. There Colly caught a glimpse of a sandy head and pair of broad shoulders disappearing behind one of the food stands. She hurried in pursuit, but when she grabbed the man's arm, she found herself looking not at Russ but at a bearded biker-type in a t-shirt with "Shoot the Snowflake Libtards" stenciled across the image of an assault rifle wrapped in an American flag.

"Sorry," Colly muttered. Cutting around a deep-fry station, she stumbled over a picnic table, nearly landing in the lap of an elderly gentleman with a white goatee. Talford Maybrey sat munching something brown and crispy off of a greasy paper plate.

His pink face beamed as he dismissed her apology with a wave. "It's quite all right, my dear. Did Iris commission a police raid?" He chuckled, wiping his mouth and whiskers neatly with a napkin. "She doesn't approve of fried foods, but the snake is particularly delicious this year. Care to join me?"

"Maybe later." Colly's eyes traveled over the faces clustered around the food trucks. "Where is Iris?"

"Off somewhere being interviewed by a San Angelo news crew."

Colly inquired about the rest of the family.

"I've seen them all at various times," Talford said. "But I don't know where anyone is at the moment. It's easier to lose people than to find them in this place."

The food court was packed. Saying goodbye to Maybrey, Colly wove through the throngs to the tent's north doorway. Jimmy Meggs had kept his word, and Colly was relieved to find Gibbins on guard there. She spoke with him briefly before ducking back inside.

The temperature under the big top was rising fast. Sweat trickled down Colly's back, and her t-shirt clung damply to her skin as she worked her way down the east side of the tent. She'd always been good under pressure, but as the seconds passed, she felt a sort of panic building in her throat. This place was too crowded for one person to search. Wondering if Avery had made it to the tent, Colly was reaching for her phone when she heard a shrill whistle and spotted her partner shouldering towards her through the crowd.

They compared notes. Avery had encountered Logan at the Ferris wheel, but had seen no trace of their suspect.

Colly plucked absently at her clammy shirt. "We've been all over this place. What are we missing?"

"We haven't tried the first-aid trailer or the toilets. They're both out that way." Avery nodded towards the north door.

"Good thinking. You check those. I'll keep looking in here. Call if you find something."

Avery brushed a tendril of damp purple hair out of her eyes and hurried off. Colly pushed forward once again. By the time she reached the holding pit, she felt dizzy with the heat. She shoved her way towards the bleachers against the wall, where the crowd was thinner, hoping to catch her breath. She found herself near the "Staff Only" entrance to the ad-hoc research room that Russ had shown her on Thursday. Pete, Felix's nephew, was standing, arms crossed, in front of it, wearing the same boots and greasy straw Stetson he'd worn two days earlier. He nodded impassively as she approached.

"Guarding the research equipment?" Colly asked.

Pete lifted his hat and mopped the back of his neck with a bandana. "Ain't no equipment now—them Aggies went home. But we can't have kids messing around back there. Got more snakes than usual this year 'cause of the early hot spell. Research pen's holding the surplus till we need 'em."

"Have you seen any of my family?"

Pete nodded. He'd seen all of them at various times within the last hour, he said. "Matter of fact, some of them are back there now." He jerked his head towards the opening behind him. "They wanted to see it."

"Who?"

His answer made Colly go cold despite the oppressive heat.

Pete's brows contracted. "You okay?"

But Colly barely heard him. "Go get help."

Drawing her gun, she darted past him and through the doorway.

Compared to the brightly lit big top, the research room seemed almost cave-like. The halogen ceiling lamps were dark. The only illumination came from a single work lamp at the opposite end of the space. It was affixed to a stand on the far side of the auxiliary snake pen, positioned in such a way that the glare obscured Colly's view in that direction. The near end of the room, where she'd seen the venom-milking station and other equipment on Thursday, was now empty except for a few portable tables and chairs stacked by the tent walls.

Colly saw no one. At first, she also heard nothing but the muffled noises of the crowd in the big top behind her and the now-familiar hum of rattlers coming from the snake pen. But after a few seconds, the stillness was broken by a sound that was, in that moment, more terrifying to Colly than all the rattlesnakes in the world.

"Are the snakes mad, or just scared?" It was a high, clear voice that Colly knew at once.

"I don't know, Satchel. What do you think?"

Colly recognized the answering voice, as well. Her skin prickled, and the gun shook in her hand. Though partially blinded by the work lamp, she now dimly perceived a dark, adult-sized figure standing on the near side of the auxiliary pen—apparently facing away from Colly, since she hadn't yet been spotted. No child-sized form was visible. Shielding her eyes, Colly began to move cautiously down the length of the room towards the snake pen.

"I think they're pretending to be mad," Satchel's voice responded.

"Why?"

"Avery says that's what you should do when you're scared."

"That's when snakes are most dangerous," the other voice answered, as Colly moved closer.

"It's not their fault," Satchel said. "People shouldn't kill them."

324

"Sometimes you have to kill things, even if it's not their fault. Even if you don't want to."

Satchel was quiet, apparently considering this point. Colly's feet felt heavy, like in a nightmare, but she forced herself forward, angling towards the wall to avoid the light. The dark figure grew more distinct as Colly drew abreast of it. Now, she could see a second, much smaller figure in front.

"Why?" Satchel asked.

"We have to stop things that will hurt people."

"It's not fair to kill them for something they didn't do yet."

"If it's in their nature to hurt people, we have to make sure they don't."

Colly took three more cautious steps, and suddenly the glare no longer blinded her. From this vantage point, the lamplight shone on the faces of the two figures, and she could see them clearly. Satchel was sitting on the edge of the pen, his arms and legs wrapped like a baby monkey's around the torso of the adult who was with him. Dressed in shorts and a t-shirt, with a partially deflated red balloon tied to his wrist, he was leaning backwards, craning for a better view of the snakes, while the other's arms were locked around his waist to keep him from tumbling in.

Colly inhaled sharply.

At the slight noise, Satchel looked up. "Grandma!" he shouted happily. "Let me down, Aunt Brenda—Grandma's here."

Brenda gasped and spun around, still holding onto Satchel. But when she saw Colly, her face assumed its familiar, friendly expression. "Oh good, you made it. I didn't think—" She froze when she noticed Colly's gun.

"It's over, Brenda. There's no way out." Colly kept her voice calm. "I've got guards at both tent exits. Put Satchel down and step away from that pen." She edged slowly towards them.

"What on earth—?" Brenda's brow furrowed. Clutching Satchel with one hand and keeping the other on the rim of the snake pen, she backed away. "Colly, are you all right?"

Scared and confused, Satchel began to cry. The half-deflated balloon, which had been rising and sinking slowly around him, now drifted in front of his face, and he batted it fretfully away. "I want Grandma, Aunt Brenda."

"It's okay, buddy. I'm right here," Colly said. "Brenda, let him go."

Brenda's arm tightened around the squirming boy. "Hold still, Satchel. She won't shoot, I promise. Grandma's been under a lot of pressure. But we're going to get her some help."

"You can drop the concerned-psychologist routine. I know about—" Colly stopped herself with a glance at Satchel's frightened face. "I know everything, Brenda. Others do, too. It's over."

Brenda's eyes narrowed. Her expression didn't change, exactly; but her features seemed to harden. "If you know all that, then you must understand why." She was retreating along the perimeter of the snake pen, holding Satchel in front of her like a shield.

"I have a notion." Colly advanced steadily to the pen's plywood wall, within fifteen feet of Brenda and Satchel. She glanced quickly inside. On the sawdust floor were at least a hundred snakes. Most had gravitated to the opposite wall under the work lamp and were basking in a tangled heap. "Put Satchel down, and let's talk. That's the only way to help yourself now."

Brenda stopped. "Help myself?" Her voice was sharp. "This isn't about me."

"Then think of Logan and Minnie."

Brenda's eyes flashed. "I am—I always have been. Do you think I *wanted* to kill Denny?"

For a second, Satchel stopped struggling. His eyes widened, and he stared at Brenda.

"Look at me, Satch," Colly said quickly. "Brenda, I'm sure you didn't mean to do it." She kept her voice soothing as she inched forward. "Remorse will go a long way with a jury—but actions speak louder than words. Let him go."

"Remorse?" Brenda seemed puzzled. "I evaluated Denny. I saw his PET scan. When Willis was that age, no one knew what he was. But with Denny, we knew. Someone just needed the will to act."

"You can't play God."

"That's what people tell themselves to justify doing nothing," Brenda said bitterly. "I sat through Willis's trial in '98, you know. The defense showed his brain scan, and it blew me away. I had no idea technology like that existed. Why wasn't he scanned at the first sign of trouble—back when he molested that Carroway boy? I wanted to stand up in court and scream, 'You mean you could've seen this coming—you could've stopped him murdering Adam Parker? What the hell is wrong with you people?'"

"Brenda, you didn't just evaluate Denny. What was the point of doing therapy with him if you were planning to kill him?"

"I had to make sure I was right about him, didn't I? There's no room for error with something like that."

"For God's sake, Brenda, he was a child—you could've helped him. No one's doomed to be a monster from birth."

Brenda grimaced. "You've been talking to Niall, I see. I used to think that way, too. But half-measures don't work with a psychopath. You of all people should know that."

As Brenda spoke, Colly caught a glimpse of movement in her peripheral vision. Someone was edging cautiously along the opposite wall, keeping in the shadows and working to stay out of Brenda's line of sight. Colly didn't dare look to see who it was. She needed to keep Brenda's focus firmly on her.

"You used to think like Niall? What changed your mind?"

"If a criminal's broke, we lock him up and throw away the key. But a dangerous psychopath can have his sentence commuted if his family contributes enough to the governor's campaign."

"You mean Willis?"

Brenda nodded. "When he got out last year, I was stunned. My kids spend half their time at the ranch. Everyone said, 'Don't worry, there's a restraining order'—like that's supposed to reassure me. Give me a break. I realized the truth—with a psychopath, there's only one solution."

The figure by the wall had paused briefly during this speech but now began to move again. Colly caught the glint of dark metal. She fought the temptation to look.

"You're talking about executing people for pre-crime. Brenda, that's insane."

"It's insane to play Russian roulette with public safety. This isn't science fiction, Colly. You saw those scans at Niall's. We have the technology to know who's dangerous—we've had it for decades. We can't afford to dither."

Brenda was so caught up in her argument that she had stopped moving, while Colly continued to inch towards her. Suddenly aware of this, Brenda scrambled back several feet. Now, with the slightest turn of her head, she would be staring directly at the person by the wall.

Keep her talking, no matter what, Colly thought. "If you're so proud of killing Denny, why'd you hide it? Why bother with the intricate cover-up?"

"Do you think I'd let Lowell raise Logan and Minnie by himself? They need me."

The shadowy figure crept closer. It was now within twenty feet of Brenda and Satchel.

"You weren't a suspect—what was the point of framing Willis?" Colly asked.

"Haven't you been listening? Willis was more dangerous than Denny ever was. The Rangers' investigation was stalled. I had to do something."

"So you planted those masks in his nightstand."

Brenda's face clouded. "I thought the one on Denny would be enough. But the DA's a Newland lapdog—he wouldn't indict Willis without more evidence."

Satchel was crying harder now and had begun to squirm. His feet clattered against the plywood siding of the pen. The snakes, agitated by the noise, began to rattle angrily.

Satchel's movements sent the red balloon bouncing erratically into Brenda's face. "Hold still," she snapped, thrusting the balloon into his arms. Sobbing, he clutched it against his chest like a security blanket.

While Brenda was distracted, Colly managed a furtive glance at the figure by the wall. It was Russ. A gun was in his hand. Their eyes met, and he nodded.

Brenda's tussle with Satchel had repositioned her so that her back was now to Russ. Colly took a step closer. "I've gotta hand it to you—those masks were the perfect red herring."

"I got the idea from Niall. He talks in his sleep."

"You mentioned that on Monday, but it didn't click for me till today. Did you steal them from his place?"

Brenda shook her head. "I bought them online. I knew if Willis was convicted a second time, he'd get the death penalty. No governor would dare release him again, even if he was a Newland." Brenda adjusted her grip on Satchel. Her fingernails bit into his arms. "I didn't plan to kill Willis—it's not something I enjoyed doing. It just kind of happened."

Colly stared at her. "You—you killed him, too?" she stammered. "The ME ruled it an accident."

"It *was* an accident—sort of. I slipped away from Iris's birthday party to put the masks in his cabin. That's all I meant to do. But when I got there, I saw him in his herpetarium, and I realized how easy it would be to get a rabbit out of the hutch and just—just toss it in." She pantomimed the action with her free hand. "That snake of his would take care of things."

At this, Russ stopped short. He swayed against the wall for a second before recovering himself and pushing forward. Outside, Colly heard the low rumble of thunder.

"The perfect murder," she said, keeping her eyes on Brenda. "Only one problem—Willis was innocent. He didn't kill Adam Parker, and he didn't molest Dave Carroway. He didn't do anything to anyone."

Brenda blinked. "You're lying. I saw his brain scan myself."

"Brain scans don't make serial killers—look in the mirror if you need proof of that."

"This conversation's pointless. You're like everyone else—talk, talk, talk. What good is that? Someone has to have the guts to do what's necessary." As she spoke, Brenda slipped one arm beneath Satchel's legs and lifted him higher.

He shrieked, and Colly's breath caught in her throat. "Brenda, don't."

"I'm sorry. He's got all the signs—incontinence, pyromania, antisocial behavior. I wasn't totally sure till he killed Minnie's hamster last night. That was the last straw."

"You can't be totally sure—you haven't done a brain scan."

"You've forced the issue. I've got no choice now." Brenda hoisted Satchel onto the plywood wall of the snake pen as he flailed and screamed. The slightest nudge and he would topple in.

"Satchel, hold still. Brenda, for God's sake—he's seven."

Russ was now fifteen feet behind Brenda. Though still by the wall, he could reach her in three quick strides. Colly silently willed

330

him to stay where he was, afraid that any sudden movement would spell disaster. She needed a distraction, something—anything—to buy time.

"Brenda, listen." She took another tentative step forward. "You don't want to do this. It's *Satchel*. Remember when Victoria got pregnant in high school and said she wanted to keep the baby? You were the first person I called. I was freaking out, and you said if we supported her decision, we'd be glad of it later."

Brenda was listening, her eyes dark and distrustful. Satchel had grown still, though he was crying quietly.

Colly sidled nearer. "That night, I told Randy what you said. It took him a couple months, but eventually he got excited about being a grandpa. And you were right. Satchel's such a great kid. I can't imagine life without him." She edged closer.

Out of the corner of her eye, Colly saw that Russ had moved away from the wall and was beginning to inch towards Brenda from behind. He was ten feet away, eight feet away. But she didn't dare wave him off. She could only pray that he would follow her lead.

Keeping her focus on Brenda, she slipped her gun into its holster and held up her hands. "We're just talking, Bren. I'm not going to hurt you. And I know you don't really want to hurt Satchel."

He had stopped crying and was staring intently at her, sniffling and hiccupping quietly. Colly took another step. Three feet more, and she'd be close enough to touch him. It took all her willpower not to reach for him now. She gave him a reassuring smile.

"Of course I don't want to hurt him," Brenda said hoarsely. "If you think I do, you haven't been listening."

"I am listening, Bren. I know you're not a bad person. You've had a stressful few years, and you've gotten a little confused."

Russ was now five feet behind Brenda. He looked like a cat crouched to spring.

Oh, shit, oh shit, Colly thought. *It's now or never.* "Let me help, Bren. Just give me Satchel."

Brenda said nothing. Thunder rolled above them once again.

"Brenda, look at his face. He's just a scared little boy. Put him down."

"I can't. He's too dangerous."

"Yes, you can." Colly reached out, intending to give Brenda's arm a gentle, cajoling tug.

But at that moment, Russ dropped his gun and lunged, flinging his arms around Brenda from behind. With a shriek, she let go of Satchel and stumbled backwards. Russ lost his balance, and the two of them toppled over in a thrashing heap.

Released suddenly from Brenda's grasp, Satchel teetered on the brink of the snake pen, flailing as he fought for balance. Colly sprang forward, but just then the red balloon, bobbing wildly with Satchel's arm movements, bounced in front of her eyes. She swatted it away and grabbed for his t-shirt, but too late. With a shrill scream, Satchel tumbled into the enclosure.

Chapter 34

As Satchel fell, Colly heard a loud bang, like a gunshot, but she had no time to wonder about it. Nearby, Russ and Brenda grunted and yelled as they wrestled on the ground. Scarcely noticing them, Colly rushed to the snake pen and peered inside. Satchel lay on his back about two feet from the wall. The majority of the rattlesnakes were still clustered on the opposite side beneath the work lamp. The area around Satchel was comparatively clear. Though agitated by the sudden intrusion, most of the snakes near him were moving away. Except for one. Three feet from Satchel's right shoulder, an enormous rattler was coiled, its head and tail erect, rattling fiercely. *That thing's thicker than my arm*, Colly thought. The red balloon lay flattened in the sawdust between Satchel and the snake. The gunshot noise must have been the balloon popping.

Satchel lay stunned and blinking at the snake beside him. He appeared uninjured except for a smear of blood on his thigh. Had he been bitten? Colly couldn't tell. She was sweating and icy-cold despite the heat of the room. Her mind raced. Satchel was too far from the wall for her to reach. She drew her gun and took aim, trying to hold the snake's head in her sights. Her hands shook. Such a small target, and so close to Satchel. What would happen if she missed?

"Satchel, Satchel." Colly kept her voice calm. "Don't sit up or make any sudden movements. I want you to slide very slowly towards my voice, okay?"

Satchel showed no indication that he had heard. He seemed frozen in place.

"Satch, you've got to try—I'm afraid if I jump in there, I'll make the snake madder."

But no amount of coaxing worked. He was too paralyzed with fear to move.

In desperation, Colly looked around. The ground to his left was fairly open. Maybe if she approached from that direction and circled around, she could draw the snake's attention away, maybe even get close enough for a kill shot.

"Okay, Satch, stay put. I'm coming."

Two decades spent facing down drug dealers, human traffickers, and murderers had not prepared Colly for the terror she felt as she climbed over the four-foot wall and lowered herself into the snake pen. A loud thunderclap sounded overhead. She flinched and glanced anxiously at the snake. It hadn't moved. *Slow and steady*, she told herself as she edged away from the wall, giving both Satchel and the snake a wide berth. The rattler swung its head in her direction. Colly froze, transfixed, watching as it unwound its long body and began to slide towards her, the umber diamond shapes along its back following one another hypnotically across the ground. It had nearly reached her when she raised her gun and fired. The shot went wide, slamming into the floor of the pen with a puff of sawdust. The snake lunged and then recoiled, poised to strike again. Colly's ears rang. She felt a stinging pain in her calf. No time to think. The noise of the gunshot had disturbed the knot of snakes beneath the work lamp. Rattling furiously, they untangled themselves with astonishing speed and dispersed across the floor. Dropping her gun,

Colly rushed forward, scooped up Satchel, and lifted him over the plywood wall.

As she set him on the ground, she felt a second sharp sting, this time behind her knee. She looked down. A gigantic rattler dangled from her leg. Its fangs were caught in her jeans, and it was writhing, trying to free itself. She kicked it away and clambered over the wall, landing almost on top of Russ and Brenda. Though Brenda was still thrashing, Russ had managed to flip her onto her stomach. He had her left wrist cuffed behind her back and was attempting to secure the right.

Satchel was huddled against the wall, in danger of being struck by Brenda's flailing limbs. Colly picked him up. Her legs felt oddly heavy. She carried him a little way, then set him down and knelt to check the bloody spot on his thigh. The room was growing darker, and she couldn't get her eyes to focus. Colly wiped away the blood and searched for fang marks. When she palpated Satchel's leg, she felt no swelling.

"Is he okay?" Russ asked. He was climbing to his feet, sweating and covered in dust. An ugly red welt scored the right side of his face from cheekbone to ear, and he was dabbing at it with his sleeve. Brenda lay face down, handcuffed and motionless beside him. The fight seemed to have left her. She was moaning quietly. Outside, the thunder growled, louder than before.

"I think so." Colly's words came out strangely garbled.

Satchel tugged her sleeve. "Grandma, you're bleeding."

He pointed to a dark blotch that had soaked through the right leg of her jeans. Her boot felt tight. Colly tried to get up, but the room spun, and she fell onto her hands and knees. A bitter metallic taste filled her mouth. She retched in the dirt.

"Are you bit?" Russ was leaning over her now. Another crash of thunder shook the ground, followed by the sharp, violent rattle of hard rain on the canvas roof of the tent.

Colly tried to answer. Her tongue felt thick and fuzzy, like a wadded-up sock in her mouth, and she struggled to breathe. She could hear Satchel crying and calling for her. She tried to stand again but fell on her side. Suddenly, she was surrounded by a frenzy of sound and light. Shapes were moving, and voices shouted over the noise of the storm. Avery, her face distorted and strange, floated into view, then vanished. Niall appeared, hovering over her like the still center in a swirling vortex. He raised her eyelids with his thumb and shone a bright light in her eyes. He spoke, but his words were garbled, like a recording played at half-speed. He melted away, and a kaleidoscope of other faces flickered around her. Colly's vision blurred. The faces spun crazily. Someone was carrying her. Then they were outside, and she felt the sting of cold rain on her skin. From somewhere she heard Russ—or was it Randy?—saying, "Hold on, hold on." And then a brilliant flash split the air, and the world went black.

The garage is cold, and a heavy odor hangs in the air. She stops. Where is Satchel? Then she spots the rusty droplets trailing up the steps. A figure stands in the doorway—a child. Naked, pale, face hidden in shadow. Not Satchel. Denny. As she stares, he turns, vanishes into the house. Setting down her bags, she draws her gun and follows.

A mist fills the kitchen. The pale figure drifts ahead of her. She tries to keep up, but her limbs are sluggish. She's wading, now—not through water, but through something thick, heavy. It hisses and writhes around her legs. She drops the gun, sinks to her knees, the viscous mass swallowing her like a wave.

Suddenly, Denny is standing beside her, his white skin glowing in the darkness. She's on her feet again, following him through the living room door, where he dissolves into the shadows.

Her gun is gone. She's alone, floating in a black void. Something is waiting for her here. She peers expectantly into the gloom. After a long time, she sees a faint, blue glimmer above her head. Steadily it expands, draws near. A familiar voice murmurs in the darkness. "Colly, Colly . . ."

"Colly, can you hear me?"

Colly opened her eyes with effort. Something was beeping steadily nearby. Light streamed through the window—not blue, but the ordinary golden light of late afternoon—and from the hallway came the squeaks of rubber-soled shoes and the clatter of metal carts. Niall Shaw was leaning over her, smiling. "You were groaning in your sleep. How do you feel?"

"Like hell." Colly tried to sit up, but her head throbbed.

"Best not to move."

"Where am I?"

"In the hospital in Big Spring. You've been out of it for a couple days."

Colly blinked. She looked around. "What happened? Where is everyone? Is Satchel—?"

"Satchel's fine—he's at the ranch with Iris. Russ and Avery will be right back. When I got here, they asked if I'd sit with you while they grabbed some supper."

With another effort, Colly struggled up onto her elbows. "What happened to me?"

Niall pushed a button, and the head of the bed rose slightly. "You should rest. Don't think too much."

"Ever tried not to think? I'll rest better if you'll answer my question."

Niall sat down in a chair beside the bed and crossed his long legs. He studied her face. "What's the last thing you remember?"

She closed her eyes, forcing herself to relax. "I was in the big tent at the Rodeo."

"Do you remember why?"

"I was looking for Brenda." Colly opened her eyes. "She killed Denny."

A look of pain crossed Niall's face. "I still don't know how you figured that out."

"Avery checked security footage of a road we suspected the murderer travelled. She saw a minivan with a Texas Tech sticker on the back."

"Brenda's."

Colly nodded, wincing as the movement made her head throb. "I realized she's the only person who could've known about the hare's mask you left on Adam. She put one on Denny so investigators would think there was a serial killer."

"But I never told her about the mask."

"Yeah, you did."

Niall's expression changed. "That's why you asked if I talk in my sleep?"

"It was the only thing that made sense. I thought I remembered her mentioning it, but I called you to make sure."

Niall's hand went to his forehead. "It was my fault."

"You're not the psychopath. Brenda is."

"She's not, though." Niall leaned forward. "She asked me to test her once, when we were dating. She's the opposite—an idealist, high on the empathy scale."

"Who cares what you call it, if it amounts to the same thing?"

"Do you remember finding her?"

Colly stared at the ceiling and tried to think back. She'd been pushing her way through the hot, crowded tent, she knew. But the specifics came only in flashes of disconnected imagery—a bucket of snake heads. Talford at a picnic table. Avery's face, tense and earnest.

She shook her head. "It's mostly a blank."

"She had Satchel in the back room. When you caught her, she threw him in the snake pit. Don't worry," he added quickly. "He wasn't bitten. He had a balloon that apparently distracted the snakes. Paramedics said there were three sets of fang marks in the latex."

Colly had a sudden, vivid memory that twisted in her gut like a physical pain—the red balloon bobbing against her face as she lunged for Satchel, the feel of his t-shirt slipping through her fingers, her hands closing on air.

"I thought the snakes got him. There was blood on his leg."

"That was just a scrape, thank God." Niall paused. "But you were bitten. Twice."

"It's coming back to me. Is that why I've been unconscious? I didn't know rattlesnake venom did that."

"One of the bites hit a major blood vessel. You went into anaphylactic shock, then renal failure. It was touch-and-go for a while."

"Everything was spinning. Avery was there—and you, too. You were shining a light in my eyes. How'd you get there? Did Avery call you?"

Niall looked surprised. But before he could answer, a man's voice behind him said, "You must've been hallucinating. That was the paramedic—we always have one at the Rodeo. And antivenom, too, fortunately."

Colly and Niall both started and turned. Russ and Avery stood in the doorway, smiling.

They crossed the room, and Russ took Colly's hand in both of his. "Look at you—you're awake." He was working to keep his voice light. "It's about damn time."

Chapter 35

Later that evening, Dr. Bhandari—the grave, dark-eyed young hospitalist who was treating Colly—stopped by to see her. He checked the bite wounds on her leg and seemed pleased.

"When can I get out of here?" Colly asked when he had finished typing notes on his tablet.

The doctor frowned. She should remain under observation for at least four more days, he told her. Snakebites sometimes had long-term effects, and her reaction had been particularly severe. "Not that you'll listen to me," he added glumly when he saw her expression. "Cops make terrible patients."

"I'm not as bad as all that. If you say four days, that's what I'll do."

In the end, she lasted three. Russ, still on leave from his job, hardly left her bedside. He seemed strangely shy and solicitous, watching her closely and leaping up to adjust the pillows or close the curtains or fetch her water if she showed the slightest discomfort. Colly found this attentiveness mildly annoying, but he seemed so eager to please that she didn't have the heart to ask him to leave.

Avery joined them in the evenings, and together they talked for hours about the case, piecing together answers to the questions that remained. Brenda had refused a lawyer and had confessed everything to Avery in the Crescent Bluff lockup before the sheriff's people had arrived on Monday to transport her to the county jail.

Avery grinned at Colly. "Here's a weird compliment for you—she told me she knew she was screwed when she heard Russ was calling you in to consult. She got the idea of trying to chase you off with anonymous texts, so she drove to Colorado City and bought that burner phone before you got here. When the texts and the snake booby trap didn't work, she got desperate and staged the break-in at the farmhouse."

At the memory of the hare's mask in Satchel's suitcase, Colly flushed angrily. "Why didn't she just murder me? It would've been easier."

"I asked her that. She looked at me like I was the crazy one—said she'd never kill to protect herself, only society." Avery shrugged.

"I can't believe she told you all this," Russ said. "Is she trying to set up an insanity defense?"

"She knows she's done for. Now she's thinking of her kids—says she'll plead guilty to spare them the spectacle of a trial."

"What'll happen to Logan and Minnie?" Colly asked Russ when Avery stepped out for a smoke. "Lowell's not exactly a model parent."

"They're at the ranch with Momma, for now. I made Lowell come clean to her about the embezzlement."

"Is she pressing charges?"

Russ shook his head. "The kids just lost their mother—she didn't have the heart to send their dad to prison, too. She fired him as plant manager, of course, but says she'll keep things quiet if he'll go into rehab and stop gambling."

"What about Jace Hoyer?"

Russ shifted uneasily and scratched his stubbled cheek. "We didn't tell her he was involved. We can't very well throw him under the bus if Lowell gets to walk. Besides, Hoyer's lost his whole family, and he's already in jail for assaulting you." He cast a guilty glance at Colly. "I know it's not by the book, but—"

Colly stopped him with a gesture. "I'm glad." She relaxed into the pillows and closed her eyes.

Each day, Iris brought Satchel for late-afternoon visits. Colly was startled by how happy he seemed. He climbed onto her bed and babbled cheerfully about horseback riding with his cousins and trips to Dairy Queen with Avery. The events at the Rattlesnake Rodeo had given him a celebrity status at school, and he'd begun to make friends. On Tuesday, he brought a new ant farm to the hospital to show Colly—a gift from Niall, who'd volunteered to meet with him daily to help him process the recent trauma.

Satchel curled beside her, fingering the thin cotton of her hospital gown. "I don't wanna go back to Houston," he whispered. "I like it better here."

In spite of all the company, Colly felt restless and lonely. She found herself hoping that Niall would visit again. But he was swamped with work—seeing Brenda's clients as well as his own until he could hire another therapist—and he couldn't get away. He rang her up each night, though, after visiting hours ended and Russ had gone home. And Colly waited anxiously for his calls.

On Thursday morning, she woke up hungry for the first time since being bitten, and she ate even the rubbery hospital eggs with gusto. When Russ arrived just before noon, Colly was dressed and sitting on the side of the bed.

He stopped in the doorway. "What's going on?"

"You're busting me out of here. I can rest just as well at home."

◆　◆　◆

Monday morning, rainy and cool. Cement-colored clouds sagged over the Crescent Bluff police station as Colly crunched across wet gravel to the front entrance. Avery and Russ were both waiting inside. Russ had insisted on coming in when Colly told him her plan.

"You sure about this?" he asked. "I could give him a message."

Colly shook her head. "He deserves to hear it from me."

"And me," Avery said.

Colly laid a hand on the younger woman's shoulder. "You've handled the interviews with Brenda. Let me take this."

Russ led Colly down some stairs and through a heavy door. "The interview room's being repainted. You'll have to talk here."

She followed him along a short passage to a pair of old-fashioned, iron-barred holding cells. One was occupied.

"Hello, Jace," Colly said through the bars.

Dressed in a dull gray jumpsuit, Jace Hoyer lay on the bed, staring at the ceiling. He lifted his head and glared. "Come to gloat, have ya?"

"I thought you might want some answers, now that we know what happened to Denny."

Jace swung his legs over the side of the bed and sat up.

"Let me in, Russ. Give us a few minutes," Colly said.

"No way. You can sit out here—I'll get you a chair."

"Jace won't hurt me."

Russ rubbed the back of his neck. "I'll be watching." He nodded towards a camera high on the wall as he unlocked the door. "Mind yourself, Hoyer."

When he was gone, Colly sat down on the cell's built-in bench. "You've probably heard Brenda Newland was the killer."

"She was down here last weekend." Jace nodded towards the neighboring cell. "Not that she said much. But I ain't stupid." His face twisted into an odd grimace. "Poor Denny. His own shrink."

"I know."

343

"And she got away with it for six months while the Rangers screwed around investigating me and Willis Newland."

"You can't really blame them. Brenda had an airtight alibi. Denny left the counseling center at one o'clock, and the ME says he died no later than two. But a dozen witnesses put Brenda in her office with clients till six that day. There's lots of cameras around the counseling center—impossible to sneak out unseen. Plus—" Colly hesitated. "The Rangers had reason to think Denny was killed by the same person who murdered Adam Parker back in '98."

"Then how the hell'd she do it?" Jace exploded. "If *you* figured it out, they should've."

"Real life's not like the movies. There can be thousands of pieces of evidence at a crime scene, and ninety-eight percent of it's irrelevant. Takes time to make sense of it all. Plus, the Rangers don't know Brenda like I do. The crime was just so contrived that it was hard to imagine. Even now that she's confessed, I can hardly believe it. But I should've solved it quicker." Colly sighed. "It's a long story."

Jace waved an arm around the bare concrete cell. "I got plenty of time."

Colly nodded. It was tough to know where to start, she said. As for why Brenda had killed Denny, her rationale was so warped that it was useless to try to understand it.

"She's nuts?"

"Not legally. She understands society's definition of right and wrong. But medically speaking, maybe. She took some crazy risks, and she wasn't self-aware enough to hide all the inconsistencies in the case."

"Like what?"

Colly shrugged. The most obvious was the body itself. There was evidence linking Denny's death to Adam Parker's. But Denny was found naked, and Adam fully clothed. That was odd—a break in the pattern. Serial killers were usually consistent about those types of details.

That wasn't all. There was an orthopedic shoe insert in Denny's backpack, though no one in his family had foot problems. And he was seen on the day he died wearing a red ballcap that Jolene swore wasn't his. "We found that cap at the fireworks stand out by Digby's Automotive, but it was stolen from the site before we could have it analyzed," Colly said. "That was the first thing that should've pointed me to Brenda. When we found it, we'd just come from the counseling center."

"She followed you?"

Colly nodded. "She hid in the salvage yard next to Digby's. We dismissed that idea because the place is patrolled by guard dogs, and the Digby's employees didn't hear any barking. But Brenda's a jogger, and she runs that way a lot. All the dogs in the area know her."

"What was the ballcap doing at the fireworks stand?"

"I'm coming to that."

There were other signs she'd missed, Colly said. Denny's therapy appointment got moved from Thursday to Friday the week of his death. Brenda said Jolene changed it. But Jolene said Brenda requested the switch. "I figured one of them just misremembered. It didn't seem relevant."

"But it was?"

Colly nodded. "Jolene always drove Denny to his Thursday appointments. But on Fridays—"

"She'd been picking up extra day shifts."

"Right. Somehow, Brenda knew Denny would have to ride his bike to therapy on Friday. He probably told her himself."

"So what?" Jace leaned forward, nervously bouncing his knees.

"Her plan wouldn't have worked otherwise," Colly said. "Jolene gave us other clues, too. She mentioned that Denny sunburned quickly, and that he was supposed to return some library books after his appointment with Brenda. But the books were still in his backpack when we found it. And when his body was discovered, his skin wasn't burned the way you'd expect if he'd ridden his bike all the way to the stock pond."

"Meaning?"

Colly met Jace's eyes. "Denny never left the counseling center."

Jace stared. "What?"

"Brenda's already confessed—she killed Denny inside her office."

"The hell she did. His Little League coach saw Denny riding his bike past Digby's."

"Sorry, I'm getting ahead of myself." Colly paused. "You have to understand—Brenda's got an obsessive-compulsive streak. She's a planner." Once she'd decided to kill Denny, she'd mapped out every detail in advance. She didn't want to run the risk of going to prison and losing her kids.

Opportunity was the easy part. Brenda spent a court-mandated hour alone with Denny each week. As long as she killed him quietly, her risk of being caught in the act was almost zero. But there was a catch—when someone walked into a therapist's office, they were expected to walk out again. And if they didn't, the therapist would be the only possible suspect. Brenda considered several ideas, from giving Denny a slow-acting poison to injecting him with a hypodermic full of air to create a pseudo-heart attack. But she dismissed them as too risky.

Then one day, Denny commented that he and she were the same height, which gave Brenda an idea. She liked going to thrift stores, and Iris had recently given her several sacks of old clothes to take to the donation center. Some belonged to Iris herself, and some to her housekeeper, Nadine. Brenda went through those sacks and scavenged an old-lady dress, shoes, hat, and a gigantic purse.

"Nadine has bad feet," Colly added. "I noticed she was limping when I was at the ranch my first night here. I found the shoe insert in Denny's backpack the same day. And Iris gave Brenda more sacks of old clothes right in front of me. I should've connected the dots." Colly shook her head. "Anyway, Brenda chose that Friday for the murder because Lowell would have the kids. When Denny arrived for his appointment, she gave him a Xanax-laced coke. And when he fell asleep, she strangled him with an extension cord. Very quiet. No cleanup."

"Christ Almighty." Jace looked sick.

"Sorry, I'm used to talking to cops." Colly waited while he collected himself. Finally, he nodded for her to continue.

"Brenda has this huge suitcase full of play-therapy toys in her office closet. I've seen it myself," Colly said slowly, watching Jace. "She undressed Denny and put him in it. That's another clue I missed, at first. Carmen mentioned she found toys all over Brenda's office that night when she came to clean. She said the closet in Brenda's office was locked, so she couldn't get the suitcase out to put them away. The Rangers didn't think anything of it, but I should've. Brenda's super-tidy—she'd never leave toys out like that, unless she had no choice."

After stowing the body, Brenda emptied Denny's backpack and put the old-lady outfit and purse inside. Then she put on Denny's clothes, plus a red ballcap she'd brought to hide her face—she'd cut her hair short the week before, so she'd look more boyish. Carrying the backpack and wearing her own running shoes, she rushed past Pearl, the office manager, and out the front door of the counseling center a little after one p.m. She'd already told Pearl not to disturb her because she'd be doing paperwork in her office until her two o'clock appointment. Pearl went off for a late lunch. Later, she swore to the Rangers that she'd seen Denny ride away on his bike and that Brenda never left the building. CCTV footage backed up her story.

Brenda didn't have time to go far—she had to be back before two. She rode north on the Old Ranch Way, passing as many security cameras as she could. "She didn't anticipate Denny's coach seeing her," Colly said. "Her only option was to blow past him and hope he didn't follow."

She hid the bike in the tall weeds behind the fireworks stand, then put on the old-lady clothes, except for the shoes—she had to run to get back in time. She left the ballcap there, but she stuffed Denny's backpack and the rest of his clothes into the purse and took them with her.

"She couldn't risk going back the way she'd come, in case Tom Gunnell spotted her," Colly said. "So she cut across the fields onto Salton Road. At least one farmer saw her from a distance but thought she was a local, since the farm dogs didn't bark—but like I said, they all knew her."

"Didn't folks think it was strange for an old woman to be running?"

"She only ran till she got near town. Then she put on the old-lady shoes and walked back to the clinic. Getting back in her office was the riskiest part. If Pearl came back from lunch a little early, the jig would be up. But Brenda's luck held. My first day here, she told me that an elderly woman wandered in from the alleyway looking for a bathroom while she was alone in the building. I was asking questions, and she got nervous that we might have a witness or footage of her coming in the rear door."

Back in her office, Brenda put on her own clothes, hid the suitcase and all of Denny's belongings in her office closet, and saw clients till six o'clock, then did some paperwork. She went home and washed Denny's clothes to make sure she hadn't left behind any evidence. In the middle of the night, she returned to the clinic and entered through the alley.

Colly shrugged. "There's a camera back there, but she gambled that the cops wouldn't check it. Why would they? Footage showed Denny leaving through the front door hours earlier."

Brenda planned to redress Denny, but by then he was in full rigor mortis in a fetal position. She put the suitcase—with Denny's body inside it—into her van, along with his belongings, and drove out to the Newland Ranch, stopping on the way to pick up the bike from behind the fireworks stand.

Wearing an old pair of Lowell's rubber boots—for the mud, as well as to make police think the murderer was a man—she wheeled the suitcase to the stock pond.

"They saw the tracks," Colly said, "smoother and narrower than a hand truck's. But the Rangers never thought of a suitcase. Neither did I."

Brenda left Denny's body and his bike on the shore and threw his backpack in the water, not knowing an insert from the old-lady shoes was still in it. "Then she planted something on Denny that she knew would make us think we had a serial killer in town."

"Planted what?"

"That's confidential, for now. It was the mother of all red herrings—a stroke of genius, Brenda thought. But it backfired, in the end. It's how we caught her."

Colly fell silent. Jace sat staring at the cell floor. After a few minutes, he looked up with a furrowed brow. "Who'd I see messing with the van at the ranch Monday night?"

"That was Brenda. She slipped away sometime after dark during our family get-together, put on Lowell's ranch coat for a quick disguise, and rigged up that rattler. I don't know where or when she got it, but she knows how to catch snakes—she does it every year for the Rodeo." Colly shook her head. "I should've guessed. She parked in the one security-camera blind spot that night."

"Then who stole the printouts in my garage freezer? Brenda didn't know about them."

"She did. Denny told her. Kids find everything. She knew you couldn't go public with them without incriminating yourself, so she wasn't worried. But when Carmen told her you'd left, she got scared we'd search the place and find those papers. She figured you took them with you, but she wanted to make sure." Colly laughed suddenly. "It's ironic—everything Lowell did to keep her from finding out about the embezzlement, and she knew all along."

"She could've destroyed him."

"Not without hurting her own kids' futures."

The cell grew quiet. Finally, Colly leaned forward. "Listen, Jace, I want to apologize. If I'd known how fragile Jolene was, I might've done things differently, questioned her differently."

Jace blinked. "Ain't your fault. She's been hanging by a thread since Denny died."

"Well, your family's suffered more than it should've, and I'm sorry."

Jace nodded, tugging distractedly at a clump of mud-colored hair. "What happens now? Y'all sending me to county?"

Colly stood and shook her head. "Avery and I discussed it. We're dropping the assault charges. You're off the hook for embezzlement, too, as long as you keep your nose clean. You're free to go."

Chapter 36

Colly squinted into the sunrise. The empty highway stretched before her, dark and straight, while high above it, red-tailed hawks wheeled against a windy sky. Already the vultures roosting on fenceposts had begun to unfurl their dusky wings, warming them in the swelling light.

A glance in the rearview mirror showed Satchel napping against the car door. Even in sleep, he clutched the ant farm, protective of its delicate lacework of tunnels and nests. He had cried when she'd woken him in the predawn darkness. Couldn't they stay just one more day? Just till lunchtime? But Colly held firm. She had said her goodbyes. She couldn't bear the thought of running into anyone she knew and having to say them again.

Iris had held a farewell cookout the evening before. Practically everyone was invited: Avery, Niall Shaw, Earla Cobb, Jimmy Meggs—and, of course, Talford Maybrey. It felt strange to be there without Lowell or Brenda. Despite everything, Colly knew she would miss having a sister-in-law as an ally against Iris's frigid courtesy. Last night, however, Iris had been warm and gracious.

"I can't thank you enough," she'd said when the two of them were alone in the kitchen. "Willis can finally rest in peace." She laid a hand on Colly's arm. "I hope you'll come back soon. Satchel needs family. Besides," she added with a melancholy smile, "you're the only daughter I have left." Then, Iris hugged her—not her usual stiff clinch but a long, affectionate embrace that Colly returned clumsily.

Back outside, she'd looked around. Niall stood chatting with Avery and Earla. Colly wandered to the grill, where Russ, in a denim apron, was cooking hot dogs for the kids. A platter of raw steaks waited on the table nearby.

"Need any help?" Colly asked.

"Propane's nearly out. Come with me to grab another canister? There's something I need to say."

Apprehensive but curious, she followed him around the house and down the footpath to the barn, waiting in the breezeway while he ducked into a storeroom and emerged with a fresh propane tank.

He set it down and dusted his hands. "I'm quitting the force."

"Seriously?"

"You were right—I shouldn't be a cop anymore."

"What will you do?"

"Momma's asked me to supervise the turbine plant. Who knows? Maybe I'll develop a knack for it. At least I won't rob her blind." He grinned, looking so much like Randy that Colly was taken aback, though the experience was less gut-wrenching than it had been.

Russ's expression sobered. "I know I disappointed you on this case. I disappointed myself." He swallowed noisily. "I care about you, Colly. More than care. I have for a long time—since before Randy died, if I'm honest. Maybe it's a mistake to tell you. I would've taken it to my grave if Randy hadn't—" Russ exhaled. "A few times since you got here, I've thought you might feel something, too." He was watching her closely. Hopefully. Finally, he looked away. "Did I misread the signals?"

"I don't know," Colly said slowly. "I probably sent mixed signals. But things are clearer now."

"Clearer?"

She sighed. "I loved—I *love* Randy. You look so damn much like him that I can't help feeling something. But if we got together, I don't think I could separate the two of you in my head. Randy's ghost would always be there."

Russ was quiet for a moment. "I get it. Don't worry, I won't make a nuisance of myself." His face was impassive, but his throat worked. "We're still friends?"

In answer, she kissed him quickly on the cheek and slipped her arm through his. They walked back to the patio in silence. Russ seemed depressed. But the party was lively, and to Colly's relief he soon grew more cheerful. While he grilled the steaks, she helped Iris fix the younger children's plates. Niall and Talford were sipping cocktails and chatting near the waterfall at the deep end of the pool. She resisted joining them. Instead, she sat down on a deckchair beside Avery.

"I want to thank you for spending so much time with Satchel while I was laid up," Colly said. "And for all your help on the case."

"Can't believe it's over. Everyone got it wrong, and you solved it in less than a week."

"I couldn't have done it alone."

Avery reddened but looked pleased.

Colly lowered her voice. "About what you told me the other night—"

Avery's shoulders tensed. She started to speak, but stopped herself.

"I'm not going to report you, in case you were wondering."

"Why not?"

Colly sighed. "I know what it's like to make a mistake and have someone die because of it. You were eight years old."

Avery chewed her lip. "Legally—"

353

"The law's not a precision instrument. Human decency's got to be considered, too. Besides," Colly added, "you've lost enough."

Avery looked away. "I still miss them both, you know. Mom and Adam. It's been twenty years, but still . . . And the weird thing is, I can't remember them—not really. I'm not even sure what I'm missing anymore. They're just an idea I've built in my head." She wiped her cheek with the cuff of her sleeve. "How can you miss something you can't remember?"

"I know what you mean," Colly said quietly. Only two years had passed since she'd lost Randy and Victoria, yet already they'd begun to seem remote, somehow—a handful of memories fading like old photographs in a family album. What would Satchel remember of them when he was Avery's age?

With an effort, she pushed the dismal thought aside. Iris was calling everyone to the table. Colly stood and laid her hand on Avery's shoulder. "Listen, I don't know what your long-term plans are, but you've got the makings of a good detective. I have lots of friends in the Houston PD. I'll put in a recommendation for you whenever you want."

Dinner was served on the patio. By the time they finished eating, the shadows were lengthening across the flagstones. The children went inside to eat ice cream and watch a movie, and the adults settled into lounge chairs by the pool with cups of coffee and thick slices of strawberry shortcake. Colly slipped quietly away from the group and headed down the footpath through the crape myrtle thicket. As she emerged into the open, she heard a voice from behind, calling her name.

Niall was striding quickly after her.

"Where are you going?" he asked.

Colly hesitated. "It's nearly dark. There's something I have to do before I go home."

"Want company?"

Colly wavered. It was her final unfinished business, some-thing she'd imagined doing alone. But she found herself nodding. Niall walked beside her in comfortable silence. They passed the tennis courts and started down the long, shallow slope beyond. Halfway to the bottom, Colly veered from the path, cutting across the winter-brown turf towards the ancient oak that stood on the hillside, spreading its branches over a cluster of white tombstones.

Niall hung back respectfully as Colly picked her way among the graves until she reached a trio of stones that were whiter than the rest. She stood by Willis's for a few moments, then moved on to Randy's and Victoria's. After a little while, she sat down on the grass in front of them and waved for Niall to join her.

"Beautiful spot," he said quietly, sitting beside her. "What was he like, your husband?"

"Funny, sweet." Colly smiled. "Stubborn as hell. All the Newlands are."

"And your daughter?"

"She was just like him. And so talented. Wanted to be a chef." Colly brushed some bits of dried leaves from the engraved letters of Victoria's name.

"Is it hard to be here?"

"This is my first time since the funeral. Time heals all wounds, supposedly. But it doesn't. The pain just becomes your new normal, and you figure out how to live with it." She paused. "It's ironic. I came here for closure. I thought I could pay my debt to the Newlands, work off my guilt, and be done with them. But every-thing's messier than ever. Satchel loves it here. He's begging to come back. Iris is already knitting him a stocking for next Christmas. One big happy family at the ranch."

Niall laughed. "Forget it. You can't get closure with family—that's not how it works."

"Randy warned me they were like a spiderweb."

"There's strength in a web, I guess."

Colly sighed and ran her fingertips over a cluster of olive-green shoots poking through the brown grass, their tiny leaves splayed out like wheel spokes.

"Are those bluebonnets already?" Niall asked.

Colly nodded. Soon the hillside would be draped in a disheveled riot of purple-blue splashed with red and pink clusters of firewheel and evening primrose. "This place is gorgeous in April. But I'm not waiting around to see it." She scrambled to her feet and dusted off the back of her jeans.

Niall followed suit. "Maybe next year." He reached out suddenly and, taking her hand, he squeezed it tightly.

"Maybe." Colly returned the squeeze. Then, after a brief inner tussle, she pulled her hand reluctantly away. Better to keep things simple—for now, at least.

She looked up. A few early stars were shining through the live oak's dark, smooth leaves. "Time to go back," she said.

◆ ◆ ◆

"Grandma!" A shrill voice brought Colly suddenly back to the present. In the rearview mirror, Satchel's face was flushed with sleep, but his eyes were wide awake.

"What is it, buddy?"

"I miss Maisie."

"Who?"

"My horse, the black-and-white one. Grandma Iris said she's mine, but she'll keep her for me when I'm in Houston."

"That was nice. Did you say thank you?"

Satchel shot her a reproachful look. "I'm sad we're leaving."

"We'll come back soon."

"You say that when you hope I'll forget. But I won't."

"Satchel, we've been gone less than an hour."

"Can we visit in July, for my birthday?" He was glaring at her in the mirror, his mouth set in a determined line that reminded her sharply of Victoria at that age.

Three weeks with the Newlands and he's as pigheaded as the rest, Colly thought, looking back at the road. The sun was higher now. The asphalt shimmered beneath it like a golden ribbon unspooling itself across the plain. She cracked the window and let the cold air rush in, flooding the car with the chalky sagebrush-scent of the scrubland—a bracing odor, clean and sharp.

Colly laughed suddenly. "Fine, Satchel—you win. We'll come back in July."

ACKNOWLEDGEMENTS

The writing of a book is a paradox—a solitary act, and yet impossible to accomplish alone. I am indebted to so many who helped to make this particular book a reality. Thank you to my agent, Marilia Savvides, and to my editor, Victoria Haslam at Thomas & Mercer, for their tireless labor and encouragement, and for believing in this book and in me as a writer. Many thanks as well to developmental editor Laura Gerrard for her insightful notes and suggestions, and to the copyeditors, designers, and everyone else involved in producing this novel.

I am also deeply grateful to my writing group—Al Haley, Dr. Debbie J. Williams, Dr. Steven T. Moore, and Dr. Shelly Sanders—for their friendship, and for the countless hours they spent reading and commenting. This book absolutely would not exist without them. Likewise, I want to thank my dear, dear friends Diane Cope, Lisa Wiggins, and Mike Wiggins, not only for serving as early readers of this book but also for listening to me talk about it for three years and never once saying, "Can we please discuss something else?"

My thanks to Dr. Greg Straughn and to Dr. Steven T. Moore for their practical and logistical support; to former Houston detective Bob Delony for his expert advice; and to the Crime Writers'

Association in Great Britain, whose Debut Dagger award furnishes new crime writers like myself with unprecedented opportunities.

Most of all, I am grateful for my family—for my parents, who nurtured my love of reading and of writing; and especially for my daughter, Emily Rankin, who encourages and amazes me always.

ABOUT THE AUTHOR

Photo © 2023 by Matt Maxwell

Sherry Rankin grew up in New Jersey and has taught creative writing and literature in West Texas since 1997. After winning the Crime Writers' Association's Debut Dagger Award and being shortlisted for the Daniel Goldsmith First Novel Prize in 2017 (for an as-yet-unpublished novel), she went on to be shortlisted in the Margery Allingham Short Mystery Competition in 2019.

Sherry has a daughter in New Mexico and enjoys gardening and walking her three dogs.

The Killing Plains is her first published novel.

Follow the Author on Amazon

If you enjoyed this book, follow Sherry Rankin on Amazon to be notified when the author releases a new book!

To do this, please follow these instructions:

Desktop:

1) Search for the author's name on Amazon or in the Amazon App.

2) Click on the author's name to arrive on their Amazon page.

3) Click the "Follow" button.

Mobile and Tablet:

1) Search for the author's name on Amazon or in the Amazon App.

2) Click on one of the author's books.

3) Click on the author's name to arrive on their Amazon page.

4) Click the "Follow" button.

Kindle eReader and Kindle App:

If you enjoyed this book on a Kindle eReader or in the Kindle App, you will find the author "Follow" button after the last page.